Jigsaw:
Piecing Love Together

John Sparrow

Jigsaw:
Piecing Love Together

by

John Sparrow

This book is a work of fiction.
Names, characters, businesses, organisations, places, events, and incidents are products of the author's imagination or are used fictitiously. Any resemblance to actual persons, living or dead, events, or locales is purely coincidental.

John Sparrow asserts the moral right to be identified as the author of this work.

Copyright © 2025 John Sparrow

Front cover created with ideas generated by Microsoft Copilot.

"Journeys end in lovers' meeting."

— William Shakespeare, *Twelfth Night*, Act II, Scene III

Dedicated to Jane Rogers, an inspiration to so many writers.

And to Pam, my destination.

Other works by the author available on Amazon

Fortune

Fortune: The Musical

Tickets Please!
(An adaptation for the stage of the
DH Lawrence short story)

Awakening Iya

Crime and Prejudice

Something and Nothing

(https://www.amazon.co.uk/stores/Prof-John-Sparrow/author/B06VSKBSQQ)

John Sparrow is a Chartered Psychologist and Associate Fellow of the British Psychological Society. He is a registered practitioner psychologist with the Health and Care Professions Council in the UK. His works of fiction draw upon key psychological issues in personal development and interpersonal relationships.

www.johnsparrow.uk

Chapter 1

Michael Lewis was loved even before he was born.
"It's the same. It's the same," Cathy called from the bathroom, her voice carrying the well-practised, received pronunciation of a traditional primary school teacher. There was an excited, if not somewhat frantic, tone to her words.
Her husband, George, shouted back, "I carn 'ear yer," his Suffolk accent clear. "The radio's on in 'ere." *Maneater* by Hall and Oates was playing loudly, and George, standing in the bedroom, attempting to look hip, snapped his fingers to the beat, expanding his coolness with a slight squirm of his hips as the song progressed.
Cathy at the bedroom door. George reached out to her, inviting her to dance. Sensing her reluctance, he smiled warmly and turned the volume on the clock radio nearly entirely off before they climbed into bed.
Cathy nestled her head on his left shoulder and repeated the words with calmness and pride. "It's the same. I am pregnant."
George reached over to the radio and turned it off. "See. I didn't think the first one would be wrong. Clever you. Tha's wonderful." He kissed her forehead and repeated, "Wonderful."
"Oh, George, I'd begun to think it would never happen. We've tried for so long. It's amazing. I'm
thirty-three, for God's sake. Everyone has babies by now. You're thirty-six." She added with an exaggerated tone. She paused, reflecting. "My dad was thirty-six when I was born, but they'd been through the war, and I think that delayed many people. But normally..."
George was counting on his fingers. "February, March, April." He continued to count silently.
Cathy squeezed him. "Yes, it will be mid-October, I think. But we'll get a clearer idea from scans and that."

Cathy Taylor had completed her A-levels and gone to train as a primary school teacher, returning to Shropham in Norfolk to teach in nearby Attleborough. George Lewis had continued to live at home in the village while studying at Otley College of Agriculture and Horticulture. He had secured a job with a refining company, persuading farmers to adjust their crops with biofuels in mind. They struck up a proper relationship in 1977 and were married in 1978. Once married, they bought a small, terraced cottage about forty miles away in Ilketshall St. Andrew, Suffolk, where they lived for nearly five years. Cathy had a job at a local primary school. Their inability to conceive had become an enormous concern.

"Sometimes these things take time, but we're there now," George said affectionately. He kissed her again on the forehead and squeezed her shoulders gently.

"We will have to love this baby, George. I mean, completely love him... her... it." She shook her head. "I don't like 'it.' What word shall we use?"

"Of course, we'll love... the bump." George felt her giggle through his chest.

"No, but I mean unerringly love. Because it's so special that there is... a bump at all."

"We will, Cathy. We absolutely will."

There was silence. George felt a quiver. Cathy was crying. He turned his head further towards her and kissed the tears on her left cheek. "It is wonderful, Cathy. Tha's wonderful."

"I know. I don't know why I'm crying. Silly. I'm thrilled."

"Will you tell your mam? Yet, I mean?"

"It's too soon. Let's wait a few more weeks. To be sure. Why? Do you want to tell your parents?"

"No, I'll be guided by you. You's right. Best to wait."

"I think my mum had given up on me... us. Last July, she said, 'You've been trying for four years. It may not be God's will.' She never talks like that about God. I mean, I think she was trying to say it wasn't our fault."

"Well, it wasn't. We're ready now. Maybe the waiting makes it even more special."

*

By the beginning of April, Cathy and George were trying to adjust to the reality of pregnancy. George treated Cathy as if she were made of glass. Cathy read, read, and read.
"You'll be more of an expert in pregnancy care than a midwife."
"I didn't dare read anything about it... before. I thought it might jinx it. Plus, after that first day, I began to worry that it was a false alarm. A phantom kind of thing. So, I still didn't read about it."
The song *Billie Jean* was ending on the radio in the kitchen. George began swivelling his hips as *Maneater* started playing. He stopped.
"I think you being sick is real enough. And now we can see the beginnings of your bump."
"Yes, but I'm reading here how important this first scan will be tomorrow. That's twelve weeks."
"I know. It will be the first actual sight of... the baby. Although I have to say, whenever I've seen videos of those images, I can't make out what's what at all."
As the song continued, George said, "I'll always associate this tune with that first day. First time I'd heard it then. I remember thinking how not like you this woman in this song is—some horror wild she-cat after his money." George said as the song continued. "Not like my Cathy, heh?" he added affectionately. "Turned out to be a big hit over the next few weeks. Seems ages ago."
"A lot has happened, George."

*

The following day, they went for an ultrasound scan appointment. A surprisingly old midwife called them through to a small room. She seemed frail and spoke quietly with an Irish brogue. "Well, now, so. I
will put this gel on your tummy. It's quite cold, but it soon warms up. Then I'll place this probe on your tummy, and we'll move it around until we see the baby."
George focused on the monitor as a jumble of random shapes danced across the screen, but he couldn't make sense of what he saw.
Cathy turned to George. "We'll see our baby. Our baby, George." She began to feel overwhelmed and was on the verge of tears. She looked at the monitor. "It's not at all clear. It's showing a blurry double image. Is it working? Is there something wrong with it? Is the baby there? Is it all right?"
The Irish nurse interrupted. "Ah, well now, see. All is fine. Working totally fine. But there isn't just one baby. You're having twins, so you are."
"I saw. I saw!" shouted George. "I can see two... things... heads and bodies and everything."
Cathy stared at the image, transfixed. Her heart raced. Her pupils grew ever larger. A tempest of jubilation. "Two babies? We've made two babies, George. It's our first sight of a miracle."
The midwife continued. "And so it is, yes. Two babies. And look here. Both sharing the same chorion, inner sac, so that means they're identical twins."
Cathy raised her head further from the bed and stared even harder at the image. And with that, the floodgates opened. The scan image seemed to etch itself into her memory instantly. She reached her hand out to George. "Look, George. Can you see? You need to see and remember this picture, too," she said through the tears.

"Ah, you'll be remembering what you've seen for sure. I've done this many times, and many mums tell me, even years later, that they can see the picture in their mind as if it was standing right there in front of them. I think it's the whole emotion of the thing. It helps put the image in your brain intact, in every detail, sort of thing. I don't know. Burns it in or something. It's true of all sorts of scenes and images we see in our lives when we're emotional."

"It is. I can tell. It's there now, even when I close my eyes. I'll remember it all, including the date—April 7, 1983. The date I first saw my babies. Will you remember it all, George?"

"Well, I can see them for sure." He turned to the midwife. "But don't we get a copy or something?"

"You will, you will. We can print out a little Polaroid-type picture for you with the date and time on it."

Cathy had calmed down momentarily. Her elation was suddenly overtaken by fear. "Are they all right? Both alright? I mean, will they be all right?"

"Look now. Listen. On this new machine, we can hear the babies' heartbeats as well as see them." The midwife moved the probe. The pulsing in the image synchronised with the rapid beating of a heart. She moved the probe again. "And here. Baby number two. Good, strong heartbeat."

For Cathy, a tide of joy. Then, a switch to a riptide of worry. "So, what will it mean? What do I have to do? Do twin pregnancies go wrong more?"

"Hush now. So many questions. Let it sink in now. We've had twins here before, you know. It'll all be fine. Let me print this wonderful picture off for you."

"We never talked about twins. We had been trying for so long, but we didn't talk much about babies other than wanting one. We never thought of twins."

"Well, now, there you have it. All that wishing and you've gone and got yourselves two," the midwife said as she handed Cathy the printout picture.

Later that evening, Cathy spoke with her mother in Shropham on the telephone. "No one I know has twins. What am I supposed to do?"

Ever practical and from a farming background, her mother cut straight to the point. "It'll cost you more. I know George has a good job and that, and he's happy about the baby... babies, but I've heard men say, 'It's the best worst thing that's happened to them.' Twins, I mean. And anyway, they're the same. Identical, I mean. I've heard that companies send you stuff if they're identical. That'll help."

"Yes, they are identical, but it's not about the money, Mum. We'll manage. We've talked about it. I'm more worried about whether we'll make it to full term, I mean. People tell you all sorts of horror stories. Nobody ever said anything like that before I was pregnant. Ha, I think they wait to let you in on it all when it's too late."

"Don't be listening to them. What do they know? Have any of them got twins? No. So, forget all that. Anyway, you've read more books and articles than is good for you. They'll only tell you every possible thing that can go wrong and scare you to death. What are the actual doctors saying?"

"Ha. You're right about getting scared. Not the books, but people. People like Mandy at work. She said her sister's husband told his colleague— a woman—who told him that her sister didn't sleep more than an hour after sixteen weeks."

"Stuff and nonsense. We all struggle to sleep. You've simply got to find the right position. That's all. It'll be the same. Just find the right position."

"Well, the doctors have been reassuring. But even they say there are additional risks, like hypertension. You're twice as likely to develop it with twins. But as they said, they monitor you. And, of course, I tell George, and he's straight out buying a blood pressure monitor, bless him. But he's right. That way, I can take it every day rather than wait for the next antenatal appointment. There are no symptoms, anyway."

"Well, that's good. I had high blood pressure in the final few weeks, and they put me on bed rest. They were worried about pre-eclampsia, I remember. Got to be careful with that one."

"Yes, again. Twice the risk. Quite a few things are twice as risky. Gestational diabetes, too. And I've already had off-the-scale morning sickness and constipation. There's even a risk of losing one. Some nights, when I'm not sleeping, I go through it all. One growing significantly slower, losing both. But you know, Mum, I'm surprisingly relaxed about it. During the daytime, I mean. The doctors are so good. They're on top of things; even premature babies pull through fine nowadays."
"Exactly."
"George has it right. He says we should focus on the positives. Nobody seems to do that. He came up with something the other day. He said, 'You're growing someone along with their best friend.' And that's true. I think twins are lucky in that."
Over the next few weeks, George and Cathy discussed possible boys' and girls' names several times. They liked some names but elected against others because they had roots in only one side of their families. They had written a list of names but hadn't felt it was safe to choose a name. They still did not know the gender of the twins.
"We need names that go together," said George.
"Like Tom and Jerry, do you mean, or Cagney and Lacey?"
George picked up the list. "We can choose a name from your side and mine now."
"Lily was my grandmother's name, and you said Rose was your mother's middle name."
"Lily and Rose Lewis. Sounds great. And for boys..."
"Well, you said you wanted Michael because that was your dad's name, so we agreed we'd choose a different boy's name as well."
"Maverick?" George joked. "Or Magnum, you know, the American PI TV series?"
"Well, not an M. Everyone would get confused. Another man's name on your side of the family, which goes with Michael?"
"My dad's middle name is William." "Michael and William Lewis. We have it, don't you think?"
"Better than George."

*

On Monday, October 3rd, 1983, Michael and William were born two weeks early. They both had breathing difficulties and were placed in incubators. Michael, in particular, was a concern. The doctor said his lungs were a bit less developed than William's. Cathy and George took that to mean he would probably die. Neither of them was particularly religious, but they prayed.
The sterile, technical, machine-driven incubator shrieked, life hanging on by a thread. But it was heartless. Cathy and George were trapped in fear, desperation, and helplessness.
"He's a fighter," George stated time and again. Cathy knew he said it more to persuade himself than as his absolute conviction. Cathy cried and begged the nurses, God, and most of all, the machine. After a week, they could touch William briefly through the side of the incubator. Each touch tried to send healing and strength.
The bond they both felt when Michael was finally able to come out of the neonatal intensive care unit was tearful, thankful, total, and never forgotten.

*

Once the babies had been allowed home, George had to return to work, and Cathy was on her own. Cathy's mother had come briefly when the twins were born and had telephoned regularly.
"Mum, Michael has cried almost non-stop for four months. I feel like I'm neglecting William because he's the easier of the two. Sleep comes only 30 minutes at a time, in between feeding, pumping, burping, and cooing each baby back to sleep. I feel like I'm losing myself in the daily grind of trying to find my footing as 'mum.'"
"It sounds hard, Cathy. I should be there more often, but I just can't. I wish you hadn't moved so far away. Is there not a friend who can help a bit?"
"No. Well, Kelly—remember that friend I met at antenatal—sometimes comes around and holds one of them while we have a coffee. But that's it. It's too much, Mum."

Cathy started to cry.
"Oh, Cathy. I'm sorry, I..."
"It's all right, Mum. I know you can't help. I'm sorry to cry. It just seems too much sometimes."
"It'll get easier, Cathy. It will."
"Everyone says that, but I'm not sure it ever will. George does what he can when he's here, but he has to be away so much, even overnight. It's too much. We should never have had children—not with us set up like this. George says he'll look at getting a different job, but there's nothing for his skills around here."
"Well, maybe he will be able to. Let's hope. In the meantime, I think you're wonderful. You're doing a brilliant job. I will try to come. I will. This is the hardest time. It will get easier. Believe me."

*

The early intense period did ease, and Michael's ongoing frailty only intensified Cathy's affection for him.
Michael had developed relatively well despite his greater tendency to pick up infections. He learnt to walk earlier than William, who preferred shuffling backwards to his desired location. Neither of the boys developed their ability to speak at the same age as many of their contemporaries, though Cathy and George had been assured there would not be any long-term consequences. Doctors' reassurances continued to be essential, as people would constantly issue doom-laden warnings that whichever twin was lagging in a particular regard might not grow up as clever as the other.
What they both did was develop excellent drawing skills. All they saw, they drew. All they thought, they drew.

*

Cathy returned to work in 1988 when the twins started at the village primary school. The boys enjoyed their time there, though they played more with each other than with other children. Back home, they both loved drawing pictures of the day. They would even swap part-finished drawings so that the other could add further touches.

"Have you seen how they intuitively, silently pass things from one to the other, and the other seems to just know how to continue?" George asked Cathy.

"Yes, they're on the same wavelength in all sorts of ways. They have cooperation down to a fine art. They are brilliant together. It's wonderful to know they'll always look out for each other," Cathy said.

One of Michael and William's favourite activities was swimming. George had taken them religiously every Saturday morning since they had started school. One Saturday afternoon, Cathy was talking with Michael at home.

"It's Daddy's birthday tomorrow. Shall we make him a card? You could draw him a lovely picture and do some colouring," Cathy suggested, taking the opportunity for some one-on-one time with him, as his twin, uncharacteristically, had a nap at 4:30 p.m. on a school day.

"I do cards at school for Easter. I could draw him a chick," Michael replied enthusiastically.

Cathy cleared a space on the kitchen table and placed an assortment of felt pens and a sheet of card on it. "OK, so shall Mummy help you fold the card so it has a proper front and inside?"

Michael nodded as Cathy took his hands and guided them to align the edges of the card before creasing it to make the birthday card. "That looks right, doesn't it? Like a real birthday card."

Michael grinned and picked up an orange felt-tip pen.

"OK, so you've picked up an orange colour. Where might there be orange on a duck?"

Michael paused to think. "On 'is beak," he shouted with glee, bringing the pen to the card.

"His beak. H. His beak." She stayed Michael's hand. "Yes, great, so where should we have the chick's head? We need to put the chick in the middle of the page." She guided his hand to the right of the card about two-thirds of the way up. "Here," she said with a warm mixture of finality and encouragement.

Michael drew the beak. "Lovely. So now his 'ead..."

"Er, 'ead? What is that? I don't know the word 'ead."

Michael touched his head. "This 'ead."

"Oh, you mean head. Again, with an H." Looking back at the picture, she continued, "OK, what colour is that?"

"Yellow. And body. And his arms."

"Wings," Cathy corrected.

Michael drew the outline of the chick.

"So now we need his feet. We could have them orange, too, heh?"

"Or red. Or blue," Michael suggested.

"Blue feet," Cathy said, laughing. "I don't think so. Maybe red, though."

Michael drew two stick legs.

"So, how many toes?"

"Five. I have five toes."

"You do," Cathy replied affectionately. "But chicks only have three. Draw three toes on his legs."

Michael drew the toes. "There," he said. "A chick." He pulled a slight grimace upon seeing the drawing, which looked disappointingly different from the image of a chick that he had in his head. "It's not very good, is it, Mummy?" he moaned.

"Well, when it's coloured in, it will be. Daddy will love it. Start colouring in the body. Stay in the lines. Do it steadily."

Michael coloured in the body, only straying slightly at a few points.

"And now the beak. See if you can colour that in. Slowly and carefully."

Michael coloured inside the beak shape but immediately crossed the outline. Anger. He tried another line. Again, it crossed the line. In total frustration, he shouted, "I can't do it!" Then, extraordinarily, he repeated the phrase, but this time in an amazingly accurate mimicry of Orville the Duck. Pleased with himself upon hearing the words, he repeated it.

Cathy burst out laughing. "That's just like him. Just like Orville. Where did you learn to do that?"

Michael recalled another phrase he had heard Orville say and added, "I can't fly," again in a perfect rendition.

Cathy laughed even louder. "That's amazing, Michael. I didn't know you could do that. Do it for Daddy later. It will make him laugh."

Michael smiled and nodded. "I will."

"And he will love his chick when you write 'To Daddy. Love, Michael.' Perhaps William will do one later as well. But he will like your joke voice, so he will."

Michael paused to think. "I would like to make Daddy laugh. He always seems so busy."

*

At age seven, Michael suddenly became seriously ill. He lost weight and became extremely lethargic. Blood tests were taken. Cathy and George sat with a child on each of their laps, Michael on Cathy's, in the GP's surgery, when the doctor used the word "Leukaemia."

Cathy's tears fell instantly. Michael turned to look up at her, sensing distress. She looked down at him. *Is he dying now?* She hugged him tightly.

George reached over to grab Cathy's right hand, and he, too, began to cry.

The doctor continued. "I know you are both upset, but there are treatments. Good treatments. He's a strong little chap." She went on to explain chemotherapy, but neither Cathy nor George heard a word.

George spent an immense amount of time looking into the different forms of leukaemia and the specific drugs being used in Michael's chemotherapy.

"It says here that Cyclophosphamide and Cytosine Arabinoside are the best treatment for acute lymphoblastic leukaemia," he repeated the sentence verbatim, clinging to the belief that saying it over and over would somehow make it work.

Cathy's immediate focus was on the extreme illness Michael experienced after treatment. *Is he getting worse with all this?* She placed her faith in home nursing and caring for Michael.

The house was full of get-well cards from far and wide. Many were from people they barely knew.

William struggled to understand why Michael wasn't getting better, unlike him when he had a bad cold.

"Mummy, I've drawn Michael a picture to get him well, like the other cards will," William said, passing his artwork to Cathy.

"George. Oh, George. Look at this," Cathy said as she passed the drawing to George.

The drawing showed Michael in his bed with William at his bedside, holding his hand.

"Oh, that's lovely. He misses him so much. What is that he's drawn above Michael's head?"

"It's an angel. We learnt about angels at school. I'm sure one will help Michael."

"That's lovely, William," George said.

"I'm sure it will," Cathy added as she was knocked backwards by a giant wave of sympathy.

Cathy and George looked at each other. While wanting to appear strong for William, they cried, and both hugged him.

Even while extremely ill, Michael and William played together.

"Have you watched 'em?" George asked Cathy as he returned from sitting by Michael's bedside with them. "They cooperate in silence. Seem to know what t'other needs."

"I think William has a real awareness of how Michael is. He seems to know what he can't do now and automatically compensates for it. It's uncanny."

"I don't believe in telepathy, but they are somehow on the same wavelength. I think it comes from all the years they've spent looking at each other as they're asked questions. They've always glanced over to sort of see what t'other one thinks. Maybe somehow, by now, they kinda know."

Cathy nodded. "I know it sounds ridiculous, but I think William is almost using his... I don't know what... psychic... energy to help Michael get better."

"I think Michael can sense the love he is surrounded by. From all of us, but especially William."

Whether it was the chemotherapy, the nursing, their

love, the love of his twin, or the angel in the picture, Cathy and George never knew, but Michael recovered.

*

The drama of Michael's cancer gave birth to a permanent fear in Cathy that lingered like a spectre, alarming her at the prospect of any danger or illness.

Nevertheless, the next four years brought laughter and joy back to the family. They found outdoor life appealing, and apart from swimming in the pool with their dad, they were so close to the coast that they could enjoy ample time on the beach and in the sea.

Michael and William began to manifest differences. William's art skills developed significantly, while Michael developed a real fondness for music. But their bond only grew stronger. They spent all their time together.

All the neighbours knew them. Imogen, from next door, in particular, raved about them. As Cathy left the cottage to take them to school one morning, she bumped into her.

"Cor, they're good-looking boys, Cath. They'll be real lady-killers; they will. And they're nice with it. You've done a stonking job. I am so glad that Michael overcame his problems. What are you up to over the bank holiday?"

"Yes, they're great. My dad keeps saying how good-looking they are. I think he used the term 'lady-killers' too. Sounds like they'll be murderers. We're off to my mum and dad's tonight. My dad's got all sorts planned for them. He wasn't so good with them when they were babies. But since they were about five, he loves it when we go up. What about you and Derek?"
"We're getting the bedroom ready. Won't be long now." She patted her pregnant belly.
"Sure. You're due in the first week of July."
"He's a boy. But only one. Hopefully, we'll get him a brother or sister soon. It's always nice for them to have a… sibling. I sound posh saying that, don't I? A brother or sister, I mean."
"Ha, mostly."

*

Weekends were hectic.
"I'm taking the boys to the shopping centre this afternoon. William is desperate to get those trainers he saw last week," Cathy said to George as they were washing and drying dishes together at the kitchen sink.
"I said I'd meet my bor for a lunchtime pint. Gordon. Don't let him talk you into the most expensive trainers in the shop," George replied.
"No. They're not. I told them both last week that we couldn't get them both trainers at the same time and that one of them would have to wait until next month, when we're paid again. Michael said straight away that he'd wait. They're becoming more and more different in little ways. The trainers William wants are called Converse and bright red," Cathy continued.
"Red? Ye gods, what next?" George replied, feigning horror. He paused. "And they talk. Converse? Be talked about more like," he quipped.
Cathy laughed. "And they're a lot less expensive than other trainers. They're canvas like pumps. Michael wants the latest Nike trainers —they are all the talk of the town. They are expensive."
"And what colour are they? Green? Purple?"

"No, just plain white. As I said, they're different from each other. William is all about colour and a 'look.' Michael is more about fitting in. And that means expensive."

"We'd better start savin' up this month then," George added.

That afternoon in town, they went to the new shopping centre. All fabulously swish—bright and clean. Their attention was drawn to a bundle of what looked like rubbish in a small alcove next to a shop space that had yet to be let. The pile included a sleeping bag.

"Do either of you need the toilet before we start shopping?" Cathy asked with a voice of many years of experience.

In unison, they chimed, "No."

In the shoe shop, William headed straight to the rack of single trainers covering an entire wall and picked up the ones they had come for. Cathy looked around for an assistant, but there only appeared to be one young lad. *Saturday staff.* Oblivious to her gaze, tilting head movement, smile, and eventual waving of the bright red trainer in the air, he finally noticed and sauntered over.

"Do you have these in a '2'?"

The boy didn't speak but turned away, carrying the shoe to what Cathy hoped was the stockroom. They waited. And waited. Had the boy forgotten and gone on his break? He reappeared carrying a box.

"We haven't got a '2,' but we have '3's."

Not so naïve, then. "OK. Thanks. They're probably too big, but we'll try them."

The lacing on the trainers was the longest and most complex Cathy had ever seen. William began lacing one, and Cathy the other.

"I need the toilet," Michael chimed.

"I told you to go," Cathy shouted, irritated by both the Krypton challenge of the lacing and Michael's plea. "You'll have to wait a minute."

"I can't. I really, really need to go. I didn't need to go when you asked, but we've been ages. We passed one a few doors back. I'll be quick."

Cathy hesitated. She wasn't sure Michael should go alone.

Even that slight hesitation prompted Michael. "I have to go now."

"All right. But straight back here. We'll still be trying them on or at the till. Look, over there," she pointed.

Michael left the shop and went to the toilets, passing the alcove with the bundle, now occupied by a dishevelled man. He had placed a beanie hat on the floor, and some coins were in it.

Michael had been told about homeless people at school and how sad it was for them. On his way back, he reached into his trousers and pulled out his pocket money. He walked over to the hat, bent down, and carefully placed his money. As he did so, he smiled at the man.

He was somewhat fazed by how dirty the man's teeth were when he smiled in return.

"Thank you," the man said. "Come with me," he added.

William declared that the shoes fit perfectly, though clearly too big. Cathy figured he'd grown into them, which was probably for the best.

They queued. They paid. But no, Michael. Cathy barked at William, "I told him to come straight back. He's a silly boy. Just wait until he gets back here."

But Michael didn't come. In a panic, Cathy asked the girl at the till to keep her eye on William as she rushed out of the shop toward the toilets. She hesitated briefly outside the Gents, but desperation led her to enter by a few meters. Then she stepped back and forward again, shouting out, "Michael. Michael. Are you here?" Silence. Again, the call, this time with even greater urgency. "Michael. Michael. Are you here?"

A middle-aged man spoke as he was leaving the toilets. "Are you all right?"

"My son, Michael. He's ten. He went to the toilets ages ago, but he hasn't returned to the shop," Cathy explained breathlessly, bordering on tears.

"I'll go back in and look," the man replied calmly.

Within a few seconds, he returned. "He's not in there. Which shop was it?" he queried.

"The... the shoe shop just there," Cathy replied, somehow losing some of her gasp as she reacted to the man's calm manner.
"Let's go back there," the man suggested. "I'm sure he's all right," he added reassuringly.
And there he was. Standing, talking to William.
"He's here. He's here," Cathy said to the man. "Thank you. Thank you."

The man walked away without comment.
"Where have you been?" Cathy shouted.
"I went with the homeless man," Michael replied.
"Homeless man? Homeless man? Who? Where?"
"Over there. That bundle of stuff we saw. That's his. He doesn't have a house. I gave him my pocket money, and he asked me to go with him."
Cathy's tone became even more desperate. "Go with him? Where? You didn't. You know you can't go off with strangers. Where did you go? Did he touch you? We'd better get the police. Where is he now?"
"He's having his dinner. He used my money to buy some lunch. He was hungry. In the coffee place just along there. He took me with him and said, 'I want to show you that I am using your money to get some food. People think we purely use money for drugs. I'm a good man. I've merely hit some problems,' he said and smiled. He had terrible teeth."
"He's no right taking money off a child and taking you away. I think we should tell the police," Cathy replied. She thanked the shop assistant. As she calmed down, she thought better of involving the police. The man hadn't known Michael had to return to the shop and was only trying to show his thanks.
"You're a kind boy, Michael. It was good of you to help a poor person. But you have to be careful in life. Kindness can trap you."

Chapter 2

On Saturday, 8th June 1985, Grace Carpenter had met the man who would change her life.
"Pardon, mademoiselle. Je m'excuse. Er… sorry."
Grace Carpenter looked up at the man who had just knocked the book out of her hand as she left the Chester bookshop. Her frantic scrabbling on the pavement to minimise the book's damage from the wet ground ended when she retrieved it. The elegant Frenchman stood over her.
"Ta," she replied, having never lost her Merseyside accent despite having lived in Chester for fifteen of her twenty-three years. Upon seeing a well-dressed man, she added, "Thanks very much," in a reduced accent.
"Oh, but yes. Les pages sont mouillées. Wet," Claude Fontrelle said, glancing back at the shop Grace had stepped out from. "Come. I buy another for you."
"There's no need. Honestly," Grace responded, her sadness about the ruined book mingling with English decency in pretending it didn't warrant troubling the man to replace it.
"I insist, mademoiselle. C'est ma faute. My faute… fault. Come," Claude persisted, heading back toward the bookshop and extending his hand back to Grace as if in a relay race, waiting for her to hand him the damaged book.
Grace obliged and followed him into the shop.
Claude looked down at the book title. "Ah, I know this book. I go tonight to this film, here in Jester."
"Right. It's not a new book. It was written yonks ago, but the new film's success has made many people buy it. Including me."
Now sufficiently composed, Grace realised that her focus on the book's fall had made her ignore that it was still raining. She attempted to pull her long copper hair into some semblance of order.

"I would like a copy of this book, please, madame. *Out of Africa*. Do you have more copies?"
Claude said to the assistant, who promptly left to fetch one. He looked around the bookshop and spotted the small café area. He looked out of the shop, then said to Grace, "It's still raining. We have a coffee. Yes?" Upon paying, he continued, "I am alone in this town. It would be nice to talk to a pretty lady. I am not danger."
Grace nodded and smiled, running her hands through her hair to straighten it further. She knew she wasn't pretty— rather plain— but she didn't feel that the suave, dishy Frenchman was a threat. And it was wet.
Grace knew the café area in the bookshop quite well. She had often wiled away an afternoon there, but not in conversation. As they took their seats, she wondered what they would talk about.
"So, I am Clod. Clod Fontrelle. I live in Paris," Claude said relatively formally.
"And I am Grace Carpenter. I live in a small town near here called Frodsham."
"Frogs-ham? This is a funny name. A town for frogs."
Grace laughed as Claude continued. "I have not seen this sign for Frogs-ham. I come here to Moll-d."

Grace found his mispronunciations charming. "It is pronounced Mold, like mould," she giggled.
"Oh dear. They also must laugh at me. I always call it Moll-d. There is an agricultural equipment centre there. I sell for... ROPA France."
"I'm sure they don't," Grace suggested, quite taken with this exotic man.
Two hours went by.
"And now, I will be bold, like mould. I will ask you to dinner and then to see this film with me tonight. Will you agree, Grace Carpenter?" Claude asked with a flirtatious twinkle in his eye.
Grace thought she was in a movie, not just going to see one.

The meal was pleasant, and the film was romantic. Grace was enchanted. Claude's request for her to come back to his hotel for a drink was greeted unhesitatingly, although Grace was not used to such forwardness. And certainly not to spending the night with a man. Ever.

On that night, Grace was the movie star. She had the leading man. They made love throughout the night. It wasn't until dawn that the realities of her mother's anger and questioning set in. Her mum wanted to know where she had been and why she hadn't said she would be staying out all night. *Stayed over at a friend's house. Didn't think you'd still be awake.*

Back at the film set. Even getting dressed was exciting. Claude explained that he had to leave for Paris early but would be returning soon. He gave her his home telephone number, and she gave him hers.

Over the following days, Grace longed to share details of her newfound romance with someone. Anybody. She thought about Claude throughout the day and especially at night. Her bed now felt like a lonely place—no body, no breath upon her neck. But she had found a man. The man. She began to plan how she would manage the next overnight stay at the hotel. Should she call him now? He had said he hated the falseness of phone calls and how hard it would be for him to wait until they could meet again. And Grace found it hard, too.

Weeks crawled by. Still, no call to say he would be coming the next day. She would have to ring. He'd understand. But he'd said not to. He might get angry. Best not to. Be patient.

By the 20th of July, Grace realised that she was pregnant. What to do? How would he react? After several days of deliberation, she picked up the phone. She didn't speak French but understood the meaning of "Ce numéro est impossible à obtenir." The true significance. In a panic, she tried to find details of agricultural equipment businesses in Mold. But there were none.

A week later, the discussions at home with her parents were a mixture of screaming anger, condemnation, and ridicule. The religious beliefs of her parents made abortion out of the question. While they all thought his name was probably Claude Fontrelle, they agreed that everything else was pure fiction. They decided that Grace should go and spend time with her mother's cousin, Gladys, in Oswestry, and return using the name Mrs Fontrelle, with a story of abandonment.

Just in case he ever did reappear. Grace duly obliged, even formally changing her name by deed poll to Grace Fontrelle and moved to Heswall.

On Wednesday, 12th March 1986, she gave birth to Claire Fontrelle—an event she greeted with total bitterness—a child she hated from a man she now loathed.

Chapter 3

Claire began climbing the tree with her usual agility and confidence, belying her not-yet-seven years. Decisions on which branches to select were rapid, as were her twists and reaches. She liked this tree. She could see that she could get high. Away from the world. That world.

But today, the tree was wet, and her mother's insistence that she always wear shift dresses rather than shorts or jeans added an additional complication as she sought to avoid dampening the fabric. Swinging toward a chosen branch, she felt her knee and dress hem rub hard against the rough bark. She glanced down, hoping against hope that all was well. She would be in trouble for marking the dress. *Oh dear.* She knew this green slime well. The lichen might wash away with water, but today her hands could not gather enough from the leaves, and her rubbing only worsened the stain.

She hitched her dress up front and back, exposing her knickers, and continued climbing. The earlier rain was more evident in the higher branches. She felt a slight slip of her fingers on the target branch. When her other hand joined in, it, too, slid. The next move would be tricky.

Perhaps most children would have turned back at this point—or indeed never even started—but Claire was driven. Driven to experience the powerful feeling of escape in the highest part of the canopy possible.

But the next branch was not possible. Not today. Not even for Claire. As she stretched, her left hand, meant to steady her, slid slightly on the branch. Enough that she could only get the weakest grip on the new one. Her face set. Her eyes widened. No way back. And her left hand was no saviour—it, too, might slip. And all the while, her right hand's grasp grew ever less certain.

Claire mustered belief and made her move.

Her grip failed. She fell. As she plummeted, she muttered aloud, her voice carrying the same *c'est la vie* attitude as her earlier inner voice. *Oh dear.*

Claire felt the impact—the deafening thud of her head on the grass.

And then... nothing. Nothing but numbness. And blackness.

Mrs. Tapping had taken her usual morning walk with her dog. It was a beautiful, bright day, but the sound struck her most. A gentle breeze hissed through the trees, and the birdsong sounded harmoniously light and airy. And yet, there was quietness in the place. Her footsteps echoed on the duckboards as she walked over a stretch with a muddy hollow. Even the gentle pants of her dog, Ellie, were audible. As she stepped off the boards, she heard the comforting crunch of autumn leaves beneath her feet.

The tranquillity was interrupted by the excited yapping of a small dog somewhere ahead in the woods. The barking persisted, and as she approached a small clearing, she saw a neighbour crouched over the body of a small child lying at the base of a tree. Mrs Greaves lived several doors away from her. Mrs Tapping walked forward.

Claire finally stirred.

Mrs Greaves comforted her. "Lie still. Don't move. Let me check that nothing is broken."

"Should I phone an ambulance? Do you think she might have hit her head? Or have some internal injury?" Mrs Tapping asked.

"I'm okay. I just slipped. I only fell from up there." Claire pointed to a branch about a metre and a half above her.

"Well, you knocked yourself out. You shouldn't be climbing trees, and certainly not on your own. And you shouldn't be here in the woods by yourself at all."

"I like it here. It's fun. I'm good at balancing and climbing. I don't fall much. And look—barely a scratch. I'm fine. Worse things happen at sea."

"It isn't nothing, Claire. It's a serious matter. You're only seven years old. You should be at home playing safely in your garden at your age," chided Mrs. Greaves.

Claire stood up, brushed herself down, and bounded off, completely unperturbed, calling behind her, "Thank you."

"Do you know her?" asked Mrs Tapping.

"No, not personally. I've seen her around. She does seem to be out and on her own a lot."

"I feel sorry for her. I don't think life at home is great for her. Do you know Mrs Fontrelle?"

Mrs Tapping shook her head. "No, I've never met her."

Mrs. Greaves grimaced. "Well, she's not right, you know. In the head. One of those who's up one minute and totally down the next. I think her daughter, Claire, tries to escape from the house. Poor kid. She could do with having a good pal. It isn't right that she spends all this time alone."

"No. She seemed like a lovely girl. She took that knock pretty well, though."

As Claire skipped her way back home, she felt the skin on her right knee tightening. She looked down and saw a bright red area where her skin had peeled.

She entered through the back door. Her mother had kicked off her slippers and was lying on the sofa, eyes closed.

"I fell," Claire said, her tone seeking sympathy. And for a moment, she thought concern had come.

"Oh dear," her mother murmured—a reply hovering between genuine and feigned sympathy.

Claire tried to elicit more care by adding, "It really hurts," as she attempted to nuzzle into her mother's side on the sofa. But it backfired.

She was immediately pushed away. "Wipe it clean and leave me in peace. Mummy's got one of her headaches."

Claire's reaction wasn't one of resentment but of excessive sympathy.

"Oh dear. Should I get you a biscuit?" she asked with evident concern.

"Just a small one."

Claire urgently sped to the kitchen, rifling through the biscuit box to find the correct one. She returned, beaming like a happy retriever.

"This will help, Mummy," she said, looking into her mother's eyes for signs of gratitude, but they signalled nothing.

Thwack!

Claire felt a sharp pain in her left thigh, followed by the sound of a slap echoing through the room.
Thwack!
A second smack, this time on her right thigh.
Claire didn't cry out. She drew in a deep breath, almost as if preparing to yelp, but the sheer shock stunned her into silence.
"So now, will you stop being a nuisance?" her mother shouted, her eyes set and full of hatred.
When Claire gathered her thoughts and willed herself to leave the room, her mother's blazing eyes had cooled. They had settled into something else—cold emptiness—as she dropped her slipper alongside the other at the front of the sofa. She lay down and closed those unpredictable eyes.
Claire imagined them burning behind her mother's eyelids, some fire raging inside her brain. Then she quickly turned and left the room, creeping upstairs to her bedroom. She looked around for something—anything—to distract herself, but all she saw were the same few books on her shelf. She lay on her bed, touching the sore sides of her legs, wincing as her fingers brushed over her raw knee. Twirling strands of her hair into small curls, she became Little Orphan Annie.
Half-whispering, half-singing, she murmured, "The sun'll come out tomorrow."
Several minutes later, she heard the front door open. She sprang into action. Sliding down the bannister as quickly as possible, she stationed herself by the door, where her mother was now reaching for her coat.
Like a dog sensing whether an owner's stance signalled walkies or an absence, Claire knew she was about to be left behind.
"Where are you going? Will you be long? Will you be all right, Mummy?"
"Shush."
Her mother had put on her everyday coat and was about to button it up. Claire reached to hold onto the hem of her mother's dress as she turned, but missed.
"Wait. Wait just a minute, Mummy. I... I don't—"
"Shush. Not that nonsense."

She reached again, this time catching hold of the hem of her mother's coat.
"I... I... I... I only wanted. I needed to tell you... something."
Her mother exhaled sharply, irritation taking over. She batted Claire's hand away.
"What?"
Claire's chest swelled with emotion, her thoughts tangling, her mind grasping for something to say. But all that came out was: "I fell."
"Stupid girl. You've told me that already. And don't go making a mess in here. Go out and play."
With that, her mother opened the door, pushed Claire back into the house, and left.
Claire recognised the confusion of feelings washing over her—but she had no words for them.
Sadness at the lack of care she had received.
And an overwhelming sense of fear, as if something terrible were about to happen.
As she stretched up to reach the front door lock, a phrase drifted into her mind—one she had heard her aunt say to her mother many times before.
She whispered it at first, then chanted softly:
"Ripples on the water. Ripples on the water."
Just around the corner from her house, Claire spotted a log from a wood-burning stove delivery lying at the edge of a driveway on Galbraith Road—the posh houses.
She was immediately interested. Logs meant balancing. She knew she shouldn't take it. But she'd give it back.
And if she was quick…
Then, she had it. She ran with her treasure back to her house, her heart pounding excitedly. On the patio, she scanned for the best spot, where she had the most room to roll.
Without hesitation, she stepped onto the log with her right foot. It was a near-perfect cylinder, so it was lively. Too lively. Her foot slipped, and she tumbled off.
Again. And again. She tried to shuffle her foot each time as the log rolled beneath her. A quarter turn. A half. And off it skidded. Then, both feet. A test. How long could she balance?

One, two. One. One-two. One-two-three. Well—a mega quick one-two-three.

Time flew. Hours. Determination, satisfaction, but mostly… fun.

This log was too good to put back. And anyway, she might get caught. She rolled it under the shed for safekeeping.

Later that afternoon, she found a pencil and, on the blank inside cover of one of her books, she drew:

Claire, the circus performer.

Claire is balancing on her log.

On a barrel.

Claire, the trapeze artist.

Bending her legs to hang over the trapeze, swinging upside down, just as she had done on her favourite tree in the woods.

That evening, there was a knock at the door.

Claire crept along the landing and crouched at the top of the stairs, craning her neck to glimpse who was calling. The log owner?

Her mum answered. Claire recognised Mrs Greaves's voice from earlier that day.

"I thought I'd pop round to see if Claire is OK. She had a nasty fall earlier."

Claire could see Mrs Greaves's face peering around the door, trying to look inside.

"No, you didn't. You've simply come to snoop. Spy on me. There's nothing wrong with Claire. Get lost."

And with that, her mum slammed the door shut.

Claire crept back to her bedroom. Anxiety.

Her mother turned and shouted up the stairs.

"Claire, get down here."

Claire put on her happy, *'I'm-no-trouble'* face. "Who was it, Mummy?"

"You know who it was. You've been making a fuss about falling over, telling everyone, trying to get sympathy. That was her—next door but two. Pretending to check on you. All she wanted was to look around the house. I didn't let her in, but even so, she was leaning in, scanning. She'll be on the phone now, slagging me off to that Mrs Tapping. Do you want people to hate me?"

Claire winced at her mother's angry snarl. "No, Mummy. I didn't say anything about it. I ran off."

"Don't believe anyone who says they're looking out for you and watching over you. No one does that unless it suits them. You look after yourself, do you hear?"

"Yes, I hear. I know. That's why I ran off."

Claire turned and hurried back upstairs, a sense of relief washing over her. She knew she'd have to stay inside for a while now, but her mind was already wandering as she sat on her bed. Where could she find some fun? Somewhere new. Outside.

Feverishly, she grabbed her notepad and began to sketch.

A tree.

An eddy of contentment.

She continued.

A tree with a whole brick house, complete with a smoking chimney, nestled in its branches.

Serenity. Safety.

Chapter 4

It was in January of 1994 that Cathy sensed something was wrong with William when she woke him.
"Many. Flowers. Sky. Happy," he said.
"What do you mean?" Cathy asked.
"Bang. Bang. Bang," William said, tapping his head incessantly, his voice growing louder and louder until he was screaming at the top of his lungs.
Cathy shouted hysterically to George, "Something's wrong. Completely wrong. Quick. Something's wrong. Badly wrong. Ring an ambulance!"
At that moment, William went into convulsions.
George ran up the stairs. "No time. We'll take him ourselves, now," he panted.
They roused Michael, threw a dressing gown around him, and George carried William downstairs. They sped off in the car. The typical forty-minute journey took thirty-four minutes. William had fallen asleep in the car despite Cathy's desperate attempts to keep him awake.
The hospital kept him in. Over the next several weeks, he underwent many tests, including a brain biopsy. The severity of his condition was apparent to everyone. The diagnosis of a brain tumour came as no surprise. But the news that it was Diffuse Intrinsic Pontine Glioma—and thus incurable—was a shock. The prognosis of only a few weeks to live after the initial onset of symptoms was devastating.
"We knew there was an increased risk of cancer for William when Michael was ill, but I thought 'e'd gotten past all that," George sobbed.
"It's because I kept praying for Michael. All his life, I have prayed for him. This is God's vengeance," Cathy lamented.
"You don't believe that. It's not God…"
"He should take me. Take me. Not William. Take me!" Cathy screamed hysterically as she paced back and forth across the floor of the family room at the entrance to the ward.

George looked on helplessly. He knew she was wrong, but he also knew he had no hope for William and no God to blame.

The speed of the decline was alarming. Michael was allowed to visit William on a few occasions.

The last time he visited, in the final week of February, William had no speech and lay virtually immobile. Michael took with him a drawing he had made. He had heard the story several times of how William had drawn him a picture when he was ill and how kind that had been. His mother had said she kept the drawing, though Michael had never seen it.

He spent a long time on his picture. He drew it as a small cartoon strip, determined to get it right—hope as magic.

In the first frame, he drew William with bandages around his head, lying in the hospital bed, surrounded by wires, tubes, and devices—precisely as he had seen them. In the second frame, he was lying on the bed beside William, holding his left hand. In the third frame, William took his bandages off and stood up. In the fourth frame, they played together on the beach, and the sun shone.

But the sun wasn't shining on the 4th of March, 1994, when William died.

*

For Michael, the funeral was a complete blur. He had been bought a new shirt. Too big. Unforgivingly stiff. He had been bought a tie—not a new school tie, but a black one. The tie was too long, and most had to be tucked away inside his shirt, the knot as wide as his neck.

They travelled in a big black car to Ellough, near Beccles, to a crematorium. He and his parents stood at the front. There were many people there—pretty much everyone from Ilketshall St. Andrew, as well as several of his teachers from school.

They sang some songs that Michael didn't know. Everyone cried.

*

The death changed everything. George had to return to work, but Cathy extended her sick leave from Ringsfield. Yet, both Cathy and George were lost. In this event, there was no wisdom from others—only pity.

Memories assaulted Cathy. Flashbacks. The scan. Two embryos. Her two boys are playing. Her two boys in their beds. Every image drained her of life.

George had no desire to take Michael swimming, as he had always done with the twins. Nothing had meaning.

They both felt totally lost.

"Do we take his things out of their room?" George asked.

"Or will that upset Michael more? Maybe he wants to have them there," Cathy replied.

Michael cried constantly. He was only willing to eat the most uniform foods—cereals, beans, and tomato soup. Anything resembling a full meal was merely played with. He ate in an almost robotic manner, as if barely present in the moment.

The play space in William and Michael's bedroom was the most distressing place for Cathy and George to see.

"He sits on the right-hand side of the table like he always did. He does drawings and writing and places them to his left as if William is there," George lamented.

"I heard him calling him when he came home from school today," Cathy added.

"And we heard him the other night, talking as if William was there," George said.

"I don't know if this is normal or something to worry about," Cathy said.

"I read that often a child can go back—almost become younger, more babyish—when they can't cope," George added, shaking his head.

"He does that," Cathy confirmed. "He sits on my lap and talks in an excessively childish way. He hadn't done that for years."

"We can only try to comfort him. Tell him he's loved. That's what he needs. It's got to be good that he's bein' comforted, hasn't it?" George queried.

But Michael didn't understand all he felt, only that he was totally alone. So alone. Sometimes, he believed William would come back. One afternoon, after returning from school, he ran straight upstairs to William's room. He sorted through William's pencil case and lifted out several different colours. He sharpened the red one. Then, he placed a sheet of drawing paper on William's side of the desk. He pulled William's chair out and went back downstairs.
"I think he's coming back tonight, Mummy. I know he will."
"He can't come back, Michael. He's gone now," Cathy replied.
"I know that he's gone, Mummy, but he is coming back. He'll surprise you. I just know he's coming."
But William didn't come back in the afternoon, and Michael searched for him that evening.
"He's hiding, Mummy. Tell him to come out. He's naughty."
"He isn't here, Michael. He isn't here."
Cathy reached out to hold Michael's hand and gently pulled him toward her. "Here, come and sit on my lap."
Days, weeks, and months passed. Cathy and George found the pain interminable. On many occasions, when Michael entered the room, they imagined it was William, only to have to bring themselves up short and react to Michael as best they could upon the realisation.
Michael's solitude was constant. He had begun to want answers for why William had gone.
"Did I do something wrong, Mummy? I once hit him on the head with a teddy. Too hard. I remember. Did I kill him, Daddy? Did I?"
"No, Michael. It wasn't anything like that. It was an illness. Inside his head."
"Will I get that, Daddy?"
"No," George replied in his most comforting voice, hugging Michael close.
"Will you? Will Mummy?" Michael asked, panic rising in his voice.

"No, Michael. Nobody else will get that. William was just extremely unlucky," George said in the same warm tone. "What we need to do is get one of your friends to come for a sleepover so you can play together," he added, attempting enthusiasm.
Michael didn't reply. He nestled further into his father's chest.
Later that evening, George told Cathy that he'd suggested it.
"He won't want it. It's like the school has been saying. He isn't engaging with other children. With William, he did. Sure, they played together, but they played with others, too. He won't now." Cathy sighed.
"Well, I'll try to persuade him to ask Kevin. He likes Kevin," George suggested.
Cathy sighed even more deeply. She shook her head and rubbed her forehead gently. "I don't think he will have him come."
George sighed heavily. "We're going to have to get him help. Professional help. The GP says it will all pass, but I'm worried."
"I'm more than worried, George. I'll do anything. Anything to help him. I want him to have a normal life. A proper life. But then... I'm terrified for him. I want to wrap him up in cotton wool and love him. Night and day."
George walked over, took Cathy's hand, and kissed her.
Cathy attempted a smile. "Truth is, George, I think we all need help."
As they drove to St. Lawrence School at the end of June, Cathy said, "We'll be seeing Mrs Potts. I can't believe it's his last parents' evening here—end of primary school. I'm worried about how he'll cope when he goes into high school. This school is tiny, but Brighthouse High School is huge. Anyway, let's see what she says about how he's getting on."
"Well, it's only early July. Barely four months. I think it's remarkable that he's even goin' in," George replied.
"It is. But we know he's struggling at home. Mrs Potts has known him for a few years now. She was lovely when I first went to see her... after... She might have noticed something. Or maybe she can suggest something."
They sat in a small queue outside the classroom.

George sensed the stares and the uneasy shuffling of others joining behind them. "They never speak," he whispered to Cathy, eliciting an even more uneasy shuffle from her, conscious of the others possibly hearing.

When it was their turn, they entered the room and were met with genuine sympathy and warmth from Mrs Potts.

"How are you both?" she asked as they sat down.

"How are you getting on?" she added, reaching out a hand to each of them across the table, gently squeezing both of their forearms.

"Well, er... you know. Getting there," Cathy replied.

Mrs Potts nodded. "Yes, absolutely. A slow process. A slow process."

George and Cathy smiled politely, lowered their gazes, and nodded gently.

"Well, Michael's been trying hard. He's not his usual self, but he's trying. He doesn't seem able to concentrate fully on his lessons. He's there, but you have a sense that he's somewhere else as well. He isn't fidgeting—he simply stares into space. Not out the window, just into space. And he's unusually quiet. He and William were pretty confident together in class and on the playground."

"Yes, William often took the lead," Cathy added.

"Well, that's right. We knew that, so we keep an eye on him in the playground. Of course, he may need some time by himself. Some children do. But we watch him, and now and then, we suggest he goes over to play with some of the other boys he knows best—Terry and Kevin."

"That's good. We've tried to see if he wants a sleepover with one or both of them, but he doesn't seem to," Cathy said.

"Well, that'd be good, maybe in the holidays. Anyway, he's a bright boy. He made up ground particularly well when he was... ill... himself. He'll get there, I'm sure. I know Jean Bebington. She's the Year 7 tutor at John Cavener School. To fill her in. She's awfully nice. Is that OK?"

"Yes, fine," Cathy replied.

"Is there anythin' we can do to 'elp him? Education-wise? Over the summer, I mean?" George asked.

"No. Maybe keep an eye on him. His distraction may lessen. I'm sure you're talking with him. These things take time to process. Anyway, here's the final report we've prepared. You can see that he's still way up there in terms of achievement. It's just that he's dipped a bit right at the end."

"Right," George replied.

After a brief pause, Mrs Potts said, "Anyway, having them here was wonderful. Lovely boys. I guess this is the end of your link with St. Lawrence. I'm so sorry about your loss."

George and Cathy stood to leave. Cathy had a sudden urge to hug Mrs Potts. She turned and approached her. Mrs Potts extended her arms to greet her. They hugged.

"Take care. Take care."

"Thank you for everything," Cathy said as she turned to leave.

"Yes, thank you," George added, turning back from the door.

"I don't know why you're making out that you're doing school stuff with Michael to her. You never have," Cathy chided as they left the building.

*

Over the holidays, Michael cut a truly solitary figure. He rarely went out and didn't want to have any friends over. Cathy and George had decided not to book a holiday away. Instead, they took two weeks off work and used the time for several day trips and treats for Michael. There were brief moments of enjoyment—at the bowling alley, Waterworld, zoo, or Thorpe Park. But a cloud hung over them. Even the sunniest of days seemed overcast.

In the first week of September, the high school allowed small groups of children from the same primary school to visit for a day.

"I was talking to Emily, Tom's mother, and Mary, Kevin's mother, about us taking all three of you together for this tour of the school. How would that be?" Cathy asked Michael.

"Yes, fine. I don't play with them so much now, though. They seem happier being just the two of them. They've got a tandem bike that they've been fixing up. They go out on that."

"Well, I'm sure they still want to be friends. You could join them on your bike, I'm sure. Maybe you could do that tomorrow. It might be your last chance. After that, Kevin's family goes to Spain, and Tom's family goes to Greece, before school starts again. What do you think?" Cathy asked, adding a bit more enthusiasm.

"Maybe. Not if it's raining. They won't go then," Michael replied.

It was raining.

Cathy returned to work in September. She was physically present but somehow not fully there wherever she went—not engaging. An overwhelming sense of dissociation

hung over her. She and George tried especially hard to talk to Michael each day after school to see how he was coping. Michael reported the topics they had covered in different subjects. When they asked if he was playing with friends or had made any new friends, the only response they could get was, "A bit."

"You should play with him more, George. I think he's tremendously lonely."

"Not just me," George snapped.

"You, too. You always want to put these things down to me. I do my best. He's just sullen. He doesn't want to have fun or do fun things. I'm sick of you having a go at me. I'm out working all day," George moaned.

"Oh, yes. Work, work, work. You hide away with work. You get home later and later. Do less and less here. I have to do everything."

"Oh, shut up!" George shouted.

By December, Cathy and George's relationship had deteriorated further. Michael was utterly alone. The parents' evening at Brighthouse High School was a watershed moment.

"We are concerned, Mr and Mrs Lewis. Michael is not concentrating. He is cutting himself off from others. He barely talks to the other children. He gives one-word answers to questions teachers ask him. We know he is a bright lad, but his marks are alarmingly poor. Pretty much across the board, as you'll hear when you meet with his teachers from the different subjects," Mrs Bebington told them.

The other teachers confirmed the situation. The English teacher, Miss Bianchi, concluded, "It may not be for me to say. I'm no expert, but maybe he needs some support from our educational psychologist. The one who has come to the school for a few other children over the years. He's good. He's helped some of our pupils—not with this, but with other things. Maybe he could help."

As they left the school, George and Cathy vowed to take action. "I'm still not sleeping. You're drinking. And Michael is desperately struggling. I think we need to start with the doctor," Cathy suggested in anguish.

"Yes. And then maybe the Marriage Guidance Council," George muttered.

Cathy corrected him. "Relate," she said.

"We don't," George replied sullenly.

Cathy and George booked an appointment to see their GP at the Medical Centre in Bungay the following week to explore their options.

"Are you sleeping?" Dr Patterson asked Cathy.

"George seems to have no trouble falling asleep, but I'm not sleeping well," Cathy replied.

"Your sleep is important, Cathy. I'll give you something to help with that."

Cathy nodded but added, "But the wider implications of it all in the family worry us."

George chimed in, "Michael is behaving oddly, and we feel like we're all not functionin' proper like."

"Well, grief is a difficult time for people. But we know it passes. The priority is to get you both functioning at your best. So, let's get sleep sorted first. Maybe make another appointment in a couple of months, and we'll see whether the tablets have helped. OK?" Dr Patterson said as he passed Cathy the prescription.

As they left the room, Cathy spoke quietly to George. "I'm not sure he understands what we're saying. I don't think we had a chance to tell him what has been happening or how we're feeling."

"No. He's pretty much saying, 'You'll get over it.' Maybe the tablets will help a bit, but I doubt it."

"Well, you sleep mainly because you've drunk so much every night. And it's not helping you get over it."

George spoke even more quietly as they walked past the receptionists. "I don't drink myself silly. Surely, I deserve a drink at least in the evening when I come back from work."

"I'm not saying that. I mean, sleeping isn't solving it, is it?"

Cathy began taking the temazepam. George drank more. They slept, but neither was fully alert in the morning or throughout the day.

Cathy lamented, "It's mid-December, and I'm not looking forward to Christmas this year. We've normally been out for a tree by now. Since the boys stopped believing in Santa, Christmas lost something. But now…"

"I know, but we've got to make it good for Michael. He's struggling more than ever. His form tutor said last week, when we saw him, that all his teachers were saying the same thing: he's in a world of his own. All his results are down."

"Yes, we'll make it special. I think we should go back to Dr Patterson tomorrow and explain that we need more help. I've been looking into psychologists who counsel families, and I think that's what we need. He seems focused on you, me, and pills. We have to be firm and demand that he refer us."

"I'm not sure we can demand anything."

"Well, a couple of people have mentioned counselling to me, so we owe it to Michael to try."

"None of that will happen before Christmas, though, so that's down to us."

George and Cathy were pleased that Dr Patterson had referred the family for therapy. Michael had been given more presents than he had ever had before, but Cathy and George feared it would be for nothing as he sat with them on Christmas Eve. They sat in silence as they increasingly did. George in his armchair, Cathy on the sofa, and Michael on the floor, with his back against the couch alongside Cathy's legs.

Michael looked over to the tree. It was no longer a magical tree. A tree of excitement and happiness. It was merely a tree. Suddenly, he cried out, "All I want at Christmas is for William to be back."

Again, without words, silent tears fell down Cathy's cheeks. The sight of Cathy's sadness provoked George to cry. He walked over to Cathy, sat beside her, positioned his feet to avoid bumping Michael, and put his arm around her shoulder. He reached down to Michael and laid his hand on his head. The moment of them all crying and consoling each other revealed some residual strength of the dying love among them, but, in truth, words failed them.

On Christmas Day, George could not escape the memories of previous Christmases and the overwhelming sense of absence. He tried to speak to Michael warmly and affectionately throughout the morning, but he knew Michael was acting. He immediately replayed his words to himself, knowing none carried any emotion. Guilt. I hate myself. He started drinking. How can I escape the torture of the familiar in these now airless spaces? He went to his garage to tinker.

Cathy tried to conjure joy before breakfast as Michael opened his presents. She told herself it was important to remember the pleasure in his eyes. There were glimpses, but she knew it was ultimately a dulled experience. She found the focus on preparations and cooking a respite.

Michael opened each present mechanically as if he were opening groceries. Upon each reveal, he raised a brief half-smile before placing it down.

"Can I help you cook, Mum?" he asked as he entered the kitchen.

"Not today, Michael. It's all too complicated. Go and play with your toy, heh."
"Where's Dad?"
"He's in the garage," Cathy replied with resigned frustration. "Best leave him there," she added.
Michael wanted his dad to love him. Either of them. He made his way to the garage.
George was organising nuts and bolts into separate compartments in a purpose-made plastic case with a Perspex lid. He had brought the whisky bottle and his glass with him.
Michael put on a cheery voice. "Can I help, Dad?"
"No, Michael." George couldn't even think of a reason he could give to justify his decision. He poured himself another glass.
Although disappointed, Michael continued. "Are there any jobs in the house I could do then, Dad?" he asked with the same chirpy tone.
"No. It's Christmas, Michael. You've got lots of new toys—expensive things. Go and play with them," George replied with apparent irritation.
Michael turned away, disappointed.
The Christmas dinner was a silent affair, other than instructions to pull a cracker. The snap of each one sounded resigned. "Put your hat on, Michael," Cathy requested as she put on her paper hat and gave George a stern look to conform.
Michael found no humour in the hats. He decided they were silly.
The decision to spend the afternoon watching the film *Santa Claus* was a welcome distraction, even though Cathy had half an eye on George as his drinking accelerated.
Michael could not understand his feelings. He, too, had memories. Strong memories of opening presents in unison with William. Constant glances towards each other. And... simply... playing. There were some games amongst his presents, but no playing. William was not there. He looked over at his dad

expectantly, but Dad was asleep. A strong sense of disappointment washed over him. He began to try to play the game himself. Then he pretended William was there and that they were playing. But, in the end, a complete conviction settled in—that William had not come back for Christmas, nor would he ever. He must have let William down. He couldn't have loved him as much as William had loved him when he was saved from his illness. He had not loved enough.

Chapter 5

Cathy and George received a letter from Dr Jenkins early in the new year. She explained that Dr Patterson had contacted her and that she was willing to meet with them to discuss their concerns. The letter included a phone number for scheduling an appointment. They called within hours of receiving it.

At their first meeting, Dr Jenkins introduced herself and immediately asked them to call her "Alison." She asked each of them to describe their thoughts and feelings, using the term "suicidal ideation."

Cathy, grasping that Alison was probing whether they had experienced suicidal thoughts, quickly responded, "No. Not suicidal thoughts . . . er . . . ideation."

George nodded, thinking this Alison person shouldn't use words like ideation anyway.

"Our goal will be to understand how both of you and . . . Michael . . . are thinking and behaving at this time," Alison continued. "We'll also explore how you believe you should be acting—each of you, separately—your personal goals. However, my broader approach is to assess how you function as a family. I'll suggest topics for discussion, possibly assign tasks and observe. We'll examine how you might like to see things change."

George and Cathy nodded.

Alison went on. "You see, I have a goal. I don't want to help you go back to how things were."

Cathy and George almost simultaneously muttered, "But . . ."

"I want you to learn how to be a new family. A family of three. Yes, a family that carries memories of William, but one that can move forward and thrive."

George responded first. "Yes. Right. I see that."

Alison smiled. "That's the goal. But learning how to be a new family will be difficult. Under normal circumstances,

people don't have to renegotiate their entire dynamic with other family members. You will. It won't be easy. But families do manage this. And I believe you will, too."

Whether it was George's response to Alison's early question about alcohol consumption or Cathy's subtle shift in her chair and slight aversion to gaze, something prompted Alison to ask that the first individual session be with George.

George's first session with Alison Jenkins proved challenging. He hadn't expected such probing questions and admitted, "When I come home, I should be pleased to see him. But all I see is one of them. Like half measures. Half empty, not half full." He startled himself as his voice cracked and tears slid down his cheeks. He continued, struggling with the weight of his guilt. "I should appreciate Michael for 'is own sake. And I do feel sorry for 'im—what he's going through—but the truth is, even seeing 'im fills me with this overwhelming feeling of . . . disappointment . . . almost, deflation."

Alison interjected. "There are no 'shoulds' or 'musts' here, George. These are your feelings, and you understand why they exist. They may be temporary. But if they persist and make you uncomfortable, that's something we can work on."

George sobbed. "I bloody do want to change this. It's not fair to Michael. It's like . . . there's a gap, not a presence in the room."

"Absolutely," Alison agreed. "What usually happens when you come home, see him, and experience those feelings?"

"I should . . . I ought to . . ." George shook his head, chastising himself. He gathered his thoughts. "I suppose it'd be good if I gave 'im some time. Played with 'im. Talked with 'im."

Alison smiled and nodded.

George's tone turned defensive. "But I'm tired. Lots of parents are tired. I come home, and I just need to chill. Work is hard. I shouldn't—" He caught himself, aware of Alison's earlier point, but the restraint irritated him. "I shouldn't 'ave to feel guilty for sittin' down with a beer." He looked at Alison, expecting judgment.

But Alison remained impassive, her expression offering neither approval nor disapproval.

*

Still, George's drinking had become a sore point between him and Cathy. Being fair to Michael had also turned into a battleground—each of them wielding the phrase as a weapon to criticise the other.

Cathy's first session with Alison was just as emotional. The word she repeated most often was 'guilt'.

"I feel guilty. I've told so many people, and I mean it—William died because I kept praying for Michael. All his life, I prayed for him. This is God's vengeance," Cathy said, echoing the exact phrases she had voiced to George months earlier.

"Are you a religious person, Cathy?" Alison asked.

"No. I'm not even sure if He's actually... out there... up there. But somehow, imagining Him admonishing me helps."

"Sometimes, we project our feelings onto others, assuming it's what they think or say. But in reality, it may only be our thoughts," Alison replied. "This belief that William's death is your fault—how do you think it's affecting you? Or Michael? Or George? How does it manifest in your behaviour?"

"I think it makes me a bit of a martyr. Like I'm determined to push through, as penance. Like I have to somehow make up for it all. Atone. I feel like I'm trying, trying, trying to fix everything. But I can't. Everything's changed.

George has changed. But maybe his leaving me to it is
just me staking another claim to martyrdom." She exhaled. "That's why we're here. It's all gone to pot. And we haven't even mentioned Michael."

Alison nodded. "Before we start building a new family that loves and cares for each other, it's important to understand where everyone's feelings lie. A loss like this can put intolerable strain on a family. It shatters everything. Our first step is to help each of you communicate your emotions—whether it's hopelessness, helplessness, confusion, anger, depression, guilt, or anything else."

"George doesn't feel the same way I do," Cathy retorted.

"No, perhaps not. However, one of the biggest strains in a family can be when members expect each other to think and act the same way. When they don't, they blame one another. If we can accept all reactions as legitimate, we can reduce that added tension... through conflict management."

"I see that. But we can't talk like this with Michael."

"We'll work with you and George as a team and focus on how the three of you interact. From what you've shared so far, you've largely avoided direct anger and hostility toward each other. But perhaps you've both turned inward instead. We'll reflect on that together when we meet as a family next time."

*

"I'm not sure I want to be examined like a troupe of monkeys," George moaned that evening.

"It was hard enough telling her one-on-one how I feel. But being watched? It's like I'm being scored or something."

Cathy walked over and hugged him. "Come on. It'll be just like Jeremy Beadle."

"Alison Jenkins can't be him, can she?" He returned Cathy's squeeze.

"She might be. Let's see."

For a moment, the warmth of old kindled.

*

Michael didn't seem fazed by being in the observation suite, even after being told they would be filmed and that they would later discuss what the footage revealed. He answered Alison's questions directly, easily expressing his emotions that surprised his parents.

"I'm scared it'll happen to me," he admitted. "I've already had it. Cancer, like William. Well, kind of the same. It could come back."

Alison didn't respond immediately, letting his words settle.

Cathy and George instinctively pulled him into their arms, murmuring, "No. Absolutely not."

Alison then turned to Michael. "Did that help?"
"No. I don't think so. I still feel scared."
Alison nodded, explaining to Cathy and George how families communicate, cohere, and sometimes clash—how, at times, showing compassion can actually mean avoiding an issue rather than resolving it.
At a later session, Michael's emotions boiled over. His frustration erupted as he blurted,
"It's like you think William was perfect, but I'm not." His voice rose in anger.
"And he wasn't. He just wasn't! I try to be good, but I can't be this perfect person you've made him out to be. It's not fair."
George met his gaze. "No, he wasn't perfect. Nobody is."
Cathy, defensive, added, "I don't think we tell you off often, anyway."

*

Several weeks into the sessions, Michael finally found the words to explain his sense of guilt over William's death.
"I overheard Mum telling Dad she'd prayed hard for me to get better. Dad told her, 'Prayer is just the old way of saying you're giving love.' And he said, 'It was our love, and especially William's, that saved Michael.'" Michael hesitated. "They didn't know I heard them. William saved me. I didn't save him."
"We only meant—" George began.
Alison raised her fingers slightly from where they rested on her lap and deliberately spoke over him. "And what did you think about that, Michael?"
"I was grateful to William," Michael admitted. "I should have tried harder to love him better."
Alison nodded and smiled.
"And now I remember . . . well, I think I remember. I'm not sure. But I think I've seen the picture William drew for me. Mum says it was magical, and she kept it. I tried to do a picture for William, but mine wasn't magical. I prayed for him, but . . . I don't know what praying is. Or what God is. I did love him. I did. I did. I tried to help him."

"Of course you did, Michael," Cathy said reassuringly, reaching over to squeeze his shoulder gently.

"I try to get better at drawing," Michael continued, his voice softer now. "And I know I love Mum and Dad very much. But I'm scared. It might not be enough. Again." He turned to his parents, his eyes pleading.

Cathy immediately sensed his anxiety. "Nothing is going to happen to us, Michael. Honestly. Nothing."

"Was it a magical picture, Mummy?" Michael asked. "I think I remember it. Can I see it? Maybe I could copy it."

"It wasn't magical, Michael," Cathy said gently. "William just loved to draw. Do you remember? He did a lot of drawings—all the time. He loved you. And you loved him. Nothing is going to happen to Dad and me. Please don't be afraid of that. We love each other. And that is what matters. Nothing else."

"We're fine. We're all fine," George added.

Alison finished making a few notes before looking up. "OK. Well done, Michael, for sharing a little of how you've been feeling. Can we see now how talking about these things allows us to say what's been buried deep down? How do you feel now that you've said this, Michael?"

"I don't know," Michael admitted. "I do love Mum and Dad—a lot. But I'd still like to see the picture. Just because."

Alison spoke with Cathy alone while George took Michael out. "I think it's good that Michael is finding ways to express his feelings. Some children find it helpful to keep a journal—a place where they can write and clarify their thoughts. A private space," she explained. "If you hold on a second, I'll give you a copy of some journalling exercises that might help him. Often, once a child makes more sense of their feelings, they become better able to express them."

*

Later that evening, Cathy and George looked through the papers Alison had given them.

"There's a list of prompts," George said. "Questions like, 'The thing that makes me feel saddest is . . .' and 'Since the death, my family doesn't . . .' and 'If I could change things, I would . . .'"

"Well, he could answer those," Cathy replied. "The thing is, we're not to look. It has to be his journal. He needs to know it's private and that he can write whatever he wants. Anything at all."

"There's a kind of template here, too," George added, scanning further. "Boxes where he can write responses to 'I wonder . . .' then 'I wish . . .' and finally, 'I hope . . .' They seem like good prompts. Maybe they'll help. We just don't want him sitting in his room writing all night."

"She said that, over time, it might help him talk more."

George flipped through a few more pages. "Yeah, I can see that 'ere. We can suggest it to him."

"Maybe we should try it too, George. Actually . . . I might."

*

At another session with all three of them, Cathy mentioned how much William had loved drawing, recalling how he and Michael had often given each other pictures. Alison turned to Michael.

"Do you like to draw, Michael?"

Michael hesitated. "Yes," he said, his voice uncertain, unsure why it mattered.

Alison nodded. "What I mean is, do you ever draw how you feel?"

"No," Michael replied incredulously.

"Have you ever started doodling with a pencil and suddenly noticed the beginning of a shape—something unintentional that you then turn into a real drawing?"

Michael suddenly relaxed and laughed. "Yeah, I do that."

Alison caught the shift in his tone. "It's fun, isn't it?" she said warmly.

Michael grinned. "I like that things just appear like they were already there, even though I didn't plan them."

"Absolutely! I do it quite often," Alison said. "And sometimes, it helps me realise something I hadn't noticed before." She paused. "I think it'd be a great idea for you to try that every day. Or at least often."

*

Michael did start keeping a journal—something he would return to at different points in his life. Cathy began to, too, but quickly lost interest. George never saw the need.

Michael continued to doodle, letting shapes and images emerge. The monthly sessions with Alison continued for six months in total. Over time, George, Cathy, and Michael developed some skills in open communication. But certain things remained unchanged.

Cathy never lost her compulsion to make Michael's life as good as possible—a drive fuelled by guilt, though she sometimes questioned its legitimacy in her sessions with Alison.

George never entirely shook his sense of emptiness nor the dulling of his emotions. And he still reached for a drink more often than he should.

Michael, meanwhile, pushed himself relentlessly—in school, in sports, in his art, though he never possessed the flair William had in life.

But the thing he worked hardest at?

Being liked.

He just loved to be liked. Always.

But how do you achieve that?

Chapter 6

By the time Claire was nine, she had attracted the attention of other girls at school, but never formed strong bonds with them. They found her amusing—but nothing more. Different and not to be copied. Walking around the playground at lunchtime only reinforced her sense of separateness.
"You're naughty," chided Dorothy, one of her classmates, in a tone that actually signalled approval as Claire was putting her tongue out behind the back of one of the teachers.
Others would echo similar sentiments from time to time. But more often than not, they played with someone else.
Dorothy confided in Margaret, "Claire is fun, but I like being with you more. You're kind."
"You're my bestie, too," Margaret replied with a broad smile. "I like Dawn and Sheila and tried to be friends with them. You'd like them too," she added. "But they go to each other's houses a lot. I think they're besties."
"I like having you as a best friend," Dorothy concluded.
Seeing them chatting, Claire bounded over. "Do you want to skip? Take turns?"
"We're just chatting," Dorothy said cheerily.
Claire turned away and approached another small group of girls. "Hi. Are you playing?" she asked brightly.
"We're finishing our game of hopscotch," one of them replied. "Just these three need to go again. You can watch if you like."
Claire took up the offer. She glanced back to where Dorothy and Margaret had now invited Sally over and held the rope for her to skip.
They sang:

> *"Eepa, weepa, chimney sweeper.*
> *Had a wife but couldn't keep her.*
> *Had another, didn't love her.*
> *Up the chimney, he did shove her."*

They laughed as Sally caught her foot on the rope and started the routine again.

Claire shrugged and muttered to herself, "Best not to think about it."

Standing idly, watching the others play hopscotch, her attention shifted to a drainpipe barely visible beyond the corner of the school dining room. She'd never noticed it before, but it led all the way up to the flat-roofed building.

She assessed it, and suddenly, her imagination took flight. In her mind, she was climbing it. She heard children's laughter as she envisioned herself gripping the pipe and climbing the first bracket. She heard their laughter shift to gasps of fear as she ascended higher. The sound of clapping. A slight slip—more gasps. But then, she made it to the top. Cheers erupted.

Claire Fontrelle's Tales of Derring-Do.

"Claire Fontrelle! Claire."

A voice cut through her fantasy. This voice was real. A teacher's voice. A telling-off voice.

For a moment, she was confused. She wasn't on the roof. She hadn't actually climbed.

"Claire," the voice boomed, closer now.

She turned to face Miss Whittaker.

"Claire, come with me to the office, please."

What have I done?

As they reached the office, a girl was waiting outside the door. She had the cleanest uniform Claire had ever seen.

"Claire, this is Penny Hall," Miss Whittaker said. "She's just moved here—to a house right around the corner from yours. She'll be in your class. I want you to be her friend. Will you do that?"

"Yes, Miss Whittaker," Claire replied, turning toward the girl.

She was greeted with a beaming smile. A needy smile.

"Pleased to meet yer," Penny said.

Claire had never heard a Manchester accent before. She wondered if Penny might be foreign.

Over the next few weeks, Penny clung to Claire like a limpet. She regaled her with stories of her life—how she had lived in Africa before her parents moved back to England.

Her tales of Africa were unlike anything Claire had ever imagined—sunshine, exotic animals, danger.

Penny basked in Claire's admiration. She was extraordinarily self-assured for her age, yet keenly aware that she was no longer in Africa. Those friends were gone.

She desperately needed Claire to like her. To be her friend.

To Claire's mind, Penny had an opinion on everything—a no-nonsense, no-doubt, move-on approach to life. She had no patience for secrets and found other children's "just between us" whispers irritating.

She was surprisingly dismissive of her parents—especially her father- for someone so young. She preferred to be away from home as much as possible.

Penny and Claire spent more and more time together as the school years passed. They went through primary school, then secondary school—Penny moving sluggishly while Claire danced around her, always bubbling with excitement.

Their growing stock of shared experiences became a source of endless reminiscences—bonding them whilst repelling outsiders.

They weren't particularly caring toward each other, but they served each other well as companions in their mutual desire to escape home.

Claire didn't know why Penny preferred to be anywhere but home.

Chapter 7

In Year 8, Michael tried to be more conscientious, primarily driven by a fear of his teachers' chastisement. But it was a delicate balance—he didn't want to be seen as a swot. He found too much enjoyment in earning laughter and approval by being silly in class.

"I expected better from you, Michael," bemoaned Mr Evans, his maths teacher, in an early attempt to curb Michael's antics. But instead, it became material. Michael mimicked his teacher's tone and posture to perfection, frequently turning to classmates and declaring, "I expected better from you, Gareth"—or whoever seemed a fitting target at the time.

Michael soon developed a knack for assessing lessons—figuring out which teachers were more observant and which provided opportunities for mischief. Mrs Graham, in particular, was an easy mark. Her lack of attention left room for face-pulling, miming puppet shows, or dramatic feigning of death. Even an impressed friend's occasional, barely contained giggle would go unnoticed.

But it was between lessons—at breaks or during lunch—where Michael truly cemented his friendships.

He had an unconscious skill for reading people. At school, it allowed him to befriend the rougher kids—even the bullies—with a well-timed aside or nod of tacit approval. And yet, within moments, he could shift seamlessly into quiet, empathetic listening to a more fragile soul.

Everywhere he went, Michael tried to be liked.

Yet, deep down, he never truly believed he was likeable. In trying to please everyone, he wasn't entirely sure who he actually was.

Despite the occasional blip—a low coursework grade or a poor exam result due to lack of effort—Michael enjoyed school. He was in no rush to go home. There were too many arguments between his parents.

Football training gave him an excuse to stay longer. He played as a goalkeeper for the second team, which meant he could be away from home on Saturday afternoons for matches.

One evening, after training, Michael sat in the changing room as Justin called over to his friend Kieran.
"What time should I come round later?"
"Half six. We can grab a Coke first," Kieran replied, tying his shoelaces. He glanced at Michael sitting beside him. "We play five-a-side at the youth club."
Michael nodded and smiled.
After a pause, Kieran added, "Come along if you want," his tone deliberately casual.
Michael mirrored the nonchalant stance. "Yeah, I might."
"Cool. Do you know where it is?"
"Yeah. See you later. Maybe."
Wednesday night five-a-side became a regular fixture. Soon, Michael swapped swimming with his dad on Saturday mornings for swimming with Justin and Kieran on Sundays. It suited George.
The three of them became inseparable.
With their bikes, they had the freedom to visit each other's houses, ride to the youth club, or explore the places they liked to hang out. Sundays became their day for a kickabout on the local sports club fields—a day they learnt to while away hour after hour, simply talking.
The kickabouts were so casual that they resembled tag wrestling. Someone might step in to join a side, prompting another to step out and resume lounging about. The format allowed endless jibes from those watching.
"You dipstick, Rodney," Michael called over to Kieran, mimicking Del Boy from *Only Fools and Horses* as Kieran lost possession of the ball.
Justin and Kieran always laughed at Michael's impressions. This time, Justin chuckled and gave Michael a playful dig in the ribs. Kieran shot him two fingers.
Michael stopped being Michael from then on, on this lazy summer Sunday afternoon.
He became Mike.

*

Cathy often visited her parents, bringing Michael with her. She still called him by his full name, as did other family members. He tolerated it, though now, Michael felt like something you got called when you were in trouble.

George usually declined the visits, preferring to see friends at the pub instead. That suited Cathy—she enjoyed private time with her mum.

Her dad adored playing with "little Michael." Michael, in turn, loved visiting his gran and grandad—and their dog, Susan.

"I'll hold her lead, Grandad," Mike said gleefully as they headed across the fields behind the house.

"Yes, up to the stile. She's fine after that—no cattle there."

"I bet she's fine with them anyway. She sees them every day. Probably just says 'hello'."

"You can never be sure. It only takes one to get spooked, and they all panic suddenly. Same as me in the supermarket—if I can't find exactly what your gran has on the list, I'm a headless chicken."

Mike clucked dramatically, spinning in circles.

Susan dutifully followed.

"Let her off now, Michael," Grandad said. "She needs a run. Dogs need exercise."

Mike loved Susan. She was never inconsistent. She was always happy to see him, always appreciative. She was well-behaved, and he knew how to guide her—sit, wait, leave, come.

So, when his neighbour, Mrs Dickinson, broke her foot, he was confident enough—and kind enough—to offer to

walk her dog, Jack, while she recovered. He asked her one afternoon when he saw her in the garden on his way home from school.

"I've said I'll walk Jack for a week or so. For Mrs Dickinson," he told his mum.

"What? Did she ask you?" Cathy asked.

"No. I offered. You said she broke her foot, so I thought it'd help if I walked Jack." Mike replied cheerily.

Cathy smiled. "You're a kind boy, Michael. She'll appreciate it. She told me yesterday that she's still in a lot of pain." She paused. "I didn't think to offer," she admitted. Then, ruffling his hair, she added with a slight nod, "But you did."
Mike grinned.

*

In Year 9, Mike and Justin liked going round to Kieran's house—he had the best stereo and the best CD collection.
One rainy Sunday, they piled into Kieran's bedroom.
Bean bags littered the floor alongside the bed, and towering speakers flanked a gleaming stereo unit. Since their last visit, Kieran had gotten a new wall unit just for CDs. It was already more than half full.
"I've got something for you to hear," Kieran announced, brandishing *Urban Hymns* by The Verve. He slipped the CD into the player and skipped straight to a particular track.
"Listen to this." The song *Bitter Sweet Symphony* started. He turned the volume up.
"Wait for it—the drums. Listen to how they fit into the music."
As the beat kicked in, Kieran slapped his leg in rhythm—one-one, one-one-two, one-one, one-one-two-three—tapping out the snare pattern.
Mike and Justin listened intently.
A minute in, Mike started trying to join in, fumbling at first, then finally nailing it before the track ended.
"Again. Play it again," Justin demanded.
They played it over and over until all three of them could anticipate exactly when the drums kicked in and tap along for the entire song.
"We could play this—if we learnt guitars and that," Justin said, suddenly energised.
"Yeah, I'd love a guitar," Mike agreed.
"And you could get drums, Kieran," Justin added. "We could practice up here. You have no neighbours, and your parents don't seem to hear the music from up here. Or at least they never say."

"Ace," Kieran replied, grinning. "And you . . . you could play bass, Justin."

Justin nodded, but his enthusiasm visibly dimmed. *No way I'll be bought a bass.*

Kieran noticed. He and Mike had spoken before about how they'd never actually been inside Justin's house. He had once muttered that his dad wouldn't like it, and they never asked again.

"So, maybe I can persuade mine to get us drums, a bass, and an amp," Kieran suggested. "And you could persuade your mum to get you a guitar, Mike. If you asked . . ." He hunched his shoulders, shrinking into an Uriah Heep impression, then tilted his head "Niiiiiicely."

Mike laughed. "Ha. Maybe. It's my birthday next month. I could try."

"But apart from that track, what else would we play?" Justin asked, injecting a dose of realism into their daydream.

"Oh, I don't know. This whole album?" Kieran suggested.

Mike grinned. "And everything by Oasis."

By the end of October, they had their instruments.

Kieran's complete drum kit was loud. Incredibly loud. And his playing left a lot to be desired.

Within the cacophony, Justin shouted, "This hurts my fingertips like hell! And it's taken the skin off my thumb as well!"

"What?" Kieran yelled over the noise, still bashing away.

Justin pointed to his fingertips, shaking his left hand and blowing on them like they were burning hot. Then he shook his right hand dramatically, his thumb sticking out in pain.

"Vinegar," Mike called out.

Justin cupped his ear, but didn't catch it.

"Vinegar!" Mike repeated. "I'm trying vinegar—it's supposed to help."

Kieran finally stopped annihilating the drum kit, realising the guitars had gone silent.

"I was just telling Justin to try vinegar for his fingers," Mike explained.

Kieran held up his own hands, revealing blisters on the insides of his thumbs and fingers.

"Bloody right. Nobody tells you about this part. I thought it was all sex, drugs, and rock and roll."

At their next get-together, Justin continued struggling to play bass cleanly—his fingers kept getting in the way.

"Hey, Justin, why don't you take the bass home tonight?" Kieran suggested. "You need more practice than just an hour here and there. You won't have an amp, but you'll still be able to hear it."

Justin hesitated. "Er . . . no. He'd wonder . . ."

Kieran frowned. "Who? Wonder what?"

Justin lowered his eyes, grimacing slightly. "My dad . . ." His jaw tensed. "He wouldn't like it." He shook his head. "He'd ask whose it was and get all aggressive about having it in the house—like it was some insult to him."

Kieran exploded. "What? Tell him to—"

"I can't, Kieran," Justin cut in sharply. "You can't reason with him. Just let it go." He shook his head. "Besides, I don't think I'll ever get the hang of it anyway."

Mike finally spoke. "It's a nice offer, Kieran. But Justin knows what his dad is like. Best we think of other ways. D'you reckon?"

Justin turned down the next invite to practice. He started suggesting they play football instead. Or just go for a ride.

Mike persisted in learning to play. Without an amplifier at home, he had to crane his neck, pressing his right ear against the top of the electric guitar to hear it properly. He was determined to get each phrase right—playing it slowly, then gradually speeding up. Over and over, he'd try, nail it, fluff it, and try again. But in the end, he got them.

That Christmas, he persuaded his mother to buy him an amp.

At the youth club early in the new year, Mike spoke with a boy named John Brompton. John was a couple of years older and had been playing guitar for four years. He invited Mike to bring his guitar over so they could play together.

John was good. He could play loads of riffs and even improvise on lead guitar.

When Mike arrived at John's house, he was taken aback by the sheer amount of music equipment in his room.

"Shit. That's ace," he breathed in awe.

John grinned, picking up his guitar. He started playing a riff and shouted over, his Suffolk accent thickening, "It's a bain tune. You could play the chords to go with it dead easy."

"It's only E minor, A, G, then D..."

Mike obliged.

"That's it. Again," John commanded.

Mike was playing real music. And it sounded good.

Over the next few months, he and John played often, learning song after song.

John introduced him to local bands, and soon, Mike, Justin, and Kieran joined him at an evening gig in the next village.

John knew the drummer, so after the first set, they went over to talk.

The drummer, a guy in his early twenties, looked like he'd run a marathon—sweat streaming down his face, his T-shirt soaked. He recognised John immediately.

"Which one's Mike?" he asked. "That's me," Mike answered proudly, relishing the recognition as a fellow musician.

"Shit. You're a baby. John's young, but how old are you?"

"Fourteen," Mike replied, suddenly meek.

The drummer smirked. "He tells me you're tight together— real neat." Then, turning to John, he added, "I said I'd mention you guys to Paul Campion. He's played bass off and on. Says he's interested. I'll give you his number when we finish." He glanced back at John.

"And he better be as good as you say, or they'll think I'm a right gawby."

As they walked away, Mike cast a nervous glance at Justin, trying to gauge his reaction. Not a flicker.

Feeling awkward, Mike muttered, "Sorry. I didn't know John was talking about getting a new bass player . . ."

"Don't be soft. It's cool. Gets me off the hook. I was never gonna get it. I'd never have bloody got as good as that guy. If this Paul's even half decent, you'll be well set."

John rubbed his chin and turned to Kieran. "So, you'd better step up. Looks like we're getting this whole thing going."

*

The band became Mike's first real passion.
Paul turned out to be great on bass—supremely dexterous. He, too, thought Mike was a bit young.
They rehearsed at Kieran's house for months before landing a spot at Mike's school show, playing three songs as an early act.
They were good.
After the set, two girls approached Mike.
"I'm Adele, and this is Stella."
"Hi."
"We liked your music," Adele said with unwavering confidence.
"That's good. Thanks."
"When and where are you playing next? We'll come. Won't we, Stella?"
"Er, yes," Stella mumbled.
"Nothing planned yet. But hopefully soon."
"Your band's ace. You looked good up there. Like a pop star. Bet you get loads of girls."
Mike, caught in a quandary, didn't want to disagree but didn't want to lie. He found his answer. "Ha."
Adele smirked. "I've seen you before. On your bike."
Mike had noticed Adele before. She was in the year below him at school, so they'd never spoken, but he'd seen her around.
And now here she was, praising him.
Does she fancy me?
Before he could figure out a response, Adele continued. "You could ask me out. If you like." She added a feigned coyness to her tone.
"Yes. Great. Er . . . cool."
"Tomorrow night. You can take me to the cinema. I'll see you outside at seven."
With that, she turned and walked off, giggling with Stella.

"Right," he shouted after her. *What is this? It'd be great to go out with her—she's probably the prettiest girl in school. But is she taking the piss? Oh, my days. I hope not. Did she hear me say yes?*

Kieran wandered over. "Do we have groupies? That Adele Boyle is fit." He gave Mike a playful dig in the ribs.

Mike smirked. "Comes with fame and fortune, Kieran. Fame and fortune."

Paul rolled his eyes. "Come on, dreamers."

"Yeah, we're not famous yet," John added. "It's us that have to pack up."

*

"Where are you off to tonight, Michael?" Cathy asked warmly the following Saturday as he headed upstairs.

"Off with his waster mates," his dad muttered gruffly.

"Going to the cinema, Dad. The cinema," Mike replied with a smile.

"What's the film?" his mum asked.

"Not sure, Mum."

"Going, and you don't even know what's on?" George scoffed. "Might be that Disney thing, *Mulan*. Serves you right for not checking. Has that war film been and gone? Saving Ryan somebody?"

"Imogen was telling me about *Titanic*," Cathy chimed in. "She said it was lovely. But very sad."

"Well, it was sad," George mocked. "Oops. Have I spoiled the ending?"

"It's a love story, George. Romance," Cathy replied, pointedly. "The sort of film to see with a girl, Michael. Not your mates."

"Ha," Mike said. "Anyway, I don't know what's on."

Chapter 8

Up in his bedroom, Mike wasn't sure if he was supposed to dress up.
It's a date. But it's only the cinema. And anyway, Dad'll take the piss.
He stuck with his T-shirt and jeans.
On the way there, he reconsidered his decision. Justified it. Regretted it. Accepted it—philosophically, then not. Over and over.
Then Adele arrived. She'd put on a dress.
His heart sank—and soared.
She looks stunning.
"Still being a rock god, I see." She tilted her cheek toward him. Mike kissed it. "Got to maintain appearances."
"Surprised you're not wearing sunglasses," Adele teased.
"You look great. I'll dress up next time."
"Who says there'll be a next time, Michael Lewis?"
"Of course, there will. We're in love." He cocked his head and fluttered his eyebrows.
Adele laughed.
The film was *Titanic*. As his mother had said, it was sad.
They kissed a lot.

*

Outside the cinema, Mike asked if he could walk her home.
"My dad's here," Adele gestured toward a yellow BMW parked across the road. "He dropped me off. You didn't spot him earlier?"
"Ha. He wasn't the old guy sitting to our left, on his own in the cinema, was he? He did look over a few times."
Adele dug her elbow into his ribs. "Don't be silly. He wants to make sure I'm okay, so he drops me off and picks me up."
"Like a posh yellow cab," Mike quipped. "Anyway, can you check if he's got any other fares next Friday at seven-thirty? Indian restaurant."
He leaned in and gave her a polite peck on the cheek—rather than the real kiss he was craving.

"I think he's free," Adele laughed before turning and crossing the road.

*

The following Friday, at the appointed hour, Adele arrived.
Another dress.
Mike had made an effort—a white shirt, pale grey chinos, and blue leather shoes.
"So, you've put on your blue suede shoes."
"So, don't step on them." He was surprised she knew music from way back then.
They talked a lot about music. Mike made a mental note to ask her to a dance next time.
Adele also told him about her new passion.
"Photography?" he asked.
"Yes, it's an after-school club. Mr Evans runs it."
"Evans? Maths teacher Evans?"
"Yeah, but he's different there. He jokes. He's actually *enthusiastic*." She hesitated. "And my dad doesn't pick me up. He's working. So we could walk back together. Maybe stop off on the fields . . . if you came to the club."
Feigned indifference. "I might be able to find the time. What night is it?"
"Tuesdays."
Mike was relieved it wasn't Wednesday—band practice at John Brompton's.
He'd have to see if he could persuade his mum to buy him a camera on Saturday.
She did.

*

The following Tuesday, after the club, Adele suggested they cycle to Worlingham Marshes to take photographs.
They left their bikes propped against a tree.
As they walked, Mike noticed their cameras—hers slung to her left, his to his right.

He wanted to hold her hand.
But it was daylight. Public.
He hesitated but kept his left hand low. Then—the touch.
An accidental brush of fingers.
She didn't move away.
He summoned his courage and reached for her hand.
Her fingers closed around his.
Joy.
They walked in silence.
Then panic set in. *Say something. Anything. Say anything.*
As the seconds stabbed at him, the terror increased. *She'll think I'm a prat.*
Adele pointed across the lake. "I love that tree."
She hadn't said anything about their hands.
"It's beautiful. That reflection is perfect." His nervousness eased.
"The silhouette is fantastic with the sun setting just behind it." Adele's voice grew more animated.
"It's the orange in the sky. Incredible."
At the exact moment, without thinking, they let go of each other's hands and raised their cameras.
Mike looked up at the clouds. "Oh, my days. Look at that. The way they're picking up the orange."
"They're cirrus clouds," Adele said. "The wispy ones. They're made of ice, not water, so they reflect the light." She paused. "I'm not a swot. We did a series on clouds last term, and Mr Evans explained it."
"Well, thanks. I didn't know that. I just thought they were beautiful." He hesitated.
His mind searched for the right word.
He decided to be brave.
"They're romantic."
Adele turned and kissed him.
He responded, still not quite believing she could like him.

In some way, his mind created a connection between her face, sunlit clouds, and this sensation of joy.

*

Back home, as he strummed his guitar absentmindedly that night, something happened.
His fingers fell into a set of chords, and a melody emerged.
Not something he'd heard before.
He liked it.
Then words came.
"When you're in love . . ."
By midnight, he had written his first song.
A love song.
The next evening, at band practice, he told them.
After the initial mockery—his schmaltzy lyrics, his over-the-top devotion to Adele—they agreed to try it out.
Kieran nailed the drumming almost immediately.
John found a harmony for the chorus.
They had a song.
Mike told Adele he'd written a song for her.
"If you come to rehearsal Wednesday night, we'll play it for you."
"Like . . . be a WAG?"
She went to John Brompton's house that Wednesday.
They played the song.
She loved it.
Mike basked in her admiration.

*

At the next photography club, Mr Evans asked them to consider images of love: photographs, paintings, sculptures—anything.
On their walk home, Mike and Adele lay down in the grass.
Mike stared at the vivid blue sky. A waft of breeze. The sweet scent of grass.
"What famous images of love can you think of?"

"Well, the first thing that came to mind was *The Kiss* by Rodin," Adele said. "It's a sculpture. I've seen photos of it. It's in France, I think."
"I know the one."
"It's passionate—so yeah, an image of love."
"There's that famous photo, too," Mike said. "A sailor kissing a girl in New York. End of World War II."
"That's not love."
"No, I suppose not." He paused. "But there's another one. A real couple. In Paris. Kissing in the street. Oblivious to the world."
"I don't know that one."
"There's also a painting," Adele said. "A Manet. A couple in a café, just looking into each other's eyes." She turned to him. "Bet I can stare longer than you before blinking."
She leaned closer.
Mike stared back.
"You're hopeless," Adele laughed when he blinked after only four seconds.
"Again."
Mike tried—but lost.
Flustered, he leaned over and kissed her.

*

That night, at home, his mum reminded him they were visiting his grandad on Sunday for his birthday.
"But Gran called," she added. "He's had a fall. He hurt his hip. He's okay, but he can hardly walk."
"Oh no. That's awful."
George scoffed. "Oh, is that this Sunday? I'd forgotten."
He grabbed the newspaper.
"Anything interesting, Dad?" Mike asked.
"Nothing you'd like. No pop stars in 'ere," George grumbled. Then he stood. "I'm popping out."
"A bit early for a drink, George?" Cathy asked.
"Just stretching my legs, that's all."
"I could come, Dad. Tell you about the photography club."

"Not this time, Michael." George's voice was clipped. "Maybe another time."

Chapter 9

The following Sunday, just as the three of them were about to set off for Cathy's parents, the phone rang.
George answered.
"Where are you? Have you waited? You might have flooded it," he said. Turning to Cathy, he added, "It's Gordon. He's stuck and can't get back to football to pick up Ben." Then, back into the receiver, "You have? Well, we're... he'll wait. Oh, well, I'll walk over and see if we can get it going."
"You're not going there... now? It's Dad's birthday," Cathy snapped.
"He's stuck, and he's worried about Ben being left. I won't be long."
Cathy and Mike waited. An hour passed. George didn't reappear.
Frustrated, Cathy scribbled a note and left it on the kitchen table.
"We've gone."
"He never bloody wanted to come. This is just an excuse," she muttered.
Mike hugged her.

*

At Grandad's, Mike was eager to show him his growing interest in photography. He scrolled through the images on his camera's display screen.
"That's amazing," Grandad said. "We had to send ours away, and you never knew what you'd got until they came back. Half of them were blurred, or someone's head was cut off. But these—these look good, Michael. Like real arty photos."
Mike beamed with pride.
Then he heard Gran and his mum singing *Happy Birthday*.
He turned to see them entering the room, carrying a cake lit with candles. Mike joined in, realising he could capture the moment. He snapped the picture just as his grandad looked up from his chair at his wife, preparing to blow out the candles.

That night, back home, he escaped to his room to avoid his parents arguing. He heard his mum shouting, his dad barking back, then his mum swearing—then crying.

He looked through the photos he'd taken.

Then he paused.

The birthday cake image.

Grandad wasn't looking at the cake.

He was looking at her.

The joy in his smile, the sparkle in his eyes—soft, boyish. Besotted.

Mike had captured an image of love.

Real love.

*

Saturday, May 6, 1998, started like any other day.

Mike greeted his dad cheerily.

"Kieran and John are coming over later to watch the Cup Final. Are you going to watch it?"

"I don't follow Arsenal anymore. You know that. Cricket's a much better game," George replied dismissively.

"Well, they were your team. That's why I support them. Bet you still want them to beat Newcastle, though."

"Were," George replied, irritation creeping into his voice.

"Should be fun. John's not that bothered, but Kieran's grandad was from Newcastle, so his whole family—including him—supports them."

"Well, that settles it," George announced, pushing his half-eaten toast aside. "I'm going down to *The Red Lion* for a nice quiet pint."

Cathy reappeared from the kitchen. "Finished, you two?" she asked warmly. "Oh, George, you've left your toast."

She reached for Mike's plate, then moved to clear George's.

"Leave it. Just leave it," George snapped. "We're not clockwork. I'll take it out in a minute. I just want to read the paper in peace if you two would just shut up."

"I only . . ." Cathy hesitated, then sighed. "Oh, go on then, George."

*

George did go down to *The Red Lion*, but not for a quiet pint. He was there to pick up Brenda.
Brenda, who was also married. Brenda, who had also had enough of family life.
They had been having an affair for six months.
George's supposed fondness for the pub had been their cover story. Brenda had been a fictional friend named Millie.
As she climbed into the car, placing a small suitcase in the back seat, Brenda's voice was urgent. "Did you tell her?"
"Not yet."
"George! But you must. We agreed. I told Malcolm this morning. He's gone all soppy and wimpy, crying his eyes out." She scoffed. "I said I needed to go out and clear my head from his constant pleading. My two were furious. They heard him sobbing and came downstairs. He told them straight out—wanted their sympathy. And he got it. Instantly. No shock. Just straight to anger. Told me to get out."
"Oh, Brenda, that's awful." George sighed. "I'll probably get the same drama. I was going to tell her today, but bloody Michael suddenly decides to have his mates round for the effing football. Thought I'd better wait."
Brenda stared at him. "George, you have to tell them."
"I will." He exhaled. "I spoke to the letting agent yesterday. We can collect the keys from the landlord at any time. He's next door—he knows we're coming today."
"Escape," Brenda whispered, eyes filling with tears.
"Freedom," George corrected triumphantly.

*

At Mike's house, he and his friends watched the match.
Arsenal won 2-0. Kieran took it well. They didn't bother staying for the celebrations. They got up to leave.

"But what about your dinner?" Cathy asked, concern lacing her voice.
"I'll get something at John's later," Mike replied casually.

*

At six o'clock that evening, Cathy's world fell apart for the third time. But this time, she was alone. Alone to face the total devastation, the loss, the uncertainty.
She had no idea that George had met another woman. Yes, she knew their relationship wasn't what it should be. But she had assumed George had just retreated—into himself, work, beer. She had thought they'd muddled through as a family. That Michael was OK.
He had friends. Hobbies. Even a girlfriend.
The announcement—and his leaving—was so abrupt that she could remember every moment.
George reappeared just as the clock—his grandad's old clock—struck six. He glanced at it, the clock that shrieked routine.
He walked up to Cathy.
"Cathy. I'm not happy here. I have tried. I can't do it anymore. I've met someone. I'm leaving."
His voice was flat. Emotionless. As if he were reading from a script.
He didn't give Cathy a chance to respond.
Just that firm, final tone.
No discussion.
Cathy blinked rapidly as though trying to clear something from her eyes. But then—a weight. A sinking sensation in the pit of her stomach.
As if she had swallowed lead.
Then—breathlessness.
She couldn't catch her breath.
Then—unsteadiness.
She reached for the kitchen counter to steady herself. And finally—words.
"Who? How? Why? Why, George? Why?" Total incredulity.

When George said, "You don't know her. I met her in the pub last year. She's lovely. She's like me. She can't do the family thing. She loves me," Cathy's tears fell.

"But I love you, George. Michael loves you. Please, George. Please. Don't do this. It's just a fancy. Not real."

She was desperately grasping for something, anything to make him stop. To rewind this moment.

"I'm sorry, Cathy. I am. But all this . . ." He waved his hand around the room. "All we've been through. It's too much. Too much for anyone. We only have one life. This cannot be mine."

"We've found a place. I'm leaving now. I'll do right by you and Michael."

"Do, right? What do you mean, 'do right'? This isn't right. None of this is right. Are you mad?"

Cathy's voice was feverish, desperate, her mind scrambling for a way to pull him back.

Make him change his mind. Make him change his mind.

But questioning, reasoning, anger—none of it made a difference.

Then, suddenly, her legs gave way. She fell to her knees, sobbing. Her arms reached for him, begging.

George turned away.

"I'm sorry. I will tell you where I am. But not today. I have to go, Cathy. I just need to go."

And then—he was gone.

Cathy remained on the floor.

Her hands—useless, pointless—flailed in the empty space he had left.

She cupped her face as if trying to comfort herself.

But there was no comfort.

Cathy was lost.

*

After several minutes, she forced herself up.

She felt ridiculous—*on the floor like this.*

She brushed herself down as if the action could restore her composure.

Flustered, she slid her hands over the worktop, the table, the shelves—wiping, dusting.

Then she grabbed a duster and began a frantic, frenzied cleaning—scrubbing at surfaces, polishing, moving objects, tidying.

The motion freed her mind—at least temporarily—from the reality.

But when she finally stopped, the silence howled.

Then came the sound.

It wasn't a scream.

It started deep, from the pit of her soul.

A moan.

A raw, animalistic wail ripped from her chest with every ounce of strength she had left.

*

When Mike returned home at 11:30 p.m., he was surprised to find his mother still awake.

As he stepped into the room, he saw it—

The tears.

The starkness.

Her eyes were locked in a permanent state of fear. Her brow furrowed as if she were struggling to see him in the dim light.

Then, her face crumpled.

Her arms reached out to him.

Like they had to George.

But this time, there was a response.

Mike reached out, too, his fingers brushing hers. He knelt in front of her, holding her hands tightly.

"Is it Grandad? Has something happened to Grandad?" he asked gently.

Cathy shook her head.

She had rehearsed this moment, running over different ways to tell him. She had even mimicked George's approach, practising different tones.

But Mike's assumption—his instant fear that her father had died—threw her.

She opened her mouth.
"Your father . . ."
But no—Mike would think she meant his father had died.
She corrected.
"Has left us."
Still ambiguous.
"He's gone to live with another woman."
Not what she had planned to say.
But the truth.
Mike's face twisted in confusion. "What? What do you mean? What's happened? He was here. Fine. He said he was going to the pub. What do you mean, Mum?"
His disbelief was total—a mirror of Cathy's just hours before.
"It's a woman," Cathy said, regaining her rehearsed narrative. "Someone he met at the pub last year. He says
they've been seeing each other and have found a place to live together. I don't know who she is or where they're going, but he said he'd let me know. Then . . . he just left."
"Left? What time did he leave?"
"Six o'clock," she said automatically. The replay started in her mind again—every second, every word.
"I tried to stop him. I begged him. But he just kept saying he was sorry. That he couldn't stand it anymore."
"Stand what?"
"Us, Michael."
Her voice broke.
"He just said it was unbearable. That you only live once. And that he was sorry."
The word felt insulting.
Empty.
A mockery of her grief.
Her sobs returned.
"I don't understand, Mum."
Mike's voice was small now.
"It doesn't make sense. Is it me? Maybe it is. I can change. I'll do more.
It'll be all right, Mum.
I promise.

I'll sort it out."

*

At school, in that first week, Mike managed to keep life going as if nothing had changed.
He was uneasy whenever the words 'parent', 'mum', or 'dad' came up in conversation, dreading the possibility that the topic might settle on him.
He feared being drawn into lying.
Or worse—confessing.
So, he didn't mention it.
Not to Adele.

Not to Kieran, Justin, Paul, or John.

*

But at home, life had changed completely. On the first evening after school, he saw it—His mother had been crying. She looked ill. When she spoke, her voice shocked him.
"I made gammon and chips for you. That's your favourite, isn't it? And peas. You'd like that, wouldn't you?"
The way she said it—soft, deliberate—was the voice she would have used when he was seven, not fourteen.
It didn't sound real.
The meal was awful, not because of the food, but the silence.
It churned his stomach.
He needed to find something safe to talk about. A neutral topic. Something trivial, but not ridiculous. Everything that came to mind felt wrong. The knots in his stomach tightened.
His chewing slowed. The gammon became chewier.
Then he realised—his mother was watching him eat. Monitoring every bite.
Not wanting to disappoint her, he forced himself to speed up, but the faster he chewed, the harder it became to swallow. He reached for his glass of water after every mouthful.

Finally, he had an idea. TV. They used to watch *The Simpsons* together. It was their thing.

"Shall we watch *The Simpsons* later?" he asked, trying for a light, breezy tone.

His mother smiled, but tears fell down her cheek before she could respond.

"I'm sorry," she whispered.

Then—

The floodgates burst. She pushed her chair back, stood up abruptly, and fled the room, sobbing.

"I'm sorry. I'm sorry."

Guilt slammed into Mike. *Stupid.* Why had he suggested that? Should he follow her? Comfort her? No. His mind flashed back to the three of them watching *The Simpsons* before.

A scene that, in itself, wasn't sad.

But now, knowing that that kind of togetherness would never happen again—

His throat tightened.

His chest ached.

His eyes burned.

He cried.

Through his tears, he cleared the table, washed the dishes, dried them, and went meekly to his bedroom.

Then—

A sudden, sharp breath.

A panic attack.

A sick, overwhelming realisation that he was trapped in disaster.

Then—

Guilt.

A tsunami of guilt.

It's all my fault.

He left because I failed to make him happy.

William did. But I didn't.

He sat on his bed, staring blankly at the wall.

Then—

A thought.

Maybe I can make him come back?

The idea made his stomach churn again. He stood up, pacing his room, circling for minutes without purpose.
Finally, he collapsed back onto the bed.
Distraction. He needed distraction.
He switched on the radio and flicked through stations.
A familiar melody—
"Just Wanna Dance the Night Away" by The Mavericks.
The upbeat rhythm pushed him to grab his guitar and play along.
Then—
"Truly, Madly, Deeply" by Savage Garden.
Melancholy. Soft.
"Turn It Up" by Busta Rhymes.
Fast. Aggressive.
"Needin' U" by David Morales.
Total energy.
For a while, he was somewhere else.
Another world.
A world of fantasy.
A world of escape.
Then, *My Heart Will Go On* by Celine Dion came on.
A haunting song of loss.
And he was back.
Back to this world.
Back to reality.

*

At around 11:00 p.m., he heard his mum close her bedroom door.
He stepped onto the landing.
She spoke first.
"Hi. I'm alright, Michael. I'm sorry about earlier. Are you OK? Goodnight. We'll be OK. We will," she said, her voice frail, exhausted.
"Yes, Mum. OK. I just wanted to make sure you're alright."
He walked toward the bathroom as she headed downstairs.

He had to make her happy again.

*

Mike didn't sleep well that night. At 1:30 a.m., he woke to the sound of the television. His mother was asleep on the sofa. He turned the TV off. Should he wake her? No. Instead, he went to the spare room, grabbed a duvet, and gently laid it over her.
Then he went back to bed. But sleep wouldn't come. He worried—Had he done the right thing? Then—Another wave of panic. Had using a quilt from what had been William's room been a mistake? Even though it was technically a new bed, a newly decorated space, maybe it would still remind her. His mind spiralled. William's death. His dad leaving. It was all so unfair. At some point, exhaustion took over.

But at 4:00 a.m., he woke again.
His mother was crying.
This time, she was in the spare room.
He was too tired to move.
Instead, he let imagined conversations with her reel through his head.
In all of them—
He didn't know how to fix things.

*

Morning came with chaos.
His mother's voice jolted him awake.
"We've slept in! We're late! You'll be late for school! Quick, get up! Skip breakfast! If you hurry, you'll still catch the bus!"
Mike rushed. Washed. Dressed. Too fast. It felt unreal.
The wind on his face as he walked to the bus stop was the first thing that actually woke him up.

*

That evening, he got home before his mum.

A note on the kitchen table.
"Was late for work. Will have to work late. Money here for fish and chips. Sorry. xx"
He ate his fish and chips.
Then, he went up to his room to do homework.
At 7:30 p.m., his mum popped her head around the door.
"You OK? Sorry about this morning. And tonight."
"It's OK, Mum. No problem."
She gave a slight nod and disappeared downstairs.
For the rest of the evening, she was on the phone.
Over and over, he heard the same phrases.
"A complete shock, yes."
"I had no idea."
"I don't know how he could do this."
"We'll manage."
Then, crying.
Then, the inevitable apology.
"I'm sorry. I didn't mean to upset you."

This became routine. For weeks. Stilted conversations. Tense meals. Loneliness. Mike didn't talk to anyone about it. Instead, he tried to fill the space. He played his guitar. He wrote songs. He buried himself in homework. But there was no magic solution. No fixing it.

Chapter 10

Weeks turned into months.
Eventually, Mike told Adele that his father had left home.
He said it was for another woman.
He didn't admit his part in it.
Adele used the words *"Rotten," "Sad,"* and *"Pity"* but offered little physical comfort.
His bandmates knew they were supposed to sympathise, but they couldn't shake the thought that the absence of their fathers' constant criticism might be a relief.
"One less person on your back," Kieran had said.
It was then that Mike realised that no one saw it as bad.
And so, he let go of the instinct to protect himself for once.
To protect his reputation.
John's complete disinterest helped.
And eventually, Mike stopped feeling embarrassed.

*

His mum still cried—a lot. At random TV scenes. At things that had nothing to do with their situation. To Mike, everything seemed emotional to her now. Comfort her? It was impossible to predict how she would respond.

Sometimes, she welcomed it. Sometimes, she batted him away in anger.
"It won't all be all right, Michael. Stop saying that."
She stopped cooking meals from scratch, relying more and more on ready meals.
She looked ill.
She barely cared for her hair, clothes, or makeup.
She was awake at odd hours.
She snapped at everything.
Occasionally, she'd ask if he was all right, but when he answered, "Yes, I'm fine, Mum," she just smiled absently.
Only conversations with his grandad felt normal.

His grandparents started staying over on weekends.
Gran would clean, iron, and fuss.
Mum would cry even more when they were there.
His grandad, though—
His grandad took him out.
They'd walk Susan, the dog.
His grandad told stories—about school, about the trouble he used to get into.
And for the first time in months, Mike laughed.

*

On one of their visits, Grandad's tone turned serious. As they walked, he said, "Your mother's not well, Michael. She's going to get some help. From the doctor."
"Right," Mike replied, nodding, though he had no real idea what that meant.
"She'll be taking some tablets." Grandad sighed. "She might sleep more. Hopefully, she'll cry a lot less, too."
"Right," Mike repeated, nodding again—this time, as if he understood.

*

Mike began taking photographs of things that symbolised deep emotion.
He wrote songs about loss.
But he didn't share them with anyone.

In October, he turned fifteen. His mum tried her best to celebrate. She had asked him what he wanted.
"Just some money for clothes."
There was no card from his father. Not a word. The silence was confirmation enough. It was his fault. He didn't talk to his mother about it.

The following Saturday, he went into Beccles to shop for a shirt and trousers. He had arranged to meet John. As he walked down the High Street, he spotted his mother. She was standing outside *Boots*, staring blankly down the road. It was raining, but she wasn't using her hood. She was standing there, letting the rain fall. He walked toward her, about to speak—Then she turned. And he saw her face.
Gaunt.
Sunken.
Empty.
It hit him.
Loss.
Pining.
Forlorn hope.
Despair.
She looked like *The French Lieutenant's Woman*. Like Tragedy herself. She was abandoned. And for the first time, Mike saw it. Total sorrow. A haunting image. And it was a stark contrast to his guilt.

*

More months passed. Mike tried his best to be there for his mum. But he also needed his friends. His music. Adele. Balancing it all was a challenge. But he persevered. And slowly, his mum came back. She cried less. She let him comfort her. She started asking about his day again. They even went on holiday.

Her life was still empty, however. She started reading again. She switched between books and TV in the evenings, filling time. She stopped demanding to know every little detail about where Mike was going when he went out. Stopped tracking him. Mike stopped feeling guilty about going out. He still glanced back at her as he left to reassure himself.

And Cathy—
Her Michael, the most important thing in her life—
Became her everything.

And for Mike—His mother became a lifelong responsibility. Doing right by her became his duty. Doing right by others became his *modus operandi*.

*

Over the next several months, Adele tried to be supportive. But they were young. They didn't talk deeply about things. They asked after each other. Offered basic words of encouragement. Then moved on. They spent time alone together, but for Adele, it wasn't as important as it was for Mike. Sometimes, she'd tag along with him and his friends—Sunday morning swims. Happy just to be part of something.

*

In August 1999, Mike got his GCSE results. He had done enough. Enough to get into the sixth form. Enough to study the subjects he wanted. More than Kieran or Justin, who had planned for vocational courses—Carpentry. Electronics.
"That's great," his mother said. "Your History grade is strong enough for A-level. And your Maths. The Psychology teacher only wanted five GCSEs, including English, so that's good."
"Yeah, I guess," Mike replied. "It's what I need, so it's fine."
"Are you sure you want that combination of subjects, though?"
"I'm good at maths, and I like history. Psychology sounds interesting. So, yeah."
"But what about after?" she pressed. "What degrees look for that combination?"
"I don't know, Mum. I haven't even started yet, and you're asking about years away."
She leaned forward. Hugged him.
"Well done. That's the thing. Well done."
Mike smiled, already regretting his brief outburst.
"What should we do to celebrate?" she asked hesitantly. "Would you like to do something? A meal? The cinema?"
"I already said I'd see Kieran and Justin. Then I'm going to Adele's. Her mum's cooking dinner."

As the words left his mouth, he immediately regretted them. The dinner at Adele's was going to be a routine event and had nothing to do with his results. But now, he could see how it would sound to his mum.

"It's just tea, like when Adele comes here. I'm sorry, Mum. I didn't think. I can change it—"

"No, no, it's fine." She forced a smile. "I should have planned something. No, you go. It's fine. I'm probably being silly, wanting to celebrate."

But her voice wavered. Her eyes welled up. She cried.

"I'll change it, Mum. I'll tell them—"

"No." She wiped her tears and straightened her posture. "You know I cry at the drop of a hat. I'm not crying to make you feel guilty. You're going."

*

Mike enjoyed studying A-levels. Psychology, in particular.
It was a subject he just 'got'. Concepts made sense to him instinctively. He could think through their implications with ease. History still interested him. Maths? Maths just got done.

But the truth was that school was a minor part of his life. He spent more and more time with Adele. He played more gigs. He constantly listened to music. And for the first time—He felt like he had found himself.

*

As well as performing, Mike, Adele, and his friends went to see other local bands. Mike always wanted to be at the front—to hear the band better, to watch the guitarists. But at the back—at the sides of the room—That's where the real action was. Mike started noticing the small drug deals. Mostly E's, but the sharp scent of cannabis was unmistakable.

*

One evening, after dropping off their kit at John's house, John pulled something out of his pocket. He grinned.
"I've got some weed."
He rolled a joint, lit it, and took a long, deep drag. Holding his breath, he passed it to Kieran.
Kieran followed suit.
Then—Mike.
Mike didn't smoke, but he took a drag anyway.
The urge to cough was unbearable, but he fought through it.
Then—Justin.
Adele refused.
And so it went—again and again.
Several joints later—
Mike understood what it felt like to be high.
His mind detached from his surroundings in a way that felt both profound and yet benign.
It was like watching the world from a new perspective—a quiet, pleasant separation.
After that night, they smoked often.

*

The band mostly played indie tracks from the charts. Mike liked learning full albums, but the band focused only on the big hits. From Stereophonics' *Performance and Cocktails*, they only played *Just Looking*. From Travis' *The Man Who*, they only played *Why Does It Always Rain On Me?* Mike's taste, however, stretched far beyond guitar music. He was intoxicated by techno—its hypnotic beats, its energy. He loved: Fatboy Slim's *Right Here, Right Now*; Basement Jaxx's *Rendez-Vu*. But the track that transported him—*Olympic Flame* by Tiesto.

The rest of the band thought techno was "okay" at best.
Adele?
She hated it.
"It's just the same thing over and over. They're not proper songs."

"But listen! There's something new every few bars!" Mike argued, incredulous.
But the real problem?
Techno had to be played LOUD.
Blisteringly loud.
And definitely too loud for his mum.
When she was out, he'd blast his music at full volume, his mind in Ibiza, dancing like he was inside a club.
Then—
"Turn it down! TURN IT DOWN!"
His mum would burst into his room, furious.
"The neighbours will complain!"
"You're going to damage your hearing!"
"It doesn't work when it's quiet, Mum!" Mike would argue, pointing at his subwoofer.
But when he wasn't blasting techno, he was writing.
Softer songs.
Love songs.
But also—
Songs about war. About the Iraq conflict in 2000.
Adele didn't like those either.
"It's clever. But it's all so... serious," she said.
"Well, war is serious, Adele. Don't you think?"
"Yeah, but you can't dance to it, can you?"
She smirked.
"Not that what you do is called dancing."

*

Being with Adele was special.
As their second anniversary approached, they discussed plans while lounging at Mike's house.
"Shall we go somewhere nice? For a meal?" Mike suggested.
"We could..." Adele hesitated.
Mike picked up on her reluctant tone.
"Or maybe the cinema?"
"We went last week."
"Or just stay in? Watch a film here?"

Adele smiled.
"Yes. Let's do that."
She cuddled up to him.
That was all she wanted.

*

Time with Adele came with problems.
"Guess you're not coming out with us later," Kieran muttered, his tone making it clear—Mike had his priorities wrong.
"Seeing Adele? Again?" Justin mocked.
Mike hated disapproval.
So, he downplayed it.
"Just for a bit. I'll probably catch you later."
Cheerful. Casual. Trying to signal that they were still important.
His mum had the same quiet disappointment.
"Oh, I didn't realise you were seeing her tonight."
"But you were with her all day yesterday."
She never explicitly said he was spending too much time with Adele.
But she didn't have to.
Mike felt guilty every time he left.
So, he'd say, "I won't be long. I'm only dropping by."
Even if it wasn't true.

*

Homework suffered a bit.
But he could do some while listening to music.
And he wrote songs late at night.
Adele-time always came at the expense of study time.
Adele, though, had her own struggles.
She had issues with her sister.
Mike spent a lot of time cheering her up.
And the months passed.
She wasn't the same confident girl he had first met.
Was she depressed?

She doubted herself—everything she did, everything she could do.
And Mike?
He told her.
"You're amazing."
"You can do this."
"You're brilliant."
But he also worried.
Not just for her—
But that she might leave him.

*

One night at the pub, he confessed his fears to Kieran.
"I'm never sure what to say. What if I say the wrong thing? What if she thinks I'm useless?"
Kieran scoffed.
"Mike, you're too hard on yourself. You're her boyfriend, not her therapist."
"But I've been reading about counselling. I could help—"
"Enough, Mike. Enough."
Kieran took a sip of his drink.
"Some people are just... hard work."
"Too hard work."
"We're too young for this."
Mike stared at his glass.
His voice was quiet.
"But Kieran, I need her to like me."

*

One evening, the following March, as they sat watching TV at Mike's house, Adele spoke.
"I'm just not happy. I don't think we should see each other anymore."
Mike froze.
"But maybe you're not happy with other things. Not me," he protested.

Adele sighed.
"I don't know. It's everything. I just... I want to be by myself."
Mike clung to her words, searching for hesitation—for doubt.
There was none.
She had spoken with no sadness. No regret.
"Please, Adele. I don't want you to..." His voice cracked. "...leave."
He broke.
Tears burned his eyes.
Adele's expression softened.
She looked sad.
But not the kind of sadness that held remorse.
It was pity.
And pity wouldn't make her stay.
As she reached the door, Mike blurted out the words he'd never actually said before.
"I love you."
Adele didn't reply.
She just left.

*

Losing Adele shattered Mike. Completely. Despite all the other things in his life, he felt utterly lost. Nothing felt fun anymore. The music that once lifted him now felt hollow. Everywhere he went—He saw couples. Laughing. Holding hands. He had never felt so alone.

*

His mother was worried. One afternoon, she confided in her friend Imogen next door.
"It's heartbreaking to see him like this. He keeps crying. He doesn't think I can hear him, but I can. I'm worried he'll get depressed. Like... clinically depressed."
"Oh, I don't think so," Imogen reassured her. "They all go through it. We did. I did. My first boyfriend broke my heart. I don't think I've ever fully recovered."

"Yes, but Mike's different. He's a sensitive soul. And he's been through so much. What if it all just... gets on top of him? I don't know what to say to him. How to help."
"None of us ever do," Imogen admitted.
"We all say the same things—You'll get over it, you'll meet someone else—but it never actually helps."

*

Admiration isn't love. Mike realised that now. What he felt wasn't just loss—It was rejection. A fall from being liked. He couldn't escape the aching question that tormented him day and night:
"I don't know what I did wrong." He said it to himself. To others. Over and over.

John, Kieran, and Justin thought booze or weed might fix him. They tried to get him drunk. They tried to get him stoned. Every time they met. But it didn't help.
Mike muttered, "The drugs don't work, they just make it worse," quoting The Verve's *The Drugs Don't Work*, almost like a chant.

*

Late at night, songs poured out of him.
Songs filled with bitterness.
Anger.
But most of all—
Loss.
Flashback. Her face and the underlit clouds.
Agony.
One song he called "*Breaking Out of a Teardrop*."
In it, he sang:
"Ain't like the books I've read... Ain't like the songs I've heard..."
Overwhelming.
A deluge of hopelessness.
The lyrics imagined a chorus of friends calling to him—
"Open your mind and find a new kind of life."

But he couldn't. His visual mind latched onto a haunting image Himself, knee-deep in tear water, heartbroken, looking out from inside a teardrop. The song, the words, the image—They entered his soul.

Chapter 11

That same year, Claire and Penny were thirteen—
And inseparable.
If asked what they did together, they would struggle to say much beyond—
"All sorts."
"Everything."
But that was the magic of their friendship. A singularity. They could talk for hours. Or walk in complete silence, totally at ease. Their togetherness fed their adventurousness. The purchase of second-hand bikes turned them into explorers.

*

Claire's mum knew her reckless streak.
"Don't go too far. It's an old bike. It's bound to break down. And Penny's is just as bad."
Words that might have suggested concern—if not for what followed.
"And I am not coming to get you back from God knows where."
"We won't," Claire chirped, already heading for the door.
Confident that—Whatever happened—they'd be fine.

*

But sure enough, one of the bikes always broke. A puncture. A slipped chain. A worn-out brake. They laughed about how they only ever seemed able to ride out, never back.
"Ride out, walk back."
It became one of their insider jokes.
But their bikes gave them freedom.
To get into the 'green', as Penny called it. Not just for an hour or two— But from morning 'til dusk. And beyond.

*

Weekends meant bike rides—No matter the weather. Claire would pack a cheese sandwich, fill her bike's water bottle, and go. Lashing rain was a joy. She loved the feel of raindrops running down her face—The taste of them as she stretched her tongue out to catch a few. The sound of tyres slicing through puddles. The way different wet road surfaces created a symphony of splashes. And the puddles themselves—That childish thrill of hitting a deep one, feeling the sudden drag, the spray flying everywhere. Especially on bare legs.
She would arrive at Penny's, soaked and grinning, announcing.
"It's raining."
As if it were a gift.

*

Living in the northwest, they became experts in rain. But other weather conditions expanded their education. When a Friday night forecast predicted strong winds, Claire had an idea.
"Let's go to Delamere Forest tomorrow."
They weren't disappointed.
Deep in the tallest pine trees, they heard groans.
The wind strained the trees.
They propped their bikes against a tree and stepped into the woods.
Their feet crunched over a thick carpet of browned pine needles.
The ground felt dry despite the recent rain.
Then—
A deep, aching creak.
A snap.
Most people would have fled.
Claire?
She lay down on her back.
Penny hesitated.
Then—she lay down too.
From the ground, they could see the tall, clustered trunks bending against the sky.
Another groan.
Another snap.

"Jeez, amazing," Penny whispered.
The battle above them raged—
But on the ground, there was silence.
Claire wished she had a camera.
But she didn't need one.
It was seared into her mind.

*

They returned again and again over the next few years.
Always with the excitement that—
Maybe this time...
Just maybe...
A tree will fall.

*

Back at school, Claire and Penny's uniqueness was not appreciated. Dorothy, Margaret, and the other girls prided themselves on being "in". They wore the right clothes. Had the right hairstyles. Their exaggerated swooning over *Boyzone* was proof of their status.

Claire and Penny were aware of the boy bands. They felt the first stirrings of attraction. But no matter how hard they tried—They just didn't like the pretty boys. Not Ronan Keating. Not Stephen Gately. Their discussions had already revealed a divide. Penny liked Keith Duffy's rougher look. Claire preferred the cheeky charm of Shane Lynch. Neither realised this slight difference was just the beginning of something bigger.

*

"Bet you don't even know who Boyzone are, do you?" Margaret sneered at Penny.
"Or their latest record," Dorothy added, targeting Claire.
"We do," they answered together dismissively.
Margaret smirked.

"So, who do you like? Do you even know their names?"
Dawn and Sheila's arrival completed the encirclement.
Two of the girls giggled—
"Ronan."
Curtsey.
The other two joined in—
"Stephen."
Giggling.
Then their attention turned to Claire and Penny—
Mockery, ready and waiting.
"Shane Lynch," Claire said.
"Keith Duffy," Penny added.
Margaret's smirk slipped.
This was not the response she expected.
So, she improvised.
"They're naff."
She sneered.
"You're weird."
Dawn and Sheila backed her up.
"Mingers. Weird. Fuck off."
And just like that—
They walked away.

*

Claire turned to Penny.
"I don't mind being weird."
She hesitated.
"I hate that f-word. I'm never going to use it."
"Me neither."
Claire thought for a second.
"Let's use other swear words. I've heard Germans swearing in films—Mein Gott and Scheisse instead of shit."
"Yeah! And in French, it's Mon Dieu and... I think Merde."
Claire grinned.
She raised her fists, shaking them toward the sky.
"Mein Gott! Scheisse!"
Penny copied her stance.

"Mon Dieu! Merde!"
"Mein Gott! Scheisse!"
"Mon Dieu! Merde!"
They continued—
Turning it into a chant.
Then a song.
Then—
A joke just for them.

*

Even after five years of friendship, home life remained a taboo topic between Claire and Penny.
The only things Claire knew about Penny's parents?
Her dad was "a bit stupid" and "basically ridiculous".
Her mum?
"Only ever says nasty things to people."
And—
"They don't get on."

*

So, the invitation to Penny's house came as a shock.
"They're going out," Penny announced.
Her voice held disbelief.
"They never go out. And never together."
Claire frowned.
"Why now, then?"
"Some party at my mum's work. She doesn't want them gossiping about her being 'single' or 'divorced' or something. But she told him he better not say anything ridiculous."
Penny rolled her eyes.
"Anyway, they say they'll rent some videos from Blockbuster. But only if you come round."
Claire hesitated. The latest report on Penny's parents didn't exactly set her mind at ease.
Penny noticed her reluctance.

"You won't have to see them or owt. They're leaving at six. Maybe you could come at seven?"
"How long for?" Claire asked, still cautious.
"Till we've watched the two films. Then you can go. They won't be back until late."
Claire brightened.
"Boss. What are the films?"
Penny grinned.
"One's a bit babyish. Remember when we saw Toy Story when we were twelve? Well, this is Toy Story 2."
"Ha! Fine by me."
Claire launched into You've Got a Friend in Me, and Penny—
With glee—
Chimed in.
"To infinity and beyond!"
For a moment, despite being fourteen, they were kids again.
But Penny quickly restored her near-adult persona.
"The other one's called Notting Hill. Supposed to be funny. It's not a U, though—it's a PG."
She straightened her shoulders.
"Sorted."

*

Claire had started keeping a diary. She'd always liked sketching, but now she wrote about events—Her feelings. That night, she jotted down: "Visiting Penny's." Next to it, she drew—A dark cave entrance. Two pairs of monstrous eyes stared out. Penny's reassurances weren't enough. Claire was still afraid.

*

Claire arrived, scanning the driveway—The car was gone. *Good*.
"Chuffed you've come," Penny said, pulling her inside. They watched the films. They loved Toy Story 2.
"They're great mates, Woody and Buzz. I like that," Penny mused.
"Like us," Claire grinned. She raised a hand. "Mein Gott."

Penny high-fived her. "Mon Dieu."
Notting Hill had fewer laughs.
"That painting was weird," Penny said afterwards, referring to the Chagall painting *La Mariée* featured in the film.
"Goats playing violins? Proper naff."
"I liked it," Claire admitted.
"Didn't totally get it, but it felt dreamlike. Like... the bride's thoughts in the painting," Penny snorted.
"Oh, is that what it was meant to be?" she shrugged. "Still. It's not proper art."
Claire let it go.
"The love story was a bit far-fetched, though."
Penny's tone darkened. "Love is far-fetched. I don't think it exists. Just something people tell themselves."
Silence fell.
Then—Claire confessed.
"Certainly not my mum's feeling about my dad."
She paused.
"Whoever he was."
Penny stiffened. She knew Claire's dad had always been absent. But she'd never asked. She could have, now—But instead, she deflected.
"Nor my mum and dad. Like I say—it's all bollocks."
Claire hesitated.
"Maybe. But I like the idea of it. Being swept off your feet. Romance. Sounds pretty magical."
She smiled.
"But we'll cross that bridge when we come to it."

*

The key in the front door lock made Penny freeze for a moment.
She leapt up—Plumped a cushion—Snapped to attention.
Claire barely had time to register before Mr and Mrs Hall walked in. Instantly, Claire stood, too.
Mrs Hall's eyes narrowed.
"You're still 'ere," she said.

A thick, Manchester sneer.
Claire swallowed.
"Just leaving now, Mrs Hall. We watched films." Apologetic. Afraid. Only now did she take them in visually.
Mrs Hall—Hair pulled back so tight, her forehead shone. Lips painted candy-apple red. A black tea dress—Patterned with clusters of giant roses. Like something out of a 1970s TV show. But Mr Hall? He was—Tiny. Dressed in a funeral suit, wide lapels and all. A garish red-and-blue tie. And the tiniest round glasses Claire had ever seen. Like a 1930s bank clerk. She was staring.
And that was when Mrs Hall said it.
"Jeez, your arms are monkey-long."
Claire's stomach dropped.
"Must have been all that tree swinging we all heard about you doing as a girl."
Claire glanced at Penny. Looking for clues. *A joke? A jab?*
But Penny was—
Gone.
Not physically.
But mentally—
A cringe so complete, she disappeared inside herself.
Claire turned to Mr Hall, desperate to change the subject.
"Did you have a nice time, Mr Hall?"
His posture shifted. Odd. He tilted his head, bent his knees—
"Ay-thang-yaw." And—curtseyed.
Claire blinked.
Years later, she'd learn this was an Arthur Askey impression—
Some comedian from the '40s and '50s.
But right then?
She thought—
He was mad.
Penny had reached her limit.
She grabbed Claire's arm—
Pulled her to the door.
Claire barely managed to say goodbye before they were outside.
And then—
She ran home.

Just in case she was being pursued.

*

Back home, Claire switched on her radio, grabbed her notebook, and scrawled one word:
Nightmare.
Her pencil moved instinctively, the strokes sharpening into a narrow figure.
Unrealistically narrow—
The face, pinched.
Then—
She added small, round black glasses.
Penny's dad.
"Pure Shores" by All Saints played.
Claire sighed.
"Twee."
She moved on—
Penny's mum.
The ridiculous dress.
She drew oversized red lips.
An exaggeration—
But unmistakably, Mrs Hall.

*

More songs—*The Real Slim Shady* by Eminem. Claire perked up. She'd heard it before, but now—She listened. The scorn for "little girl and boy groups." The defiance—"A million of us who cuss like me don't give a fuck like me..." Liberation. Claire jumped up, singing along—
"Will the real Slim Shady please stand up?"
She shouted it again louder—And louder.
Another track: *Take a Look Around* by Limp Bizkit. She had liked it when she'd heard it before. But now—She felt it. Life was "just a blast" that was "movin' really fast." The rage. The urgency.

Claire picked up her pencil again.
This time—
The bullies.
Dorothy's ears, stretched.
Margaret's eyes, narrowed.
Dawn's lips, bloated.
Sheila's curls, springing in terror.
Caricatures—
But clear as day.
Claire didn't know she had it in her.

*

The next day, she didn't mention the drawings to Penny.
She just said—
"I love that Eminem and Limp Bizkit stuff."
Penny shrugged.
"It's just talking. Shouting. Lost on me."
Claire scoffed.
"I hate all that 'happy, jolly' boy-and-girl-band crap. And the soppy, whiny ones too."
"Truth is, I don't listen to music," Penny admitted. "Not much. Not bothered."
Claire stared.
"The drive, the energy, the excitement—how can you not love it?"
Penny smirked.
"Merde. Hysteria. You're welcome to it."

*

Claire and Penny still did everything together. But now—Boys were noticing them. Everywhere.
"It's weird," Claire muttered. "You can feel their eyes boring into you."
Penny nodded.
Claire paused. "They behave like robots. Programmed." Paused again. "Do you... like it?"

Penny considered. "Better than not being noticed." She tilted her head, musing. "If they weren't interested, they'd just scan the horizon for something better."
Claire laughed.
"Yes, Dr Freud."
Penny rolled her eyes.
"Your hair gets you the most attention, though."
Claire ran her fingers through her auburn strands, frowning.
Penny pouted. "Mine's just mousy."
Claire grinned. "Me and Sabrina the Teenage Witch, huh? And anyway, I like your hair."

*

They tested the game.
Glanced back at the boys.
Penny commented on what she saw. "Some just look away immediately. Some even get embarrassed. But the cocky ones? Straight over."
Claire sighed. "It's all about how long you hold eye contact, isn't it?"
Penny grinned. "Programmed, like I said."
She raised her arms, moving stiffly like a robot and, in a Dalek voice, chanted, "We are all programmed."
Claire shook her head. "Well, I'm not."

*

Boys stayed at arm's length.
Claire and Penny liked it that way.
Claire's journal helped her make sense of things. She classified boys—

Category	Definition
Chav	Tracksuit. Loud. Thinks he's funny.
Poser	Acts like he's in a boy band.
Wicked	Actually cool. Rare.
Funny	Can make her laugh. Mega rare.

Category Definition

Bore   Talks about football. Nonstop.

Stupid   Self-explanatory.

Can't tell Jury's out.

She tracked them. Some boys rose in ranking. Others bombed. Girls? She mostly wrote about 'unfairness'. Some had 'more freedom'. Some were 'mean for no reason'. 'Hate' appeared often. 'Love'—Only when someone was bold. When they stood their ground, she despised blind obedience.

*

TV was ridiculous. Her sketches filled with caricatures—But none were self-portraits. By sixteen, Claire knew—What she liked. What she hated. What she wasn't. But who was she?

Chapter 12

Adele was a constant in Mike's life. And then she wasn't. Inarticulate mutterings about not feeling the same, Mike spent months grieving Adele. He analysed every second they'd been together. *Maybe I didn't do enough. Maybe I wasn't exciting enough.*

His mother tried to console him.
"It's not your fault, Michael. Sometimes people... need change."
But Mike didn't believe that.

*

Walking through the village was torture.
Every girl in the distance—
Could it be her?
He saw her twice—On the top deck of a bus.
Did she see me? Maybe. She didn't smile. Dissed.

*

Mike stopped going to places she might be.
Hung out at friends' houses instead.

*

He applied to university.
Psychology.
He knew he needed to leave.

*

"Manchester as your first choice?" Cathy asked.
"Not Norwich?"
Mike hesitated.
"It's just a train ride, Mum."
She sighed.

"Just be careful. You're a bit... gullible."
Mike smiled, appreciating her concern.
"I will, Mum. I will."

*

He got the grades.
He confirmed his place in the halls. He was set.
A new chapter.

*

Walking around the village in the final days before he left, Mike wondered what he might miss about Ilketshall St Andrew—his village. The image that came to mind? St. Andrew's Church. The pale stone. The octagonal tower. Against a bright blue sky. Small. Quaint. Somehow—Comforting. Home.

*

Mike's mum drove him to Manchester on Sunday, September 16th. The events in America the previous Tuesday only deepened her fear.
"This 9/11 thing—"
"It's terrifying."
"It could happen here next."
"They might target big cities like this one."
Mike sighed.
"Mum, stop."
As they approached the residence halls, Cathy stiffened.
"You're not in a tower block, are you?"
Her voice was on the edge of hysteria.
Mike forced a laugh.
"First floor, Mum."
"Not the 110th, like the Twin Towers."
"I'll be fine. Stop worrying."
But Cathy was relentless.
"The other floors could still come crashing down on you."

Mike groaned.
"Mum—"
They parked. Mike hauled out two suitcases. His mum carried his guitar and coat.
"This one—Cass House," he pointed.
They walked through the ground-floor café area.
Students buzzed around—
Boys and girls, laughing and chatting.
Cathy paused, wary.
"Your flat is just boys, though? Right?"
Mike rolled his eyes.
"Yes, Mum. Just boys."
"There's the lift."
They reached Flat 1.
Mike was in Room 1—
"Nearest the stairs," Cathy noted.
Mike shot her a look.
"Mum."
She raised her hands.
"Okay, okay. Sorry."
They stepped into his tiny new room.
Cathy walked straight to the window.
Surveyed the view.
"Okay. Not the Twin Towers. You could jump from here. Maybe break a leg." She nodded, reassured.
Mike winced.
He needed to get her out before his flatmates heard this. He ushered her toward the lift.
"Don't bother coming back down," Cathy said. "The lift will take ages."
Mike leaned in. Kissed her on the cheek.
"Drive carefully. Stop at the same two places we did on the way up. Take good breaks."
Then—
"And thanks… for everything."
The lift doors opened.
Perfect timing.
Mike stepped back, watching—

His mother's eyes filled with tears.
Then—The doors closed.

*

Mike returned to his room. Turned the key. Opened the door. And—Felt a wave of unease. He was alone. Completely alone. For the first time in his life. He scanned the room. Small. Bare. Monastic. The narrowest bed he'd ever seen. *Two feet six inches? Seriously?* He flopped onto it. Stretched his legs. *Not quite Goldilocks. It'll do.*

*

Then—Voices. Outside.
"Is she here? Knock on Tiffany's door and see."
A girl's voice.
Mike frowned.
Tiffany? One of the flatmates' girlfriends?
He heard a loud knock at a nearby door.
"Hi, has she arrived? Flat One. Did you see her?"
"Yeah, she's here. I didn't see her, but I heard her talking to her boyfriend or dad, Something about the Twin Towers."
Mike froze.
Thin walls. My conversation with my mum. Wait—what?
"So, we have our sixth Ace of Bass," a third girl joked.
"Bass House rules!" another chimed in.
Mike heard a group of girls singing, "*All that she wants is another baby. She's gone tomorrow, boy,*" from the band Ace of Bass.

It's Cass House. I saw the sign.
Then—
"The boys swapped the letter again. It says Cass House now."
Realisation slammed into him.
Oh, shit. No way. I'm in the wrong bloody flat.
Then—
A soft knock on his door.

How can I get out?
"Let's go say 'Hi'," Mike heard alongside the sound of the girls shuffling to leave the room. And then the knock on his door. He simply couldn't think straight. *Apologise, Explain. They know the sign has been changed.*
He opened the door.
And—
Five girls.
One in only underwear.
She shrank back, arms crossing over her chest.
Mike froze.
"Oh? Sorry. Is she in? You must be the boyfriend."
A curly-haired girl held several sheets of paper.
"You are…?"
Mike swallowed.
"Mike. But—"
The girls craned their necks, peering into his room.
"Has she gone out?" a dark-haired girl asked.
"I thought you left," said the girl in underwear, folding her arms across her chest and now crossing one leg in front of the other.
"No. It's me. That was my mum. I thought this was my room. There's been a mistake."
Silence.
Then—
The girl with the papers raised them.
Read aloud—
"Fooled you."
And—
Laughter.
Several lads walked up behind the girls, laughing. One of them pushed to the front of the group at the door. "Hi, I'm Jason. Did you like our script?" he asked, with a broad beam. The girl with curly brown hair raised the papers and then waved them.
"What. So? Am I in Cass House"
Jason beamed. Different voices.
"We saw you arrive."
"You were the last one."
"So, we wrote the prank downstairs."

Mike shook his head.

"There is no Bass House, Mike," added the girl with papers.

Jason continued. "We persuaded the girls to play along. We sat downstairs and wrote the script. We knew you were the last to get here. We saw you arrive."

Mike said, "I was thinking," and then continued in his best Homer Simpson voice:

"I'm normally not a praying man, but if you're up there—please save me, Superman."

The group exploded with laughter.

Jason's elaborate scam sealed something—

A friendship group of immense strength.

Mike—

The gullible one.

But a great sport.

The girls?

Loved playing along.

Especially Tiffany.

Mike turned to her.

"What's your name?"

"Tiffany Montague," she said proudly.

"Did a bit of acting back home in Chelsea."

"You were good," Mike said.

"Fucking good. I thought you were actually shocked when I opened the door."

Tiffany took a bow.

"I'm definitely joining the drama group here."

And—That was Tiffany. A star in every way. She found the drama club. And—Was lost to Flat One, Cass House.

Chapter 13

The most striking thing about Mike's Psychology degree was its sheer scale. The lecture theatres were massive—Just like in the movies. Mike half-expected *Will Hunting* to appear and answer one of the professor's questions.

*

Most of the lecturers were surprisingly young. Dr Paul Cavanagh—mid-twenties, sharp, energetic. He taught Research Methods and Data Analysis. Professor Adrian Carpenter—ancient, eccentric. He lectured in Social Psychology and loved to remind them: how he 'knew Michael Argyle, you know.' A 'legend in non-verbal behaviour studies.' Yet despite his age, Carpenter's mimicry skills were electric—He brought the subject alive.

*

But it was Mrs Margaret Wells who truly inspired Mike. She was the lecturer in Developmental Psychology. Middle-aged. Super mumsy. She didn't stand or hide behind the lectern. She sat on a chair like a children's storyteller. She didn't lecture—She painted vivid stories of children and developmental struggles. It was so real, so emotive. Mike was hooked.

She talked about issues she had seen. It was all so imaginable in Mike's mind. He loved it. It all deeply touched him. Two of the lectures in that first year stayed with him throughout his career. In one, Maggie Wells had shown a video. It was a video made in the 1950s by a psychologist called Harry Harlow about attachment. It showed a monkey having a choice between the wire-framed manikin that had milk available through teats and a manikin covered in coarse hair. When alarmed, the monkey would run to the latter for comfort, not the former. Comfort and security as a bond. Mike was deeply moved by the video.

But it was another video that affected him most. It was a recent recording Maggie Wells had made from behind a two-way mirror of a young mother attempting to play with her baby. Maggie had explained that the girl had not experienced a loving bond with her mother as a child. Watching this girl, knowing in theory what mothers should do to play with a baby, yet with no eye contact or warmth, was a profound sight. Mike cried in the lecture.

In addition to the interpersonal aspects of psychology, Mike also enjoyed the discipline's logic. This was most evident in Cognitive Psychology, where details of human mental processes—memory, perception, and problem-solving — were revealed through carefully constructed experiments.
Mike's love of psychology made all the coursework easy for him.

*

Mike was surprised by the amount of free time.
Mike filled it with music.

*

Jason played guitar, too.
They wrote songs together and harmonised effortlessly.
One night in Jason's room—
"We're good enough to play open mic nights, d'yer think?" Mike asked.
Jason hesitated.
"I dunno. I might get nervous."
"You'll blow people away."
"Maybe."
"Trust me."

*

They played a few venues.
And loved it.

*

As first-year students, Mike, Jason, and Will lived in Fallowfield, catching a bus into the city centre campus every morning.
Nights followed a pattern:
Quick dinner in the shared communal kitchen with different people taking turns cooking. Followed by a brief chillout in one's own room. Mike often elected to spend that time playing his guitar. Then—9:00 pm, out to a bar. Sometimes, they'd stay there all night. Thursdays were student nights—Free entry to small clubs. They'd rollback home at 2:30 am.

*

On one Thursday night in March, around 9.30 pm, Mike and Jason were walking through town when they noticed some homeless men settling down in doorways for the night. Gaunt faces. Sunken eyes.

A four-wheeled cart clattered down the pavement. Two young guys pulling it along. They stopped at a shop doorway—Spoke to a man curled up in a sleeping bag. Then—The cart was opened. A waft of hot food. The guy passed him a meal, then closed the lid. The logo on the cart was "The Food Mission."
Mike caught one of the helpers' eyes. A guy in a Manchester United beanie. Mike smiled. The guy nodded, moving on.

"That's ace," Mike said.
"Must make a huge difference."
The other volunteer turned toward them. We can all make a difference." He pointed at the logo. "You can donate online."

Mike nodded.
"I will."
"Me too," Jason added.

The United fan spoke next—
"Or volunteer."
Mike paused.
"How many nights do people usually do?"
"Mostly one."
"We need more hands."
"We get hot food from local restaurants—proper stuff, good hygiene."
"We just distribute it."
"Ring Jake. His number's on the website."
Mike didn't hesitate.
"I'll do it."
The guy nodded, rolling the cart forward.
Jason exhaled, pulling his hood up.
"I'll donate."
Mike watched the streetlights reflect in the puddles.
He felt the emptiness of a doorway at night.
"I'll volunteer."
Jason hesitated.
"Maybe," he muttered.
Then—
He glanced at Mike.
Saw him nodding to himself.
Smiling.
Like he'd just won the lottery.

*

The pattern of events at weekends was more varied. Mike and Jason started to play open-mic or paid gigs quite often on a Friday night. They'd even been offered a regular slot at a little bar that wanted an acoustic mellow vibe, which they enjoyed. Saturdays meant watching a band at the Students' Union or going to a party, preferably both.

*

Mike started volunteering every Wednesday evening at The Food Mission. Jason always full of praise—But never joined. Never said why.

*

Jason, Will, and Mike memorised the city—Student bars. Cheap clubs. A grapevine of party spots. The No. 99 bus was the lifeline—Until it wasn't.

*

That April night, in the pouring rain, they needed the No. 99 to Sale. Jason spun around.
"It's here!"
They sprinted to the stop. Will caught the driver's eye. Success. They dashed upstairs, dripping like wet dogs.
"I didn't know the 98 went to Sale, too," Will muttered.
Mike's head snapped up.
"What?"
Jason shrugged.
"I swear it said 99."
Will muttered, "Uh... it said 98."
Mike froze. "Shit. We could be going anywhere."
Will jumped up. "Ring the bell. We're getting off."
Mike lunged for the bell. The bus jerked to a halt. The middle doors hissed open. Mike stepped off. Then, Will bent to tie his shoe. Jason grinned. Then—The doors slammed shut. The bus pulled away. Mike stood alone in the rain. Jason and Will? Laughing their asses off through the window. Mike trudged to the next stop.

*

Later, Will said, "Made it up. Should be in RADA like Tiffany."
Jason grinned.
"I'd have fallen for it, too."

Mike sighed.
"Fuck off."
With a smile.

*

First-year exams—smooth. Second-year subjects? Decent. But no Maggie Wells. Mike's favourite? Health & Clinical Psychology. Mental health. Therapeutic approaches. Fascinating.

*

Mike liked playing guitar with Jason, but it was Jason who suggested he respond to an advert pinned up in the Union, seeking a guitar player to join a band after a guy had left the group.
"It won't stop us doing our little things, but you've said you'd like the chance to play gigs again," Jason suggested.
"It doesn't say what sort of stuff they play. Merely says 'pop and rock covers,'" Mike replied.
Jason read through the flyer. "It says just roll up to their rehearsal space. What's to lose?"
Mike went the following evening. As he entered the room, the band started to play *SK8er Boi* by Avril Lavigne. Although they sounded a bit odd without a guitar, the drummer and bassist were tight. Mike was spellbound by the girl singer. She was tall and slim, with shoulder-length blonde hair. She was wearing a floral pink halter-neck crop top with blue jeans. At once, she looked elegant and yet casual. She had perfect features and, as her attention turned to Mike at the door, extraordinarily pale blue eyes. Mike was also struck by her fantastic voice. Fuck, she's amazing.

Lydia smiled and signalled 'one minute' with the finger of her right hand as the band went seamlessly into *Family Affair* by Mary J Blige. Mike looked on in admiration. Brilliant. After a few bars, they stopped playing. The beautiful girl walked over.

"Hi, sorry. We just wanted to get that transition right. My name is Lydia. Lydia Clarke. And we are . . . Covers," Lydia said with a small curtsey.

Mike reckoned she was from London. The bassist walked over and said, "I'm Pete." But Mike couldn't work out where he might be from. The drummer raised a stick and said, "Fraser" in the broadest Glaswegian accent Mike had ever heard.
Mike grinned.
"You guys sound great."
Pete nodded.
Fraser shrugged.
Mike plugged in. Strummed once to check tuning and sound level.
Fraser counted in.
And—
They tore through Sk8er Boi.
It sounded tight.
Lydia said, "Bangin'."
"We've got a gig Saturday."
Mike blinked.
"What?"
"Yeah. Thought we'd have to cancel."
Lydia smirked.
"But now? We're on."
Pete shrugged.
"If you're in, that is."
Mike hesitated.
Lydia raised an eyebrow.
"We can do this, country boy."
Mike laughed. *Suffolk accent—fair enough.*
Then—
He nodded.
"We can."

*

The gig went well. Mike was enamoured with Lydia. Top-tier singer. Drop-dead gorgeous. What could go wrong?

*

At gigs, the setup was standard—Pete played bass, standing to Fraser's left. Mike was on the right. Lydia? Front and centre. Roaming. Owning the stage. Mike found himself watching her more. The way she moved—Tight jeans. Snaked hips. Hair swishing. Head tipping back on high notes. She was intoxicating. He wanted her.

That night, they played a gig far away. Fraser drove them all back in his van. Late. Too late to head home. They dropped Pete off first. Then, as Fraser pulled up at his place, he groaned—
"Too late to haul drum kits now."
He turned to Lydia.
"Take my room? I'll crash on the sofa. Alright, on the floor, Mike?"
Lydia shook her head.
"Nah. I'll be fine on the sofa."
Fraser shrugged and disappeared upstairs.

*

Lydia shivered.
"It's fucking freezing in here."
She bent over in front of the gas fire, clicking the ignition.
Mike watched.
The flame flickered to life.
Heat.
Still, he muttered—
"Sofas are too short. Let's use the cushions on the floor."
Lydia nodded.
As Mike pulled seat cushions onto the floor, Lydia disappeared to grab coats from the front door.
"Going to the Khasi," she called.

Mike stripped to his boxers, stepping closer to the fire, desperate for warmth.
When Lydia returned, she laughed.
"You must be bloody mad."
She tossed coats over their makeshift beds.
Mike grinned.
"We'll warm up soon."
A pause.
"If the fire doesn't kill us with carbon monoxide first."
They both laughed.
"I guess," Lydia said, peeling off her clothes—
All of them.

*

She flopped onto her makeshift bed.
Pulled coats over herself.
Silence.
Then—
"Better if we snuggle up."
Mike didn't hesitate.
He pushed his cushions against hers and slid under the coats.
Lydia moved closer.
Warm.
Skin on skin.
No words.
Just instinct.
They made love.

*

Around nine-ish, Fraser wandered in. Barely looked at them. Stepped over their tangled bodies. Disappeared into the kitchen. "Coffee?" he asked. Like it was just another morning.

It wasn't for Mike. The image of Lydia's half-lit naked body from the previous night had etched itself into his mind.

Chapter 14

At sixteen, Claire Fontrelle was officially a "naughty child"—
According to teachers. To the rest of the world? She was simply playful.

*

She had enjoyed school once—some of it, anyway. Games—or PE, as they insisted on calling it—was fun. English had been fun before it got all serious and grammatical.

But there were more important things than school. What were they? Obvious. One look at her rough book told the whole story. Identity was everything. And in school, your rough book cover was your identity—Designed with love and precision. Football teams. Pop bands. Song lyrics. Each word written in different fonts, every letter shaded, shaped, and stylised. Claire glanced at hers. Something was missing. She saw a space—Something needed to go there.

*

At the start of the school year, she had filled the cover with band names—
Some of which now made her cringe.
That band? Old news.
That one? Split up.
Claire had moved on.
These days, she prefers drawing to writing.
Faces.
Postures.
People together.
She liked it.

*

She wanted to add her latest artistic impulse. She was in art class, after all. Silence had filled the room as students concentrated on the apples, oranges, and lemons in front of them. Claire frowned. *Why a lemon? Why draw fruit at all?* She much preferred sketching people—Expressions. Interactions. Real things.

*

Then, she couldn't help herself. She drew faces on her fruit— Not just any faces. The apple looked sad. The orange and lemon mocked it, gazing smugly at the sky. Claire grinned to herself. Mr Roberts did not.

*

"This isn't funny," he scolded. "You're wasting your time. You can draw them properly at lunchtime."
He sounded annoyed—But then something caught his eye. Claire's rough book sitting open on her desk. He picked it up, flipping through the pages—Then paused.

*

Claire watched him closely. Was he going to slam it down in frustration? Scold her for doodling instead of listening? No. He studied it with interest. Set it down gently. Looked at her.
"You don't like lessons, do you, Claire?"
Not a question—a statement.
She said nothing.
He didn't wait for an answer.
"We have an art club on Wednesday evenings. Not lessons— just a chance to explore different kinds of art. Come along. Ask your parents."

*

That night, Claire surprised herself. She actually bothered to ask her mother if she could stay after school. To her even greater surprise—Her mother said yes. She went. And it changed everything.

*

The following Wednesday, Claire strolled into the art club—
With nonchalance, of course.
But inside?
A swirl of excitement, curiosity, and doubt.
She liked art.
But did she belong here?
Was this betraying her "too cool for school" friends?
She pushed the thought away.
The room felt different from the daytime art class.
Older students were working on their own projects.
Mr Roberts wasn't lecturing—
He was just talking casually to the students.
And the supply cupboard?
Wide open.
People walking in and out freely.
So weird.
So… freeing.
Then, Claire saw it.
A painting—
Mounted on a massive easel.
She stared, transfixed.
The left side was a riot of primary colours—
Bold, abstract, alive.
The right side? Empty.
Just a vast expanse of blue.
Except—
A single hand reached out from the painted side.
Reaching toward the emptiness.

*

Claire felt something click inside her.
This painting was perfect.
The emptiness.
The contrast.
The longing.
She understood it completely.
She took a step closer—Drawn in.
Wanting to see every detail.
Then, suddenly A figure stepped in front of the painting.
Claire froze.
Tall.
Dark-haired.
Wearing an oversized, faded-blue cotton jacket. Creased. Shabby. Almost like a smock. His hair was long and messy. His black jeans were ripped. His red shoes stood out—a statement.

He turned. Looked at her. Irritated. Then expressionless. Blank.

But Claire felt it. An undeniable connection. This boy. His art. Something about him. Something about this place. She belonged here.

*

As weeks passed, Claire found herself immersed in art club.
Not traditional storytelling.
But fragments—
Images that seemed disconnected but weren't.
She played with space and contrast.
Balance and chaos.
She started bringing clothes she didn't wear to school—
Things that felt more like her.
For the first time—
She felt like she had a place.
A spiritual home.

*

Brian was nearly two years older than Claire, close to finishing his A levels, and entirely indifferent to the world's expectations. His style of dress wasn't a conscious rejection of trends or school cliques—it simply wasn't something he cared about. He didn't comb his hair. He still had to be reminded by his mother to brush his teeth in the morning. But he could paint.

Brian saw the world as objects, textures, and patterns. His vocabulary was limited, and his speech often stilted, but his hands never stopped moving. If there weren't an opportunity to sketch, he would observe, committing everything to memory.

Claire admired his uniqueness. She learnt quickly that talking too much would lead to being ignored, but simply existing alongside him felt effortless. Their time together began in Art Club, where she worked beside him in companionable silence, but soon, without any real plan, they started leaving together.

At first, it was just a habit—packing up their things simultaneously, walking the same corridors, stepping out of the school doors into the afternoon air, and following the path to the gates. Then, one day, Claire broke the pattern.

"Where do you live?" she asked.

"Arcadia Avenue." Brian nodded left, signalling the direction.

Without another word, they turned and began walking.

*

Halfway down Wood Road, Brian froze mid-step.

Claire followed his gaze to a girl crossing the street, pushing a massive pram.

She recognised her immediately—Cath, from their year. Claire's mind spun.

"Cath doesn't have siblings. That's not her mum's baby. Then… is it… hers?"

But Brian's reaction was different. While Claire's thoughts spiralled toward gossip and implications, Brian stared at the pram itself—not Cath, not the baby.

To him, the scale of the pram was fascinating. Massive. Disproportionate. Almost comically large compared to the petite girl pushing it.

Without hesitation, he pulled out his sketchbook, flipped it open in one fluid motion, and began drawing on the spot.

Claire watched as a few rapid pencil strokes captured something she hadn't even noticed—the way Cath's body tilted under the weight, how the effort warped her posture, how she leaned too far forward.

The figure in his sketch had no face —just a blank oval — suggesting a bowed head.

Claire had been about to ask about the baby. About Cath. About Brian's reaction. But something shifted.

Seeing him, lost in his art—seeing what he saw—she felt something different instead.

Without thinking, she slid her arm between his and squeezed gently.

They walked the rest of the way in silence.

*

Brian noticed. He didn't know why she had done it, but he liked it. Liked the feeling of warmth and connection. Liked the idea of it. He smiled to himself. He had a girlfriend.

They parted outside his house, still silent. As Brian walked up his driveway, he glanced over the hedge.

Claire was skipping down the street.

*

When she got home, she ran straight upstairs.

Adventure.

A boyfriend.

She wasn't sure how she felt about Brian, exactly—but she liked the idea of it.

She had no desire to tell anyone. Not her mother. Not even Penny.

Penny had mocked her for going to Art Club in the first place.

"Art is pointless."

"Artists are weirdos."

Claire doubted Penny would approve of Brian at all.
Still, a few days later, she casually mentioned him—only as someone from Art Club who happened to live on Arcadia Avenue.
Nothing more.

*

They spent the next few months together. Brian never visited her house. But Claire spent a lot of time at his. During the summer holidays, they spent entire days sitting in the local rugby field, watching the sky shift. Claire talked. Brian listened. She didn't notice that she did most of the talking. Brian didn't feel the need to speak. He wasn't hiding anything—he just didn't have the same kind of stories. Claire saw funny, strange, exciting things everywhere. Brian saw patterns and shapes. She filled the air with words and movement. Brian simply watched her move. He loved hearing her voice. But more than that, he loved the way she just existed.

*

One day, Claire leapt up and did a cartwheel, landing on her feet with uncontainable energy.
"Let's look for four-leaf clovers," she announced, collapsing back onto the grass.
"They'll bring us luck."
Dutifully, Brian combed through the clover patches, fingers grazing leaves, scrutinising each one.
"Ta-da!"
Claire's voice turned pirate-like, a ridiculous, exaggerated accent.
Brian looked up.
She was grinning, a long reed stem clamped between her teeth, eyes gleaming with mischief.
"Arrr, he be lookin' for treasure."
Brian laughed.
An honest, full laugh.
Not just a breath or a chuckle—a proper laugh.

Encouraged, Claire kept going, her accent turning Scottish.
"Arrr, but Long John Silver's been 'ere afore ye."
And then, without warning, she threw herself into a perfect handstand.
Brian was entranced.
He loved all of it—the performance, the silliness, the way she inhabited space like no one else he knew.
When she flopped back down beside him, she leaned over—
And kissed him on the cheek.
Brian turned his face toward her—
And they kissed.

*

Penny was intrigued. "So, he's a proper boyfriend, then?"
"Well, of course, he is."
"So, have you...?"
"Kissed? Yes, sure. He's a good kisser."
"But have you...?"
Claire's face flushed with indignation. "Mein Gott! Certainly not!" The sharpness of her own tone caught her off guard, so she softened. "We're mainly just friends... I don't know. It's all a bit confusing."
"Yes, but you've got one."

*

A few weeks later, Penny made her own announcement.
"Nigel from across the road has asked me out."
"That's great, Penny. Who is he?"
"He's two and a half years older than me. He didn't go to our school. He works for his dad's car sales business."
"Do you fancy him?"
"Well, he's quite good-looking. He wears glasses. I'd never thought about him that way. But now..."
"You'll have a boyfriend too." Claire grinned. "Better practice your kissing. On your hand, I mean. Come on, pucker up."

Penny duly obliged, planting a loud, exaggerated "Mm-wa" onto the back of her hand.
"No, I mean proper kissing. Longer."
"I know."

*

Claire and Brian kissed often on the rugby field, but their kisses were tentative, uncertain.
Claire tried to introduce variety, experimenting with techniques she had heard about.
"Kiss me more gently."
"Open your mouth a bit more."
"Would you like to kiss for longer?"
Brian always tried. His responses were usually short and factual.
"Alright."
Their approach to kissing became matter-of-fact, almost procedural. Occasionally, Claire would lean in and kiss his neck, and over time, Brian learnt that this was his cue—he would turn towards her, they would kiss, and then they would continue as if it hadn't happened at all.
The cinema became their primary place for kissing, not because of passion but because that's what couples did.
"Why do you think Lois Lane did that?" Brian mused after a scene on screen.
"Because she fancies Superman, silly." Claire rolled her eyes.
"And not Clark Kent, just because he wears glasses?" Brian scoffed. "She'd have to notice, wouldn't she?"
Their mockery of romance became a game. They enjoyed sarcasm and enjoyed each other's company, but the idea of passion? It still felt foreign.

*

Penny and Nigel continued dating, but the four of them never met up. Brian had no interest in the idea.
One day, Penny pressed Claire again. "So, have you gone past first base?"

Claire hesitated. She hadn't.
But Penny was already talking over her silence. "I let Nigel touch me." She looked over, watching for Claire's reaction. Seeing her surprise, Penny quickly clarified. "Only up top, I mean."
Claire blinked, not sure how to respond.
"Well, that's boyfriends and girlfriends, isn't it?" Penny reasoned. "We've both got one. It's kind of like having a badge, I think."
Brian. A badge.
That weekend, Claire told Brian he could touch her breast. He agreed.

She felt naughty. But mostly, she felt like she had earned something.
Another badge.

*

That autumn, Claire stepped into a new world—Brian's world, a world of art and expression.
She visited his house often, watching his latest paintings take shape. One afternoon, she found him working on a scene of people walking down a street—but one figure was walking backwards.
"Why have you added that?" she asked.
"She walks that way," Brian replied as if the answer were obvious.
"What does that mean?" Claire pressed.
"Not everyone walks the same way."
Claire felt like his words carried weight—like they held some hidden truth—so she nodded as if she understood.
Over time, she stopped asking questions.
She saw what he saw.
His work inspired her own.
She began experimenting, scribbling without direction, then searching for emerging patterns—as if the artwork itself was trying to reveal something.

She didn't call her pieces "finished" but took a few to show Brian once she was done with them.
He never asked questions.
Instead, he would point.
"I like this."
Or, "This works."
Sometimes, just a nod.

*

They kept going to the cinema, spending time on the rugby field, and kissing in their usual rhythmic, unspoken way.
Then, in early December, Claire arrived at Brian's house and noticed his easel was covered with a cloth.
"What's that?" she asked. "Something new?"
Brian stepped in front of it, blocking her path. "It's nothing. Just an idea. Leave it."
Claire's curiosity spiked.
"We're writing about—" she started, but with a dart forward, she whipped off the cloth before he could stop her.
She stared.
The painting looked upside down.
The top of the image was a floor—a table and chair, positioned as if hanging from the ceiling.
But the floor itself was wrong.
It looked… soft.
As she stepped closer, she realised—it was made entirely of teddy bears.
Hundreds of tiny stuffed bears formed a plush, comforting surface.
Claire laughed. "Brilliant. I love it."
Then, her gaze travelled downward—to what should have been the ceiling.
Instead, it was jagged glass bottles, smashed and glinting with sharp edges.
A slow unease settled in.

"Oh my…" she whispered. "That's clever, too. But… weird. Why is everything upside down? And why…" She hesitated. "Why the contrast?"
She turned to Brian.
"It's… how I feel." His voice was small.
"Feel about what?"
"About us." Brian's eyes stayed fixed on the painting. "About you."
Claire frowned, trying to make sense of it. "I don't get it."
Brian exhaled sharply, rubbing the back of his neck. His face flushed red.
"It's love," he blurted.
Silence.
Claire stared at him.
Then, at the painting.
Then back at him.
"Love? Love is… this? This weird, chaotic place?"
Brian nodded. "Yes."
Claire's expression softened, confusion morphing into something else.
She shook her head.
Slowly.
Then again.
"Poor you."
She turned back to the painting, feeling as lost as the world he had created.

*

That night, lying in bed, Claire's thoughts drifted back to Brian's painting.
She pictured his brushstrokes, the way they swirled and blurred, like a dream on the edge of clarity.
She tried to understand what he had felt while painting it.
Had he been confused?
Was she confused, too?
She shook her head as if to shake the thought loose—but it lingered.

Reaching for her sketchpad, she wrote:
Love is confusion.
She stared at the phrase.
Then, she began to draw—stretching streams of looping 'L's above the first letter in love, arching them around the full stop, looping them back beneath the word.
She gazed at her doodle, then laughed aloud.
"Silly word," she muttered.

Chapter 15

Although she still spent time with Brian, Claire was sure she wasn't in love.

She felt no different about him than she did about anyone else. Nothing inside her shifted when he said he loved her. They were just words.

She liked that someone had said it. No one had ever told her they loved her before. But at the same time, did that mean she owed something in return? Was she supposed to feel different just because someone else did?

Claire never mentioned the painting again. Brian never used the word love again.

And after Christmas, things began to change.

She sensed that Brian expected her to come over on Friday nights and that they would always go to the cinema.

She had enjoyed her first term in sixth form—especially Art. She started talking to other students more and found their ideas interesting.

She noticed Penny had started going to live music events.

Claire felt like she was missing out.

*

By February 2003, Brian wasn't the Brian she had first met.

His art had returned to that theme, but now it felt repetitive. He called them studies, but she couldn't understand why he kept painting the same thing, over and over, with only minor differences.

He talked more about irritations. Distractions.

His room was never fully dark, never fully light.

He started arguing with his parents.

"It's all noise. The same noise."

Then, one night, he was sullen. Tired. Distant.

A week later, his mother met Claire at the door.

"He's sleeping, Claire. You'd best leave it tonight. He isn't sleeping properly... he says everything is too bright."

When she saw him that Friday, he was muttering.
He repeated her last few words as if they had some hidden meaning.
He told her about his nightmares and how he preferred not to sleep.
"I can't concentrate. I can't paint."
"Maybe some fresh air?" Claire suggested. "A walk, maybe?"
"A walk. A walk. Go for a walk. Too tired to walk. Maybe tomorrow. Tomorrow. See you tomorrow."
Claire left.
She walked home, knowing the fun had gone.
Would she miss him?
Na.
He was just a boyfriend.
Everyone needs to have one at some point.
And she had.
She might go with Penny to the pub with live music on Saturday night.
That will be fun.
I can get dressed up.
Two weeks later, at school, she heard the news.
Brian had been taken to a mental hospital.
"Schizophrenic, apparently," Penny said.
"Yes, rotten."
"You had a good time with him, though. He was nice, in his way."
"We did," Claire admitted with a faint melancholy.
Her mind wandered. A flashback. His painting of love. Just a jumble.
"But I didn't love him or anything."
She shook her head quickly and smiled.
"*C'est la vie*, hey?"

*

GCSEs came and went.
Other than Maths, Claire's results were good.

Even Maths was a decent enough pass for her to stay in sixth form.
Art was her outstanding success.
She chose to study Art, History, and English for A-level.
Her mother was not convinced.
"You'd be better off doing Geography. Art won't get you anywhere. If you had Geography as well, you could train as a teacher."
"I don't want to be a schoolteacher, Mum."
"I'm good at Art. Mr Roberts says I could go on after A-levels."
"Mr Roberts. Mr. Roberts. What does he know? Go on to do what? Anyway, I don't care what you do. Just don't come back moaning when you can't ever get a proper job."

*

Penny chose a different path—Economics, Business, and Geography.
Not that Claire ever told her mother what Penny was studying.
Penny talked a lot about work, jobs, and careers.
She made it clear she wasn't going to university.
Claire suspected Penny's parents had decided that for her.

*

Since their timetables differed, they saw each other less in school.
But that didn't stop them from meeting up for lunch.
Life outside school still mattered more.
They still spent weekday evenings together.
But Friday and Saturday nights were different.
Claire faced a choice—be a gooseberry or be alone.
She chose, whenever possible, to be alone.
Penny barely talked about Nigel anymore.
"He's so funny," she would say.
"We had a great laugh."
"He totally likes me."
Claire never asked for more details.

She didn't want them.
Over the summer of 2003, Claire got a job at McDonald's.

*

When school resumed, she kept a few weekend shifts. The job was naff, but she liked the money.
What surprised her most was how blatant boys had become in chatting her up.

One Saturday lunchtime, a guy stepped up to order.
"You look just like that dead woman in that painting."
He laughed.
"I mean, she was mega pretty. Just like you."
Claire blinked, struck by his confidence.
He's older than me. Maybe three years. Posh. Not as good-looking as he thinks. And he's got a cheek.
"I'm Caspian," he continued, glancing at the badge on her uniform. "Claire."
"What dead woman?"
"*Ophelia*. By Millais. You've seen it, I bet. I'm surprised you didn't ask if she was a relative or something at the time."
"I do know it. Pre-Raphaelite painting. So there, smart arse."
"And?"
"And what?"
"Do you agree with me? You're the dead spit. Same hair. Everything. Have a look. I'll check back with you next Saturday, Ophelia."
And he did.
That following Saturday, he asked when she finished work. They met up.
He told her he was training to be a solicitor in his father's practice.
He had just finished his BA in Jurisprudence at Oxford.
Whatever that was.
So maybe four years older.

Claire had long stopped categorising boys in her old system. But if she had, Caspian would be labelled intriguing.

*

She told Penny a bit about him.
"He comes in on Saturdays after football. With his mates."
"What? He's a football jock?" Penny scoffed, flashing back to their early-teen dismissal of such types.
"Not like that. The others are. He dresses differently. Writes poetry, for fuck's sake. He gave me one about me. It was… dead good."
"And you're sure he's not a prat? So, are you seeing him? Am I going to meet this Caspian? Not sure what Nigel will make of him—poetry and that."
"Well, he's practical, too. Training to be a solicitor, remember? We went out last night. And yes, I'm seeing him again. And no, you can't meet him. Yet. I'll see."
Claire couldn't hide her satisfaction.

*

At school lunch, Penny wouldn't let it go.
"So, what did you do on this date? Did he bring his Zimmer frame?" she teased.
"We went to the arts cinema at the college."
Penny raised an eyebrow. "Arts cinema?"
"We saw *Pollock*. Caspian thought I'd like it. He's into art, too. It was good. A bit bleak, but painters can be. Anyway, like I said—Caspian is… well, Caspian. Unique."
"A footballer at an arts cinema. You're not kidding." Penny scoffed.

*

Caspian was an enigma.
Claire had watched him play football. On the pitch, he was aggressive. Brutal.

And yet… he wrote poetry.
The biggest mystery, though?
The way he was with her.
He cared.
He listened to her.
If she was upset, if something annoyed her, he actually asked about it.
Claire felt cared for.

*

Because Caspian was older than Penny and Nigel, Claire thought he might find it awkward to meet them.
One Friday night, she and Caspian went to The Swan, a town pub where a lot of the sixth-form girls hung out.
She wasn't sure if Penny had ever mentioned it—but there she was.
Ensconced in a corner.
Snogging Nigel.
Should she leave?
Before she could decide, Caspian returned from the bar—at the exact moment Penny left for the toilets.
They locked eyes.
"Ah! So you're Caspian."
Caspian, catching her playful tone, slipped into a perfect Cockney accent.
"It's a fair cop, guvna."
Penny burst out laughing.
Claire quickly introduced them and pointed out Nigel, who was now staring at them from across the room.
The evening went unexpectedly well.
Caspian was at ease with Penny and, surprisingly, with Nigel, who Claire still found obnoxious.
Despite her reservations, the four of them started meeting regularly at the pub.

And whether Nigel mellowed, or Claire softened—or they both grew up—the four of them got along well.

*

Claire entered a new phase in her art. Her theme, much like her sense of self, was ambiguity. Her paintings held both playfulness and uncertainty. Her figures were unresolved, androgynous, caught in strange, exaggerated postures. She used colour sparingly—only where it drew attention to the piece's greyness. In one, she painted a figure wearing a green beanie hat like Caspian's. Caspian loved her paintings. She loved his poetry.

*

Time flew by. Caspian was always a gentleman. His kisses were more confident than Brian's had ever been—but never progressed further. They never discussed it. But both knew their relationship would end when Claire left for university. Caspian briefly tried to dissuade her. But ultimately, he admitted it was best she go—so long as she didn't forget him.

A-level results. A in Art. B in History. C in English (embarrassing, disappointing). But enough to get into WMU. And so, without sadness or regret, Claire thanked Caspian for being kind to her—and left.

Penny stayed true to her word. She left school to work in a bank. Nigel joined his father's solicitor partnership firm. Claire paused—briefly—to reflect. She was surprised to find that no vivid images came to mind. How had she felt about Caspian? She had liked him. She had liked feeling cared for. Nurtured. She would miss that. But being cared for isn't love. And so, she set her hopes on a new life in Birmingham.

Chapter 16

By the summer of 2003, after months of knowing Lydia, Mike had formed a clear impression of her: carefree, unpredictable, and electrifying. And the more time they spent together, the more he realised—she was the most spontaneous person he had ever met.
"Let's go to 'V' tonight."
The words shot out of Lydia's mouth with urgency.
Mike frowned. "We won't get into a festival without tickets."
"We will. People leave early on Sundays and might give us theirs."
"No way."
"Yes, they will. You'll see. And it's the Chillies, so it'll be great."
Mike hesitated. "But it's in Chelmsford, isn't it? Big trip if we don't get in."
"No time to lose. Let's go!"
And with that, they set off. And Lydia was right. Some people did give them their tickets as they were leaving. Mike began to love being with Lydia. Her vibrancy. Her unpredictability. The sheer variety of things she thought up for them to do.

*

John Brompton had stayed in touch with Mike and occasionally visited. At the start of the new term, he came to Manchester.
"Right, let's see if this band of yours is as bostin' as you say it is."
"We're pretty good. You'll see. Lydia is amazing."
John smirked. "And nuts, from what you've been telling me. A total live wire."
"A bit of a contrast with Adele," Mike admitted.
"She's still moaning that she's not happy but never wants to do anythin', from what I 'ear."
"Adele's nice. A bit too quiet, maybe. But nice. Yes?"
John raised an eyebrow. "Mike, you'll never have a bad word to say about her. That's you, Mr Nice Guy."

"Sometimes you need to see things through plain glasses. Not rose-tinted ones."
Mike grinned. "So, you've seen my Elton John glasses then?"

*

That night, John came to watch *The Covers* play. The pub was tiny, the band crammed into a tight corner with barely half a metre between them. But the atmosphere was electric. When they went mellow, it oozed a cool jazz-bar feel.
And then, Lydia sang. Her rendition of *Beautiful* by Christina Aguilera blew John away. As they packed up, John turned to Mike.
"Fuck, Mike. She's amazing. You need to stop doing covers and play your own stuff. With her, you could definitely go somewhere."
Mike nodded thoughtfully. "Yeah. You're right. I have thought about it. I'll ask her sometime."
At that moment, Lydia ran up. She threw her arms around Mike, oblivious to John.
"That was bangin'! We were fucking on it tonight. I feel amazing. Let's go out somewhere. I'm wired!"
John watched as Mike switched gears, matching her hyperenergy.
"And dance, dance, dance!"
John chuckled.
"Hi. I'm John. From Ilketshall. Mike's hometown."
Lydia spun round to him.
"I'd love to go! See all of Mike's old haunts. He's talked about you. Maybe we could drive there tonight and spend the day there tomorrow! Let's go now!"
John blinked.
"Er. Maybe. I've come up here for the weekend. Maybe next time."
Shit. She fuckin' is as mad as a box of frogs.

*

John helped pack the gear into Fraser's van, then tagged along as they walked to a nearby club.
Mike and John walked at a normal pace.
Lydia skipped, jumped, balanced on curbstones like tightropes, and hopped along the double yellow lines.
Once inside, she gave everything to her dancing.
She was impossible to ignore.
Absolutely beautiful.
Utterly wild.

*

The following morning, over coffee, John didn't mince words.
"Does she do speed? Is that what it is? Mescaline?"
Mike laughed.
"No, that's just how she is. She gets more psyched after a gig, but she's always great fun."
John wasn't convinced.
"I always have a sense, though—like the Kaiser Chiefs—that I predict a riot."
Mike grinned.
"She's amazing. And I think she kind of likes me."
John exhaled slowly, watching him.
Then shook his head.
"It looks like you're dancing with a whirlwind."
Mike liked that phrase.
"Dancing with a whirlwind."
Perhaps she was dancing with a whirlwind when he had watched her the night before. Something was giving her energy. Maybe now she is the whirlwind.
He nodded. "I'll write a song with that title."

*

The house Jason, Wal, and Mike rented in their third year was cheap.
It was relatively close to the Fallowfield halls but a million miles away in terms of cleanliness, warmth, and furnishings.

One of many run-down terraced houses built in the 1900s, it had long since fallen into the hands of landlords looking to rent to students rather than locals.

The kitchen was barely functional—a couple of cupboards on the wall, two under the sink—nowhere near enough for cookware, crockery, and food.

Pans lived on the draining board, making washing up an ordeal. Dirty plates and cutlery piled up in the sink, only washed when there was no other option but to clean a dish for immediate use.

*

One December morning, Wal shuffled groggy into the kitchen, searching for a bowl of cereal. He rattled around in the sink, trying to find the least disgusting bowl to clean Finding a spoon was a blind man's game—fishing through murky water, touching food remnants, feeling for the right shape. The white scum floating on the water was too gruesome to look at, so he tilted the sink, drained off the worst of it, then refilled it. As he attempted to scrub a bowl under the freezing tap, Mike walked in.

"Any warmth in that water?"

"Nope. Stone cold," Wal grumbled, tipping the sink again to drain the overnight bloom that had grown on the surface.

"We need to put the immersion heater on at some point. And the heating. It's bloody freezing in here."

"Yeah, well, we'll have to find some coins for the meter first. Maybe we should each chip in a fiver and see how long that lasts. I'll tell Jason. Where is he, anyway?"

"Stayed over at Natalie's. It's warm there."

"Tea?" Wal asked, reaching for a cleanish mug.

Mike scanned the drainer. Not a single washed cup in sight.

"No thanks. I think some of those mugs haven't surfaced since September. I'll pass."

Wal chuckled. "We must have the best immune systems in Britain."

"Famous last words . . ."

Later that morning, as they walked down the street, they ran into Tom—the elderly man who lived alone in one of the terraced houses. Over the months, they'd gotten to know him a little. Never married. Lived in the house where he was born. Had been on his own since his mother died twenty years ago.

"Heading to the shops?" Mike asked.

"Gonna try," Tom sighed.

"I can grab what you need if it helps?"

"Nah, I don't need much. Meals on Wheels are bringing my tea later. Young Katie, my carer, gets most things in for me. But thanks, though."

Mike hesitated.

"What are you doing for Christmas? Do Meals on Wheels do a Christmas meal?"

Before Tom could answer, Mike blurted,

"You could come to ours. Wal and I are cooking turkey and all the trimmings. Why not join us? We'll even break out the champagne."

Tom chuckled dryly.

"Never drank champagne. And I don't do Christmas. They'll bring me something. That'll be fine. But thanks."

"But you'll be on your own," Mike pressed. "At least come by later for a sherry or something. A mince pie."

"Don't like sherry. Don't like mince pies. I'm a miserable old bugger, aren't I?"

Tom turned away and began shuffling down the road.

Mike sighed.

"Offer's still there, Tom. We'll clean the place up, special like—just for royalty."

*

One evening, over dinner, Mike brought up his future.

"I guess I need to start thinking about what to do after graduating. Finals are in May, which means three months to go. Then, I'll need to start something by September."

Lydia smirked.

"Get a job, like me."

"Ha. Well, if I want to become Chartered, I need to do a Master's, then a doctorate, plus supervised practice. It's more about where to go and which area of psychology I want to specialise in."
"Any thoughts?"
"There's talk of scholarships here for Health Psychology or Clinical & Health Psychology. Staying here might be best."
Lydia lit up.
"Nothing at The Sorbonne? I'd love to live in Paris."
She dramatically mimed a Parisienne—smoking from an invisible cigarette holder, running her fingers through her hair. Then, she paused.
"But not Hull. Anywhere but Hull."
"Ha."
Lydia leaned forward.
"Truth is, do we seriously want to move? The band? My job? The job's a crap little engineering company, but it suits me. I think we're best staying put."
Mike nodded immediately.
"Fine by me. If I get the scholarship, we'll stay. I'll find out about it."

*

The following week, he booked an appointment with Professor Scholes. He spoke with Lydia that evening.

"So, I went to get an appointment to see him. His secretary was sitting at her computer. I guess it must have had his calendar on it. Anyway, she sits and starts typing." Mike pretends to type on the dining table, miming the secretary typing earnestly. "Fuck knows what she's needed to type in. She went on for thirty seconds. I honestly expected her to do a Carol Beer from *Little Britain* and announce . . ." Mike adopted the stance of the actor, David Walliams, and used the character's favourite phrase, "Computer says, 'No'"

Lydia laughed and laughed. "You've got her to a T. Brilliant."
She continued laughing, spluttering, "I can just see her."
Mike chuckled.
"Anyway, after all that, she finally tells me I can see him next Tuesday morning. I'm guessing he only does one appointment a day!"

The following Tuesday evening, Mike had big news.
"He says if I get a First, they'll consider me for the Clinical & Health Psychology scholarship."
Lydia grinned.
"Pressure's on, swot."

*

Despite playing gigs, Mike still found time to study.
Swimming, though?
That had gone out the window.
But he got his First.

*

His Master's was a different beast. He enjoyed it, but for the first time, he began questioning whether psychology was the right path. The band had started playing his original songs, and they were going down well. Lydia wanted to gig more. Even tour. If she had said, 'Let's do it,' Mike probably would have. But Lydia liked things as they were—except for Monday mornings.
"Shit, I'm shot," she groaned. "We need more sleep."
Mike smirked.
"It's not the gigs—it's you, partying on afterwards every time."
Lydia laughed.
"I know! But it's killing me."
She grinned.
"I get so psyched when we play. I can't just come down straight away."
"So, smoke a joint."
And she did.

A lot.

They continued playing local gigs regularly. Lydia took to smoking joints those evenings and, increasingly, every other evening. Mike joined in a few times.

Overall, he enjoyed his Master's degree. He was told there would be a job as a research assistant in the department on some contract research that one of the professors had received funding for if he did well on the course. It would enable him to do his doctorate in clinical psychology.

He managed to fit in a swim at some lunchtimes at the university's sports centre. Despite a chronic lack of sleep, he passed his Master's degree well. Lydia's frenetic activities and skunk obsession made life difficult, but he didn't say anything.

Chapter 17

In September 2004, as Claire arrived at West Midlands University, she was starkly reminded that she was in a big city.
As she wended her way toward the Arts Building, her mind conjured up a Paolo Nutini lyric:
"These streets have too many names for me. I'm used to Glenfield Road and spending my time down in Orchy."
The light was different. The sky was smaller. No whiff of the coast. *Not sure about this. Forget the whole idea. Yes, a silly mistake. I'll just go home. Fewer streets. So, yes, Penny will be pleased. We could keep going to The Swan on Fridays and Saturdays. I could easily get my job back at McDonald's.*

*

Her body followed the signs pointing new students toward something called 'Induction.'
A big room with a queue. She dutifully joined the line. Everyone was staring into space, fidgeting with documents or playing with phones. Then—
"Well, doesn't this make yee feel propa glad you've come, the day?"
The girl behind her had a thick Geordie accent.
"Should have had a bar."
Scheisse, what a feeble thing to say.
"Whay aye, I'll need a drink after all this, mind. Fancy?"
"Count me in."
The girl nodded toward the street.
"I passed a pub called The Swan a few streets away. Back down Margaret Street, then Edmund Street, then down that long, wide one—Newhall Street."
She frowned in thought.
"Looked pretty buzzin'. Thought about getting palatic and forgettin' all this."

Then she added, offhand, "It's all creepily Victorian round 'ere. I passed somewhere called Gas Street Basin last night. I'm Jill."
Claire glanced around the ornate, old building.
"Victorian, yes. And this feels like some boarding-school-cum-orphanage."
Then—finally—she turned back, offering a half-smile.
"I'm Claire."
She took in Jill properly. Curly brown hair, confident posture.
Her gaze dropped to Jill's feet.
Full-on sparkly trainers.
This girl's wicked.
"Where are you from? You sound like Donna Bell from *Byker Grove*."
Jill grinned.
"And this, comin' from yee—looking like a dead ringer for her, bonnie lass. I'm a Geordie. Are you Scouse?"
"Ha. No. I'm from across the water, the Wirral. Heswall. Near Chester."
Then, teasing, "That's like me saying you're from Wearside."
Jill gasped in mock horror.
"Howay, a Mackem? Didn't mean to be that rude."
She brushed a stray curl behind her ear, smirking.
The queue shuffled forward.
Claire slipped her phone into her pocket, but Jill caught sight of the case.
"Mint case. Propa mint."
"Yes, I'm a glitter girl."
Jill stretched out her foot and pointed to her sparkly trainers.
"Like me."
Claire laughed, then dropped into her best Gollum voice:
"My precioussss."
Their joint laughter lifted the awkwardness.
They were going to be friends.

*

They did go to the pub.

It was still late morning, so there was space.
They found a raised section where students clustered together, balancing drinks and paperwork.
Then—loud, raucous laughter.
Claire and Jill turned.
A corner of the room.
A group of students, but older.
They looked shot—probably straight from a party.
The focus of their chaotic energy?
One man.
The King.
Tall. Good-looking.
But not normal.
Not conventional.
This man was *out there*.
He spoke again, and the group erupted.
Claire, without thinking, nodded to herself.
Jill followed her gaze.
"They're ahead of us. Want another bevvie, hen?"
"Yes. Gin. Rhubarb and ginger. I'll get the next."
Claire's eyes drifted back to the King as Jill headed for the bar.
Their gazes met.
For a moment, held.
Then his friends pulled him back.
The group chatted; someone mentioned the tutor's speech, and someone else commented on the art.
But Claire's focus shifted again.
The King's group was moving.
And she knew.
Even before she looked up again, she felt him approaching.
She lowered her gaze, but only briefly.
When she looked back up, he was brushing past her.
More than a glance.
A smile.

*

Back to Jill.

A few more drinks Then—food.
"Somewhere cheaper than here."
"Chips will do for me," someone declared.
Everyone agreed.
"Sorted."
But what started as a quick food run turned into a full-blown expedition. No local chip shop in sight. People they asked didn't even know if there was one in the city centre. Then—finally—someone did. Directions. Then confusion. More directions.
"We've been on this street already," someone groaned.
More laughter. More aimless wandering. Then—victory. A neon sign. Tasty Plaice. Stephenson Street. They stumbled inside, half-starved, half-hysterical. And, by the time they left, bellies full, they were no longer strangers. They were friends. And they would always call it the 'tasty place' for years to come.

The following Thursday, Claire and Jill's workshop had finished at four, and they had no formal fresher's activities on Friday.
As they stepped onto the pavement outside the building, Jill threw her arms up and shouted—
"We're free. Free!"
Claire twirled in a circle, singing—
"I've got a feeling that tonight's gonna be a good, good night!"
Jill laughed, linking her arm through Claire's, half-skipping down the road.
"The weekend starts here, bonnie lass!"
Claire tilted her head up, sighing—
"And it's been a lovely day, and we've been stuck inside."
She grinned. Like that word—'mint'.
Jill smirked. "Well, let's start early. There's nowhere outdoors at The Swan, though, so you'll have to save your rays 'til tomorra."
"No tanning at four o'clock in September."
"Onwards."

*

As they stepped inside, the *Swan* swallowed them whole.

Virtual darkness.

A place that didn't register the time of day or night.

The bar glowed, the music pulsed, and the place was rammed.

The instant effect?

Claire lit up.

"This place feels like home already, doesn't it?" she shouted over the music.

Jill grinned. "Canny. Second home, and we've only been in Birmingham a week."

Claire swayed, singing two notes from I Gotta Feeling—

"Woo-hoo!"

She shook her hips, catching the attention of a group of lads in front of them.

They pushed and weaved through the crowd, heading for the battleground bar.

The noise was even louder there—

Shouted orders.

Shouted conversations.

Shouted above the shouting.

Claire spotted a space at the bar and lunged for it—

But in a split second, the gap closed, her arm and shoulder trapped against the counter.

Then—

A lad to her right glanced down at her, laughed, and shifted aside, making space for both shoulders. His kindness was rewarded as he shouted his order.

Claire spotted Maz behind the bar.

"Maz is on! We're in," she called over her shoulder to Jill.

"Get a few, then. She'll serve quick, but the others might not later. She's a fast worker, getting a job in 'ere in days."

"She's worked in bars before. Spent the summer in Ibiza. Says she has no money, so has to."

Claire caught Maz's eye, managing a minimal wave—her elbows pinned by the crowd.

"Three—no, four—Blue Balls and four Mind

Erasers," she shouted, smiling.
"Good start."

*

More jostling.
She nearly lost her place but managed to wedge herself in.
Could bars have rails to hold onto?
Some of the lads used their bulk to muscle in.
A challenge for her.
"Four *Mind Erasers!*" Maz announced, expertly carrying two shots in each hand.
Claire hesitated, then quickly formed a plan.
She reached for two, turned, and handed them to Jill.
Then—two more.
She turned back just as Maz placed four *Blue Balls* on the bar.
Claire didn't catch the price over the sudden spike in noise, so she just handed over her card.
Maz scanned it, nodded, and returned it.
Now—
A new challenge.
Jill had the *Mind Erasers*. Claire had to grab all four *Blue Balls*.
She succeeded.
Now—retreat.

*

They found a space away from the chaos. No seats. They raised their hands in mock surrender.
Claire spotted an empty table where a staff member had just cleared glasses.
She hurried over, setting her drinks down.
Jill followed, passing her the others.
A quick shuffle—
Now, two neat rows of three.
Jill lifted her shot.

"Cheers."
"Cheers."
They clinked glasses and threw back the *Mind Erasers*.
Claire exhaled sharply. "I always feel like a proper melt at the bar."
Jill grinned. "You did well. They're animals up there. I'll go for the next round."

*

As they scanned the room, Claire was surprised by how many faces she recognised.
She glanced up toward the corner booth—
And there he was.
Again.
Perched in prime position.
Holding court.
She turned back to Jill, about to mention him—
Then hesitated.
I don't even know him.

*

More shots.
More banter.
More glances.
Claire felt annoyed with herself.
She was looking over too much.
Jill caught on.
"Do you know them?"
Claire shook her head.
"No, none of them."
As she spoke, a low voice murmured in her left ear—
"Evenin', gerl."
She turned—
But he was already walking away.

Headed toward the toilets.
Jill's eyebrows shot up.
"Fucking hell. What did he say, hen?"
Claire shrugged.
"He just said 'evening'—that's all."
Jill grinned. "Fuckin' A. He's fit."

*

Penny came to visit.
"So, did you talk to him?" Penny asked the following afternoon as they arrived at Claire's room in Halls.
She had travelled down for the first weekend at university, just as planned, and was following up on Claire's hazy retelling of the previous night.
Claire unlocked the door and stepped inside. Penny stared.
Smart but spartan.
Bed. Wardrobe. Cupboards.
The desk space?
Functional—if you were a science or social science student.
For an Arts student?
Completely useless.

*

They went out.
"No," Claire admitted, flopping onto her bed. "Jill and I kept downing shots, and with all the noise and the place getting more and more packed, I was just kinda... in the moment. I think it was a good night, but honestly, the rest is a blur."
She paused.
"He must have left at some point. Or maybe we did. I don't know."
Penny raised an eyebrow. "Mon Dieu. Proper student now."
She plopped onto the edge of the bed.
"Did you do any actual classes last week?"

Claire laughed, shaking her head. "Nope. Just induction stuff—different faculties, different campuses. Students' Union, societies... all that jazz. But no actual work yet."
"Dosser."
Claire groaned, rolling onto her back.
"Scheisse, I shouldn't have done that."
"Done what?"
"Shaken my head too fast." She winced. "Room's spinning."
She reached gingerly for the glass of water on her bedside table.
Penny smirked.
"Still hungover? You did party."

*

Penny glanced around, taking in the bare white walls.
"Jeez, it's like Strangeways." She shuddered. "White-painted breeze blocks? Have people topped themselves in these places?"
"So, how would you decorate, then?" Claire asked, mocking her.
Penny snorted, launching into a rambling response about posters, fairy lights, and possibly pink curtains.
Claire thought about her words.
She's not good at putting her point across.
Disjointed.
Incomplete.
Scheisse. Am I that used to students already?
Still, Penny had a point.
The halls did look like a cell block.
"You're right, though. I hadn't thought about it." Claire admitted.
"I'll put up some posters or something. Not that I'm here much."
But as Penny kept talking, Claire felt something shift.
A gulf.
A distance she hadn't noticed before.
Penny doesn't belong here.
Freshers' Week had built bonds overnight. Friendships cemented in seconds.

She and Jill felt like old mates already.
But Penny?
Penny felt like a visitor.

*

The weekend turned into a chore.
Claire played tour guide, walking Penny through the city centre and pointing out places that no longer felt new.
Every time she said, "Jill and I...", she saw Penny's face falter.
Stop waxing lyrical about Birmingham.
Penny had come to make sure she wasn't lonely.
But she wasn't lonely.
Penny knew it.
Claire had gone.

*

By Sunday afternoon, Claire welcomed Penny's suggestion to catch an earlier train home.
"What with work and everything. And you start proper studying tomorrow."
They stood on the platform, waiting.
A silence fell.
Claire found herself willing the train to arrive.
The chug of approaching wheels—
Penny brightened.
"Here it is!"
Claire winced at her own inappropriate enthusiasm.
"So...," Penny started.
"So...," Claire echoed.
The train doors hissed open.
Penny hesitated. "I'll see you—"
"When I come up for the weekend, in a few weeks," Claire cut in.
Her voice was gentle. Comforting.

Like when you feel guilty for not feeling as sad as someone else does.
She pulled Penny into a hug.
It felt false.
Resist patting her back. That'd make it worse.
The doors slid shut.
The train pulled away.
Taking the past.

Chapter 18

When Claire arrived at the School of Art at WMU the following week, she came as a student.
The fleeting trips last week?
She'd been a visitor.
Now?
She belonged here.
The words from induction week played in her mind—something about it being "the masterpiece of some local architect at some date in the previous century and now listed."
Something about it being "the first Municipal School"—whatever that meant.
Something about "pioneering" because women could study here.
And how it had "changed art and design education"—somehow inspired by Arts and Crafts principles.
Yes, yes, yes. Yawn.
Now, it just looked old.
And it sounded old.
That weird, echoing hush that older buildings have.

*

Claire studied the materials.
The ceramic tile floors have patterned borders of brown, beige, black, and white squares.
A mahogany staircase spiralled up several floors, dipping down into a basement with much larger black-and-terracotta tiling.
Hence, the echoes.
She climbed the stairs and noticed brass studs embedded in the bannisters.
Her fingers reached out instinctively.
To stop people from sliding down them, she thought, grinning.
She rechecked her papers and kept going, searching for the lecture theatre.
Most doors were open.

She glanced inside one—white walls, banks of Apple computers, light pouring through tall windows.
Then, back to the hallway—mustard-coloured paintwork, dark wood, a clash of centuries-old architecture and modern tech.
Had she been to this room last week?
Would it be medieval or space-age?
She stepped inside.

A revelation. The room wasn't old-fashioned. It was designed.
Dark brown slatted wooden panelling softened the space, mirroring the mahogany in the main staircase.
Giant rectangular LED lights hovered overhead.
A massive white projection screen glowed against the wall.
Chrome chairs, sleek and grey, lined the floor in perfect symmetry.
It was—unexpectedly—beautiful.
Maybe these arts people did know what they were doing.
She liked that the place had history, however obscure.
She liked that it embraced modernity.
This could be home.
A place to be herself.

*

The first lecture was a revelation.
This was no schoolteacher.
Claire had studied art history before, but this was different.
Standing at the lectern was a stunningly beautiful woman—slender, Indian, and perhaps a bit younger than her mother.
Her voice lilted, emphasising the wrong syllables in words, making them sound musical.
She wore a fitted blue dress with delicate patterns of tiny flowers and stems trailing across the fabric.
Claire glanced at her timetable.
Manisha Mahajan.
The name fit.
She spoke effortlessly, weaving stories of artists, influences, encounters, and rivalries.

Not just their techniques—their lives.
A room full of riveted students, eyes slightly widened, leaning forward.
A world away from boredom and fidgeting in school classrooms.
The lecturer's eyes flicked toward Claire—often, it seemed.
Claire focused harder.
Cool.
For a thirty-something-year-old.

*

Manisha leaned forward, resting an elbow on the lectern.
Her sleek black hair fell over her shoulder—and with a deft flick, she tossed it back.
A red bangle glinted on her wrist.
Metal.
Claire frowned, studying it.
Glass inlay? Enamel?
Not sure.
But—it had a story.
A personal one.
Something that mattered to her.
Claire was sure of it.

*

The bangle became an obsession. Manisha never took it off.
It didn't match anything else she wore. But no matter the outfit or any other jewellery she had on, the bangle stayed. Why?
Claire was sure—this wasn't just an accessory. It had been given to her by someone important. Someone whose passion had entranced her. And she was still infected by it. Freed by it. Claire felt drawn to her.

*

Manisha Mahajan wasn't like any woman Claire had ever met.

She wasn't a cold, distant mother.
She wasn't a fuddy-duddy teacher, drained of all enthusiasm.
She was at ease—
With herself.
With her past.
With life.
More than that—
She was open to it.
As lectures continued, Claire felt buzzed—as if she'd been mainlining caffeine.
Her mind spun with ideas.
Things she could do.
Things she could create.

*

The next session? The studio. She bounded in. Vibrant.
A collision of colours, shapes, and overlapping spaces.
Artists at work—each absorbed in their own parallel world, yet moving as if part of an unspoken choreography. The boy in the lilac-print shirt dragged his brush across the canvas in rapid, sweeping strokes. The blonde girl in blue overalls stepped back, assessing, then jabbing her brush forward in staccato flourishes. The scruffy redhead, endlessly sketching circles within circles, eyes locked in intense focus.
Claire heard the sound of art—
The creak of easels.
The thud of brush against canvas.
The shuffle of feet as the painters adjusted, shifted, and flowed.
But beyond all that—
She felt it.
The pleasure.
The intensity.
And she wanted in.

*

"OMG. You look happy," Jill's voice broke through, joining Claire in the studio. "The lecture wasn't that good."
Claire barely turned, still absorbed.
"I loved it. And just look around. Total buzz. We're here, Jill."
They scanned the room together.
Then—
Claire glanced at Jill.
Shit.
Jill looked too put together—wearing a black ribbed roll-neck jumper and smart jeans.
Claire glanced down at herself—a printed silk headband, a striped knitted jumper in shades of blue, grey, and beige.
Jill smirked.
"Fashion, whoops," she grinned. "We look like proper wazzocks. At least you didn't turn up in a school uniform, Hermione."
Claire blinked.
Jill sighed dramatically.
"Hermione Granger? Emma Watson?"
Blank stare.
"Harry Potter? *Philosopher's Stone*? Have you seen the movies?"
"No."
Jill gasped.
"Well, we must. They're ace."
Claire smirked.
"So, why Hermione? Me?"
Jill gestured at her head.
"The hair. Your lovely hair, darling."
"Ha. Right. So now I'm not just Donna Bell?" Claire teased. "I'd better check out Hermione Granger. Make sure you're not dissing me."
Jill laughed, then glanced around.
"Anyway, where can we buy old, dirty clothes?"

*

A voice cut through the studio hum.
"Sorry. Squeezing through. Squeezing through."

Claire turned.

A woman—middle-aged, compact, efficient—navigating the crowd with practised ease, her voice well-worn, like a market vendor calling out familiar phrases.

Then—

A gentle nudge at Claire's left side.

She shifted.

The woman slid past.

Then—

She turned to face them all.

"Right. Here we are."

She was the tutor.

"Hi, everyone. If you can just squeeze in."

Claire and Jill watched her gesture around the studio.

"I'm Kath Kanter. This is where you'll be working on your major fine art project this semester."

The students followed her sweeping hand.

"We won't be doing Jackson Pollock walls or three-by-four metre canvases like those second-year guys." She nodded toward a cluster of students..

"Instead, we'll be using sixteen-by-twenty-inch canvases—pinned around the walls."

Claire's eyes flicked toward them.

"These pieces you see here?" Kath continued. "They're from other groups. Mainly fashion design students. Now—looking at them, can anyone guess the three themes we'll be working with?"

Claire felt Jill's elbow.

Then, Jill's not-so-subtle finger pointing at a canvas.

Dripping streaks of pigment cascading from the top.

Nothing else.

"People with blue heads?" someone joked.

Kath chuckled.

"Jagged edges?" another student guessed.

A voice from the back cut through.

"Bullying. That one."

"Yes! And that one."

More voices joined—

"And maybe that one."
Kath nodded.
"Great."
A student gestured toward the far-left canvases.
"And what the f— are those meant to be?"
Silence.
Then—
Claire surprised herself.
"Self-harm."
Her voice was steady.
She pointed at the dripping paint canvas.
Jill—quick on the uptake—added, "And that one."
Another canvas.
Kath acknowledged them.
"Yes, absolutely."
Then—
A confident booming voice from the crowd—
"And those three bits of buildings."
Kath clasped her hands together.
"Yes—urban decay."
She paused, scanning the group.
"So, we have bullying, self-harm, and urban decay. Three compelling themes for you to get your teeth into."

*

Claire's decision was instant. *Bollocks. Not bullying. Not self-harm. Not psychological distress.*
The memory of Brian surfaced—his decline, his muttering repetitions, his retreat into darkness.
A visceral wave of repulsion hit her.
No. Fuck that.
Urban decay, it is.

*

Right on cue, Jill leaned in.
"Urban decay?"

Her exaggerated grin—now with a sarcastic edge.
Claire rolled her eyes.
"Yes. A bit of history."
She mimicked a posh voice.
Jill snorted.
Claire relaxed.
"She's a barrel of laughs," she muttered, nodding toward Kath.
"I was all set for something bright and cheerful."
She smirked.
"Maybe I'll paint flowers growing from cracks in old window frames—just to piss her off."
Jill grinned.
"That's life."
Later that morning, Claire and Jill found themselves at a table with a couple of lads from their course.
The boy in the white tee, with a Warner Bros. blue-and-yellow logo, suddenly announced—
"A friend of mine committed suicide."
The reaction was instant—
"Bloody hell," one boy muttered.
"Howay, man," Jill whispered.
"Scheisse," Claire blurted.
Then—
The whole story spilt out.

*

"She was picked on. Constantly. Quiet. Unsure. Everything she did got noticed—in the wrong way. She struggled to connect with people, but it was the Facebook stuff that broke her. She made the mistake of reacting. Once. Just once. And that was it. Trolls. Relentless. I told her—come off it. All of it. But it was like she was addicted. She just wanted crumbs. Crumbs of comfort. Someone in her corner. I tried. Her parents knew. They tried banning her. Everyone knew it was killing her. But nobody knew she would."
Silence.
Then—

"Bloody hell," his mate muttered again. "I think bullying is the pits."
"Mein Gott, yeah," Claire added.
Jill—hesitant, softer—"Are you gonna do bullyin' then?"
The boy nodded.
"Yes. For her."
"I've seen it too. On a smaller scale." His mate added. "I think I'll do it too."
Claire hesitated.
"It could be pretty intense. Are you okay with it?"
She meant it.
"It's real. Raw."
The table fell quiet.
Jill fidgeted.
Then—cracked first.
"We're doing urban decay," she said, too loud at first but fading at the end—as if regretting trying to lighten the mood.
Claire sighed.
"Plenty of decay around parts of Birmingham."
"Yes. Bleak."
"Rough."
"Sad."
Then—someone snorted.
"Ha. Maybe we should've done graphics."

*

Over the following four lectures, Manisha Mahajan introduced them to Contemporary Indian Artists. She spoke of—The clash between traditional Indian art and modern rebellion. Zarina's minimalism. Thukral and Tagra's pop aesthetics. Reena Kallat's bureaucratic symbols woven into art. Wondrous. Claire was enthralled.

*

When she next entered the fine art studio, something had changed.

The small theme paintings were gone.
In their place—
Large canvases. Tall easels. Works-in-progress.
Then—
A voice.
"Claire," called Kath Kanter, waving her over.
She was standing in front of a landscape painting.
"What do you think of this?"
Claire studied it.
The colours. The composition.
The texture.
"I think it's balanced. The colour, the composition—" she paused. "And… the texture. I like the sky—it's expressionistic. The horizon and land—more minimal."
She surprised herself.
Had he just sounded like an art critic?
She glanced at Kath, expecting a reaction.
Nothing.
Kath's face remained neutral—neither approval nor disapproval.
She just…looked.
Then—
She leaned in closer, her gaze fixed on a section of the painting.
"Minimal, yes," she murmured. "But the texture works. The thick paint—it's effective."
A pause.
"But…"
She traced a finger over a section.
"This detail—deliberately unresolved."
Claire turned—Kath's focus had shifted.
Her gaze was fixed behind Claire.
Then—
A shift in tone.
"Ah. The man himself."
Claire spun around.
It was him.
The boy from the pub.
A flutter in her stomach.

Not because of him, but because of the incongruity—
Pub life and art school discussion did not mix.
Not in her mind.
Yet—here he was.
His eyes met hers.
Then—back to the painting.
Kath's hand hovered over the canvas.
A gentle circular motion.
A single finger lifted.
"Simon, come tell Claire and me—what are you trying to achieve here?"

*

"The painting is about motion," Simon said, his accent thick.
He was earnest.
"Aspects of the landscape seem fixed—like the sky.
Other elements... pass us by—like when we're in a car, speeding past."
He pointed at a section.
"But some objects freeze—they catch our attention. Hold us."
Claire listened, intrigued.
She hadn't expected...this.
The rowdy pub boy, Simon, talks about art with depth and nuance.
She liked his words.
She liked the way he thought.
"So...you don't know exactly how you'll finish it?" she asked.
Simon shrugged slightly.
"I know what it's about. The rest?"
He gestured vaguely.
"The elements I'll add... they come from the painting itself. From me."
Then—
"It's not actually a car's-eye view. It's about big things in life. Skies. Mountains. The permanent.
And the things that feel impermanent."
Claire stared at the painting again.

"I like this," she murmured.

*

Kath nodded approvingly.
"Watch this space."
Then—she moved on.
Simon turned back to Claire.
For a moment, she didn't know what to say.
But he kept talking.
"Deciding when a painting's finished … it's an internal feeling," he said, adjusting his stance.
"I keep seeing things I want to change.
But also this feeling—like I shouldn't have the last word.
Like… the painting should decide."
His accent seemed stronger now that Kath had gone.
Claire interrupted.
"That's so true."
She leaned in slightly.
"I hear this little voice inside. It tells me to stop.
But then—sometimes, I step back.
And the painting laughs at me."
She grinned.
"Like it's saying, 'Only kidding.' Like it's playing with me."
Simon chuckled.
"Sound. Listening to the painting—not dominating it."
"Exactly," Claire nodded.
She was closer to him now.
Unthinkingly—
She squeezed his forearm.
A reflex.
A gesture of shared understanding.
She met his gaze.
His eyes—brown, flecked with green.
And alive.
He didn't flinch at the touch.
Instead—
He adjusted his stance, turning more fully toward her.

A slight rise in pitch in his voice—
"Serious… and playful?" he mused.
Then—a slight smirk.
"My, my…"
The next day, Claire spotted Manisha Mahajan approaching. She was chatting with a couple of students as she made her way through the clustered tables at the front of the room.
Claire tracked her.
The bracelet caught her eye again as Manisha casually perched on the edge of a table, flicked her hair back, and adjusted her sleeves. Then—
A surprise.
Manisha looked straight at her and smiled.
Insistent brown eyes.

*

Manisha spoke to the class.
Confident. Warm. Engaging.
Claire shifted in her chair. Settling in.
She was going to absorb every word.

*

"There has been a fad in interpreting contemporary art in recent years," Manisha began, her voice rich with subtle rhythm.
"This trend suggests that people should deconstruct a piece. See everything as a metaphor.
Some latch onto a specific theme—like a diagnosis—and then congratulate themselves for 'cracking the artist's code.'"
She paused.
"But is art ever this simple?
Anyone?
Karl? Bhaiyya Ji?"
All eyes instinctively turned to Karl midway down the room.
All eyes, except Claire's.
She was watching Manisha.
She saw how she read Karl's face.

The small smile. The nod of reassurance. The subtle widening of her eyes urged him to continue.
When he finished, Manisha responded.

*

"Ace. Emotion. Yes."
She shifted slightly.
"There are artists whose work is conceptual.
They follow a blind process—accumulating and layering ideas almost intuitively until they are struck by a meaning—a purpose.
Then, they build from it.
But—has art always been like this?"
A pause.
"In my lecture, I talked about Leonardo's distinction.
Do you remember what it was?"

*

Claire saw Manisha scan the room.
She knew what was coming.
Students suddenly found their fingernails fascinating.
Or the notepad on their desk.
Or—the window.
Claire held her gaze.
And—
As expected—
Manisha's eyes locked onto hers.
The scanning stopped.

*

"Claire?"
"Seeing as and then seeing that," Claire replied.
Manisha lit up.
"Wicked. And what does that mean, precisely, Sakhi?"
Claire's heartbeat kicked up a notch.
But her voice remained steady.

"That from a mere scribble, we can suddenly get a sense of something—we see the scribble, or part of it, as something."
She leaned forward slightly.
"A glimmer of form."
"And then," she continued, "we see that—if we add an element here, a clearer line there—we can fully create the object we initially sensed."
A silence.
Then—
"Wow," Manisha breathed.
"That is great, Claire. You put it extremely well. Top of the class."

*

The words hit like a wave.
Recognition.
And then—
Heat.
Claire could feel it creeping up her neck.
Everyone's eyes turned.
They'll see how red I am.
Manisha will see.
Bollocks.
Her heart pounded.
She thumbed feverishly through her notebook.
Stared at it for what felt like minutes—
Until—
The tingling subsided.
But she remained uneasy for the rest of the seminar.
She avoided Manisha's gaze.
Because—If those brown eyes caught hers again—
She would die.

*

At the end of the session, Claire tried to escape.

But the queue at the door stretched forever.
Then—
A gentle grasp on her elbow.
A soft voice, close.
"I am sorry, Sakhi.
I did not mean to embarrass you."
Claire turned.
"I'm silly," she muttered. "Ridiculous.
People will think I'm a real divi."
"They will not, Claire."
Manisha's tone was gentle.
"We have all been there."
She squeezed Claire's arm lightly.
"You are a bright girl.
You will have to get used to praise.
And you will."
Then, softer—
"I am sorry."
Claire forced a smile.
Manisha had been kind.
And that threw her.
She left with an unease she couldn't shake.

That evening—
Alone in her room—
Why was I embarrassed?
It was nice of her to come up afterwards.
Her hand touched her cheek.
The faint heat returned.
She shuddered.
Then, stood up.
Spoke aloud.
"Ripples on the water.
Quickly effaced."
Then—
She went for a run.

Chapter 19

The incident left a more lasting effect than Claire had expected.
She felt closer to Manisha.
And—there were many opportunities to bump into her.
To chat.

*

Their conversations always started with art.
But gradually—
They opened up.
Manisha asked about Claire's social life.
And—boyfriends.

*

"So, what impact did Brian have on you?" Manisha asked one afternoon.
Claire hesitated.
"What did you do after he was put in an institution?"
"I painted."
A pause.
"I read."
Another pause.
"And—like I always do—I simply went out."
"Oh, surely not?" Manisha's voice was gentle but probing.
"No support from your family, Sakhi?"
Claire snorted.
"Scheisse, no."
A shake of the head.
"My mother may have said something like, 'I told you he was odd.'
And that was it.
Always was."
A beat.
"Truth is—" she exhaled, "it did affect me."

"I just . . . couldn't say how. Not in words."
"I still can't."
Her voice dipped.
"But I could sense it in my art."
"I use bright colours. It comes out of making the world—my world—less . . ."
She paused again.
"Less depressing."
"There is a lot more to your art than that, Claire," Manisha replied, leaning in slightly.
"You have an unmistakable style. I can see you in what you create. Others can see it too."
Claire frowned slightly.
Manisha continued, "Do you not notice? Others are trying to copy what you do."
A shrug.
"I suppose it is not fair to say copy, but you open up new avenues for them have seen it. Even in Simon."
Claire's head snapped up.
"He is older than you. And he has his own way."
A small pause.
"But he has picked up on it."
"I do like Simon," Claire admitted.
"We talk a lot."
A knowing look from Manisha.
"Cool."
"I kind of wish we could be more than friends."
Manisha's brows lifted slightly.
"And you stop, why?"
Claire sighed.
"I hang around with Jill all the time. And Simon—he's always out with a crowd. I don't think he's looking for a girlfriend."

*

Manisha tilted her head.
"Some men play things that way," she mused.
"I know he has had relationships here."

"He's popular with the girls."
"He's good at chat."
A slight hesitation.
"Sorry. I don't mean to be rude."
"No, no—that's OK."
Claire forced a smile.
"What I mean," Manisha continued, "is that sometimes, to men, girls are simply . . . fun."
"Maybe he sees you differently."
A pause.
"I think you might find—he's scared of anything serious."
Claire's eyes narrowed slightly.
"The voice of experience?"
A moment of hesitation.
Then—
A small smile.
"Not completely."
A beat.
"Well—in a way."
Claire tilted her head.
"What way?"
Manisha sighed.
"Well, my partner."
A pause.
"David."
"He's much older than me."
"We met at university."
A flicker of something—perhaps memory—crossed Manisha's face.
"He's American."
A tiny smile.
"A Texan."

*

Claire listened, intrigued.
"He seemed the same way you describe Simon."
"On the outside—terrifically jolly."

"Almost shallow."
A longer pause.
"But—"
"There is depth there."
A glance away, as if unearthing something long-buried.
"We knew each other a long time before we . . ."
She trailed off.
Then—softly—
"But it was more complicated."
Claire said nothing.
She waited.
Manisha inhaled sharply.
"Not because of our cultures."
"He respects mine.
And I, his."
Another pause.
Then—quietly—
"He was one of my lecturers."

*

Claire went home to her flat, still mulling over what Manisha had said. She headed to the kitchen and heard Dawn's voice.
"That's not love. That's sex. Even I know that."
Funny how I know all the different accents now.
The room was filled with the now-familiar sight of seven or eight people sprawled across various surfaces—leaning, sitting, slumped.
There had been a time when she had felt daunted walking in.
The proximity of so many people.
The way they positioned themselves—legs spread across the floor, perched on countertops, resting against cupboards—made something as simple as reaching the sink feel like navigating a minefield.
But now—
Now, she had the confidence to focus on her own purpose.
And she had learnt how to be instantly upbeat and fun.
She switched herself on.

"Hi. Love? Sex?" Claire queried, her voice light, teasing—signalling comfort with the topic.

She scanned the room.

Dawn was on the worktop, her legs dangling on either side of her boyfriend Mark's head as he slumped against the cupboard below.

Sian and Alex had pushed two chairs together, holding hands as they created a web of legs stretching across the floor.

Rani—petite as she was—was climbing onto the worktop further along, sitting cross-legged near the wall unit.

Afet, the much taller Turkish girl, leaned beside her, checking to make sure Rani had a good view of the discussion.

Rachel and Paula, meanwhile, had somehow found the oven and fridge doors to be restful surfaces to lean against.

A jungle scene of limbs, laughter, and easy camaraderie.

Claire loved this.

The blend of cultures, the mix of perspectives.

The way they had moved past the initial days of teasing each other's accents, the light-hearted jabs about where they were from.

Now—it was just natural.

A melting pot of backgrounds and experiences.

And then she thought of Heswall.

Stupid Heswall.

She spotted a gap near the sink. Ideal.

She had only come to wash her cup.

Placing it on the drainer, she turned back toward the conversation.

Dawn was mid-sentence, her foot digging playfully into Mark's shoulder.

"He—" she gestured toward him, "just said that he loves me because he fancies me like hell!"

Laughter.

Mark grinned.

"It isn't just sex," he protested, feigning indignation.

"Sex is just an act. A physical thing."

"So, infatuation then?" Rachel challenged.

"Don't knock it. You need infatuation," Mark shot back.

"Well, passion, anyway."

He squeezed Dawn's ankles affectionately.

"Besides, Dawn knows I love her—truly, madly, deeply."

A chorus of groans.

"I remember when I first fell for a boy. Back home." Afet sighed, eyes glazing over.

"It was so intense.

All-consuming.

Furious."

"I was obsessed with him.

I couldn't get him out of my head."

"Like it," Rani nodded.

"But then—I got love-sick."

"I'd heard of the term before, but I was seriously ill with it."

"Probably just a dodgy meal you both ate," someone joked.

Laughter.

Rani continued, shaking her head.

"No—it was like . . . I ached for him."

"Being apart from him made me feel so totally sad."

"Eat? I couldn't eat."

"Sleep? Forget it."

"The crazy thing was that the more time I spent with him—"

"The feelings went away."

"The shine wears off," Dawn remarked, giving Mark a mock warning kick before offering an exaggerated c'est la vie shrug.

"Yeah, but this is all early stuff," Sian added.

"Look at people who've been together for ages—you can tell they love each other."

"Well, yeah—they've put on weight."

Laughter.

"No, but totally tell," Sian said. "My dad inordinately cares about my mum. And she cares about him." A beat. "Love is putting the other person first," she concluded.

Responses.

"It's selfless."

"Not blind lust."

"Does that mean my gran is in love with her cat?" someone quipped.

"She'd do anything for that cat."
"That's companionship."
"Cats don't love back," Claire added.
"You're right, Claire," Alex chimed in.
"Love is about giving and receiving."
"Thought you'd gone all shy on us, Alex," someone teased.
"Tell them the story of your real love back home in Towyn, boyo," Mark smirked.
Alex merely smiled.
Sian looked at him questioningly.
"He's gone shy on us," Dawn noted.
"He told us all about it at our flat."
"He has this best mate back home," Mark started dramatically.
"He sees him go all quiet—you know, love-struck."
"Proper sick, like Rani said."
"But—it's a small place, apparently."
"He sees her a lot."
"But—" Mark drawled, dragging out the pause, "he never speaks to her."
"He just—"
"You tell them, Alex," Mark mocked, grinning.
All eyes turned toward Alex.
He merely shrugged.
Then, he twirled his finger in circles around his temple.
"Oh, go on, Alex, you haven't mentioned her to me," Sian pressed.
A slight unease settled over the room.
"Oh, for fuck's sake," Mark sighed, exasperated.
"I'll only give you the gist."
A dramatic pause.
"Anyway—one night, he's finally with her."
"And it's instant."
"He's all over her."
"Mad with passion."
"Alex!" Half the room gasped in mock horror.
"So, he goes back to see his mate—"
"And he's kind of embarrassed."
"He doesn't even know her name."

Mark grinned.

"His mate just laughs."

"'I know her name,' he says."

"'It's Eunice.'"

"E . . . W . . . E . . . N . . . I . . . C . . . E!"

The room erupted.

Every time someone repeated "Ewenice," the laughter renewed.

Claire clutched her stomach, breathless.

"You bastard!" she wheezed.

"I couldn't think what you were on about—"

"I knew you were making it up, but I couldn't see where you were going."

"Back to love," Sian managed, wiping tears from her eyes.

Claire leaned against the sink, listening.

She felt an obligation to say what she thought love was.

But the truth?

She didn't know.

So—

She didn't speak.

*

Claire tromped her way back to her room, agitated.

Irritated.

Complicated discussions.

Not knowing what I think about so many things.

She muttered under her breath, shifting into a Pooh-like voice, imitating the old Disney cartoon:

"For I am a bear of very little brain."

She flopped onto her bed, reaching instinctively for her sketchbook and pencil.

She wrote:

What is love?

Her mind went blank.

She doodled.

Aimless squares, circles, triangles.

Then—smaller triangles inside squares, squares inside triangles.

She linked a set of circles around the objects, like a flower's petals.
The image's femininity irritated her.
She scribbled it out.
And in doing so—
She saw something.
The scribble, the masked geometric shapes, the distorted angles—they formed something.
A building.
A ramshackle barn.
A barn, standing alone in an empty field.
A barn with an open door.
The image enchanted her.
It meant something.
But what?
That's it—a run.
I need to be outside.
She stood, looking out her window.
It was raining.
No matter.
Actually, she'd enjoy the rain on her face.
She pulled on tracksuit bottoms, a loose hoodie, and glanced at her feet.
These trainers will do.
She grabbed her quilted jacket, picked up her phone, and headed out.
The corridor felt even more like a prison than usual.
Banks of closed doors.
Plain white walls.
The heavy, solid door at the staircase exit.
Hard concrete steps.
And then—
Out.
Out into the open air.
She breathed it in.
Not country air.
Birmingham air.
But at least—

Not stale air.
The first drops of rain ran down her face.
Cold—but not icy.
She started jogging, leaving her troubles behind.
But some thoughts persisted.
Love.
What is love?
I like Jill.
I liked Penny.
But love?
What's that?
She reached the park gates.
The rain had eased.
She turned right, following the path along the park's edge.
The roar of traffic faded.
The soft drumming of rain against pavement was barely audible.
And then—
Silence.
Only her footsteps.
Her steady breathing.
She brushed against an overhanging shrub, feeling the raindrops flick onto her hands and face.
She started to wipe them away—
Stopped.
Instead, she waited.
Let them trail down to her lips.
She swept them up with her tongue.
Tasty rain.
She sped up.
The rain stopped.
Small puddles ahead—
She splashed through them.
A bush sticking out into the path—
She vowed to brush against it—
And did.
But then—Thoughts. Again. *I didn't love Brian. He said he loved me. Loads of times. I thought he was silly for saying it. Did he even mean it? He didn't know what he was thinking most of the time. And at the end—*

He hardly thought at all. Heh ho.

There were more people on the path now. Obstacles. *Where the hell were they before? Sheltering? Can't think where—*

The café's on the other side of the park.

She laughed aloud—

Imagining them rising from the ground like some sped-up mushroom growth time-lapse.

Brushing themselves down—

Casually strolling along as if they had always been there.

Maybe they had.

She ran on.

What happens?
Is love like a bolt of lightning?
Or do you just wake up one morning, lovesick?
Like Afet said?
Like that song—
"I just can't get you out of my head."
Pure obsession?

Her phone rang.

She kept jogging, fumbling into her pocket.

Finally—

"Hi, Jill."

"Are you having sex?"

"Nooooo. I'm out running."

"In the pouring rain?"

"So?"

"You're mad. Your clothes will be soaked. And your hair—"

Claire grinned, shifting into her best posh teacher voice.

"There's no such thing as bad weather, only unsuitable clothing."

"Mad. Do you fancy meeting up?"

"What time is it?"

"Five."

Claire slowed to a stop.

Meet where?

The union? That's easiest.

All in—an hour.

"See you at the union at six."

"I'm bored. Hurry up."
"Five forty-five, then. See you later."
"See you later. Don't be late."

*

The evening with Jill was the usual escape into oblivion.
Once they'd warmed up, they had totally gone for it.
Now—
Claire stumbled up the stairs to her floor.
Trying to remember—
That joke.
What was it?
It was hilarious.
"Hi, Claire. Been out?"
Sian and Alex squeezed past, still holding hands.
"I'm staying at Alex's tonight. See you tomorrow."
"Goodnight," Alex added—sheepishly.
Claire stared after them, brain fogged.
What's the PC response to that?
"That's nice?"
I'm not that drunk.
She got her keys into the door seamlessly.
Flopped onto her bed—
Expecting to sleep.
These nights are doing my head in.
I need to grow up.

Chapter 20

On May 7th, 2005, Mike's university held its May Ball.
He still had his dinner jacket, dress shirt, and bow tie from his undergraduate days.
And now, as a master's student, he found himself back—reluctantly dressed in it.
A couple of guys from his course had mentioned they were going.
"Are you coming?"
He had said he would.
Despite having seen it before, the transformation of the university buildings still felt remarkable.
Various rooms had been turned into music stages: A string quartet in one. A solo acoustic guitarist in another. A jazz trio in a dimly lit lounge. Darkened rooms pulsing with pop and rock bands.
The room he stood in now—A cocktail bar, complete with a pianist.
The formal attire still felt alien to him.
He thought he looked good in it—but its strangeness kept him pulling at his collar as if loosening it would make him feel normal.
His characteristic self-consciousness kept his mind looping back to how he looked.
He scanned the room.
No sign of the others yet.
He glanced at the stage.
The pianist was playing The Girl from Ipanema.
He knew the song well.
He often played it on his guitar.
His imagination kicked in.
In his mind—
He was on stage, playing it.
The crowd applauded.
His imagination transported him further.
A larger venue.

An even bigger audience.
More applause.
Back in reality—
That damn collar.
Where were they?
A jab in his ribs—
Len and the others had arrived.
A six-foot-three rugby player, Len looked wildly incongruous in a white tuxedo.
Joe, on the other hand—
A bright purple velvet suit.
Mike watched him shift uneasily, looking around, half-expecting mockery.
All three of them started the night feeling guarded.
As they realised, they didn't look out of place—
They relaxed.
Slightly.
Mike spotted Suzanne, a girl from his course.
She usually melted into the background.
But here—
She looked stunning.
Her hair was pinned up.
A navy-blue cocktail dress, flowing and elegant.
And beside her—
A girl he didn't recognise.
"Hey, that's Suzanne," he said.
"So it is," Len replied.
However, Joe seemed startled by the idea that people they knew—especially girls—were here.
He subtly stepped behind Len as if hoping to disappear.
Mike realised—
Suzanne's friend had noticed his staring.
She leaned over, whispering something.
Suzanne turned to look at him.
He smiled.
Waved.
They spoke again—
And started walking over.

Mike glanced at Len—expecting to see Joe too.
But—
Joe was already gone.
Slipping out the door like a ghost.
"Doesn't everyone look super?" Suzanne said with a playful smirk.
"Absolutely. Even Len has brushed up well."
Len raised a fist, pretending to throw a punch.
Suzanne laughed.
"This is Briony," she said. "She shares my flat."
Len nodded, flashing a brief smile.
"Well, since we're in a cocktail bar—" Mike grinned.
"Let's get some."
The four of them moved to the bar.
Mike glanced back, half-hoping to spot Joe—
Round him up.
But he hadn't returned.
The next hour—
Drinks. Talking.
Suzanne casually mentioned that her boyfriend, Terence, was supposed to be there, but had broken his foot playing football.
She made it clear—
Mike didn't stand a chance.
Oddly—
It relaxed him.
They wandered from room to room.
More bars.
More music.
They danced until late, moving wildly to the rock band.
On May 7th, 2005—
Mike was not Mike Lewis.
He was someone else.
The carefree, confident man in a black tuxedo.

Chapter 21

On that same day, in Birmingham, WMU also held its May Ball. As first-year students, Claire and Jill had initially dismissed the idea when tickets first went on sale.

"That'll be lame. It'll just be all the social science wazzocks," Jill had concluded.

"Or the science dorks," Claire had added.

Over the next few days, however, they had overheard people talking about how much fun it would be to dress up.

"I suppose it is kind of just a fancy-dress party," Claire had mused.

"Me? In a posh frock? Nobody in Newcastle wears them," Jill scoffed.

"They do, too. I saw an episode of *Wire in the Blood* where Dr Tony Hill—Robson Green—goes to a ball, and there's tons of them all preened up.

Jill laughed and winked. "Whay aye, you're right. Of course, we do."

They had talked each other into it and spent quite a bit on dresses. They also agreed to style each other's hair. For days, they had practised taking the other's hair up, curling the sides into loose ringlets.

As they walked into the university's hired banqueting suite, they were struck by the transformation. The venue gleamed with soft golden lights, the polished floors reflecting clusters of elegantly dressed students. Different rooms housed various stages, including live music, jazz, and a lavish cocktail bar.

Claire felt completely different in her almost-Grecian pale cream dress. She moved more slowly, more gracefully. The boys in their tuxedos looked like something out of a 1920s film.

She and Jill walked over to the bar and picked up a list of the cocktails on offer.

The boy beside her placed his order: "A Mint Julep and a Gin Rickey, please."

Claire turned to Jill, her eyes gleaming. "I know those drinks. They're from *The Great Gatsby*. Daisy Buchanan drinks them. I am back in the 1920s."

Jill feigned smoking with an invisible cigarette holder in her sleek, long black dress.

The image triggered something in Claire's mind. Holly Golightly. *Breakfast at Tiffany's*. The glamour, the elegance. Without hesitation, she turned to the barman.

"Two Manhattans, please."

The night unfolded like a movie scene—twirling in shimmering candlelight, laughing over crystal glasses, the weight of the world forgotten. An evening of pure happiness. One of the happiest nights Claire had ever known.

On May 7th, 2005, Claire was not Claire Fontrelle.

She was a sophisticate in a beautiful evening gown.

Chapter 22

Life, however, quickly returned to normal. Over the next few weeks, Claire found herself increasingly impressionable. She had caught herself using the word cool more often than usual. She knew exactly where she had picked it up. An image of Manisha Mahajan surfaced in her mind. One night, as she was getting into bed, she heard her inner voice saying the word:
"Cool."
She fell asleep thinking of Manisha—her poise, confidence, and wonderful accent.
The following day, the first thing Claire thought of was Manisha. Her mind immediately conjured the image of her standing among a group of people, effortlessly at ease. Cool.
Flashes of Manisha from various encounters at the university. Moments not fully recalled, yet vivid enough to bring back how she stood and smiled. What does Manisha look like in other settings?
Claire opened Facebook and searched for her. Common name. She applied filters. First Birmingham under City. No luck. Maybe she lived outside of town? She tried Place of Work. And there she was.
Claire scrolled down Manisha's timeline.
Knew it. She has loads of friends. She goes to such mint places. She searched for signs of Manisha's partner. The same man appeared in multiple photos. Wow, he's a lot older than she is. Thirty? He looks fifty.
Claire switched to Instagram. Nothing. Back to Facebook. She zoomed in on the photos where Manisha and her partner stood together. They don't look that close. One picture showed him with his arm around her. She scrolled further. Not one where she held his hand or leaned into him. She's so serene. So cool. Self-contained.
Her gaze drifted to Manisha's clothes. And there it was—the bracelet, always on her left wrist.
Another fine-knit jumper. Cashmere. That's what it's called. She must have them in different colours.

Claire scrutinised the older pictures. Manisha's hair had once been cropped short. I like it longer, the way she has it now. A fleeting thought: Maybe I should grow mine.

I look such a mess compared to her.

She closed the app.

I need new clothes. Classy stuff.

"Hi. You look shit," was Jill's cheerful greeting as they stood outside Kath Kanter's morning lecture.

"Thanks," Claire shot back sarcastically. "I need to stop getting so wasted. I end up looking fucking meff."

"Dunno what meff is, but if it means 'dragged through a hedge backwards,' then yeah."

"It does. Thanks," Claire replied, mimicking her earlier tone.

It was just friendly banter, but the words reinforced her growing self-doubt. I look nothing like Manisha.

Then, to her horror, Manisha appeared in the corridor.

No. Not now. Not looking like this.

She wasn't doing this class; she was only passing through. But she would see her. No way to hide. No way to escape.

Claire's mind raced. Pretend to hug Jill. Turn us around, her back to the corridor.

In a flash, she threw her arms around Jill. "You love me, really," she said.

Jill responded warmly, singing, "I do, I do, I do."

Claire felt her heart rate slowing as she risked a glance over her shoulder. Manisha had turned down another corridor. She was gone.

Why am I so self-conscious?

She barely followed the lecture. Her mind wandered to clothes.

Where can I buy better ones?

After class, she told Jill she wasn't feeling great and was skipping the rest of the day.

She headed straight to town. She had heard of Harvey Nichols.

Claire wandered into the shoe section of the store. She loved the layout—elegant purple upholstered benches, tall black metal racks with marble bases, and soft lighting that made the shoes look like an art installation. The bright white cabinets displayed single shoes, not grouped by size, and their sporadic placement created an artistic effect.

She immediately thought of Damien Hirst's pill cabinet paintings. Each shoe was like a prescription, lined up in its little box.

She hesitated. Do they even have price tags?

Dare I look?

No. She wasn't going to buy shoes. And if she looked too closely, a sales assistant might approach.

She laughed, imagining security asking her to leave because she looked too scruffy.

She hurried off.

As she approached the knitwear section, her confidence surged. I'm buying something here. And if anyone suggests I can't afford it, they can sod off.

And there it was.

A neon green jumper.

Not a colour she had seen Manisha wear, but somehow—it was so her.

Claire strode toward it, suddenly gripped by the irrational fear that someone else might snatch it first. The fact that the store was nearly empty wasn't the point.

She grabbed it and held it up. Examined it closely.

Bollocks. I'm not looking at the price. I'm having it, no matter what.

The fabric was incredible.

One-size crew neck, dropped shoulders, ribbed cuffs. The curved hem looked like piping, but when she touched it, she realised it was rolled fabric. Her fingers traced a tiny, almost imperceptible stitching detail—ten one-centimetre bands in brown, yellow, olive green, black, beige, pale blue, pink, lime green, black, and white.

Lush. I love it. Love it, love it, love it.

What is this fabric?

She checked the tag: No. 53 Crew Cashmere-Blend Jumper.
Cashmere.
She finally flipped the price tag over.
£215.
Her breath hitched.
Her mouth fell open.
That's what I spend on food in a month.
She turned toward the fitting room.
But I'm doing it.
As she walked to the checkout, she spotted a photo of a model wearing the same jumper, paired with off-white trousers.
She looked amazing.
The sleeves pushed up. The hem curled slightly.
She looks so cool. So, Manisha.
In the fitting room mirror, Claire copied the model's pose.
She beamed.
This is the new me.
She'd grab some trousers at Primark on Corporation Street. They'd be fine.
And she'd look mint in this.
Claire bought the trousers the next day.

That evening, she drenched herself in perfume and, with near reverence, dressed in her entire ensemble.
She stood before the mirror.
Good. Sophisticated.
And for the first time in her life, she half-believed she looked attractive.
She smiled wider and spun around, viewing herself from different angles, moving fluidly—like a model.
Then, carefully, she undressed, draping the outfit over the chair with almost ceremonial precision.
She grabbed her old jeans and a grey hoodie from the floor.
She dressed.
Back to just me. Dowdy and dull.
As usual, Claire sought immediate distraction when faced with emotions she didn't like.
She grabbed her phone.

No messages.
A couple of Facebook notifications.
Nothing interesting.
She glanced at the sketch she'd been working on.
Nothing struck her as needing modification.
She reached for her reading assignment.
Glazed over after the first paragraph.
She blew her lips in a loud, bored sigh like horses do.
The sound amused her, so she did it again.
Then again, louder—until it sounded like a raspberry.
She caught her reflection in the mirror.
She stuck her tongue out at life.
"Enough of this. Where is everyone?"
She grabbed her jacket and set off to find people. Anyone.
As long as it meant having some fun.
The kitchen was practically empty.
Only Rani was there.
Can't be doing Rani right now.
She was sweet. Gentle. But twee.
Rani turned from the kettle, offering a warm "Hi"—followed by an uncertain silence, unsure what to say next.
Claire nodded.
Rani turned back to the kettle, clearly willing it to boil faster.
Claire knew that agonising feeling from when she first moved in.
She had no real reason to be in the kitchen.
She turned to leave.
"Would you like some tea?" Rani called just as Claire reached the door.
"No. I was just checking to see if I left a book here earlier. Cheers."
Half a second later, she added:
"Thanks, though."
That settled it.
She was going out.
Another night down the pub. Some good laughs but no genuine desire to make a night of it.

She gave her usual excuse as she left the crystallised group in the corner.
"Got to go. Got a nine o'clock lecture."
The chorus was universal.
"Ooh. Get you."
Not meff now.

*

On Monday morning, the first lecture was delivered by a guest speaker.
Claire had been unsure about attending when it was announced weeks ago. A 9:00 am lecture? Unlikely.
But here she was, 8:45 AM, strolling into the building, bright as a button.
This was the new Claire.
Suave. Sophisticated.
The biz.
As she walked through the corridor, she could feel eyes on her.
She laughed to herself as she overheard:
"That must be her. We'd better go in."
She watched a group of students pivot toward the door, thinking she was the guest speaker.
I just parted the seas.
The power of appearance.
And then—
A voice.
Soft. Close. In her ear.
"Holy shit. You look stunnin', gerl."
Simon.
She turned.
His eyes were full of her.
He stepped back, hands gesturing along his body as if acknowledging the entire ensemble.
Claire surprised herself with her assured response.
"Thank you, kind sir."
She turned and entered the room.

She chose a seat toward the back—plenty of space further forward, but—
It is still me, then. Not being a swot at the front.
The lecture?
Something about entrepreneurial skills for creatives.
Claire's interest waned fast.
She scanned the room—sets of bleary eyes struggling to focus.
Who thought 9:00 am was a good idea?
Most of her friends weren't even there.
Her real focus for the day?
Talk with Manisha.
Not gushy. Casual.
Like with Simon.
She'd reference Manisha's last lecture. That would seem natural.
The speaker wrapped up. Claire stayed seated.
She adjusted her posture.
And then—
There she was.
Sweeping into the room.
Graceful. Confident. Effortless.
Claire could only dream of moving like that.
Manisha stopped to speak warmly to a student further down the row.
"That will be ace. Go for it."
Who is that?
Claire stiffened.
Am I… angry?
No.
Jealous?
She wanted to be with Manisha.
Just her.
Before she could register whether Manisha had noticed her, she was gone.
Claire barely glimpsed the bracelet.
But she knew it was there.
Manisha wore light-grey chinos, a long dark-grey fine-knit cardigan that flared open as she walked, and a crisp white shirt with an open collar.

Rad. Très French.
This time, Claire concentrated.
The lecture was on friendships, rivalries, and artistic exchanges in Impressionism.
Manisha focused on Pissarro and Cézanne.
Claire jotted down notes:
- Cézanne was a hopeless dreamer, withdrawn, shy, boisterous, exuberant, and unstable.
- In letters to Zola, he admitted his fear of appearing inferior made him withdraw, using his art as a sole refuge for true inner contentment.

So familiar.

Manisha continued:
- Pissarro was nine years older, deeply committed to painting, and endured extreme poverty for his art.
- At 31, he was seen as a mild-mannered patriarch, eager to teach and learn.
- Cézanne saw him as a teacher, friend, and second father.

Claire froze mid-note.
Epiphany.
She knew now why she admired Manisha so much.
She was her Pissarro.
Claire had never experienced a mother figure.
But Manisha understood her.
Her feelings for Manisha—the confusion, the intensity—
It wasn't infatuation.
It was admiration.
She was finding herself.
Redefining herself.
Manisha was a role model.

Manisha continued:
- Over the course of ten years, Pissarro and Cézanne influenced each other.

- Pissarro began incorporating Cézanne's structured compositions.
- Cézanne refined his technique, layering small touches of colour to approximate delicate sensations before nature.

Claire reflected.
It was about artistic relationships.
How interactions and collaboration create revelations.
At that moment, she knew what she wanted.
She wanted to be Manisha's friend.
To learn from her. Work with her. Create alongside her.
To become an artist.
From that moment on—
Claire wanted to learn.
Voraciously learn.
With others. Through others.
Like Pissarro and Cézanne.

Chapter 23

In the event, Claire only wore the cashmere jumper a handful of times.
When she was with Manisha, she felt self-conscious about copying her.
And there weren't many other occasions where it felt right to wear it.
She kept it wrapped in tissue paper.
As the summer term was ending, Claire and Jill started laying out plans for how they'd spend the summer.
One evening, sitting in Jill's room, Jill asked:
"Are you not going 'ome at all, hen?"
"I don't think so." Claire paused.
"There's not much for me there now. Penny and I... we've kind of grown apart. And my mum won't be bothered."
Then, snapping on a bright face, she added:
"Why don't we go abroad for the summer? Bum around. For months."
"Ha. Ace." Jill grinned.
"I could go for four weeks or so. I think I need to go 'ome at some point. I fancy somewhere hot. Like Malaga or somewhere. Hotter than Newcastle, anyway."
"We're on!" Claire replied excitedly.
"But don't forget, we've got this uni trip to Florence in the last week of August," Jill reminded her.
"We'll be back by then! It still gives us July and August. Maybe even the last week in June, too." Claire said brightly.
The following week, Claire looked into flights.
They could show up at the airport and get on any plane with space if they were flexible.
The uncertainty thrilled her.
She told Jill, who agreed immediately.
That weekend, they went clubbing as usual.
Jill met a boy.
Claire barely saw her in lectures after that.

When she finally caught up with her, Jill was sorting through her pieces in one of the studios.
"So, who is he?" Claire asked.
"I remember his name was Jake, but that's all."
"He's at Aston. He's a bonnie lad. Just finishing his second year. He's doing sociology. He's from Kent. We're ultra good."
Jill smiled, almost dreamily, then added:
"He says where he lives, he just pops over to France all the time. We said we'll do that at some point in the summer."
"But we said we'd go to Spain."
"We will. We will. Just… not for the whole time. Maybe a couple of weeks or something. Yeah?"
Claire paused.
"Well, I still plan to go for longer."
Jill hesitated, then offered:
"I could meet up with you wherever you are. That'd be great. Yeah?"
"I guess. It'll all work out in the end," Claire said flippantly.
Claire went to Spain.
She found bar work in Malaga.
Jill contacted her, and they tried to plan a meetup, but it never worked out.
As August arrived, Claire felt in her element.
Breezing about.
I might actually stay here forever.

*

She did return for the trip to Florence.
The city's beauty overwhelmed her.
She had been transported back to the Renaissance.
I am touching the buildings Michelangelo touched.
The Italian names of the streets, squares, and landmarks echoed in her head.
She was reminded of the city's history each time she heard them.
On their first afternoon, the tour began at Piazza del Duomo.

They passed Giotto's bell tower, then entered the Museo dell'Opera del Duomo to see the original golden doors of the Baptistry.

An hour later, she almost ran to The Bargello before heading into The Uffizi—

The gallery of her dreams.

The sheer scale of Botticelli's *Birth of Venus* overwhelmed her.

Then Raphael.

Da Vinci's *Annunciation*.

The joy was endless.

That evening, the group ate at Café Rivoire.

The staff warned them not to stay out too late—

"Busy schedule tomorrow!"

Planned highlights included, the Duomo itself, with Brunelleschi's cupola and a shopping trip down the iconic Via Sant'Elisabetta.

Because there were so many of them, it was clear that people would split off into smaller groups.

"Early to bed? I don't think so. Life is for living!" Claire shouted over to Jill.

"Count me in. Home of The Godfather cocktail, and all that."

They decided to go to a small club they'd spotted on Via dei Servi.

It's a low-key place with a live band.

"Wicked. Feels more authentic than just a DJ," Jill said.

"Ha, yes. A proper dive bar," Claire added.

At 9:00 pm, they entered *The Bebop Club*.

It was not a dive.

It was classy—a cave-like venue styled after a 1960s London nightclub.

Low ceilings.

Great acoustics.

A lit-up dance floor, its glass tiles pulsing with light.

Claire had never seen anything like it.

Cocktails and beer were served in a back room.

They managed to grab a table near the bar.

The club was decorated with photos of famous musicians and guitars strung on the walls.

The band played everything from The Beatles to Vasco Rossi.
At 11:00 pm, the crowd thickened.
And then—
"Fuck me, there's Manisha Mahajan," Jill blurted out.
Claire turned.
Manisha looked incredible.
The little black dress.
The way she moved.
And she could dance.
She was with a group of older women, but Manisha looked the most at home.
"Let's go somewhere else. Feels weird with staff here, an' all," Jill said.
The other girls didn't seem bothered either way, but Claire frowned.
"That's crazy. She's nice. Why can't she be out having fun? Why can't we both be here?"
Jill rolled her eyes.
"Bollocks. Not me. We'll find somewhere else. Let's go."
Claire hesitated.
Then, Manisha caught her eye.
And smiled.
"She's seen me now. I'm not going to be rude. I'll see you there."
Jill scoffed.
"Bootlicker. Or worse…"
Claire stuck her tongue out like a kid.
After they left, Claire wandered over to where Manisha was dancing.
Manisha immediately shifted, making space for her.
Claire watched her every move.
Began mirroring.
Free. Effortless.
They danced for over an hour.
Eventually, Manisha's friends left.
She waved them off.
Then turned back to Claire.
Beaming.
They kept dancing.

Just the two of them.
The club faded away.
The ambient light from the floor made it feel otherworldly.
Everyone else was a blur.
All Claire could see—
All she wanted to see—
Was Manisha.
They danced
only for each other.
After a while, Claire signalled that they should head to the bar.
It was slightly quieter there.
"Would you like a drink?" she asked, her enthusiasm evident.
"No, I had better not. I have had enough, Sakhi. We had a couple of drinks before we came here. Coffee for me."
Manisha paused, then added:
"I am only staying around the corner. Want to join me for one?"
Claire's heart skipped.
Tonight can't get any better.
As they entered Manisha's hotel room, Manisha headed over to the sofa, gesturing for Claire to sit next to her.
Her short dress slid up as Claire sat, revealing more of her legs.
Manisha's eyes followed the movement, lingering at the furthest point visible.
A sudden surge of desire.
Desire to touch.
Her right hand began to move toward Claire's thigh—
Then she turned pleadingly, looking into Claire's face.
Claire did not adjust her dress.
If she wants to touch me... that's OK.
Manisha's gaze flickered downward—then settled on her bracelet.
The bracelet she always wore on her left wrist.
"I always wear this one."
"I know... I noticed."
"Do you know why?"
Manisha's voice was soft, hesitant.
"It was a gift from my first love... Margaret."
Claire's breath hitched.

"But I thought you have a partner? A bloke. I've seen photos of you together."
The moment she said it, she realised—
She had just admitted to looking at Manisha's social media.
Manisha didn't seem surprised.
"Yes. I mentioned him to you once. David. He's lovely. We are great."
Then, more quietly:
"But love is a complicated thing. It is not straightforward."
A pause.
"I am bisexual."
Then, Manisha's gaze locked onto Claire's.
Deep. Searching.
Claire didn't know where she found the courage.
She just knew—
She was going to be kissed.
She had never done anything like this before.
But she was comfortable with the idea—
With Manisha.
Manisha leaned in.
Claire held her breath.
Would she kiss her gently?
Softly?
Or fiercely?
Manisha's kiss showed the way.
A warm, intimate kiss.
A kiss unlike Brian's.
Unlike Caspian's.
Fulsome lips. A softness Claire had never felt before.
Manisha stood, holding out her hand.
Claire took it.
She was led to the bed.
Manisha's fingertips grazed her shoulder.
She began to undress her.
A flicker of childhood memory.
But this was nothing like the rough, impatient hands of her mother.
This was careful.

Gentle.
Claire reached out to reciprocate—
But Manisha's hand pressed hers away.
A silent instruction.
Let me.
Then, in her nakedness, Claire was guided to lie down.
She watched as Manisha undressed.
Cool air drifted over her skin as Manisha bent to place her blouse on the floor.
Claire was entranced.
Then—
Manisha's body touched hers.
A shiver.
Her silken black hair tangled with Claire's red curls.
Her hand traced a path—
Circling.
Her breasts.
Her nipples.
Her belly.
Her buttocks.
Her thighs.
Until—
A sharp intake of breath.
Claire's body responded instinctively.
Manisha's hands were so gentle.
Then—a shift.
Not hands.
Manisha's tongue.
Following the same path.
Exploring.
Building.
A gasp.
Claire's body arched.
A rush of ecstasy—
A feeling of being seen.
Totally, wholly appreciated.
Never in her life had she felt this cared for.
Is this me?

Is this who I am?

Their time in bed was the most tender and romantic experience Claire had ever known.

Somehow, they spurned sleep all night.

At first light, they shared memories.

Claire lay in Manisha's arms.

Manisha explained how she had found love with Margaret—how she had discovered her bisexuality.

"I had sex with a boy before Margaret," she admitted, stroking Claire's back, "but I had never experienced love."

Claire thought about Brian. About Caspian.

About the enjoyment of being in a relationship.

But she did not use the word love at any point.

Manisha tilted Claire's chin up.

"How do you feel about me being a woman?"

Claire hesitated, searching for the right words.

"I don't know. I'm kind of... fascinated by you."

Manisha smiled softly, waiting.

"I love your accent. Your walk. Your gentleness. But also..." Claire paused, her voice lowering. "You give me such care. I think you're wonderful."

Manisha brushed a curl behind Claire's ear.

"And the sexual side of our relationship, though?"

Claire's breath hitched.

"I don't know..." she said honestly.

Then, more quietly:

"I like it when you touch me. The tenderness. Yes, it arouses me and..."

She blushed, hesitating.

"I was in heaven when you made me... orgasm."

Manisha leaned down and kissed Claire's forehead.

"Many girls have sexual encounters with another girl," she said gently.

"Some, like me, enjoy being with both men and women. Some realise that a lesbian relationship is all they desire. And some... go on to live entirely heterosexual lives."

She paused, searching Claire's face.

"Maybe you need to think about your identity."

Claire exhaled, snuggling closer.
"I don't know what I'll do," she admitted.
"I know I'm happy. This may be me. I guess... what will be, will be."
She kissed Manisha's cheek.
Then, in the quiet, she whispered:
"You are all I can think about. You are everything."
Manisha smiled, running her fingers through Claire's hair.
"And everything is you."
Claire grinned.
"Ha, like the song."
"Yes, just like that, Sakhi."
Claire reached for her sketchpad, rolling over to capture the moment.
She began to draw Manisha's naked form—
The curves. The serenity.
A meandering, gentle stream of sensuality.
After a few minutes, Manisha leaned forward to look.
"Goodness, am I truly that sexy?" she teased.
"We say... kamottejak."
Claire laughed, biting her lip.
"You are, for sure. But you're also... pure, delicate, and completely feminine."
Manisha smiled, her fingers tracing slow circles through Claire's red curls.
"Your hair," she murmured.
"You know it drew me to you from the moment I first saw you."
A pause.
"It's magnificent. Like Elizabeth Siddal's hair."
Claire blinked.
"Beatrice? Proserpine? Rossetti?"
Manisha nodded approvingly.
Claire liked the feeling—
That Manisha was attracted to her.
That it was different from Brian.
Different from Caspian.
This was... deeper.
A few hours later, Manisha sat up in bed.

"I know Florence quite well," she said, smiling at Claire. "Want to go for a dawn walk?"
Claire beamed.
"Ace," she said, using the word she had heard Manisha say.
Manisha pointed at two plaques high up on a wall at the Piazza di Santa Croce.
The top one marked the 1966 flood.
The lower one—1557.
Claire tilted her head, running a finger along the stone.
"Michelangelo was still alive."
"Yes. His hometown. Though he was living in Rome when he died."
Manisha's voice softened.
"You have a particular interest in Renaissance art, don't you?"
Claire smiled.
"And artists. I love that so many of them knew each other. I'd love to have heard their conversations."
"Ha. Even though they were in Italian?"
"That's a minor problem."
Manisha linked arms with her.
"Let's cross the Ponte Vecchio. I won't spoil it. Just come and see."
They climbed Via di San Niccolò, taking the steps behind the tower.
As they reached the top—
Manisha gestured.
"Turn around, Claire."
Claire did—
And gasped.
The most spectacular view of Florence unfolded before her.
A sea of terracotta rooftops glowing in the early light.
Manisha took Claire's arm—
And they kissed.
They breakfasted at *Samambaia Café*.
Afterwards, Manisha suggested they pay a quick visit to the Palazzo Strozzi.
"There's an Anish Kapoor sculpture I want to show you before we meet the others."

Claire watched her eyes dance as she spoke.
That same passion.
That vibrancy.
Claire loved it.
As they headed back into town, Manisha grew serious.
"And now, the hard part."
Claire tensed.
"We have to act normally for the rest of the trip."
Claire's chest tightened.
"Know that I want to be with you. We will be together. But we cannot be seen like this."
Claire stiffened.
"I'm not ashamed of us."
"Nor am I, Claire. That's not what I mean."
Manisha squeezed her hand.
"I'm proud of who I am. And I'm glad you feel the same."
A pause.
"But I am your lecturer. We are not supposed to enter relationships with students. In any form."
The words hit like cold water.
Claire's stomach sank.
She wanted to show this new identity.
To declare it.
To be with Manisha openly.
She opened her mouth—
Then, with a quick shake of her head, she stopped.
She inhaled deeply.
Exhaled.
"Such is life," she said quietly.
Then, calmly:
"I understand."

Chapter 24

Now twenty-two, Mike was thrilled to begin his doctoral studies. Professor Nolan had secured a research council grant to explore creativity in children aged five to seven, and Mike had been appointed as a research assistant on the project.
Mike and Lydia were having dinner.
"I told my mum we'd go down this weekend," he said, glancing at her. "She wants to know more about what I'm doing. And, you know, what we're doing."
Lydia raised an eyebrow. "So, more like an inquisition, then?"
"Ha. You passed the audition when we visited last Christmas. She'd started to think I'd made you up. She likes you. You'll be fine."
Cathy had prepared a full Sunday lunch and was getting anxious. 12:35 p.m.
Mike and Lydia were cutting it fine.
She walked into the kitchen, opened the oven door, and checked the leg of lamb, trying to judge if it was cooked.
Not quite.
She turned the oven down by ten degrees.
The doorbell rang.
She turned it back up before heading to greet them.
"Hi. I was beginning to worry. Was the traffic bad?" Cathy asked as Mike leaned in to kiss her cheek.
"A bit," he admitted. "But we're not late."
"Hello, Cathy," Lydia said, mirroring Mike's greeting.
"Hello. Have you changed your hair? I haven't seen you since last Christmas."
She turned toward Mike. "You should come down more, Michael."
Lydia smiled, tucking her hair behind her ear. "It's a bit shorter."
"I came down for your birthday in April, Mum. Lydia couldn't get time off work. It was a Thursday, remember?"
Cathy waved a hand dismissively. "Well, it's good you're here now, but it's a shame you can't come this Christmas."

"We said we'd go to Lydia's parents this year. Just to be fair, you know."

Lydia quickly added, "I haven't seen them in fifteen months." Hoping to make it clear—no favouritism.

"Right. Well. Yes. OK."

Over lunch, Mike explained his research.

He told his mother how he and Lydia were still playing in the band and that they had started performing some of his original songs.

He asked how she was.

"Oh, well. You know. OK."

Not much more than that.

Then Cathy drifted into reminiscing.

"Remember all those November 5ths? Writing your name in the air with sparklers?" she asked, smiling fondly.

Mike grinned. "I do. Loved it. And the treacle toffee. Never see that anywhere these days."

"I can make it. Next time."

She paused.

"Oh well. You may not be here next Guy Fawkes... but I'll make it anyway."

"Fireworks? Did somebody say fireworks?" Lydia lit up.

She turned to Mike, eyes wide with excitement.

"We could go get some now. Set them off in the garden later. Shall we? Shall we?"

Mike laughed. "We could. But we'll have to head back soon."

Lydia pouted in mock disappointment. "Oh, spoilsport."

Then, brightening up, she pushed back her chair. "I'll do the dishes. Give you two time to reminisce."

As Lydia left the table, Cathy lowered her voice.

"So, are things good with Lydia, then?"

"Er, yes. We're great."

Cathy studied him for a moment.

"It's been three years now, Michael. She's extremely pretty. And nice in many ways. But I don't think she'll settle."

Mike frowned. "Settle? Mum, we're young. We don't think about things like that."

"I know, but I don't think she's the marrying kind. Ever, I mean."

Mike's frown deepened. "Marriage? I'm not sure I'll ever get married, Mum. People don't. Not anymore."

Cathy sniffed. "Some do. It's a good tradition."

Mike leaned back in his chair. "Tradition? Traditions come and go. Look at UK car making. I heard on the radio this morning that MG Rover is moving to China. That was a tradition, too. Things change."

Cathy's brows lifted.

"And what about today? November 5th. That's 400 years ago today. That's tradition."

Mike sighed. "You mean celebrating burning someone alive? Lots of traditions are ridiculous."

A long pause.

Then Cathy leaned forward, voice quieter.

"What about children, then?"

Mike blinked.

"You want children, don't you?"

"I guess... yeah."

"Have you ever asked Lydia if she wants kids?"

Mike hesitated.

"We've never talked about it."

Cathy pursed her lips.

"I'm sorry, Michael, but I don't think Lydia will. She's too... flighty for that. You need to ask her. You need to know these things."

Mike looked away, suddenly uncomfortable.

"Maybe," he muttered.

A beat.

Then he stood.

"I'll go see how Lydia's getting on."

"I would have done the dishes, you know. She didn't need to."

Mike shrugged. "We just wanted to help."

As he walked toward the kitchen, his mother's words lingered.

"You need to ask her. You need to know."

Mike felt a strange unease settle over him.

Can I see Lydia as a mum?

He shook his head.
I'm not sure I can.

Chapter 25

As December approached, Claire had spent four months bewitched by Manisha.
She had learnt how to give pleasure as well as receive it. The clandestine nature of their meetings added a frisson, an excitement that sustained her desire to continue.
But none of these words were ever spoken.
Claire expressed fragments of her feelings in her art, but even there, she knew she had to work in abstraction—disguising the subjects. The figures in her paintings hovered over a precipice, staring into a grumbling, molten volcano—a chaotic place of raging intensity.
"What is that?" Jill asked, frowning at a canvas of violent swirls. "It's got... a blackness to it."
"It is what it is," Claire replied enigmatically.
Later, when Simon saw it, he merely said, "I think you're lost... in space."
Beyond excitement and the need for discretion, Claire didn't analyse her feelings too deeply.
The sexual side of their relationship was more about an awakening—discovering new facets of herself she hadn't known. She felt cared for.
But was she giving in return?
She had a vague sense that her identity was forming, but one thing was clear—she was not in love.
Some weeks later, Manisha asked if she could sketch Claire.
"Sit naked on the bed," she said softly, retrieving her sketchpad and a box of pastels.
For the next hour, she worked in silence.
When she was done, she passed the drawing to Claire with a gentle smile.
"For you."
Claire's breath caught as she took in the image.
Deeply.
"Mein Gott. You've made me look... beautiful. And elegant. But I'm not elegant. Do you actually see me like this?"

Manisha nodded. "I do."
Claire stared at the portrait, trying to comprehend how anyone could find her worthy of such praise.
She hesitated, then asked, "Do you love me, Manisha?"
It wasn't a question she was sure she wanted the answer to.
Manisha paused. "I care about you deeply. Enormously deeply."
Claire exhaled, relieved.
"Yes, that's it," she said, almost triumphantly. "That's enough, isn't it?"
Manisha hesitated, then smiled faintly. "It is, Sakhi."
But Claire sensed something missing in her tone.
Manisha's gentleness was ever-present.
One evening, as they sat together in Manisha's flat, she quietly turned and began stroking Claire's hair.
Over and over, pulling the strands through her fingers, letting them slide to the ends before starting again.
"That's nice," Claire purred, sinking into the comforting rhythm.
Manisha found it sensual.
"I care so much for you, Claire. Our time is... different from when I am with David."
She paused, then whispered, "I love being with you... both."
Claire felt she should say 'I love you' back.
But love was not a word she used lightly.
Instead, she murmured, "I know. That's nice."

*

The feigned distance at university was exhausting.
A constant vigilance. A forced disinterest.
"That's a wicked top Manisha's wearing," Jill remarked one morning, noticing Manisha in the coffee queue.
Claire barely glanced up. "I guess."
Jill frowned. "I thought you liked Manisha Mahajan."
"Like? Sure. She's alright. A good teacher... lecturer... whatever."
Jill shrugged, looking back toward the queue. "Well, it is a nice top."
Then she nudged Claire, smirking. "But I know who you totally like. What happened there? I thought you'd cop off with him."

Claire followed her gaze.

Simon.

Her heart skipped.

She flicked her hair instinctively, straightening it. "Yeah... I suppose I do."

She did.

From that moment, Claire visited Manisha less and less.

Excuses piled up.

"I said I'd go to the cinema with Jill."

"I have an essay to finish."

Until one evening, Manisha found Claire alone in the fine art studio—and cornered.

"It's okay, Claire," she said gently. "I know the big rush is over. Don't worry."

Claire forced a smile. An apology?

Instead, she shrugged, nodded, and said, "Life goes on."

It was meant to sound lighthearted, but it came across as callous.

A pang of guilt.

She quickly added, "Something will work out in the end."

Manisha nodded, saying nothing.

Claire had loved being mothered, cared for, and guided.

But being mothered was not love.

And yet, she had her memories.

And the pastel drawing of her—Manisha's touchstone of tenderness.

Chapter 26

On the first day of the second term of her second year, Claire met Jill for lunch.

They arrived at the second-floor coffee area nearly simultaneously, immediately scanning the seating spaces for something—anything—with some privacy.

Jill spotted a table where several chairs had been pulled away by a larger group, leaving a pair of seats. She glanced at Claire, their silent telepathic communication kicking in before she made a beeline to claim ownership.

Seated, Jill mouthed the words "Tea" and "Chicken Caesar Wrap" to Claire, who was standing in the queue.

Claire grabbed a tray, ordered the same, paid, and carried their food over.

"Hello, stranger," Jill remarked sarcastically, a not-so-subtle reminder that Claire had been MIA for a while.

Then, with an exaggerated bright tone, she added, "Oh, thanks. How much?"

"Don't worry about it. I think we might just eat here again," Claire joked.

Jill laughed and nodded. "Possibly." Then, her tone shifted—her eyes full of eager expectancy.

"So, tell me, hen. Who is he? Is he a belta? Is he dead posh? Is he why you've gone all designer? And vanished?"

Claire snorted, shaking her head.

"Ha. Nobody. No, he. There's nobody. I just got tired of being in scruffs."

Jill arched an eyebrow, glancing down at her own casual outfit pointedly. "Thanks."

"Ha, ha. No, I just wanted to put some colour into my life. I don't know. I've kind of worn downbeat clothes all my life. Wanted a change."

"We said we'd fit in," Jill smirked. "Well, it's been noticed. Not just by me. Simon's been milking me for information about you. He kept asking what bands you like and where you go. Expect an approach."

"Ha. I bet he's all EDM. Electro-house or Future-Garage. What did you tell him I liked?"

"Well, that's just it. I don't know what you like. Like, mainly like. I remember us joking about you loving Atomic Kitten when you were young."

Claire grinned, launching into the chorus.

"You can make me whole again…"

Jill joined in, dramatically pointing both hands like in the promo video.

They burst into laughter.

"Ha. We've spoken a few times about Katie Melua and Dido tracks, but we've not actually got anything that stands out, have we?"

"Atomic Kitten was when I was thirteen or fourteen," Claire admitted. "I guess I like Katie Melua and Dido tunes out right now."

Then, with sudden enthusiasm, "I like Maroon 5."

She paused. "Or even worse, I bet he likes sombre stuff like Damien Rice." Her tone dripped with mock disapproval.

"He didn't say," Jill mused. "But then, I didn't say Maroon 5 either. I guess you'll both have to find out, Bonnie Lass."

It didn't take long for Claire to find out.

That night, as she and Jill were drinking in the Union bar, Simon and a couple of his friends ambled over.

"Alright? What are you doing later?" He directed the question at Claire, then quickly added, glancing at Jill, "The two of yous."

He continued before they could answer, "There's a massive party over in Stechford. Loads of people are going. Do you fancy it?"

"Where the hell is Stechford? Whose party? Will they let us in?" Jill fired back, her tone split between confusion and excitement.

Claire glanced at Jill, already knowing her answer.

"OK. How do we get there?" she asked casually.

"Bus on Priory Queensway. Number 14. Takes about half an hour. We'll go as soon as Frank's girlfriend gets here."

The boy called Frank took that as his cue to move, muttering something before, unnecessarily, adding, "Hi. I'm Frank."

Half-hiding, the shorter guy behind him piped up, "And I'm Dar... ren," his embarrassment evident.

Jill took pity on him.

"Hi, Darren. I'm Jill, and this is..."

Before she could finish, all three—Jill, Claire, and Simon—spoke in unison.

"Claire."

They burst out laughing, dramatically bowing and curtsying at their accidental synchronisation.

There was a lot of jostling and positioning on the walk to the bus stop.

People wanted to be next to someone. People didn't want to be left out.

Claire watched it all with quiet amusement, opting for nonchalance.

Upstairs on the bus, things settled into order.

Frank and his girlfriend claimed the back row of the three-tier seating.

Simon and Darren took the middle, while Claire and Jill sat at the front.

The only discomfort was the constant craning of necks—people trying to make eye contact with one another.

Claire and Jill turned around more than once, leading to Claire sliding halfway off the seat.

"This is ridiculous," Jill muttered, straightening herself up.

Every minute or so, they turned back forward, chatting between themselves.

By the time they arrived, they had gathered that the party belonged to "some great bloke" who was "from Birmingham" and whose "parents were away."

They got in.

Everybody got in.

The place was packed.

Not just with students. Some were much older.

Claire spotted someone picking their way downstairs, weaving through hordes of people sitting on every stair.

The main impression?

Loud.

Vibratingly loud.

Simon cut a path through the crush of bodies, leading them toward the kitchen.

Claire stopped short.

Her feet stuck to the floor.

She looked down—checking if she had stepped in something.

No.

The entire floor had become a sticky mosaic of spilt beer, wine, and lemonade.

She winced, pushing forward.

Through a clutch of bodies, she saw a kitchen table pushed against the wall, littered with cans, bottles, and a bowl of orangey crisp-like snacks—that nobody touched.

She had a twinge of embarrassment. None of them had brought anything.

Simon handed her a plastic cup of warm white wine.

He turned back to fetch drinks for Jill and Darren, but Darren had already manoeuvred his way forward, grabbing his own.

Another jostle.

Another push.

Suddenly, Simon was pressed against Claire, and she was against the sink unit.

She could see his face directly in front of hers for the first time that evening.

She couldn't hear him but could see his smile, wavy dark hair, and brown eyes.

Excitement.

Being chatted up.

A proper boyfriend.

And sexy with it.

As she looked at him, she took him in. This experience. This memory.

She smiled back just as another shove from behind him pushed him closer.

He put his hand against the wall, pushing back just enough to shield Claire from the crush, keeping their private space secure.

The kissing zone.

Half an hour later, Frank and Darren appeared at the kitchen door, shouting something.
Claire thought it sounded like "TSO."
Another shout. Was it "Tiopo?"
They turned away, arms waving in the air.
Simon leaned in, shouting over the music.
"Dance!"
Then, something that sounded like "Olympic Flame."
With that, he grabbed her hand, pushing through the crush of bodies, parting a way for Claire to be pulled through.
Into the lounge.
She hadn't thought it possible, but the music was even louder here.
Somehow, in the centre of the room, people were actually dancing.
A dim lamp in the corner gave just enough light to make out faces.
Simon was transformed.
He oozed energy, his smile wide, his eyes sparkling.
He lifted his arms in the air, waving them to the beat.
Claire spotted the girl without a name.
She danced with a calm, effortless rhythm—a skip step with alternating step-outs.
People shifted to make space on the floor—tiny, temporary dance floors opening and closing as bodies moved and adjusted.
She wasn't sure if it was deliberate or unspoken dance etiquette.
Frank made a straight-arm point downwards, arching his back, bending his knees slightly, and swaying rhythmically.
Seconds passed. Excruciating.
She felt like a complete outsider.
Didn't know this music.
Didn't know this style of dancing.
Simon turned fully in front of her, dropped his hands, and crisscrossed his arms in time to the music with his palms facing down.
She smiled.

Another guy was swinging his arms across his crotch, then shifting into small, circular movements with his right arm, skip-stepping left.

Another alien dance move.

Claire was at a loss.

She shuffled from side to side.

Simon grinned wider, nodding.

Self-consciously, she raised her arms in the air, mimicking the lasso-like movements others were making.

Simon leaned over, touched her hair, and grinned.

"Not your 'Spice Gerls', heh, gerl?"

Claire laughed.

He smiled.

Straightening up, she noticed—he was watching her dance.

She tried the skip-step thing.

Simon gave an approving nod.

The next hour was a blur.

They danced and danced.

She loved the upbeat energy.

Gradually, she forgot herself.

Claire was lost in complete euphoria.

Happiness.

A hypnotic happiness.

She wasn't sure where she was getting the energy from.

The girl without a name shouted something in her ear, and suddenly, they were facing each other, dancing in sync.

The girl raised a hand—

High five.

Simon moved closer.

He put his arms around her.

They kissed.

Mesmeric.

He took her hand and led her into another room.

A dining room by day, now completely stripped of furniture.

People sat on the floor, leaning back against the walls in the low light.

A softer, ethereal track played—muffled beneath the pounding bass from the lounge—but somehow, it created its own atmosphere.

And she could hear.

"Are you enjoyin' it?" Simon asked.

"Totally."

"A good party."

"Ace."

They kissed again.

Darren, Frank, and the girl without a name appeared.

"Last bus. We'd better all go."

Darren announced it, and just like that, they were off.

Back into the blare of the dance music.

Then, into the cold air.

Quietness.

A muffled quietness, the remnants of music still ringing in Claire's ears.

The girl spoke.

"Love that music. And the dancing. Don't you, Claire?"

Claire couldn't stall it any longer.

"Yeah. Brill. I didn't catch your name. Maybe I didn't hear it."

"Ha. I still can't hear properly, either. It's Josie."

Simon piped in.

"Didn't know you liked Tiesto. Love that *Olympic Flame* song. Did you see him on TV at the Summer Olympics opening ceremony?"

Claire smiled to herself.

The previously misheard words finally made sense.

"No. Missed it," she admitted, feeling oddly guilty.

"I asked your friend Jill what you liked, but she didn't say anything other than Atomic Kitten," he mocked.

"Where is Jill, anyway?"

"Seemed pretty full-on with some guy."

"D'you think she's OK?"

"She's sound."

"Good." Claire paused, then added, "Anyway, she's taking the piss. I like all sorts. Soft stuff like Dido and Katie Melua, but I also like techno, like tonight. I just don't know the bands."

Simon smiled.

"Wait there. Wait there. They're not bands. They're DJs—like, goin' right back to Fatboy Slim, Paul Oakenfold, all that big-beat and breakbeat stuff. Tiesto's huge in progressive trance."

"I felt like I was in a trance," Claire replied warmly.

"And no drugs, neither."

They walked back from the bus stop through side streets lined with terraced houses.

"Our palace," Simon quipped as Darren unlocked the front door.

They filed in.

Frank and Josie headed straight upstairs.

Darren hovered for a moment, then shrugged.

"I'm knackered."

He disappeared into his room.

Simon didn't say a word.

He simply took Claire's hand—

And led her upstairs to his bedroom.

Any uncertainty or hesitation on Claire's part was swept away by Simon's mastery.

She felt her clothes being removed—a brief pause while Simon undressed himself.

She slid under the covers—

Only for him to pull them back, rendering her bare.

His touch—electrifying.

Her heart rate rocketed.

An overwhelming desire—

To kiss.

Hard.

Harder.

Then, his intimate touch—

Rhythms of pleasure rippled down her spine, converging at the point where his fingers played.

And then, in a moment—

He was inside her.

He pushed through, and Claire let out a small gasp.

The movements of his body over hers—

She let her forearms drop to either side of her head.

She surrendered.
Completely.
And when he quivered and sighed—
She knew.
She was now a woman.
No words were spoken as their bodies separated.
Simon reached for the quilt and gently covered her.
Such tenderness.
Within minutes, he was asleep—
But Claire lay in reverie.
She felt the seeping wetness.
Shifting under the covers, she caught a faint aroma—
Sweet yet salty.
The smell of sex.
Was this love?
The memory of her sketch of Manisha.
But now, very different feelings.

*

Some four hours later, at the first light of dawn, she felt Simon stir beside her.
Without words, he caressed her hair, his hand sliding down her back.
Her body recognised him now.
Again, he was inside her—
This time, gentler.
The warmth of the quilt, the soft rhythm of their movement—
She reached for him as he moved in her.
Her hands glided over his back.
She felt his breath quicken, his body tense.
And then—
A sigh, a climax.
They remained in an embrace, their lips trailing over each other, kissing everywhere they could reach.
Perhaps this was love?
A tear formed in the corner of her right eye.
She wiped it away with the back of her hand.

A tear of womanhood.
A tear from being desired.
From being wanted.
"I didn't know you had never…"
Simon looked at her, his voice hushed.
"You're nineteen."
Claire smiled but then quickly looked down, a flicker of embarrassment overtaking her.
"Are you OK?" he asked gently.
She wanted to tell him about Manisha.
But she had promised. Manisha had made her swear never to mention their relationship.
"Yes. Fine."
She kissed his neck.
They separated, settling into the silence until sleep descended once more.
She woke.
An absolute pleasure in the way her body touched his.
Desire.
Sheer comfort.
At ease with the world, with herself.
She turned her head, studying Simon.
His stubble had started to show.
His masculinity stirred something in her.
She noticed a painting on an easel—
A promenade reminiscent of his landscape painting at uni.
But this time—cruder, more blocked out, almost sketch-like, yet still conveying motion.
His words echoed in her mind—
Motion. Fixity.
She was different now.
Sex had changed everything.
The bedroom, the view through the window—
All fixed in her mind, freezing like a painting.
She looked back at Simon.
His tousled hair covered most of his face chaotically.
Gently, she brushed it aside, wanting to see him fully.
As she did, he woke.

He took her hand—
And again, with no words, they made love.

*

When they finally got out of bed, they went downstairs to find something to eat.
Claire was surprised to see Darren, Frank, and Josie already in the kitchen, fumbling around with tea, coffee, toast, and cereal.
Such talented people—
And yet, as her mother used to say, "Couldn't boil an egg."
Their disinterest in her presence was comforting.
They must know what happened.
But they didn't seem to care.
Then, a sudden thought.
Maybe Simon brings back a different girl every night.
Was that why no one reacted?
Josie dispelled the fear.
"Come on, you two lovebirds—stop cooing and help us get breakfast sorted. These two guys act like they've never seen a kettle or a toaster. And their hunt for cereal bowls has proved fruitless. Want coffee and toast?"
"Yes, brilliant," Claire replied.
"I'm starving."
Another wave of embarrassment.
Frank sensed her unease.
"So, you enjoyed the night... as a whole?"
Claire hesitated—
Saved by Darren.
"Yeah, some great music. I saw you giving it large."
"Yeah, it was good," Claire answered.
Simon grinned, nudging her playfully.
"Made up. Good party too, heh, Claire?"
Claire giggled, giving him a dig in the ribs.
He put his arm around her.
She felt drawn to him—
But in a way entirely different from Manisha.
This was desire.

They were boyfriend and girlfriend now.
In every sense..

Chapter 27

Claire spent more and more time at Simon's house.
She had come to realise that sex was not love.
She enjoyed sex, but simply because it was fun.
It wasn't Simon she loved.
It was sex itself.
He did fun things, too—
But it was the fun she relished, not him.
Beyond their time alone, Claire loved their conversations.
They were unlike any group of people she had ever met.
They partied. They drank. They laughed.
But they were also intense.
Passionate about art.
One evening after a day at college, Darren burst into the house—
Almost hysterical.
Claire tried to comfort him, but all he kept saying was—
"It's rubbish. All rubbish. I hate it all."
She couldn't get through.
Then, she saw Simon transform.
A therapist. A healer.
"What do you feel you're not conveying?"
Darren's agitation lowered.
"The relationships. I'm not linking things the way I feel them in my head. This whole series of paintings is a joke. I've taken months. But they're too disparate."
His agitation shifted into depression.
"I'm useless. Useless."
Simon was calm.
"Wait there. Wait there. It's not you that's useless. If you think they are useless, sod 'em. Do something else. Remember Baldessari."
Simon looked over at Claire—
She had no idea who he meant.
He smirked at her blank face, then turned back to Darren.

"John Baldessari. The godfather of conceptual art. In 1970, he burned all the paintings he had done between 1953 and 1966. Cremated them. He'd moved on."

Claire nodded in admiration, muttering, "Wow," as she shook her head.

"So, burn them," Simon continued.

"You've got the others upstairs. Let's go into the garden and burn them. You can burn the one at college tomorrow."

And then, more forcefully—

"Come on, la. Burn them."

Darren laughed—and then ran upstairs.

When he returned, paintings were under his arms, and he laughed harder.

Simon laughed, too.

And then Claire—caught in their energy—

Began laughing.

She found herself acting the part of a French diva artiste, flicking her wrist dismissively—

"Pah!"

They burned the paintings.

A week later, she and Simon reflected.

"The extraordinary thing is, he's so happy. He's up there working day and night. He's found his métier. And they're brilliant. I can't believe he's assembled an entire new portfolio in a week."

"I knew he would. He'd see the bigger picture once he freed his head from those earlier paintings."

"He has. I have. I love the theme I'm following now."

"Yeah, it's good."

"You're a genius."

"As Baldessari showed, just point out a meaning. Every concept is art."

"Scheisse, that's so clever. Yes, every concept, every idea, every thing is art, if we can show it."

"Absolutely. That's why I'm persisting with my impermanence theme."

"And why I love my threads. The threads that link different people. I can see them everywhere now."

She turned back to her latest piece.
Other people had links—strong connections.
Claire?
She lived on the web—but had no connection to anyone.
Despite the tapestry of interactions, she felt—
Alone.
At WMU, a new lecturer, Saul Roper, led a session on Impressionist depictions of Parisian café society.
Then, he posed a challenge—
"Take what you've learnt from your Photography module. Capture a café scene through your interpretative lens."
Claire had bought a second-hand Sony Alpha digital SLR for photography class.
At first, the expense had seemed huge—
But now?
A bargain.
She was hooked.
The art of photography was opening new doors.
She had learnt to see—
Not what was there—
But a perspective on it.
A psychological framing.
That afternoon, Claire went to a large coffeehouse near the university.
The Victorian building still held onto its architectural beauty.
She snapped photos—but then froze.
A memory.
Brian's paintings of faceless people.
She no longer saw the details—
Only an assembly of colours.
Garments. Shapes.
And suddenly—
It was all rectangles.
Long, short, squat.
Bodies in motion.
Angles of arms, backs, thighs, calves—
A dynamic snapshot of life.
A moment in time.

That evening, she began her piece.
It flowed effortlessly.
She studied the screen on her camera—
Then, each figure was reduced to five simple shapes.
Pantone cards are cut into rectangles.
A person mid-sit—a diagonal tilt.
Two people leaning close—a mirrored arc.
A group of three backs to chairs, laughing—a kaleidoscope of warm tones.
The counter—a long, narrow strip.
To the untrained eye, it was just an arrangement of colours.
But at another level—
It was pinpoint-accurate.
A psychological framing of the café—capturing the micro-moment.
Claire loved it.

*

At the end of February, Manisha Mahajan found an opportunity to ask Claire to come to her office.
Claire sensed the formality of the occasion despite the jumbled surroundings—art crowding the walls, books strewn across the shelves, and papers piled high on the desk.
A single daffodil stood in a rose vase—an unexpected, gentle touch in the chaos of academia.
But it did nothing to ease Claire's tension.
"What is the matter?" she asked earnestly.
"What do you think?" Manisha replied enigmatically.
"Nothing, so far as I know."
"Well, I know that you and Simon are together, Sakhi. And I am pleased about that, Claire—I am. For you."
Manisha hesitated—suddenly unsure how to handle the situation she had orchestrated.
"I know in love, you can lose yourself, but . . . "
"Love?" Claire cut in, her tone dismissive.
Manisha was taken aback.

The apparent admission that Claire was not in love with Simon threw her.

She continued, "I told you I care for you, Claire, about you. I'm simply trying to help. I want you to know that you can talk to me about these things. I know our history, but that shouldn't stop me from being your . . . ally . . . friend . . . I don't know—counsellor, even."

Claire sensed the warmth in Manisha's voice.

"That's nice, Manisha. Kind."

"Oh, I don't know, Claire. I suppose I've seen a lot of girls in their first love here, and they lose themselves. You get a sense that a friendly voice—helping them keep their feet on the ground—can help."

"But I don't love Simon," Claire protested.

"We have fun. Sex. A lot of sex. So, yes, I guess it has clarified a few things. About you, us, me. I think I am heterosexual. But we spend much time with his housemates, just chilling."

She paused.

"And okay, partying. But love? You know, I don't know what that is. I'm simply having fun. A new kind of fun, that's all. To me, Simon is sex."

Manisha smiled faintly.

"Like I said, Claire. I don't want to interfere. But I felt—still feel—that we can talk. Like, properly talk... openly with each other. I know you're friends with Jill . . . "

"I don't see much of Jill at the moment. She spends a lot of time with Jake from Aston. He's doing Sociology or something. She met him at a party we went to."

"So, maybe a friend could be a good thing?"

"Yes, you and I are good with each other. Open, like you say. I've found it a bit tricky to reach you, but I still really like you. You know that."

Claire smiled warmly.

"Merely being able to talk openly is a special thing, Claire. I know we have the tutor-student thing and our past, but I think I could be... would like to be... your confidante, counsellor, consigliere, or whatever you want. I want you to know that. We can find a way to be in touch. Proper touch. And I want you to know that... I'm here for you."

"Yes. Okay. I know that. I agree. I do miss being able to talk to you. I did like it. I like it. It's a way of relating that I don't have with anyone else. So, for so long as you don't become all teachery or something, it would be nice to meet up . . . "

"Oh, I am pleased, Claire. I think that will be lovely."

"As friends. Okay? See how we go."

"Okay," Manisha replied—with an air of resignation.

*

Claire soon discovered that Simon's acerbic wit masked a deeply scathing attitude toward others and himself.

He didn't like himself.

Once, he told her he could see through himself just as clearly as he saw through others.

Claire had no idea whether or how to help him with his self-deprecation.

Part of her chose not to think about it.

Simon, for his part, avoided thinking about it, too—except when he was painting.

He loved quoting Picasso's belief that art is a lie that speaks the truth—a distortion and encapsulation.

But Simon believed he had gone even further.

His art allowed him to fully immerse himself in a lie—presenting an obvious interpretation "for the fools" while embedding his true meaning beneath.

Claire liked that she was one of the few who understood his more profound messages.

She also didn't mind the hours he spent painting.

His dedication encouraged her to spend more time on her own art.

Recalling the painting Brian had once done about love, Claire asked Simon one evening, "If I asked you to paint how you feel about me, what would you create?"

Simon didn't say a word.

Instead, he stood up from the sofa, walked over to his easel, grabbed a piece of charcoal, and, in a few quick, fluid strokes, sketched a vulva.
Claire laughed.
"Trust you," she said.
In a way, that's all there was between them.
She felt relieved.
For all his inner demons, Simon was good company.
With her.
In bed.
But also, among friends.
He could always find humour in any situation, turning any evening into a fun one.
Claire knew that she loved fun.
Most students went to parties.
They went to every party.
People made it their business to let Simon know about upcoming parties.
Claire had learnt when to stick close to him as he played the jovial entertainer and when to leave him to his sarcastic, cutting assassin mode.
She liked the freedom that came with roaming.
She liked the carefree feeling of being in a relationship, of a sort.
In May, Simon received his final exam and assignment schedule.
He stormed into the flat, shrieking as Claire made tea in the kitchen.
"No way. I'm not fuckin' doin' it. Writing all this history shit."
Claire inhaled sharply.
"What? What do you mean, not doing it?"
"I have to submit some stupid essay by next week and sit exams."
"Well, of course you do. You know that. You're doing a degree."
"I don't need a degree. You don't need degrees to paint."
"It'd be such a waste. You're nearly there. You don't need high marks or anything, but you'd be crazy not to give them a go."
"You're the one who's fuckin' crazy. You like this history crap. Theories. Critical thinking. What use is any of it? None."
Claire backed down.

"Well, it's up to you, obviously. I guess you're free to choose."
"Damn right," Simon muttered, grabbing the half-empty bottle of whisky from the counter.
Watching Simon drink himself into a stupor had become routine.
Claire was sure he had alcoholism. Addicted.
For Simon, drinking before, during, and after parties was just the warm-up.
Alcohol was his first thought every evening—the party itself was secondary.
A drink always got things off to a good start.
A drink made a good nightcap.
Drinking didn't just fuel his social life—it liberated his painting.
Despite their constant partying, both Claire and Simon still found time to paint—and paint well.
The tutors would have kicked them out if their work had been any less impressive.
As it was, their attendance was abysmal.
Claire had barely scraped through Year One.
Year Two?
It was touch and go.
A few days after Simon's outburst, Manisha Mahajan asked Claire to stop by her office.
"You are a wonderful free spirit, Claire. Your art is developing brilliantly. But you're bright. You're barely twenty. You could do so much more with your life—if you have the . . . academic underpinning too."
"Life. Who knows where I'll end up? Under a bus, probably."
Manisha laughed.
"Yes, you're right. We don't know. But in Year Three, you must start deciding where to go next. You could pull things around and give yourself real choices."
"Simon graduates this year. If he does his finals, he's talking about heading off to South America in the summer. I've never thought that far ahead—let alone years ahead."
Manisha smiled.

"Yes, well, let's hope he has the sense to finish. And travelling is good. I went travelling after my second year. Not with a boy, but with my best friend. We had a brilliant time. And yes, we thought about not returning—but we did."

She paused thoughtfully.

"I sometimes wonder what would have happened if we hadn't. If I hadn't. I did come back—but I was set to leave again. But then I met David back here in the UK."

"Your partner?" Claire prompted.

"Yes. He's older than me, as you know. A wiser head. He persuaded me to stay. And although we both still love to travel, he helped me see that staying here was best. All these years later, we're still together. Still happy. It turns out he was right."

"You stayed for love? Wow. That's romantic." Claire paused.

"I don't love Simon. But he's fit. We have a great time. Simon certainly isn't a wise head, though."

"No, that's it, Claire. You'll have to be the wise head. Keep your spirit. Keep . . . you. Simon will have his life—the way it's bound to be. But you? You need to safeguard your future. Have all the things you are capable of."

"I don't know what that is."

"That's the point. You and I are similar in so many ways. Especially me when I was your age. I sound overly protective, but I still have feelings for you. Special feelings. Don't blow it all, Claire."

Claire wasn't sure what Simon would do.

But she felt sure she wouldn't simply walk away from her degree.

"Well, you're not like my mum," she said lightly.

"It's good of you to think about me. Yes, I will think about what you've said. I will."

Simon showed up for his finals.

He submitted a half-hearted assignment.

They didn't go travelling that summer.

They just kept on living the same life.

Chapter 28

After Mike and the band finished their gig on a Saturday evening in September 2006, two guys approached as they packed up.
The scruffier of the two spoke first.
"You guys are good. Not too fussed about some of the stuff you play, but overall—fuckin' good."
"Ta. Do you play?" Mike asked cheerily.
"Yeah, we play rock, though. Loud."
"Where do you play? We'll come and watch," Lydia said enthusiastically.
"We're playing The Eagle Inn on Cooper Street in Salford tomorrow. Only about eighty people and a bit naff, but it's a good crowd."
Mike glanced over at Lydia and saw the excitement in her eyes.
"Yeah, sure. We'll come."
Mike and Lydia went.
It was loud.
Painfully loud.
The band thrashed and bashed more than anything else, but the crowd loved it.
"We should play harder-edged stuff, Mike. Like them. What are they called? Heartstopper, I think, he said. So, like for us—stuff like Garbage," Lydia shouted over the noise.
"Yeah. Maybe. Not everything this loud, though."
The following Tuesday, Mike came home from the university late to find Lydia lying on the sofa, smoking a joint.
And her hair.
She'd cut it short.
Dyed it with henna.
"What do you think? A bit more … "—Lydia punched the air—"hard-edged."
Mike studied her for a moment.
"It's good. Different. But you look good," he said, supportively.
"I'm sick of being 'pretty-pretty.' Like a right plonker. I want to be more like Shirley Manson. In Garbage, you know? Saying something. Maybe we could write some songs like that. Yeah?"

Mike hesitated.

"We could try," he said obligingly.

But he wasn't sure he could.

Over the next week, Lydia began to care less about her appearance.

She wore hoodies and jeans all the time.

She suggested they see Heartstopper again.

Mike wasn't that keen but agreed.

After the gig, one of the guys invited them back to his place to chill.

Probably smoke a few joints.

Mike froze when heroin was produced.

Chapter 29

In September 2006, Claire started her final year, and Simon signed on.
New Year's Day 2007 was a revelation for Claire—an awakening to the true extent of Simon's drinking.
The night before had been one of wild revelry; all she wanted now was quiet. The idea of drinking again made her feel nauseous.
But when Simon staggered downstairs at midday, he immediately reached for a bottle of vodka.
He grinned at her.
"Hair of the dog."
He took giant gulps straight from the bottle.
By the hour, he was raucous, insisting they go to the pub.
"Come on, let's have some fun."
"There'll be nobody there," she protested. "Everyone's sleeping it off."
"Nah, plenty of other people will be there. A good bit of craic. A laugh."
"I don't want drunken laughs. Let's just chill."
"Drunken laughs? What's wrong with that, you miserable twat? You used to be fun. Fuckin' hell. Lighten the fuck up."
He grabbed her arm, swaying on his feet.
"Come on."
"My coat. My coat."
"Fuck your coat. Come on."
She was dragged down the road to the corner pub.
She sat in silence while Simon held court, laughing louder and louder.
When she returned from the toilets, they were all raising their glasses, shouting 'Cheers' to something.
A wave of dissatisfaction crashed over her.
The scene reminded her of the '*Hip, Hip, Hurrah!*' painting by Kroyer—where a group of men and two women toast with joy while a third woman sits apart, uninvolved.
That's how I feel. Uninvolved.

The crowd thinned, but the drinking continued.
Now, the sinister image of *'The Drinkers'* by Van Gogh surfaced in her mind—inebriation on the edge of stupor.
More drinks. More self-destruction.
By the end of the night, all she could picture was *'The Drunkards'* by Ensor—a man, head in hands, slumped over the table. Another barely sitting upright, legs splayed, stability hanging by a thread.
Simon.
Pathetic.
Since Simon had graduated the previous summer, he had lost any structure to his days. Days, weeks and months, His art deteriorated.
His sales dwindled.
And still, he drank.
January 2nd was no different.
He started the day with a drink and a chant:
"I'm going to paint. I'm going to paint."
Claire watched as he approached the easel, daubing paint over a finished piece.
He turned to her, wild-eyed.
"It's better. Much better. I like it."
She shook her head.
Artists and alcohol. How frequently are there stories of excess accompanied by words such as 'genius' or 'best work.'
Not convinced.
Is this now Simon's best work? Control is lost. Precision is lost. Crudity confused with profundity.
She left Simon to it.

*

Where was it all heading?
Claire and Simon lived parallel lives.
She still joined him at times for his Bacchanalian escapades, but more and more, she slipped away mid-afternoon when his aggression surfaced.
She ran.

Ran to forget.

Ran away from everything.

By Spring 2007, Simon spontaneously decided to go to Ireland 'for a wee while.'

Claire was relieved.

Her term wasn't over despite his castigations—"Jack it in. It's all a load of shite anyway,"—she stayed.

Her tutors kept her motivated.

They encouraged her to apply for a doctoral scholarship in art history.

She needed a 2:1.

She was confident.

Through the summer, she worked at a pub.

Not her local, but close enough.

She liked watching the bohemians—people who could enjoy themselves without ending up in the gutter.

She joined them sometimes after closing.

Life felt simpler without Simon.

He returned in August, claiming he'd found a new style.

Claire saw only deterioration.

Primitive.

Raw to the point of being meaningless.

Simon sensed her lack of enthusiasm.

"You're a disapproving, sanctimonious bitch," he snapped.

*

When she got her results, Claire was stunned.

She had earned a first-class degree.

She called Manisha.

They arranged to meet.

Manisha greeted her with open arms.

"My beautiful, wonderful student."

Claire smiled, but was never comfortable with praise, so she brushed it off.

"It's a surprise, to be honest. Maybe it's a mistake."

"No mistake, Sakhi. You were at the top the whole time."

"Thanks to you."

"A couple of wobbles maybe, but your talent and drive always win through."

Claire shrugged.

"Perhaps. But not without you."

She hugged Manisha.

Manisha held her tightly.

"Like a mum, heh?"

"No."

Claire snapped.

Then softened.

"Well . . . yes. Suppose a mum is someone who looks out for you. Mentors you. Guides you. Because they care. Like the only person I ever depend on. And always will."

Manisha stroked her hair, nodding.

"I hope you mean that, Sakhi. 'Always' sounds good."

Claire was invited to discuss her doctoral scholarship with the Department Head.

"We think you'd make an excellent PhD student, Claire."

She shifted uncomfortably.

"Well, I'm pleased with my results."

"Your lecturers agree—you have a real future in art history."

She listened as he read the proposed research topics:

"Contrasting Egyptian and Roman Art."

She grimaced.

"Political Views in Sculpture."

What?

"Gothic Stained Glass."

Oh, bloody hell.

And then—

"The Role of Social Capital in Renaissance Art."

Renaissance? Yes.

Her face lit up.

"With Professor Stewart—Julie Stewart. She was impressed with your previous work in this area and is happy to be your supervisor."

"That would be ace. Er, great. Er, decidedly . . . interesting."

"Good. You have all the financial information from the application pack. You'll start with a Postgraduate Certificate in Research Methods, yes?"

"Absolutely. Yes."

"Congratulations. See you in October."

"Thank you, er, Prof."

Claire left the office pleased—but uneasy.

She had known doctoral students.

They were brilliant.

Super-intelligent.

I'm not like them.

Am I?

Chapter 30

On New Year's Day 2008, Mike and Lydia visited her parents in Sale.
They had cancelled their planned stay over Christmas, with Lydia claiming she had been ill.
Now, out of nowhere, she snapped.
"You're pathetic, Dad. Expecting everything to be bright and cheerful all the time. It isn't. Life isn't!"
Her tirade came from nowhere.
"Don't shriek at your father!" Mrs Clarke shot back.
Lydia ignored her.
"I don't know how you put up with him. Mr. Jolly. It's ridiculous. If you, I, or anyone has a problem, he just says, 'It'll be alright.' No help at all."
"So, tell me, what is the matter, Lydia?" Mr Clarke asked pleadingly.
Lydia fell silent.
"Tell me." His exasperation grew.
Silence.
Mike, embarrassed, stepped in.
"She hasn't been well over Christmas. She's a bit run-down. Spent Christmas Day in bed," he offered, hoping to defuse the tension.
"Well, we all feel a bit below par sometimes, but we don't bite people's heads off," Mr Clarke grumbled. "A terrible way to start the New Year."
Lydia exhaled sharply.
"Sorry. Mike's probably right. I'm just feeling off. Sorry, Mum."
"It's your father you should apologise to," Mrs Clarke scolded.
Lydia turned toward him. "Sorry, Dad. Sorry."
Mr Clarke hesitated, still hurt. "It's okay. But if something is wrong, you know I'm here for you. We both are. And we do try to help."
Lydia's eyes flickered with emotion, but she shut it down.
"I know, Dad. It's me. Sorry for putting a damper on the day. Especially since we need to be going now."

Mrs Clarke sighed. "Well, at least we're parting on a better note." She turned to Mike.
"And poor Mike. Hearing all this. We're not normally like this."
"I know. Things get fraught. I'm glad we came. Thank you for the lovely meal. We'll come back soon."
With forced smiles and polite farewells, they left.
Mike said nothing as he drove.
At the first motorway service, Lydia finally spoke.
"Can we stop? I need the loo. Sorry."
Mike pulled in.
He waited outside the ladies' room.
She took ages.
When she returned, he studied her face.
"Are you okay? I wasn't sure if you'd been sick. Are you still unwell?" he asked gently.
"Fine. Fine. Just tired."
"You can nap. I'll wake you for the second half of the drive."
"Okay. Thanks."
She was asleep in minutes.
Mike thought about waking her halfway.
Then again, two-thirds of the way.
But she slept the entire journey.
Even when they got home, she mumbled that she just wanted to go to bed.
Mike didn't bring it up again.

*

But he noticed.
Lydia was not herself.
Her voice cracked at their next band rehearsal.
She struggled to hold notes.
"Maybe you're coming down with something. You sounded blocked up this morning," Mike suggested.
"Maybe. I'll be fine by Saturday." She dismissed it.
But Lydia wasn't fine.
Far from it.
She had changed.

Once vibrant, loud, laughing—now, she was sombre.
She missed work frequently.
The summer brought some relief, but as autumn set in, she grew worse.
One evening, while they were watching TV, she turned to him.
"Can you lend me a couple of hundred quid until the end of the month?"
Mike answered instantly.
"Of course. Did work not pay you for the days you were off?"
"No, it's not that. I must have miscalculated, that's all."
He lent her the money.
He expected she would pay him back on the first of the month.
She didn't.
Instead, one night, she muttered, frustratedly—
"I'm going to sell these old dresses. All that pretty-pretty shit I used to wear. Some people will like them. I'll put them on eBay. Hopefully, they'll sell quickly."
Mike tilted his head.
"They are nice. Are you sure? You look good in them."
Lydia's face darkened.
"I told you. They're not me. Get used to it. I've changed."
Her sharpness startled him.
"Are you short on cash again? I can help out a bit."
Her face twisted.
"Oh, so you're angling for your money back? I'll give you your fucking money!"
She stormed out of the lounge.
Mike waited.
Let her cool off.
He went upstairs.
Two hours passed.
He returned.
Lydia was slumped in a chair.
Her right hand draped over the armrest, limp.
On the floor:
A box of matches.
Crumpled tin foil.
Mike's stomach dropped.

"Lydia! Lydia! Are you alright? What have you done?"
He rushed to her side, cradling her head.
She stirred, barely.
Her eyes fluttered open.
They weren't her eyes.
They were vacant.
Soulless.
Her voice was slurred, scarcely coherent.
"I'm fine. I'm fine."
Her eyes shut again.
Mike's mind raced.
Drugs. Heroin.
Shit.
Heroin kills people.
Had she overdosed?
He didn't know.
"Lydia! Lydia, talk to me!"
She shifted slightly.
She smiled sluggishly.
"I'm fine, Mike. I truly am."
He stared at her, completely at a loss.
After a long moment, he blurted—
"Do you want a cup of tea?"
Mike sat with Lydia for a couple of hours.
Gradually, she came around.
"How long have you been doing heroin?" Mike asked.
"I'm not doing heroin," Lydia snapped. "I've only used it a few times. Just a few months. Not much. It helps me sleep better. That's all."
"But... do you inject it? That's dangerous, Lydia. Bloody dangerous."
"No. I just chase the dragon."
"Chase the dragon? What the fuck is that?"
Lydia sighed, shaking her head.
"Oh, Mike. You're such a good boy. Burning black tar heroin and chasing the fumes."
"Like snorting?"
"No, just inhaling the fumes, Mike. It's harmless."

"It's not harmless, Lydia. It's dangerous. And addictive. And expensive. People can't stop."
"I can stop anytime," Lydia insisted.

*

Mike didn't notice any signs of Lydia using heroin over the next few weeks, aside from a lingering cold.
He assumed it was just a flu virus she couldn't shake.
She still went to work, as did he.
But on weekends, she was restless.
"Shit. I forgot my toothpaste," she cursed. "I'll pop out to the convenience store."
"Want me to come?"
"No. I'll only be a few minutes. Put the kettle on in ten."
Lydia kissed him on the cheek and left.
She was gone for half an hour.
"What happened?" Mike asked.
"They didn't have my brand, so I tried a few other places. Got it."
She held up a tube of toothpaste.
Other times, she would say she was going for coffee with a friend, only to return exhausted, claiming she was coming down with something before disappearing for a nap.
After two months, Mike finally confronted her.
"You're using heroin again, aren't you? Yes?"
"No. I told you. I stopped."
Mike studied her face.
The tell-tale pupils. Pinprick small.
"I can see that you have."
Lydia rolled her eyes.
"Oh, for fuck's sake, Mike. Get a grip. It's just rec... recreational. You smoked dope... when you were fun."
Lydia's finances crumbled.
She borrowed money from Mike. From friends. From her parents.
She started selling whatever she could on eBay.
She even bought lottery tickets, chasing a miracle win.

Nothing helped.

In mid-April, she finally broke.

"Mike. I need help. I have to shake this. It's wrecking my life."

Mike's heart clenched.

He put an arm around her and kissed her forehead.

"You can, Lydia. We'll get help. You can beat it."

Mike felt a profound duty to stand by her.

Lydia went to her GP.

She was referred to a drug advisory clinic.

She attended counselling sessions.

She was prescribed methadone.

Every morning, she had to go to the pharmacy to take her dose under supervision.

But the old Lydia wasn't back.

She was now wholly drugged up on a controlled dose of methadone.

She had to do regular urine tests to prove she was clean from heroin.

After two months, she was allowed to self-administer.

She diligently took her methadone.

In the summer, she seemed brighter.

The dosages decreased.

Gradually, she seemed to enjoy life again.

Mike confessed to visiting his friend John Brompton.

"I feel like I have to keep everything steady. Be loyal. Help in any way possible. I feel guilty that I didn't see it coming before she started using. Now, Lydia is my total focus."

John listened carefully.

"But Mike, in all this—does Lydia love you?"

Mike froze.

Two images crossed his mind.

Lydia's naked form in the half light.

Her slumped body after the overdose.

No image of her care for him.

"I don't know. Maybe. I don't feel loved. I feel like it could happen. Just out of reach."

He reached into his guitar case, pulled out a printed sheet of lyrics, and played his song *For Love Was Almost Here*, on the guitar.

> *Couldn't wake up to see that you weren't there*
> *Couldn't wake up to hear you didn't care*
> *Felt love was always near.*
> *For love was almost here.*
> *Wrote a new yesterday*
> *Lived in a dream and wouldn't wake*
> *Felt that if you'd just stay*
> *Something could change, and I could say*
> *Love was here*
> *Love doesn't just come to order.*
> *Love can sometimes elude*
> *Love lies somewhere in the ether.*
> *Love may not come in twos.*
> *Wrote a new yesterday*
> *Lived in a dream and wouldn't wake*
> *Felt that if you'd just stay*
> *Something could change, and I could say*
> *Love was here*

John sighed, shaking his head.

"It's a beautiful song, Mike. But sad. I know you want to do right by her, but in the end, she has to be right for you."

Mike lowered his gaze.

"I know. But as I wrote, I couldn't leave."

"And what's all this about 'writing a new yesterday'?"

"That's how you hang on. You have a bad day, but the next day, when you look back, you rewrite it so it wasn't so bad."

John was quiet for a moment.

"But it was, Mike, wasn't it?"

Mike exhaled sharply.

"Well, you have to try."

Mike kept holding Lydia's burdens.

*

But he couldn't control everything.

In July, Lydia's mother was killed in a car accident.
Mike was terrified of what that would do to her.
Summoning his courage, he asked directly—
"I know you're devastated. But we have to get through this—without drugs. No matter how bad you feel. Promise me, Lydia. Talk to me. Don't go back there. I'm here. We'll get through this together."
Lydia's expression softened.
"I won't. I can. We can," she replied.
Mike wanted to believe her.
By late August, Mike recognised the signs again.
This time, Lydia didn't deny it.
She was far more accepting of her dependence.
"This is my life, Mike—my choice. I tried stopping. I'm just going to manage it better this time. I like how I feel now. I like hanging out with people like me. You're too straight, Mike. Too fucking straight."
"It'll kill you, Lydia. We can get you off it again. We did it before. I should have helped more when your mum died."
"I'm not going through that again. You can like it or lump it."

*

Over the next few months, Mike watched her fade.
Her drugged stupor became normal.
Still, he stayed.
His loyalty wasn't just about Lydia anymore.
It was about him.
A loyalty fuelled by fear.
A desperate need to avoid the feeling of rejection that had haunted him since Adele.

Chapter 31

At the start of her second year of her doctorate, Claire was pleased to have passed the Postgraduate Certificate in Research Methods. When she had first reviewed the course content, she had been daunted. It mentioned epistemologies, ontologies, and methodologies in research and referenced computer-supported qualitative data analysis—a foreign language, if not an alien one. Yet, in the end, she found it fascinating. It forced her to think critically about the nature of data in her PhD and how to analyse it effectively.

However, she hadn't anticipated a discussion with Julie Stewart about using computers to explore artistic influence—specifically, analysing similarities in facial depictions across different artists.

"I don't want to analyse my data that way," Claire protested. "I'd rather study overall composition, materials, brush strokes—things like that."

"Yes, I know," Julie nodded, leaning back in her chair. "But this research shows that by focusing narrowly on faces, we can examine composition, proportion, position, and expression. It suggests you're on the right track by looking closely."

"I was thinking of using a grounded theory approach—developing categories or sets of aspects where influence might be revealed."

Julie smiled approvingly. "I like that. See if you can find a solid set of precedents for using that approach to compare artists more broadly."

"Yes. Right. I can do that. I'd enjoy that. Thanks."

"I thought you would."

Claire left the discussion feeling proud.

She understood the differences in research approaches, used the correct terminology, and clearly articulated her ideas.

She rushed home, eager to tell Simon about her supervision session and new research direction.

She found him upstairs in their studio, painting.

"I don't know why you waste time studying artists who just copy others," Simon muttered, not looking up. "You should focus on what's new. The truly innovative."

"It's not about copying," Claire argued. "It's more subtle than that. We've all experienced the art of others—it shapes us."

Simon shook his head dismissively.

Claire felt deflated.

She turned to head downstairs but paused at the bottom of the steps.

That's only his opinion. Everyone's entitled to their own.
That's life.

Chapter 32

On Monday, January 5, 2009, Mike started work as a postdoctoral researcher in the department.

His PhD viva had gone well, and the university seemed keen for him to stay.

A new era had begun—actual employment rather than study.

His mother called on his first day.

Mike chuckled to himself. She thinks it's like my first day at school or something.

But he was touched by it.

"It went well, Mum. Thanks. It's an interesting research area—creativity in a crisis. Don't know much about it yet, but I'll enjoy researching it."

"Will they pay you properly?" she asked.

"Yes. Proper pay. But it's only a fixed-term contract."

"For how long? You've got rent to pay," she said, her voice edged with concern.

"Six months initially. I'll figure out what's next soon."

"How's Lydia?"

"Not good," Mike admitted. "She's still on methadone. Seems stable, but it's wearing me down."

"Mike, you can't go on like this. Are you looking after yourself? Swimming, at least? Not just... being there for her. She's not going to change. You need to have it out with her. Once and for all."

"Yeah, I still swim at the university," he replied.

Then, in his best Homer Simpson voice, he declared:

"From now on, I'm going to be like Krusty and tell it like it is, Marge."

"I'm serious, Michael."

"I know."

On Sunday, January 18, Mike woke to find Lydia had gotten up before him.

He went downstairs.

Horror.

A flashbulb moment.

Lydia lay motionless on the kitchen floor.
A syringe rested near her right hand.
Her face was ashen.
Mike recoiled, his mind blank with shock.
Terror.
He ran to her.
"Lydia. Lydia!" He shouted in desperation.
He crouched, lifted her head, and slid his arm beneath it.
She didn't stir.
"Lydia. Wake up. Wake up!" He pleaded.
Nothing.
He bent closer—her breathing was weak.
Panicked, he laid her head back down and sprinted to the phone.
"Emergency? Ambulance. My girlfriend—she's overdosed. She's unconscious on the floor."
The day was a blur—ambulances, A&E, and then Lydia being taken away.
No one told him anything.
Finally, a doctor approached.
"She'll survive. This time."
The admonishment in his tone was unmistakable.
"No way to live," he muttered, shaking his head as he walked away.
Mike looked down, ashamed.
Guilt.
Failure.
Again.
Later, he called his mum.
"Mike, you can't make someone love you."
"I know," he said.
But he didn't believe it.
"I just can't help but wonder why I'm not enough."
Mike hoped that Lydia might be contrite.
Instead, she was casual.
"It was just cut with something. There were one or two others. Nobody's using him anymore."
Mike stared at her, incredulous.

The following day, as he drove to the university, he felt the weight of it all.

No one at work has any idea what my life is like.

Frustration.

Injustice.

Self-pity.

Then—

A road sign.

Pedestrians on the road.

A simple icon: an adult holding a child's hand.

Responsibility.

You have to take care of a child.

But Lydia is not a child.

She got herself into this.

I am not responsible.

But then—

I do have an obligation to see she's okay.

His mind flashed back to the sign.

A man and a girl. Not necessarily his daughter. Not necessarily someone he loves. But someone he's obligated to watch over.

As he pulled into the car park, the memories flooded in.

The shock.

The fear.

The helplessness.

It's not just obligation. Caring for a child doesn't harm you. But this? This is harming me.

He put the car in reverse.

A driver honked—he had nearly backed into her.

He straightened the car.

So—

Am I selfish because I'm being inconvenienced?

She was great once. Was.

As he stepped out, his face must have said it all.

"Weight of the world, heh?"

Angus McCabe, a lecturer, gave him a knowing look.

"Ha. No. Miles away," Mike replied lightly.
So much for Homer Simpson's honesty.

*

The overdose incident was never discussed.
Mike sensed Lydia's guilt.
She didn't seem to be using as much.
But she was out more—primarily for drinks with Nora.
Is she taking drugs?
He oversaw her for slurred speech and dilated pupils.
Months rolled by.
Then—
Lydia didn't come home.
Not all night.
The next evening?
Still no sign.
Mike debated. Should I check *The Dog and Partridge?*
It's too much like checking up on her.
The following evening, near closing time, he went.
Nora.
No, Lydia.
She muttered something to a man beside her.
Mike approached.
"Have you seen Lydia?" He tried to sound casual.
Nora hesitated.
"Tonight?" she asked defensively.
She's lying.
"Er, she was here. Earlier."
No eye contact.
Mike bit back the urge to press for details.
"Okay. Thanks. Just wondered."
He turned to leave.
The man caught up to him.
"Hi. Alright, mate?"
Mike stopped, puzzled.
"Er, so... The thing is," the man started awkwardly.
"Nora likes you. And Lydia. And she's seen her a lot recently."

Mike nodded. Yes, I figured.
A silence.
Then—
"But... yeah. Like I say, Nora likes you. So, she wants me to say—"
A deep breath.
"She feels bad about it, mate. But..."
Mike waited.
"She's with another bloke."
A punch to the gut.
"Gone, mate. Sorry."
Mike froze.
"You may know him. Plays with *The Spikes*, from Attercliffe. She's been seeing him for a while."
The man shifted uncomfortably.
"Nora doesn't think it's fair. So, she wanted you to know."
Then, almost relieved to have said it, he shrugged.
"Women, heh?"
Mike looked at the ceiling and exhaled.
A tut, like it didn't matter.
"Er, yeah. Right. Thanks."
Mike turned to leave.
He caught Nora's glance.
She looked guilty.
He nodded—a small, tight smile of thanks.
But inside?
Hollow.

Chapter 33

On Sunday, September 13, Simon sent a text from Ireland.
It simply read:
"Decided I'm not coming back. Happy here."
Claire didn't reply immediately. She felt no need to dissuade him. She didn't even need to know why. She made a cup of tea. After twenty minutes, she finally texted back:
"OK. Bye."
That evening felt the same as many others in recent times.
She was alone at home.
But now, he wouldn't be coming back. Ever.
So, what had Simon been to me?
She thought for a moment.
Sex.
Am I sad?
She paused as if consulting her mind..
The image of him at that first party. Images of drunkenness. His body in bed.
No. I'm fine. Sex is not love.
She slept well.
On Monday morning, she headed to the university.
Will this keep crossing my mind all day?
It didn't.
On Monday, September 28, Claire had lunch at the café in the Arts building.
Her friend and colleague, Emma, joined her.
"Hi. Alright?" Claire asked.
"No. Terrible."
"What's up?"
"My ex has shown back up. Pleading for forgiveness. Telling me he's changed. He's a gambler. Well... a loser. We split up last year when I told him I couldn't deal with it."
"Oh, right. So... has he stopped?"
"He says he has. But he's said it before. Truth is, I've been happier without him. I don't want to go back."
"Were you married?"

"No. We were like you guys—a longstanding relationship, but no marriage. I'm glad I didn't. Anyway, I told him last night to stop pestering me. But he's still texting. Still leaving messages."
"Well, if you're sure, reply one last time. Then block him."
"I guess. I just get flustered when I see the messages."
Emma took a breath.
"How are you two, anyway?"
"It's only me now. He left a couple of weeks ago. He'd been away in Ireland for months and decided not to return."
"Shit. You guys were together for ages. I remember you telling me. You were good together."
Claire shook her head.
"Not good. Not bad. We just rubbed along."
She smirked.
"But with a lot of friction. C'est la vie."
Emma scowled.
"Bastard. All men are bastards. I've decided."
At that moment, Emma's friend Sarah appeared.
Claire had seen her around, but they'd never spoken much.
"Bastards, all," Sarah said, laughing.
"Have you still not stopped him?"
"I sent another message this morning," Emma replied.
"Claire says I should block him."
"Yeah. Block 'em all, I say."
Claire started hanging out more with Emma and Sarah.
Over coffee one day, Sarah asked:
"What's happening with your flat? Is he going to think he can roll up whenever he likes?"
"No, it's all in my name. He was always on the dole. I paid for pretty much everything. His money was only for his drinking."
"Fuck, we're all mad, aren't we? I subsidised Gordon for years, too," Emma said.
"I guess I was," Claire replied.
Then, with a flippant shrug, she added,
"But that's me."
Sarah grinned.
"Well, I'm happy with the three of us," she declared.
"Let's go out. Have some laughs. Dancing. But no men."

That Friday, they hit the bars.
Then a club.
When *If I Were a Boy* by Beyoncé came on, they leapt up to dance together.
Then, *Girls Just Want to Have Fun* by Cyndi Lauper.
Followed by *Sisters Are Doin' It for Themselves* by Annie Lennox and Aretha Franklin.
They whooped with joy.

*

At WMU, Claire had a supervision meeting with Julie Stewart.
"So, this term, I think you should put together a research paper on your work. For a conference."
"Me? On what? Where?"
"Yes, you. Your research is solid. You could easily present a developmental paper at a creativity-in-art conference."
"What's a developmental paper?"
"One where you present your ideas and planned analysis. Then, other delegates discuss the merits with you."
"Like, people critique me?"
"More like a discussion. These sessions are beneficial. They help you practice defending your work. Arguing your case. They're totally informal."
"Do you think I'm ready for this?"
Julie smiled.
"I know you are. You just need to start believing in yourself."
Later, Manisha called.
Claire asked about her trip to Mumbai with David.
She also mentioned her nerves about presenting a paper.
Manisha, ever supportive, reminded her of her own capabilities.
Claire began to believe it.
Her PhD was progressing well.
She was enjoying a spontaneous, carefree social life.
She felt independent.

Chapter 34

Mike's desire to start fresh had finally materialised. A new city. A new university.

He had secured accommodation in Plymouth with the university's help. He decided to share a house with Bruce, a guy from the Finance Department at Devonport University. Bruce was pretty quiet, spending most of his time at his girlfriend Sophie's flat. She stayed over occasionally, but Mike was often unaware they were even there.

In his first week at Devonport, Mike was invited to an ice-breaker session for new doctoral students and postdoctoral researchers.
Upon arriving at the first floor of the Engineering Robotics building, he entered a large foyer where only a couple of people hovered about.
He walked over to the buffet table to grab a cup of coffee.
One of them approached him.
"Hi, I'm Dean. I'm studying music. My doctorate is about nonverbal behaviour within string quartets."
Mike paused, trying to recall his own experiences watching string quartets interact.
"So... like tempo setting and emphasis?"
Dean looked pleased.
"Absolutely. I'm a cellist. Are you a musician?"
Mike laughed.
"Ha. Not like you. I've played guitar in pub bands, pop covers, and some of my songs. But I get what you mean. We have a drummer clicking sticks to start us off. Not mega subtle. But we give each other the eye when a change is coming."
"Well, that's the same kind of thing, in a way," Dean replied.
Then, with curiosity, he asked, "What's your PhD research?"
"I've done my PhD. I'm here as a postdoc. I'm researching the psychology of creativity—specifically, how early childhood experiences of ambiguity and variability influence it."

"Oh, right. Sorry—I thought you were a PhD student. Creativity... in music?"

"Not exactly. We use psychological measures of creativity. We incorporate neuroimaging more and more. But honestly? I haven't fully decided yet."

Dean nodded thoughtfully.

"Every time I say that, my supervisor just tells me, 'Great. You shouldn't decide everything too quickly.'"

Mike grinned.

"Sounds like good advice. Anyway, we should check where we're supposed to sit. The email said they mixed disciplines on purpose."

Together, they walked over to the seating chart pinned to the wall.

Mike chuckled.

"Looks like a wedding. Circular tables of eight. Are you Dean Kershaw?"

"That's me," Dean replied. "Sounds like you've played a few weddings."

"Yeah. In Sheffield. Plenty of gigs—including weddings."

Mike scanned the list.

"You're on Table 3. I guess we should head in. See you later."

Mike lingered near the side wall, watching Dean take his seat and greet his tablemates.

He glanced around.

Four other tables, all filling up.

Forty new PhDs. That's good going.

A man stepped forward.

"Welcome, everyone. I'm the Director of Research. I would like to introduce our first speaker of the day, Dr Sherifat Patronne. Like all our guest speakers, she's a recent PhD graduate and now a postdoctoral research fellow at Devonport."

Mike's attention locked onto her.

She's Beyoncé's sister.

The beautiful Black woman stood confidently in a cream-fitted jumper and brown suede skirt.

She adjusted the overhead projector to match her monitor.

The screen displayed her first slide:

"Structural Racism and Its Effect on Health Inequalities in the UK: A Qualitative Study"

Beneath the title: Her full name and degrees.

Then she spoke.

"I am Sherifat Patronne, and I got my PhD in Sociology in this place last year."

Her Nigerian accent was unmistakable. Mike found himself mesmerised. She was confident, relaxed, and articulate. She spoke fluently about alternative methodologies, using highly technical language that remained engaging. She explained how she had used focus groups in her research.

Still, despite his best efforts, Mike drifted into periodic reveries.

She's stunning.

And her accent...

How sexy is that?

After the talk, they moved into an icebreaker session.

The task: Collectively write a story about a new PhD student starting university.

Each person at the table had to add one sentence until they had a 48-sentence story—concluding with a moral lesson.

Mike overheard Sherifat asking for a volunteer to be the scribe.

The group discussed it briefly.

Dean agreed to do it.

Sherifat laughed.

"You don do? OK, so you will be the one to have punchline and tell us the moral."

Mike took his cue and headed to Table 2, as instructed in the invitational email.

He introduced himself, explained the task, and confirmed the scribe for his group.

They made a good job of it.

There was plenty of humour, and they ended their story effectively.

"That's brilliant. You did well," he told them.

He could sense their pride.

He was pleased he'd played his part.

During the coffee break, the facilitators left their groups and met up.
Since they were all from different departments, it was their first meeting.
"Hi, Sherifat. I'm Mike Lewis. Psychology."
"Mohammed Haq. Computing."
"Xiang Yun. Biological Sciences."
"Well done on your presentation," Mohammed said. "I'm a bit nervous about mine. I'm not the best at presenting."
"My English. Hope it all OK," Xiang added.
"I'm sure we'll be fine," Sherifat reassured them.
The day went smoothly.
At 6:00 p.m., someone called, "Anyone up for a bite to eat?"
About a third of the group muttered a 'Yes'.
The rest headed for the door.
"There's a nice pub down this road. They do good food. Oya, I reckon at this time, we get in OK," Sherifat suggested.
As they set off, Mike overheard Xiang asking if this was Sherifat's first year as a postdoc.
"It's my third," she replied.
The pub food was excellent.
The day had served its purpose—everyone was relaxed.
At 7:30 p.m., someone picked up a microphone at the bar.
"Open mic night is about to begin!"
Mike was impressed with the first two performers.
The first guy played "Stuck in the Middle" by Stealers Wheel.
Then, a girl stepped up and sang "Valerie" by Amy Winehouse.
Dean turned to the group.
"Anyone here play? Like Mike?"
One person said, "Not well enough for here."
Another repeated the phrase.
The next act was a duo—a guy with an acoustic guitar and a girl with a violin.
"This is an Irish classic," the guitarist announced.
They played "Paddy on the Railway" by The Dubliners.
Mike grinned at Dean.
"See if they've got a cello out the back," he joked.
Everyone looked at him quizzically.

"He's a proper cellist at the School of Music," he explained.
Dean laughed.
"Does anyone play the violin here?"
"I do," Sherifat said. "But nothing like that. I can play OK—but not to Conservatoire standard."
Dean's eyes lit up.
"Over to you then, Mike. Mike plays in a band."
Mike sighed playfully.
"Alright. I'll ask the last guy if I can borrow his guitar."
He walked over to the duo who had just finished.
"Any chance I could borrow your guitar?"
"No problem, mate."
"Got a capo?"
"Sure. In my gig bag. Hang on."
The guitarist rooted around and then handed over the capo and guitar.
Mike walked up to the front, sat on a stool, and clipped the capo onto the third fret.
"This is Scarborough Fair by Simon & Garfunkel—but without Art Garfunkel," he quipped.
He played it well.
The university group clapped vigorously.
Some cheered.
"Your turn, Sherifat," Dean said, grinning.
Their group immediately started chanting.
"Sherif-at, Sherif-at!"
She laughed in protest but finally relented.
She walked over to the girl from the duo, who handed her the violin.
She muttered under her breath as she took her place on the stool.
"God, no, go shame us."
She looked up at the crowd.
"Well, this lot have insisted I play. But there aren't many pop songs that suit solo violin, so I'll play a piece by John Williams—from *Schindler's List*."
She began to play.
The pub fell into an immediate hush.

Everyone was transfixed.
At least half the audience inhaled as she hit the octave jump—a collective, breathless moment.
Mike was not just impressed.
He was physically moved.
He had always loved the film's soundtrack, but hearing it live—played with such depth and emotion—brought a silent tear to his eye.
The applause erupted.
Mike recovered himself.
The cheering was deafening and lasted over thirty seconds.
As Sherifat returned the violin and walked toward their group, Mike was still lost in the moment.
The sight.
The sound.
An abiding memory of being spellbound.

*

The first term flew by.
Mike visited his mother for Christmas.
"She was too pretty for her own good, Michael," she suggested. "I could tell. She had stardom in her eyes—like life was just sex, drugs, and rock and roll."
"She's extremely talented, Mum," Mike replied defensively.
"But drugs like that... it'll all end in tears. For her, I mean. Well, she's already lost you because of it. And you were as loyal as they come. It'll only get worse. Mark my words."
"I think you may be right there. It's certainly out of control. I tried everything I could, but ultimately, I had to admit defeat. To myself, at least."
Failure.
Guilt.
"Nothing to blame yourself for. I know you tried, Michael. You certainly tried."
"Anyway, now you can meet a nice girl in Plymouth. Plenty of fish in the sea. Ha! See? The sea! Ha!" Cathy laughed at her unintentional joke.

"An 'alrite my luvver' kind of girl," Mike replied in a pretty accurate Devon accent, mustering a smile.
"But one that speaks proper-like," Cathy added in a far less convincing attempt at the accent.
"Anyway, I'm off girls, at the moment. I'm enjoying the calm of my own space. I keep fit, and work keeps me busy. I've written two papers from my doctorate and submitted them to good journals. They take forever to get back to you, but fingers crossed."
"That's marvellous, Michael. You must show me when they're published," Cathy said, her pride evident.

*

Mike returned to Devon in the new year.
The barrage of 'Happy New Year' wishes served to lift his spirits even more.
For the first time in a long while, he felt at peace.
For the first time, he could please himself.
At the end of the month, after another research student workshop, Mike stood with a glass of wine in hand when an odd urge struck him—he felt the need to turn around.
As he did, his eyes met Sherifat's.
She had been looking at him.
But the moment their eyes met, she looked away.
How do people know when they're being stared at?
He took the opportunity to walk over.
"Been a while. You, OK?" he said brightly.
For a split second, he thought he saw her bristle.
Then, her curt reply:
"Yes. Fine, thanks."
Without another word, she turned away and walked toward a group of female researchers in the corner of the room.
Mike stood there, puzzled.
What was that about? Bit rude. What have I done?
A guy from the geology department—one Mike had met a couple of times before—walked over.
"Too late to say, 'Happy New Year'?"

"Well, I'm still saying it, so no. Happy New Year."
"Good. I'll keep going until February, then," the guy said with a grin.
Mike stayed at the event a little longer, milling around.
Just as he had decided to leave, that odd feeling returned.
He turned left.
Sure enough—another stare from Sherifat.
The moment she realised he'd noticed, she looked away again.
This time, Mike smiled and waved as he walked toward the door.
To his relief, she smiled back.
But the feeling lingered.
That grinding discomfort.
That knot in his stomach that he hated whenever he sensed someone didn't like him.
Still don't know what I must have done.

*

The next time Mike saw Sherifat was at a Costa in the town centre on a Thursday afternoon in March.
By sheer coincidence, he found himself behind her in the queue.
She was with someone who was clearly her sister, holding the hand of a little girl, about three or four years old.
"Oh, hi, Mike. This is my sister Funmilayo and my niece Orisa," Sherifat said.
Mike sensed it felt more like an obligatory introduction than a warm one.
Still, he reached out his hand toward Funmilayo, who grasped his fingers lightly in a polite handshake.
Then, leaning down, he offered a gentle fist bump to Orisa, pleased when she reciprocated.
"And hello to you, too," he said warmly.
As he stood back up, he caught Sherifat's gaze—and was pleased to see that enchanting beam he had noticed the first time they had met.
"Mike is a postdoc, too. In psychology," Sherifat added, this time more cheerily.

Then, bending down, she tucked a stray piece of Orisa's hair behind her ear and spoke softly, "And did Mummy say you can have orange juice?"

There was such affection in her voice, and Mike found it endearing.

As they paid for their drinks, he smiled.

"Lovely to meet you both," he said. Then, leaning down, he gave Orisa one last farewell fist bump—her delighted giggle making him chuckle.

"Catch up some time, yes?" he suggested to Sherifat.

To his surprise, she responded cheerfully:

"That shall be nice, Mike."

Relief.

By sheer fluke, he ran into her again the next day—again, standing in the queue at a campus café.

"Hi. Is your sister here for long?"

"Back to Lagos tomorrow." Then, pushing her lower lip out in an exaggerated pout, she added, "And Orisa."

"Wasn't she just a little darling?" Mike said.

"I absolutely love her. Funmilayo is my younger sister. I am achingly jealous," Sherifat admitted with clear feeling.

"We don't see little ones in our lives, do we?" Mike mused. "In universities, I mean. As students or staff."

"It is true. We live in a weird bubble. Not like normal people. It makes you wonder."

Mike nodded thoughtfully.

"Do you have family? Sisters? Brothers? Nephews? Nieces? You seem terrifically good with Orisa."

"No. Just me. I had a twin brother, but he died when we were ten."

A pause.

"I don't know. Maybe I just . . . relate to kids. They enchant me."

"Na so. I know what you mean. They are so cute, but they can be little monsters, too. Orisa can have real tantrums."

"Yeah, but you let it go 'cos they're only young."

"You are a psychologist, are you not?" she said, mocking his discipline with playful teasing.

They talked for hours.

At one point, as Sherifat went to fetch another coffee, Mike had a sudden realisation.

So much of my life has been the language of youth—teen stuff, student stuff, academic things. But not human things. Not real, adult, family things.

And for the first time, he wanted that conversation.

"Tell me more about you, though," he asked when she returned.

"Ah, well. Me. I have been at a crossroads to get here."

She sighed.

"Funmilayo's coming has reminded me—I have had a lot of wahala in my life."

"Wahala?"

"Sorry, sometimes I use Lagosian. I mean trouble. Problems."

"What? You? Seriously?"

"Na so. When I was younger, you don't know. I spent many years messing about. Not proper jobs, no steady boyfriends. Just fun, fun, fun. For a long, long time. Then, I let all that go. Focused on getting a career. A good education."

She paused, then sighed again.

"But it all adds up to a lot of wasted years. In the normal adult female world, I mean. E choke. And I get annoyed nowadays when guys want to get off with me only because of how I look."

Mike noted the shift—her voice was more staccato, and her Nigerian dialect more pronounced.

She felt strongly about this issue.

And he got it.

"Yes. I must admit that I finally feel like I'm growing up. Old, even."

Then, with a grin, he added, "Was I hitting on you?"

"Na so. Maybe I was a bit short with you at first. I can overdo it sometimes."

A pause.

"And anyway, you seem like a nice guy."

Then, as an afterthought, she added, "I am older than you, you know."

Mike walked away from that afternoon with her feeling something strange.

Something revelatory.

For the first time, he knew what he wanted.

He wanted a simple life.
A content life.
A life with a like-minded partner.
With someone like Sherifat.
Stability.
Safe.
Secure.
By May, Mike and Sherifat had bumped into each other many times. They'd gone for coffee a few times.
He liked her—so grounded, so genuine.
Eventually, he asked if she'd like to go on a date.
She agreed.
They went to a local pub for a drink.
"It is well. Good here. Quiet. You can talk properly," Sherifat said, looking around approvingly.
"Yes," Mike nodded. "The days of shouting in someone's ear, trying to get to know them, and barely even hearing their name correctly—won't be missed."
Then, with a grin, he added, "Though I am an expert on ears, you know."
"Ha."
A funny guy. A gentle man. Courteous to a fault.
She watched as a little boy, no older than four or five, tried to play dominoes with his parents at the next table.
He accidentally knocked over a massive swathe of tiles, sending them clattering to the floor.
Before the parents could react, Mike immediately got up, knelt beside him, and helped collect them.
As he counted aloud, the boy copied him, giggling.
Sherifat observed.
Kind, even.
Mike found her company just as captivating.
She had so many stories—stories that revealed who she was at heart.
A caring person.
A family person.
As they were leaving, they had their first kiss and agreed to continue dating.

Over the next few months, they shared everything.

Sherifat was moved by Mike's experiences as a child. She related to his first heartbreak with Adele and admired his loyalty to Lydia.

Mike, in turn, found her honesty refreshing—especially her willingness to admit guilt over her wayward, rather promiscuous past as a travel rep in Lagos.

He respected how she had left that life behind, embracing maturity and purpose.

They spent more and more time together.

Eventually, they gave each other keys to their homes.

One evening, Mike was alone in his house, strumming his acoustic guitar.

He hadn't noticed Sherifat arrive—until she leaned against the doorframe and grinned.

"Wetin dey happen? You gotta see if you can get a band going here," she teased.

"Yeah? You think?"

"Your songs are great, Mike. That was lovely. Maybe a more mellow band than you had with Lydia—based on those recordings you played me."

Then, with determination, she added, "And your songs. Not covers. Maybe a twosome, like you said you first did with your friend Jason in those early days."

Mike laughed, shaking his head.

"A duo, you mean? Maybe I'll ask around—check the union, see if there are any notices."

*

The following Wednesday, with some free time, Mike headed over to the Students' Union building.

It turned out that there was a weekly open mic session on Wednesdays at lunchtime.

He stayed to listen.

A young student stepped up to the mic.

"I'm Jennie. This is one of mine."

She played.

A nice voice. Good tune.

It reminded him of Smile by Lily Allen—or maybe that was just the London accent.

She got a lot of applause.

After she finished, Mike went over.

"I'm not hitting on you or anything, but that was fuckin' good," he said with an easy smile. "I'd like to set up a folk, melody-first sort of duo. Would you consider it?"

Jennie looked taken aback.

"Uh . . . OK," she hesitated. "Let me hear one of yours first."

"Sure. Can I borrow your guitar?"

Jennie handed it over.

Mike walked up to the mic.

"Hi, I'm Mike. And this is one of mine, called "*For Love Was Almost Here.*"

He played.

It went down well.

Afterwards, he told Jennie he was a postdoctoral researcher in Psychology.

She told him she was a second-year student in Biological Sciences.

He gave her his number.

She said she'd think about it.

A few days later, Jennie got back to him.

They started playing together at open mic nights.

Then, one evening, a café-bar manager approached them after their set.

"You guys are good. Ever considered doing a regular spot?"

They were offered a residency on Saturday nights.

They agreed.

Jennie and Sherifat got on well.

One evening, after Mike and Jennie had wrapped up a rehearsal at his house, Sherifat made a suggestion.

"I think you are amazing, Jennie. Abeg, we try a threesome?"

Jennie's eyes widened in shock.

Mike burst out laughing.

"I think she means a trio," he said, turning to Sherifat. "Not a twosome or a threesome, but a duo and a trio."

"Right, yes! A trio. Just for me, for fun."

She was utterly oblivious to the alternative meaning.

Jennie exhaled in relief. "Oh, thank God."

When the laughter died down, Sherifat grabbed her violin and played along with them—running through some songs she and Mike had already tried together.

It was good.

It was fun.

And maybe, just maybe, it was the beginning of something new.

Chapter 35

Claire's first development paper had gone well. The feedback confirmed that her research was being conducted appropriately. Since the conference, she had finalised her data collection and begun the full analysis. Julie Stewart suggested using software to map connections, highlighting key text extracts as she developed her framework of artistic facets that evidenced influence from other artists. She found the writing-up period of her PhD intense and all-consuming. Her social life with Emma and Sarah? Nonexistent.

But in May 2010, she submitted her thesis.

And passed.

Her external examiner, from Sherwood University, urged her to publish her findings in the journal he edited.

Following the viva, Julie Stewart mentioned that Professor Ferguson had asked about her teaching experience.

Claire had completed the short training course for doctoral students at WMU, covering teaching and learning. She had even run several seminars in her final year, including lectures for undergraduates—one on research methodology and a couple on her own research. And she had enjoyed it. Lecturing could be a thing. With time to paint. Then Julie added that Professor Ferguson had hinted Claire might fare well in interviews for lectureships over the coming weeks. Claire applied.

When she met Emma and Sarah, she told them everything.

"I passed. My external says there might be a lectureship job at Sherwood Uni."

"Ace," Emma and Sarah replied in unison.

Followed by a chorus of, "So long as we're still meeting up."

"Of course we will," Claire said, stepping between them and throwing an arm around each of them.

"We're a team."

That evening, she called Manisha.

Manisha was ecstatic.

"I'll send you a card, Sakhi—a bottle of champagne and a big kiss."

That night, Claire, Emma, and Sarah celebrated the only way they knew how.

Pre-loading with drinks at Claire's flat.

Then, clubbing at their favourite spot.

At the end of the night, they went back to Claire's and gathered around her kitchen table.

"I love . . . us," Emma said.

"I do, too," Claire replied.

"I love the things we do. I hope we'll continue somehow when you move, Claire," Sarah added.

"We will. We will," Claire assured them. "We'll just have to plan for me staying over with one of you. Or you guys coming to Nottingham?"

"Or we could meet in other places, like the seaside. Do activities and that," Sarah suggested.

"That'd be a laugh," Emma agreed.

"I've always fancied paddleboarding," Claire said, eyes lighting up.

"Let's do that," Emma grinned.

"We all deserve a holiday," Sarah continued.

"We can do that before I leave. The sea is supposed to be warm in September."

They loved their trip to Porth Eirias.

Emma? Never quite got the hang of it.

Sarah and Claire? Managed better.

Mostly, though?

They spent the day falling off their boards.

Climbing back on.

And laughing.

They agreed to do it again in the spring.

*

Claire's move to Nottingham in September was surprisingly straightforward.

Sherwood University assisted her in finding accommodation and funding her move.

A one-man-and-a-van, advertised at the Students' Union at UWM, had been all she needed.

Unlike her arrival at university all those years ago, surrounded by hundreds of fresh arrivals, this time, she was one of only a handful of new staff at the induction morning.

Many of them? Much older.

Not their first lecturing job.

And the atmosphere? All decidedly serious.

No welcome drinks at the local pub.

Just formalities all morning, then back to her new flat.

She had set up the basics, but the place still felt soulless.

After sitting on her bed for a while, Claire decided to go for a run.

At the induction, someone had suggested joining the university sports centre near her flat and right across from Wollaton Park—a place with great running paths.

She found it easily.

As she ran, she spotted a sign:

"Parkrun every Saturday at 9:00 AM."

A good way to meet people.

As she picked up her pace, reality hit.

This wasn't just a new city.

It was a new life.

No longer a student.

This job meant she was supposed to be an adult.

Mature.

Serious.

All labels I've avoided until now.

Will I be good at this?

Her teaching practice at UWM had been acceptable but not quite the same.

Back then, everyone knew I was only a bit older than they were—still a student myself.

Will my students see me the way I first saw lecturers?

Can I be as cool as Manisha was?

Running helped.

Always did.

She finished, walked over to the sports centre, and signed up for staff membership.

All ultra adult.

The following day, Claire had an appointment with Professor Ferguson.

But what to wear?

She had spent years sticking to student garb.

Now?

Time to smarten up.

And then—she remembered.

The neon cashmere jumper she had bought years ago.

Still pristine.

Still just 'perfect'.

I'll go looking like Manisha did.

She put it on.

It still looked good.

The white trousers felt like too much, so she settled for her new pale blue jeans—smart enough but comfortable.

"Welcome, welcome. Good to see you again, Claire."

"Thank you, Professor Ferguson."

"Fergus. Fergus. All first names here."

She hesitated.

"Fergus."

Erm. Admiring too much.

Fergus?

He bellowed:

"Fergus Ferguson. My parents had a sense of humour," he added with a forced chuckle.

"Oh, I see. Like Magnus Magnusson," Claire said, grasping for a response.

"Absolutely. Very good, very good. Absolutely."

Claire took his overenthusiastic response as a warning signal.

She didn't smile.

Instead, she sat in silence, waiting for him to continue.

"So, you've had the lowdown on the place. We run a buddy system in this department, so I've paired you up with Stephanie Kourakakis. She's been here three years and knows the ropes. Steph is your source for anything you need or aren't sure of. I've asked her to pop along in a minute."

"Regarding your work this term, I've kept your teaching light—mainly seminars helping Steph, plus some lectures on her classes. But I'm sure she'll explain all that."

"We're a friendly bunch. We have an informal coffee break at 11:30am—people pop in when they can—plenty of opportunities to meet everyone. I'll introduce you formally at our next staff meeting—Friday at 12:30pm. Okay?"

"Yes, fine."

Too dismissive.

"Great. Sounds good. I'm . . . looking forward to it . . . all."

"Oh, and yes—almost forgot. We've kept your teaching light because we want you to focus on publishing your thesis."

He leaned forward.

"As you know, we put a lot of stock in research here. Hopefully, you'll get two or three top-class journal papers submitted by the end of term."

Pressure.

His words were friendly enough, but the message was clear.

This wasn't about a development paper.

Or a conference paper.

Or just any publication.

"Two papers minimum. In a top journal."

Mein Gott.

"Right. Yes. I'll set about that right away."

"Good. That's the spirit. Ah, here's Steph. Right on cue."

Claire exhaled quietly.

She couldn't get comfortable with Professor Ferguson.

And then? Surprise.

She had assumed Steph was young—just a few years older than her.

But Stephanie?

Closer to fifty.

Not quite a peer.

More like a guide.
Help, then.
Rather than a friend.
The first six months were intense.
Although she had been given minimal lecturing, Claire hadn't realised how much preparation a single hour of teaching required.
Somewhere between one and two full days of work.
She often found herself working late into the evenings.
Drafting journal articles was even more challenging, though she was grateful for guidance from Stephanie Kourakakis.
She had planned to start new artwork and had even set up a studio in her spare room.
Her easel was ready.
A 24 x 30 canvas set up for a landscape painting.
But day after day, week after week, it sat there.
Untouched.
She hadn't gone out locally with colleagues from the university.
Most lived far outside town—north, south, east, or west—and didn't stick around after work.
Luckily, she had stayed in touch with Emma and Sarah, and they had managed to meet up a couple of times. In January, Sarah suggested another trip to Porth Eirias for paddleboarding in the spring.

*

In April, the three of them went.
When they met their instructor at the watersports centre, he didn't recognise them.
"Is this your first time paddleboarding?" he asked.
Sarah replied proudly, "No, we were here last September."
Emma added, "And we were brilliant... honest," flashing a grin.
Claire laughed and looked out at the sea.
The waves were bigger than last time.
The instructor noticed.

"Yeah, the sea's quite choppy today. The wind's picking up. We probably won't be running lessons later, so we should get started soon. Good thing I don't have to go over the basics."

The rougher conditions made for even more laughter—and even more falls.

Back on the beach, they looked out at the water.

No one else was paddleboarding.

"Look at him!" Emma shouted.

"Is he waterskiing?" Claire asked.

The man was lifted out of the water.

Sarah gasped.

"No, he's on some kind of skateboard... snowboard thing!"

"And there's no boat. Look—he's being pulled by that giant kite!"

They watched in awe as the man controlled the green kite, which hovered twenty meters above him.

He bent his knees, pulled on the trapeze-like bar, and suddenly launched into the air.

Two meters.

A twist.

A smooth landing.

Within seconds, he was airborne again.

This time, he somersaulted before landing with effortless grace.

Claire turned to their instructor, excited.

"What do you call that? Kiteboarding?"

"Sometimes, but on the surf, it's kitesurfing. We just call it kiting. That's Eddie Thomas. Local guy. One of the best. He'll probably switch kites soon—wind's getting stronger."

They watched as Eddie sped toward the shore, expertly releasing one side of his kite to kill the wind.

Moments later, he packed away the green kite and pulled out a red one.

In no time, he was back out on the water.

"I thought a smaller kite would slow him down," Claire mused.

"Nah. That's a hybrid for higher winds," the instructor explained.

Emma shrieked.

"Look! He's going even faster!"

Then, Eddie launched again.
Higher this time.
Twenty meters up.
A flawless landing.
Claire was awestruck.
His balance.
His strength.
The way his body contorted through every manoeuvre.
What fun.
Eventually, Eddie returned to shore, packed his gear, and walked over.
"Hi, Owen. Alright?" he greeted the instructor with a nod.
"Yeah, good. No more lessons, though—too much wind."
Eddie glanced over at the girls, his gaze lingering on Claire.
Claire held eye contact.
She could see how fit he was.
Lean muscle.
Toned arms.
She didn't look away.
"Have to settle for coffee, then," Eddie said, his Welsh accent lilting. "Are you shutting up?"
"Might as well."
"Tidy. You guys coming? There's a great little place over there."
He pointed down the seafront.
Claire answered first.
"Yes."
She glanced at Emma and Sarah, who nodded.
They sat for hours in the café, talking.
Claire asked Eddie everything about kiting.
He told them about his other adrenaline-fueled sports.
He was clearly a thrill-seeker.
And?
Incredibly fit.
"You guys coming back next weekend?"
His gaze locked onto Claire's, then flicked to Emma and Sarah.
"I could give you a little go if the wind's low."
"I can't," Sarah replied. "Family thing."
Claire looked over to Emma, who smiled and nodded.

"But we can. On Saturday."
Back at her flat, Claire couldn't stop thinking about Eddie.
His voice.
His laugh.
And, of course, how good he looked.
She walked over to her easel and felt compelled to paint for the first time in months.
The gyrations of kitesurfing.

A flurry of cartwheeling limbs—every possible angle.
A torrent of enthusiasm as she recalled Eddie's body.

*

The following Tuesday, Emma called.
"I have to work this weekend," she said apologetically.
Claire hesitated momentarily before deciding—I'll go to Porth Eirias on my own anyway.
The conditions were perfect when she arrived—a barely perceptible breeze, the waves minimal.
Ideal for paddleboarding.
But...
No kiteboarders.
No, Eddie.
She headed to the watersports centre.
"Just me, I'm afraid," she told Owen.
"No problemo. You'll have to tag on to a small group—I've got four people going out in half an hour. That, okay?"
"Sure."
As Owen made a quick phone call, Claire walked out to the promenade, gazing at the open sea.
Suddenly—
A tap on her right shoulder.
She jumped.
Turning to her right—
Nothing.

She swung around—
Eddie was grinning at her from the left.
He had tricked her.
She rolled her eyes, but a smile spread across her face.
"Fancy meeting you here."
"I said I'd come. Emma just couldn't make it."
"Well, I'm glad you did." His grin widened. "Going for another paddleboarding session? Barely a breath of wind—pretty perfect, I'd say."
"Yeah. Owen's taking a group out in a few minutes."
"I'll stay and watch."
"Not kiting today?"
"Nah. Not enough wind. But you know what? This kind of day is perfect for ballooning. I bet they're going up later once the thermals pick up. I know some of those guys—if you ask nicely, they might take us up. Fancy that?"
His accent.
She loved his accent.
"Wow. That would be amazing. Never done it before."
"Stick with me, girl. Loads of fun."
Claire reached into her bag, grabbed her towel and swimwear, and effortlessly changed.
A quick knot around her waist, jeans and panties off in one smooth motion.
Then, her blouse and bra, pulled out with practised ease, still concealed beneath the towel.
She fastened her bikini top, let the towel drop, and stretched.
Completely at ease.
Completely aware of Eddie's subtle interest.
He was trying not to stare.
Trying oh-so hard.
Claire smiled to herself.
Eddie watched as she walked down to the water.
Then, he made another phone call.
When Claire finished her session, she jogged back to him, still dripping from the sea.
"I rang them," Eddie said. "They're going up soon. Quick bite to eat, then we're off. It's not far."

"Ace."

Claire ran her fingers through her damp hair, giving it a quick shake to fix it into place.

Eddie watched, unblinking.

She reversed her under-the-towel dressing trick, and they walked off to lunch.

That afternoon, Eddie drove them to the launch site.

The balloon was massive.

Up close, it felt otherworldly.

"We can actually go up?" she asked, wide-eyed.

"Yeah, they said it'll be fine."

They climbed into the basket.

The roar of the burner sent shivers down Claire's spine.

Then—

A continuous burn.

Heat radiated around them.

The basket tilted slightly—

Then lifted.

Higher.

Higher.

Claire's breath caught in her throat.

She turned to look at Eddie.

The wind tousled his fair hair.

His face was golden in the fading light.

Enamoured—

She was kissed.

They stayed up for hours.

The world—a silent expanse beneath them.

They landed in a field.

Eddie spoke to the pilot and crew and thanked them.

"You guys good to pack up?" he asked.

They nodded.

Then, he turned to Claire.

"Let's hitch back to the launch site."

She was still buzzing.
Still on a high.
They made love in his car.

Chapter 36

Bruce packed up his final suitcase, standing by the front door of their shared house.

"It's only a small affair—immediate family. I hope you understand," he said.

"You've said. Of course. I'm sure it'll be great . . . even so."

Bruce laughed. "But seriously, thanks. You've been a great housemate. I'm sure the new guy, Adam, will appreciate you, too."

"Hope so. He doesn't move in until the end of the month. Anyway, have a fantastic wedding and honeymoon. Love to Sophie. And Sherifat and I will see you both as soon as you invite us to your palace. I'm assuming you never want to see this place again!"

Mike stepped forward with open arms.

Bruce hesitated, surprised. Then, he set his suitcase down and returned the hug.

About half an hour later, Sherifat arrived.

"Sorry, I'm late. Have I missed him?"

"Not by long. Just a few minutes ago."

"Chai, I wanted to wish them well."

"I gave him a hug and said we'd catch up soon."

"I'd have liked to go to the wedding. I like weddings. I'd have cried, though. I always do."

"My dancing is not that bad."

"Ha. It is."

They laughed, made dinner, and sat down to eat.

"We're good, aren't we, Mike?"

"We're really good."

"I'm not proposing or anything, but you should know—I'd want to be married. To have kids, I mean. Are you against marriage?"

"Against it? No. Not at all. I don't think you have to be married to be happy with someone, but I don't rule it out."

"Just wondered. You can relax now. I just wondered, that's all."
They kissed.

*

Adam arrived like a hurricane.
They managed to move some of his belongings into his room, but his coats, boxes, and other random items were scattered across the lounge.
Mike was keen to finish unpacking, but Adam had ground to a halt.
"I'm a pig, I know. I'll finish later. I will. Thanks for helping so far."
"No problem. Probably best we get this last bit done, though, yeah?"
"I will. I will. It's just—I said I'd meet a couple of the lads at the pub around the corner. Just to, y'know, get to know the place. My new regular."
"Right."
"You could come if you like. They're a bit rough, mind."
"Ha. That'd be good, but I said I'd go to Sherifat's for dinner. I'll see you later, though."
Adam was out the door in seconds.
Mike looked around the disarray. Some of the clothes smelled strange—sweat, dampness, and something else he couldn't quite place.
Mike came home around 11:30 p.m. to find the house full of people.
His music system was blaring rap music.
"I linked up my phone. I'll set my stuff up tomorrow—hope you don't mind me plugging in."
Mike forced a smile and scanned the room.
Three guys were crammed on the sofa, and another appeared asleep in a chair.
"No. Fine. Welcome. All."
Mike left for work early the following day.
When he got home that evening, the house was still a mess.
He tidied up.

Adam didn't improve.

Mike started staying at Sherifat's as often as possible.

The one benefit—sharing rent with Adam meant Mike could save a little from his salary.

Sherifat had already started talking about renting a place together.

Their leases wouldn't allow it yet, but they could make it happen in a few months.

In the first month, Adam crashed his car.

"I'm fuckin' struggling with rent this month, Mike. I need to get the car fixed to get to work. Not worth involving my insurers. Any chance you could cover it until next month?"

Mike sighed. "Yeah, I can do that. Bad luck with the car. Maybe give me half back in May and the rest with June's rent. Okay?"

"That'd be great, Mike. You're a pal."

A couple of weeks later, Mike checked in.

"Did the car get sorted?"

"Bloody hell. As I said, I got a quote, so it didn't go through insurance. But when they took a look, they found damage to a steering rod—wanted more money. I won't be able to pay you back next month after all. Sorry, mate."

Mike exhaled. "Okay. No problem. I don't need it right now, anyway. You can still cover this month's rent, though, yeah?"

"Yeah, I'm pretty sure I can do that. Oh, and did I mention—I've got a few of the guys coming over on Saturday for the rugby and that?"

Mike raised a brow. "Oh. Okay. I'll stay at Sherifat's then. Yeah?"

"Yeah, sound."

On Sunday afternoon, Mike and Sherifat returned to the house.

It was completely trashed.

Dozens of empty bottles littered the lounge.

The kitchen table was covered in random junk—

An ashtray.
An empty whisky bottle.
Wine glasses.
A tin of shoe polish.
Screwdrivers.
Two unmatched socks.
Mike shook his head.
They walked toward his bedroom. His bed had been slept in. On his bedside table, there was a note.
'Sorry, mate. I think I'd be better off kipping on friends' floors for a while. Sorry.'
Mike stared at it.
Then, in a perfect impression of Ted Hastings from Line of Duty, he muttered,
"Jesus, Mary, and Joseph, and the wee donkey."
Sherifat laughed, assuming it was nothing serious.
Then, she read the note.
Her face dropped.
"Chai! This is not funny, Mike. He has hopped it. He owes you all that money." She gestured around the room. "And look at this mess!"
"Sorry. I know. The phrase just came to me. The lease has months to go, and we're jointly and severally liable. If he doesn't pay from here on . . ."
"You will be stuffed. What a bastard. Total bastard."
Mike spoke to the landlord, who confirmed the worst—
He was liable for the full rent.
But he should try tracking Adam down.
"I doubt you'll see a penny from him, though."
Sherifat remained supportive but couldn't help financially.
Mike knew she was still paying off student loans and supporting family obligations.
His mum was less sympathetic.
"Goodness, Michael, this is yet another occasion where your kind nature gets the better of you. People will exploit you if you keep going on like this."
Mike did not argue.
She was right.

Chapter 37

During the final few months of covering the entire rent, Mike and Sherifat discussed their options for when his lease ended. She was living with another university colleague, and moving in with her wasn't feasible.
They viewed several rental houses, but none were as well-maintained or well-located as Mike's current home. Like most university properties, her lease also ran until September, so they decided she would move in with him at that point.
The transition was seamless.
Although they had already spent much of their time together at each other's homes, living together brought a newfound sense of privacy. They relished the freedom to create their own space, free from housemates and compromises.
The biggest realisation? They got on exceptionally well.
Both were easy-going, naturally considerate, and willing to compromise—a harmonious existence.
They moved in together at the start of September and volunteered extra hours on campus to help with Clearing for undergraduate programs.
Their warm and approachable personalities were ideal for the role—welcoming accepted students and offering support to those who didn't meet the required grades.
Their decision to volunteer was partly influenced by Sherifat's suggestion—sacrificing some summer break time so they could visit her hometown, Lagos, at its best in November.

*

The night before their flight, they debated what to wear.
"I guess we dress lightly. D'yer think?" Mike asked. "I know that feeling—stepping off the plane and getting smacked by a wall of heat."

"For sure," Sherifat nodded. "But hopefully, the harmattan will be blowing. Remember? The cool, dry wind from the Sahara? Lagos is on the coast, so it's never unbearable, but the breeze makes all the difference—even if it kicks up a bit of dust."

"This top, then?" Mike held up a lemon short-sleeved shirt.

"Perfect."

"And these summer-weight chinos?"

"Yes. A true . . . holidaymaker," she teased.

Sherifat had already packed and laid out her travel outfit.

"I can't wait to show you everything," she said, smiling. "I'm glad we'll see Funmilayo and the family, but I want time—just us."

Mike walked over and kissed her. "It'll be lovely."

The flight was smooth. The heat hit immediately.

"London times two," Mike muttered, staring at the traffic chaos.

"Now you see why we're staying on the island—Lekki," Sherifat grinned.

"Ha. You did mention tranquil in your travel blog."

"And it is. You'll see."

It was.

ResortLife wasn't a typical hotel—more of a beach retreat. Nestled among trees, their cabin was a short walk from the lagoon and mango forest.

"Oh, my days, it's a tropical paradise," Mike said, taking in the palm trees and golden sand.

"Told you." Sherifat smiled. "Tomorrow, we swim. Idyllic. But tonight, we see Funmilayo for dinner."

"A quick snack first?"

"Sure. I'll get my tour guide outfit."

"Ha. I'll spot it if you slip into sales mode. How long did you work here?"

"Four years. But not my best years. Too much partying—it got out of hand. I'm more suited to being an older guest now."

"Everyone has a past," Mike said, brushing it off.

"Chai. I don't think you and Lydia were as full-on. You were holding down a job and playing gigs. I didn't know one day from the next."

She brushed down her dress as if shaking off the past. Then, in mock seriousness, she switched to her tour guide voice—
"You wan chop? Our first stop—Glover Court Suya."
"Lead on."
"Suya, heh?"
"Uh-huh," Sherifat replied, her mouth full.
"So, it's like a kebab with different meat?"
"It's ram, seasoned with salt, onions, ground peanut, pepper, and spices."
"I can taste paprika and cayenne."
"Well done, Jamie Oliver."
They exchanged smiles, settling into their island paradise.
They arrived at the restaurant early.
"It's booked under Funmilayo's surname—Ngozi," Sherifat said as they approached the entrance.
Inside, the atmosphere was a blend of fine dining and casual warmth.
They didn't wait long before Funmilayo, her husband Sobowale, and little Orisa arrived.
Mike watched as Sherifat and Funmilayo embraced tightly and repeatedly. He shook Sobowale's hand, then bent down to greet Orisa, who beamed at him.
When he stood back up, Funmilayo hugged him, and he kissed her cheek in greeting.
The evening unfolded with stories and reminiscing.
Funmilayo met Sobowale at *ResortLife* years ago when she and Sherifat worked there.
Throughout dinner, Sobowale remained polite but expressed reluctance, as if he'd rather be anywhere else.
On their way back to the resort, Mike finally voiced his thoughts.
"Are your sister and her husband okay? He seemed... off. Like they'd just had a row or something."
"Well spotted," Sherifat sighed. "She told me in the ladies' room—things are coming to a head. I mentioned how they met, but the truth is, he was a guest, she got pregnant, and they married out of obligation. He's been resentful ever since. They don't get on. They're completely different. Only Orisa has kept them together, but..."

"But that might not be enough anymore," Mike finished.
"Exactly. He wants out."
"That's such a shame. She seems lovely. And little Orisa..."
"She is a sweetie, yes? I told Funmilayo I'd meet up with her before we leave—just the two of us. I think she needs to talk."
"Absolutely."
Mike and Sherifat spent hours at Africa's longest swimming pool the following day.
In the afternoon, they explored different activities.
Mike loved the Perspex-bottom canoe, peering at the marine life below, but being dragged around in a giant rubber ring by a speedboat was the real winner.
"No wonder you stayed here so long. It's amazing," he said.
"A lot of fun, for sure," Sherifat replied.
But Mike sensed something unspoken in her tone—a half-truth. He let it go.
They enjoyed a romantic dinner that evening, the ocean stretching endlessly before them.
The next day, Sherifat was eager to show Mike the city's culture. They visited Terra Kulture, where exhibits showcased the richness and diversity of Nigerian languages, arts, and history.
They wandered through the Lekki Arts and Crafts Market, admiring wooden sculptures, intricate masks, jewellery, and Ankara fabrics. They picked out a few pieces for their home.
That night, after dinner, Sherifat left to meet Funmilayo.
Mike stayed back, relaxing in their cabin.
When she returned, her expression was troubled.
"She should never have married him," she said quietly. "He's verbally and sometimes physically abusive."
Mike frowned. "That's awful. What will she do?"
"She's weighing her options. But she knows she has to leave."
Determined not to let the news overshadow their trip, Sherifat arranged a mangrove boat tour for the next day.
They spent hours gliding through the water, then explored Lekki Conservation Centre, walking its breathtaking treetop canopy trail and spotting monkeys, tortoises, crocodiles, and rare birds.
The forest was magnificent.

Mike knew this memory would stay with him—a paradise, untouched and serene.

Back home, Christmas crept up on them.

Mike loved the simple joys of the season—getting a tree, decorating their home, and hanging lights and cards.

One evening, as they sat on the sofa, Mike noticed a card on the table—a couple sitting before a blazing fire, wrapped in the glow of Christmas lights.

"That's us," he murmured. "Peaceful. Happy together. Just... happy."

He closed his eyes, absorbing the moment.

Stability. Tranquillity. Happiness.

Nine blissful months passed.

One evening, Sherifat hung up from a phone call with her sister, shaking her head.

"She's filed for divorce. Unreasonable behaviour. Damned right."

"Good," Mike said firmly. "He's clearly a shit. I don't know what she ever saw in him."

"It just proves marriage isn't the key to raising a child," Sherifat sighed. "What matters is a healthy relationship."

They sat in the lounge a few nights later, music playing softly in the background.

"Mike. We said we're good, didn't we?"

"Yeah. We are. We said. You know that."

She hesitated, then said, "I was thinking... should we try to have a baby? Not get married or anything. Just... I'm not getting any younger. And I'd love to have your child."

Mike blinked. "A baby? Are we ready for that?"

She watched him carefully.

"I mean... if that's what you want—then yeah, I do too. I totally do." He chuckled. "Okay. What does it involve, exactly?"

Laughing, she poked him in the ribs. "So, that's a 'yes, maybe'?"

"It's a yes from me," Mike replied, resisting the urge to say it in Simon Cowell's voice.

Chapter 38

Claire and Eddie had settled into a routine of seeing each other often. More often than not, Claire went to his place.
His lifestyle was intoxicating—a whirlwind of adventure and adrenaline.
Since their ballooning trip, Eddie had introduced her to hang-gliding, jet skiing, sailing, and kiting. She had even attempted rock climbing.
Weekends were exhilarating—a rush of motion, risk, and energy.
Adrenaline. Invigorating. The sex was good.
It lacked the raw passion she had once had with Simon—but somehow, there was more to life than that.
Eddie was excitement.

*

Claire found lecturing easy. Being close in age to her students worked to her advantage. Preparation for sessions became second nature. Another encounter with the lascivious Professor Ferguson.
"Well done on submitting those papers. I knew you were good."
"Thanks. Yes, I was pleased that both were accepted. Not many amendments. They won't be in print for ages, though."
"Yes. Longer delays with better journals. Probably time you opened up a new avenue for your research. Come and chat with me about it."
"Right. Yes. Right."
Claire had no intention of visiting Fergus in his office. *Just creepy. Still, I should extend my research.*
Instead of meeting with Fergus, Claire discussed possibilities with Stephanie Kourakakis. She decided to delve deeper into creativity within historical networks of artists.

*

The following weekend, she brought it up with Eddie—but his reaction was lukewarm.

Eddie rarely talked about work.

He had an admin job at Conwy Council and had been doing it for years. He never mentioned career aspirations—never spoke of promotions or changes.

His life was about his activities—his thrills.

In many ways, Claire liked that—their relationship was light, uncomplicated, purely fun.

But this time, his lack of interest disappointed her.

Chapter 39

Mike and Sherifat had settled into their relationship and routines.

Sherifat continued to build her career as a lecturer.

Earlier in 2013, the university had hinted at an upcoming lectureship vacancy and suggested that Mike would be considered favourably.

In the meantime, he continued his postdoctoral research, publishing several papers and submitting work to international conferences.

Outside of academia, Mike and Jennie kept their regular slot at the local bar. Their performances led to invitations to play at private parties, booked by people who had heard them at the bar.

By September, however, there was still no sign of Sherifat getting pregnant.

A couple of late periods had sparked hope, but each time it led to nothing.

That morning, yet another negative test.

Sherifat walked back into the bedroom, holding the test in her hand.

"I think we had better both go for tests," she said firmly. "Something isn't right, Mike."

Mike exhaled heavily, running a hand through his hair.

"Yeah. I think you're right," he admitted. "It's disappointing. We've tried everything we've read about. But there are treatments—things that can help on your side, too."

"I am sure we will be fine," she reassured him. "But it's better to get help now than to wait any longer."

After speaking with their GP, they were both referred for tests.

The waiting period felt like forever.

Weeks passed. Then, finally, a call.

Sherifat's results came first.

Her gynaecologist found no immediate reason for her difficulty in conceiving. The GP assured her they were still waiting for Mike's results and promised to chase them up.

Another two weeks dragged by.
Then, at 6:00 PM on a Tuesday, Mike's phone rang.
He listened in silence, his grip on the phone tightening.
Several long minutes passed.
When Sherifat arrived home an hour later, she immediately sensed something was wrong.
Mike sat at the kitchen table, his face pale, eyes bloodshot, and he stared at nothing.
"Wetin dey happen? What is the matter?" she asked, her voice laced with concern.
Mike blinked slowly, his voice hollow.
"The GP called. It's me. I can't ever have children."
He swallowed hard.
"I'm infertile. Permanently. Full stop."
His voice cracked, and he started crying again.
"I'm sorry. So sorry."
Sherifat rushed to him, wrapping her arms tightly around his shoulders.
"Na so. Not 'sorry.' It is not your fault." She pulled back slightly, looking into his eyes. "What exactly did she say? How can she be so certain? We know there are treatments. We have read about them. She has no right to make you feel like this."
Mike shook his head.
"No, she's right."
He exhaled sharply
"I need to go in and get the full report, but I remember the key terms. Azoospermia—zero sperm count. Absolute zero."
He rubbed his forehead as if trying to steady himself.
"It's from my chemotherapy. The leukaemia treatment."
He picked up a scrap of paper on which he had scribbled medical terms.
"The drugs I had—Cyclophosphamide and Cytosine Arabinoside. Boys treated with those almost always end up permanently infertile."
He swallowed again, his Adam's apple bobbing.

"Apparently, although puberty happens normally, the chemicals cause irreparable damage to—" he glanced down at the paper again—"the seminiferous epithelium. The lining of the testicular tubules. The part responsible for sperm production. End of story."

"Oh, Mike."

Sherifat tightened her embrace.

"We will see. What a shock. I am sorry I wasn't here when you got the call. But we will see. We will get second opinions. Do not give up. We will see."

But Mike had given up hope.

He tried to put his feelings into words.

"I feel... inadequate."

His voice was low, almost a whisper.

"I just feel totally inadequate."

He leaned back against the sofa, staring at the ceiling.

"It's not like I ever thought my purpose in life was just to have children. But now that it's been taken away from me, I can't see the point of anything. Anything."

Sherifat exhaled softly, watching him.

"You are bound to feel like this, Mike."

She reached for his hand and squeezed it gently.

"It is a man ting. I understand. Men never want to feel inadequate. Ever."

Her voice was warm and steady.

"But this is all a shock. We will need time to come to terms with it."

Mike sighed deeply, rubbing his hands together.

"But I feel so guilty."

He looked up at her, his eyes filled with pain.

"It's not just about me. I'm depriving you. You've always said how much you want to be a mother. And now, because of me, that can't happen. I just feel... terrible."

Sherifat shook her head firmly.

"It is all just a shock, Mike. Just a shock."

But it was more than that.

Chapter 40

Claire found her new research topic on creativity fascinating, but finding the time to focus on it was a challenge.

As the term ended, she had assumed she'd spend Christmas with Eddie—until he called to say he needed to handle "a lot of boring stuff" repairing his equipment.

"Usual winter job," he explained. "Christmas break's the only chance. I'd be daft not to."

Claire had mixed feelings.

No fun, but at least I'll have time to finish my paper.

In the final week before the holidays, Claire dropped by Stephanie Kourakakis' office to discuss publication options.

She breezed in, grinning.

"Hi, Steph. Where might be best for that paper I was telling you about? Any ideas?"

Stephanie's face lit up—genuinely pleased that Claire had sought her advice.

"Absolutely! Great. Yes!" She leaned forward eagerly. "You should submit it to the top international creativity conference. It moves locations every year. I think it's a three-day event in the U.S. next year. And I'd bet you're just in time for submissions. They usually close around the end of January."

She quickly pulled up the website and scanned for deadlines.

"Yes, here! End of January. It's at Randolph University in Indiana."

"Fantastic!" Claire exclaimed. Then, a thought struck her. "Who pays for international conferences, though?"

"The department does. You have to apply for funding."

"Oh! I will, then. But do I even stand a chance? It sounds expensive—conference fees, accommodation, travel..."

"Absolutely. Professor Ferguson is always keen to get new researchers out there. It's great for your career, boosts your CV, and helps the department's research assessment rating. Win-win."

"Wow. Amazing!"

"Grab the form from the Research Office," Stephanie advised. "Get it to him this week. He'll think he's giving you a Christmas present."

*

That weekend, Claire met up with Manisha to share the news.
"So, the real academic now, heh?" Manisha teased.
"Ha."
"And an international globetrotter. Look at you!"
"Right? Sometimes I ask myself—'Who would've thought?' Not anyone who knew me back at WMU. Jill? Simon?"
"Well, I would've thought it," Manisha replied matter-of-factly. "I told you back then—you were special. Are you still in touch with Jill? I assume not, Simon?"
"Simon? No way. I don't want him anywhere near my life." Claire shook her head, amused. "And Jill? We just drifted apart. She'd never believe any of this. Never."
"Shame."
Manisha squeezed Claire's hand, her expression warm.
"Anyway, tell me everything, Sakhi. This masterpiece of yours."
They talked for hours.
A little about the paper.
A lot more about Claire's nerves over presenting at an international event.
As always, Claire soaked in Manisha's wisdom. They reminisced, laughed, and caught up.
As Claire got up to leave, Manisha put her arm around her and kissed her cheek.
"I love it when you visit. Let's do this again soon."
"Me too. You've always been so good to me."

*

Claire bumped into Professor Ferguson in the corridor on the last Friday of term.
"Ah, Claire. Good, good," he said, nodding.
Claire stopped in her tracks.

"Your application for Randolph crossed my desk," he continued. "And yes, that will be fine."
"Oh, great! Thanks. Brilliant!"
"I looked at my schedule," Ferguson added, stroking his chin. "Might be possible for me to attend as well. If I shuffle a couple of commitments around. I like to keep my hand in, you know. Might not present, but it's always good to see what the bright young things are up to. Let's hope, eh?"
Claire forced a polite smile.
"Right. Okay."
Scheisse.

Chapter 41

By January 2014, as Mike continued to grapple with his infertility, he found himself trapped in the same cycle of self-blame that had haunted him since childhood.
Couldn't love enough.
His failure with William.
His failure with his father.
Leaving his mother to cope alone too much.
Genuinely do enough to help Lydia?
And now this.
Hurting Sherifat.
Christmas had been particularly hard. They'd gone to a few gigs together, including one of Jennie and him, but he could sense the weight of it on Sherifat. The centrality of children during the season screamed 'gap' at her. As the weeks passed, the fear crept in—the fear that Sherifat would leave.
Why wouldn't she?
He vowed to be kinder. Even kinder. Please her in every way he could.

One evening, he called his mother.
"I'm trying to make it up to her, Mum. She's so lovely. She shouldn't have to deal with this."
"She's not alone, Michael," his mother replied gently. "Many couples go through this. They muddle through. You want to do everything for her now, but you can go too far. Like you did with Lydia."
"What do you mean?"
"Everyone has to take responsibility for their own feelings, Michael. You can't carry it all for her. Sherifat has to find her own way with this."
Mike felt comforted. For about an hour. Then, the guilt flooded back. *Deprived my mum of ever having a grandchild.* Fresh guilt. Mike recognised his inability to come to terms with it. He tried to recall Alison Jenkins' words—the counsellor from his childhood—but her advice felt hazy.

Except for one thing.

"Write it down, Michael. Try to make sense of it on paper."

And so, he did.

He wrote endlessly, hoping to find a way through it all.

Life with Sherifat changed dramatically after the diagnosis.

Things didn't recover.

The news fractured their intimacy.

Sex became stressful.

She felt that sex before trying for a baby had been fine and that sex with a goal had made sense, but now?

Now, it felt pointless.

Contrived. False.

A sense of loss consumed her—a grief for the child she had been deprived of.

She imagined the future they might have had.

She thought of her sister, Funmilayo.

How lucky she was.

No partner, but a child at least.

Sherifat's love for Mike faded.

Slowly, irritation crept in.

Then anger.

Until she saw their entire life together as futile.

She never said those words out loud.

But the last time she spoke to him, she simply said—

"This is not my future. It cannot be. I have to leave."

And Mike understood.

But understanding didn't make it easier.

*

Coming to terms with losing Sherifat was a slow, grinding process.

It wasn't just losing her.

It was losing the future he had imagined.

The image of the Christmas card. The memory of her playing *Schindler's List*. His memory of breaking out of a teardrop. The news of Lydia going off with the other guy. Torrents of negativity.

He had almost believed she cared for him.
And yet—this.
Alongside his self-blame, anger simmered.
And so, he wrote.
A song entitled *You*.

> *You. You were the lighthouse*
> *Me. I was at sea*
> *You gave me direction*
> *A place where I should be*
> *Found my way to you*
> *My chance for rescue*
> *By you*
> *You. You could see further*
> *Free. No storms at sea*
> *You turned your light from me*
> *Saw a place you should be*
> *Found your way to where*
> *Everything could be there*
> *For you*
> *Is it better now for you*
> *Doing what you want to do*
> *Isn't life about not you*
> *But helping other people to*
> *Live the lives they couldn't do*
> *Do all the things that they can't do*
> *Without you*
> *You. You are the lighthouse*
> *Me. I am at sea*
> *You could give me direction*
> *A place where I should be*
> *Can't find my way to you*
> *No chance for rescue*
> *By you*

*

He spent months trying to make sense of it all.

Had he ever truly been in love with Sherifat?
Or had he just been comfortable?
He realised something.
Being settled and at peace with someone—
That's not love.
But gradually, over the months, he started to see positivity in his world again.
He was twenty-seven.
He had secured his lectureship.
His research papers had been accepted for publication.
And now—
He had the chance to present at a conference in America.

Chapter 42

Claire worked hard over Christmas and finished her conference paper. She had spoken to Eddie about it on the phone, but he had seemed distant. Apart from writing, she hadn't done much over the break—just went out for runs. When term restarted in the second week of January, she rang him.
"Are you coming to see me, or am I coming to Conwy?"
Eddie hesitated.
"Neither. Er, not this weekend."
Silence.
"Well, actually, Claire, I've decided this part-time lover thing isn't for me. Too much time on my own, you know? Get up to mischief. Anyway, sorry. I've met someone here. Lovely girl. We get on brill. I saw a lot of her over Christmas, and it kind of settled it. That's what I want. Sorry."
Claire froze.
"But when we spoke on Christmas Day, you sounded fine."
More silence.
Realisation.
"Oh, I see. You've been seeing her. A girlfriend. That's why we didn't meet up? You lied. You just wanted to be with her?"
"Er, well. Not totally. I did plan to do those jobs. I did some of them. But not 24/7, so yes, I did see her. Sorry."
"Bastard. You lying bastard. You've been seeing her for ages, haven't you?"
"Not ages, Claire. I'm sorry."
"Sorry? Piss off with your 'sorries'. You're a bastard. Get lost."
She hung up.
I'll find things to do around here.
I might carry on doing some of the things we did.
I don't fucking need him.
He was boring anyway.
Later that evening, memories of all her relationships.
What had they been about?
Relating?
Being cared for?

Mothered?
Sex?
And now, fun and excitement.
Excitement is not love.
How different people are.
She considered calling Manisha.
But then, not big news.
These things happen. Move on.
She returned to the university on Monday.
She submitted her paper for the conference.
Walking down the corridor, she spotted Professor Ferguson stepping out of his office.
No escape.
"Ah, Claire. Bad news, I'm afraid. Randolph."
Bloody great. Crap year this has started.
She forced a smile, turned away, and started walking off.
"I can't make it, I mean. I couldn't sort it. You'll have to go on your own."
Claire stopped.
Turned back.
"What a shame."
Maybe there is a God.
Surprisingly, Claire quickly settled back into single life.
She hadn't gone out much with the girls in her department before, but they welcomed her.
She hadn't lost her *joi de vivre*, and the four of them went clubbing most weekends.
She reconnected with Sarah and Emma in Birmingham.
Emma had moved in with a guy.
Sarah invited her over a few times, and they shared a bottle of wine and slagged off men.

Chapter 43

In August 2014, Jeff, a colleague from Mike's department, popped into his office.
"So, tell me about this conference presentation of yours."
"It's about children's relationships with their parents and their subsequent adult creativity. But with a twist."
"In what way?"
"It's well known that musical composition involves continual experimentation with elements like notes, chords, and rhythm, and compositional rules like modes, scales, forms, and tonality. That means novelty can exist in a single piece or extend to creating an entirely new genre of music."
"Picks up on your love of music."
"Exactly. And at last year's Paris conference, there was a paper on jazz improvisation and freestyle rapping. It was refreshing to see research expanding beyond classical music."
"And remember a few months ago, Jeff, when we talked about the team at Cambridge developing relative novelty measures?"
"Yeah?"
"So, I picked classical, jazz, and rock music. Using relative novelty measures, I identified three musicians who were significant in terms of both historical novelty—meaning a clear departure from established patterns—and psychological novelty, meaning how their own music evolved over their lifetimes."
"Cool."
"The paper focuses on Rachmaninoff, Charlie Parker, and Jimi Hendrix."
Jeff nodded. "Well, that's a diverse group, for sure."
"Ha, yeah. I also analysed their childhood experiences with their parents. Since all my subjects are male, this study technically only applies to boys' relationships with parents."
"That's because of sex-role stereotyping throughout history, including in the arts. Maybe you could explicitly seek examples of female composers in a follow-up study."

"Definitely. That said, this research highlights the impact of strong maternal influence in the absence of fathers. It aligns with previous work on psychological androgyny, in which artists draw on both masculinity and femininity to express sensitivity and empathy. As Kemp (1985) suggested," Mike adjusted his voice to quote precisely, "the task demands of music and other creative arts highlight the need for artists to utilise a full range of cognitive and emotional responses in their work."
"Yes, I've read those studies."
"In this case, it's not that the mothers intentionally feminised their sons. Rather, the children were exposed to a broader and deeper range of feminine perspectives, which expanded their cognitive and emotional capacities."
"Excellent stuff, Mike. This will go down a storm, I'm sure."
"*Fortissimo*, perhaps?"

*

Mike flew to Indiana to present his paper. At O'Hare Airport, he found the Hertz rental lot easily enough—a cornucopia of cars. But not American cars. Nissans. BMWs. Mercedes. He'd opted for the "Free-To-Go Pass" and picked something from their "Fun Collection." A BMW 3 Series. Not just a fun car. But at this price? Why not?
"Welcome to Hertz," the clerk said.
A spirited manner for 6:30 AM.
Despite his best efforts, Mike couldn't match the enthusiasm.
"I have a reservation—Mike Lewis," he said, at least warmly enough.
He handed over his documents.
Hearing his accent, the young man perked up even more.
"Welcome to America, Sir. I'll have you on your way... in a jiffy," he added in a clipped English tone, like Hugh Grant in a rom-com.
Mike smiled.
"All good. Just sign here, here, and here, Dr Lewis."
Mike signed.
"Your car's been brought up, Sir."

"OK with the controls? Just remember to get in on the right side—"

"No, I mean the left," the clerk grinned.

A stock gag for visiting Brits.

Mike got in, flicking through the controls.

"All good? Full tank. You're good to go. Have a great trip."

"Thanks. I will," Mike replied, his attempt at enthusiasm landing somewhere between mild pleasure and polite obligation.

Once on the road, he set the satnav, connected his phone via Bluetooth, and pulled up the playlist he'd downloaded back home.

He eased off the forecourt, cautious at first.

After a few high-alert minutes, he relaxed.

He smiled to himself.

"OK, Google. Play the 'USA Road Trip' playlist."

Sunshine.

Harry Nilsson's *Everybody's Talkin'* started.

He loved the chord progression in that song.

He imagined himself playing it on guitar.

Next, *Turn! Turn! Turn!* by The Byrds.

A playlist put together by a fifty-something-year-old?

Not necessarily.

He'd seen students at his university memorise these classic songs.

Wouldn't have happened in his day.

Back then, students would rather be caught dead than enjoy something from twenty years ago.

But now, in a world of limitless streaming, artists aren't as tied to their era.

The age of a track? Irrelevant.

And anyway—these were great songs.

Song after song.

They made him feel good.

Life was good.

The miles rolled by.

The drive from O'Hare to Lafayette was uneventful.

It was a 120-mile trip, almost entirely down Interstate 65.

He didn't bother stopping.

So little traffic compared to UK motorways.
Not much concentration needed here.
His mind wandered.
He imagined he was in a movie.
Crossing the state line into Indiana.
The phrase conjured possibilities.
A road movie—maybe police in pursuit.
Or—
A Western.
Indiana. The land of the Indians.
For a moment, he pictured himself riding through the 1860s, riverboats drifting down the Wabash River, French being spoken in the streets.
Then—back to reality.
Lafayette was modern and bustling.
A couple of careful turns—conscious reminders of how to approach right-hand turns.
Or lefts.
No room for idle thoughts now.
As Mike drove through the campus entrance, he was struck by how familiar it all felt.
The university's vast swathes of lawns were as immaculate as ever, and the trees—so many—stood proud and full, their leaves bursting with colour, silently declaring their age and permanence.
The white buildings, gleaming in the sunlight, seemed even brighter.
Perhaps it's just a trick of the light.
Though he sat in the cool comfort of his air-conditioned rental, he knew that stepping outside would bring the full force of the morning heat.
It was 8:30 AM.
The sky was a flawless blue.
No wonder the buildings gleamed.
Clear signage led him in the right direction.
A bold yellow sign read:
IMCRC PARKING →
The lot was enormous.

Despite arriving later than many other delegates, there were still plenty of open spaces.

He followed the flow of parked cars toward the Parisher section, where most attendees had clustered.

And there it was—the familiar conference scene.

Small groups gathered in conversation, colleagues reuniting to exchange pleasantries, handshakes, and nods.

Only then did he notice the breeze that seemed to belong to this place, ever-present, causing shirts and dresses to flutter involuntarily.

And this was America.

Men in light, sophisticated, cream-coloured suits stood among those donning bright, boldly patterned shirts.

The women brought their own vibrancy—stylish dresses in understated yet elegant patterns, the air buzzing with quiet excitement.

As Mike put the car into Park, something caught his eye.

A scene that seemed to pull him magnetically.

Just beyond the bordering ridge of grass, he saw her.

A woman, mid-laughter, her long copper-coloured hair catching the sunlight, a flutter of movement as she brushed a strand from her face.

For a moment, the rest of the world faded.

He barely noticed the group around her.

Just her.

The joy in her expression, the grace of her motion, the effortless radiance of her smile.

And then—had she sensed him?

She turned toward his car, though he doubted she could see him clearly inside it.

Still, he found himself smiling back.

The moment had lasted only a fraction of a second.

But somehow, it burned into his memory.

A face of life, warmth, abandon.

As he walked into the heart of the campus, he passed several chapels.

Not something you'd find at most UK universities.

The old buildings rose around him—American old, at least.

One hundred fifty years, maybe?
And yet, she was back in his mind.
Not her—just her hair, her hand, her smile.
What colour was her dress?
The dress had moved in the wind; he was sure of that.
Was it blue?
His imagination drifted forward.
Blue? Then her eyes must be blue.
He is meeting her.
That smile again.
She brushes her hair back.
And then—whoosh.
The thought vanished.
Back to reality.
The Psychological Sciences building stood ahead.
Three stories of solid concrete.
Seventies, perhaps?
No matter.
The conference welcome desk sat just inside the hallway.
"Mike Lewis, University of Leamington," he said brightly.
By 8:30 am, he found he could muster a chirpy tone.
The team snapped into action.
A doctoral student checked his details on a laptop.
Another handed him his name badge.
"Welcome to the International Multi-Disciplinary Creativity Research Conference, sir."
A third student passed him the standard conference bag filled with:
A printed copy of the proceedings
A notepad and pen
Flyers—so many flyers—advertising upcoming related conferences
"Welcome to Randolph. Coffee is on the second floor. Elevators through the double doors on your left. Enjoy the conference, sir."
"Looking forward to it," Mike said, turning with a casual half-wave.

He knew that it would be hard to find a quiet moment to plan his day once upstairs.

Conferences like this were huge, with multiple parallel sessions. Each track followed a theme, organising related presentations into distinct blocks throughout the day.

A quick skim of the program confirmed his session:

"Creativity in Music"—11:30 am to 1:00 pm.

Which floor? Which room?

He'd figure that out later.

He wanted to pick a morning session before the first break at 11:00 AM.

He scanned the options.

Too many technical composition papers in his own track.

Then—something else.

A talk on Renaissance to Impressionist artists.

Perfect.

But—damn.

It ran at the same time as his own paper.

He sighed. What a bummer.

Maybe he could track down the author at the evening Gala dinner later.

He scanned for name badges.

No sign of her.

*

Later that night, back in his hotel room, the girl with the copper-coloured hair was back in his thoughts.

Just imagination of her.

A hotel bar.

Chatting her up.

And then—sleep took over.

Day Two.

Following the final plenary session, Mike took the chance to explore.

He asked around and was told:

"Martell Forest is stunning this time of year."

So, he drove the few miles out.

The golden leaves.
The fiery red.
The exact shade of *her* hair.

Chapter 44

A busy work year passed. In the autumn of 2014, Mike attended another creativity conference, this time in Glasgow.

His latest research, expanding on childhood experiences and creativity in music, had been accepted for the symposium.

The event was brief—just an afternoon and the following morning—but the travel time to Scotland made it feel longer, despite Glasgow being an easy train ride for him.

Over time, he had come to prefer these short, focused conferences.

When he was younger, they had felt like exciting opportunities—chances to socialise, network, and escape the daily routine.

At thirty-two, he found that conference attendance only delayed his work. The longer he was away, the more tasks piled up.

As he sat on the train, he caught himself wondering—

Have I become a workaholic?

All around him, a choreographed routine played out.

Passengers unzipped their bags, flipped open laptops, and immersed themselves in their screens.

Across the aisle, a family of four—parents and two children—each performed their ritual device-opening, their gazes glued to screens.

No conversation. No interaction. Just tasks in hand.

A flicker from his laptop—an incoming email—snapped his focus back.

But still, his mind wandered again.

It's not just task focus, he mused. It's anti-social behaviour.

Once upon a time, reading a book in public was an invitation to a conversation—someone might interrupt to ask, "What are you reading?"

Now?

Interrupting a laptop user felt like a violation—as if you were trespassing into their private world.

Maybe that was the point.

Perhaps laptops were shields designed to ward off invaders.

He chuckled to himself.
He listened closely, tuning in to the sounds around him.
How much real conversation is happening on this train?
The answer: almost none.
Only a pair of older women exchanged pleasantries, sharing their reasons for travel.
Everyone else? Silent. Transfixed.
Ever the scientist, Mike devised a theory.
People deeply engrossed in their screens were genuinely working.
But those who glanced around now and then?
Distracted. Unfocused. Perhaps even pretending to work.
If he could measure the time between each person's casual glance away from their device, he could determine whether their laptop was a "Taskmaster" or a "Shield."
The hours rolled by.
A few emails were answered—a quick scroll through BBC News.
And yet, truth be told, he preferred observing people over reading the news.
Then, a new variable struck him.
How long had someone been on the train?
How could he measure it?
He glanced at the scrolling time display on the back of the seat in front of him.
That's it.
The frequency with which people checked the time was a dead giveaway.
Not everyone was nervous about missing their stop—some wanted time to move faster.
The impatient ones? They had been on the train for too long.
As he rechecked the time, he smirked.
Like me.
The cold Glasgow air hit him as he stepped onto the platform.
It was fresh. Brisk.
A steady breeze rolled through, invigorating.
Is this how freedom tastes?

A taxi ride. A hotel check-in. A sigh as the door clicked shut behind him. Relief. And yet—
Why do I do this?
Every time, he asked himself the same question. Every time, he vowed to stop attending these unnecessary work events. And yet—here he was again.

The symposium's refreshments were scheduled from noon until 1:30 pm. Skipping the tea-making in his room, he headed straight down. At least they had fresh milk. A cup of tea. A sandwich. A familiar voice behind him.
"Mike!"
He turned.
Ben Shaw from Cardiff. True to form, Ben had already made the rounds. Within minutes, he rattled off who was there, who had cancelled, and which papers were worth attending.
"Oh, and Christopher Bevan's over there."
"Great! I haven't seen him in ages. I'll come over in a sec, yeah?"
But first, Mike needed to check the schedule. He scanned the programme booklet. Timing is everything. There—her paper was before his.
Perfect.
That meant he could catch her during the mid-afternoon break. He glanced around, hoping to spot her name badge.
Not yet.
He headed toward the main lecture theatre to upload his presentation.
Up on stage, he spotted Mohammed Shami, the symposium's chair.
"Mike! Good to see you. Looking forward to your paper."
"Hey, Mohammed. Thanks! The programme looks fantastic."
"You're up second," Mohammed said, gesturing to the computer setup.
Mike stepped forward, plugged in his USB drive, and dragged his PowerPoint file onto the desktop.
"So, we just need—"
Mohammed's voice trailed off.
His gaze shifted over Mike's shoulder.

"Ah. Here she is."
Mike turned around.
The person he'd been wanting to meet for months.
But it was *her*.

Chapter 45

Mike listened intently to her presentation, yet his gaze remained fixed on her rather than on the PowerPoint slides.
He admired the light, effortless way she moved—graceful, confident. Clearly fit.
Her voice carried a brightness, a slight Liverpudlian lilt, but mild—perhaps the Wirral?
And that smile.
And that hair.
He forced himself to refocus.
She spoke about artistic connections in the Renaissance—how artists knew one another and how techniques were transferred between them, leading to creative breakthroughs.
Fascinating.
But then she described how she imagined herself rising above them all in a hot-air balloon, seeing the threads that connected their work.
His mind drifted.
She's been ballooning. She must have.
He pictured her excitement—that same light in her eyes as she soared above landscapes.
Even as he began his own presentation, her presence lingered in his mind.
Years of public speaking had trained him to address the entire room, ensuring equal eye contact across the audience.
Yet, he found himself returning to her too often.
The nods of approval.
The beams of encouragement.
He spoke about creativity in musicians and the influence of early childhood experiences.
Building on his Randolph University paper, he emphasised maternal relationships and their role in shaping artistic sensitivity.
As the third and final paper in the session ended, the usual post-presentation bustle ensued.

Attendees rushed to capture the presenters—to ask questions, exchange contact information, and discuss possible collaborations.

Mike was immediately intercepted.

He glanced across the room—Claire stood surrounded by her own eager audience.

A queue.

Hope I can catch her later.

My findings on music and maternal influence may also apply to visual artists.

Would she be interested?

At large conferences, finding a specific person again was never guaranteed.

Mike searched for her during the afternoon break but didn't spot her.

He checked the programme—an upcoming session on computational creativity seemed interesting enough.

He heard a voice calling out as he made his way through the labyrinthine corridors.

"Dr Lewis! Dr Lewis!"

He turned.

There she was.

"Hi. I was hoping I'd catch you!"

She beamed, eyes alight with enthusiasm.

"I enjoyed your paper. I didn't get a chance to ask a question, but I wondered—have you done anything similar with visual arts creativity?"

"Great to meet you. It's Mike."

"Claire."

She extended her hand.

He shook it.

"Funny you ask," he said, smiling. "I was wondering if any of my findings might apply to visual arts."

She tilted her head. Intrigued.

"Are you set on going to this computational creativity session?"

"No. Just seemed a little more interesting than some of the other talks."

"Ditto. Want to grab a coffee instead?"

"Absolutely."

They settled into a corner sofa in the conference lounge.

Conversation flowed effortlessly.

They discussed creativity in art—how inspiration strikes, the role of intuition, and the intersection of psychology and artistic expression.

And he noticed—My God, she smells nice.

"How do you know what to do next in a painting?" he asked.

"Do you have a plan from the start?"

"No way," she said, shaking her head.

"Art is about not knowing. That's the whole point. It's a state where everything is possible. Every colour, every stroke—just options. The moment you're certain, you've lost the magic."

"Wow. Is that right?"

He leaned in, fascinated.

"Psychologically, not everyone can handle that," he mused. "We call it 'tolerance for ambiguity.'"

God, I sound like a textbook. Stop.

But she was hooked.

"I never thought about it that way. That's interesting."

He saw the spark in her eyes—' I want to know more' expression.

"'Art is a lie that tells the truth,'" she continued.

He blinked.

"That's Picasso."

She nodded.

"It's a lie because, in the end, it's just painted on canvas—but it reveals something real. A new truth."

He smiled.

"I love that. A lie that tells the truth."

God, she's fascinating.

"I always wonder—what makes something truly original?" she mused.

"That's exactly it. The difference between novelty and paradigm-shifting creativity."

Stop. Even worse.

"I guess we all analyse things psychologically, even if we don't mean to," he said quickly. "I've dabbled in photography, but put a paintbrush in my hand, and… well."
She laughed.
"Maybe you should try. You could see creativity in action."
He hesitated.
"Maybe I could get a few others to join, too," she added.
His mind raced.
How I'd love that. Watching her think and watching her create.
"Art is risk-taking," she said suddenly.
"So is research," he countered.
She nodded.
"What sort of things do you paint?" he asked.
"All sorts. I work through an idea or a theme and see what my art reveals. There's no separation between my art and my life. It always surprises me."
"Like your paper. The threads. You love threads."
Her eyes lit up.
"Exactly! And balloons."
"Balloons? Hang-gliding? Climbing? Risks?"
"Yes!" she laughed.
He grinned.
"Okay. Let's do it."
"Not the climbing, though," he added quickly. "I'd be scared to death."
A few days after the conference, Mike emailed Claire at her university address.
Initially, the emails were academic, discussing potential research collaborations.
Then, they shifted their focus to creativity in general.
Then, personal interests.
He asked to see her paintings.
She asked for his music recordings.

*

Within two weeks, their emails doubled in frequency—from weekly to twice a week.

They shared stories from their past.
Mike told her about his housemate conning him.
Her response was thoughtful and kind.
She decided—he was a good man.
One of the good ones.
He joked about her travel habits—"Are you heading to Birmingham by balloon or hang-glider?"
She laughed.
She liked this light-hearted, intelligent man.
Unlike Eddie, she felt a connection to him.
Mike admired the way she saw art in everything.
He loved that she appreciated his music.
And though she was polite about his photography, he sensed a pause in her praise.
Yet—he could hear her voice in every word she wrote.
He found Claire easy to be around.
She felt she could truly relate to him—to his mind and his world.

Chapter 46

On December 30th, Claire's phone rang.
It was Manisha.
Her voice was frantic, almost unrecognisable.
"Claire. Claire. It's David. David. He's dead. Claire—dead."
Claire froze.
"Wait—what? What happened? Where are you?"
"It's on the news. I'm still in Birmingham. I was flying out to meet him tonight. Texas. His family and all that."
"Right, so…?"
"He went earlier. I was going to join him for New Year. But this storm—it's killed people, Claire. It killed David."
Claire's breath hitched.
"His parents told me. It was a nightmare storm—blizzard, ice storm, tornado. The whole thing. Yesterday. It took out half the wall of their house in Garland. The wall fell on David. He's…he's gone, Claire."
"Oh my God. Manisha, I—"
Claire clutched the phone tighter.
"I saw it. On the news. The storm. But I didn't—"
Her stomach twisted.
"Shall I come up to see you? What time is it? I could—"
"No. No. I have to go. I have to get out there. See him. Sort things out. I don't know. I just—I won't be calling on New Year's Eve. Like I always do."
"Of course not. No. Right. When should I call you? Over there?"
"I can't say, Sakhi. That's why I'm ringing now. Just to let you know."
"Oh, Manisha. Yes. Thank you. I'm so sorry. So, so sorry. Please—just let me know when we can talk. If there's anything—anything I can do."
Manisha spent weeks in the States.
She told Claire they'd arranged a small family funeral there—what his parents wanted.
Then, from Texas, she would fly straight to Mumbai.
"I just need to be with my family for a while."

Claire understood.
"Take your time, Manisha. I'm here when you need me."

Chapter 47

By the end of December, Mike had come to appreciate the efficiency and structure at Devonport University. He had been assigned one of the department's doctoral student bursaries, which allowed him to start supervising a PhD student immediately under the guidance of the department's research professor responsible for doctoral students.

Mike's student was from Libya, and his research focused on: "Minority Culture Influences Upon Creative Thinking: A Study of Copts in Libya."

The department had also encouraged Mike to outline his personal research interests, which were listed alongside Marcos Yunam's details in his academic profile.

Marcos was bright and eager, and his passion for research was genuine and driven. Coming from a Coptic family himself, he often shared with Mike the challenges Copts faced as a minority in a predominantly Muslim country.

Late on Sunday night, around 11:00 p.m., Mike received an urgent email from Marcos.

'Hi Dr Lewis,
I am leaving the country temporarily to try to help my parents flee Libya, given the ongoing attacks on Christian communities—continuing from the murders in the Derna region last year. I won't have access to my mobile, but I can be reached at this email.
I apologise for any inconvenience.
Marcos'

Mike replied immediately.

'Hello Marcos,
I understand. Please be careful. Let me know as soon as you and your parents are safe.
Mike'

A response came within minutes.

'Hello Mike,
Thank you for your kindness. I am trying to raise funds to assist them. I've set up a JustGiving page, and I know I shouldn't ask, but if you can make even a small donation, it would help tremendously. You can click here:
[Link to donation page]'

Mike didn't hesitate. He clicked the link, read the JustGiving appeal, and immediately donated £300. Still uneasy, he turned on the news, scanning for updates on IS-related attacks in Libya. Nothing new was reported.

The following day, Mike arrived on campus, still preoccupied. At 10:30 a.m., he spotted Marcos sitting in one of the campus cafés.
Shock. Confusion.
"Hi! Are you okay? When are you leaving? I thought you'd already set off. Any news from your parents?"
Marcos looked at him blankly.
"Leaving? My parents? I don't understand, Dr Mike, sir."
"The email. Last night. You said you had to leave—"
Marcos' face darkened.
"Dr Mike, I have not sent email, sir."
A cold wave rushed through Mike.
He grabbed his phone and pulled up the messages.
"Look. Here. And here—my donation to JustGiving. This is your personal email, isn't it?"
Marcos leaned in, frowning.
He studied the sender's email. His expression shifted.
"No, sir. Look. There is an extra letter.
'marcusayunam@hotmail.com'. This is not me."
Mike's stomach dropped.
"This may be scam," Marcos muttered.
He copied the donation link, opened a new window, and pasted it.
A fake website. Not JustGiving.
"This is fake. Look. Not the real site. A personal account. It's bogus. How much did you give?"

"Three hundred pounds," Mike admitted, feeling sick.
"You must go to the bank. And the police. This is big scam."
At the bank, he explained everything to the cashier.
"I made a donation last night, thinking it was JustGiving. It turns out to be a scam. Can we stop the payment?"
The cashier pulled up his account.
Her expression changed.
"Dr Lewis, you have withdrawn all the funds from your account. Over £9,000."
Silence.
"What?"
"There are multiple transactions. Large purchases. And you have now maxed out your overdraft limit—£10,000."
A dizzying wave of panic hit Mike.
"But that's not possible—I didn't do this. What about the £300 donation?"
The cashier checked.
"There's no £300 payment. Dr Lewis, did you provide all your banking details?"
Mike's chest tightened.
"I typed them into the JustGiving site, yes—"
The cashier's face hardened.
"I need to call the manager."
Mike was ushered into the manager's office.
She was calm, but her voice was grave.
"Dr Lewis, I've reviewed your account. You appear to have set up multiple direct debits for loans over the weekend. They total £20,000."
Mike felt dazed.
"Loans? I didn't take out any loans! I never received any money! Where was it sent?"
"We don't know yet. But, Dr Lewis, you have been the victim of a serious fraud. I can freeze further payments immediately, but I have to be honest—I'm not hopeful about reversing all these."
Mike's pulse pounded.
"This is—this is thousands of pounds!"
"£39,000, Dr Lewis."

Mike's hands clenched.
"How did this happen?"
The manager studied him.
"You tell me. Why were you making a payment to JustGiving?"
Mike swallowed hard.
"I was trying to help a friend."
The police took down the fraudulent email address and website. They explained that tracing the scammers would be almost impossible.
"This kind of fraud is becoming more sophisticated," the detective admitted.
"How did they know I knew someone named Marcos Yunam? And that he was linked to Copts in Libya?"
The police sergeant frowned.
"Do you have this information online anywhere?"
"It's on my university research profile," Mike said.
The sergeant sighed.
"Very clever."
Mike shook his head.
"Very stupid. I'm immensely stupid."
That afternoon, he called John Brompton.
"Hello, Muggins here."
John groaned.
"What have you done now?"
"Got conned. Forty grand."
"Jesus Christ, Mike. How?"
Mike explained.
"They're bastards. They prey on nice people like you. They're on the huh. They're sick."
Later, he called his mother.
She was less sympathetic.
"Michael, I've told you—you're too kind for your own good. A mean man would be fine."
"But I'm not a mean man, Mum."
"No. I don't suppose you ever will be. Poor, but kind."
That night, an email arrived.
From Claire.
He had asked if she'd like to meet for a meal in London.

She had agreed.
For the first time that day, Mike smiled.
Maybe life was still good.

Chapter 48

On 9th January 2016, Claire turned right into Brick Lane. The dry pavement was a relief, but the cold night air quickly cut through her lightweight coat and dress. She knew it would be a long walk down this famous old East End street, having heard about the large market there.
She had bought both the coat and dress earlier that afternoon from Ted Baker, just three miles away on Floral Street in Covent Garden. A quick trip back to her hotel had given her enough time to shower, get ready, remove the sales tags, and be on her way.
Claire focused on finding Fika, the Swedish restaurant where she had arranged to meet Mike for their first actual date. She had looked it up on Google Maps and knew it was some way down the lane. Checking her watch for the fifth time in ten minutes, she reassured herself—she was just on time.
As she briskly walked, different aspects of the street struck her in waves.
The narrow road, a mismatch of architectural styles, had a surprising brightness—the lights of bars creating a dance floor of colours. She instinctively lightened her step.
Only then did she become aware of the noise—a drone of voices, punctuated by laughter and the lively tone of conversations, as different groups talked more loudly to involve each other.
She stepped on.
A quieter, more intimate conversation.
The anonymous hum of the street was interrupted by restaurant staff urging her to look at their menus, inviting her inside their "beautiful places."
Street sellers, occupying shop doorways, closed storefronts, or gaps where buildings should be, instantly called out their offers whenever her gaze lingered.
It all lifted her mood further.
Her steps became lighter, her movements brighter—bordering on skipping, close to spinning into a twirl with a stranger.

Her heartbeat quickened as she tuned into the urgent rhythms of multiple overlapping songs.

The occasional jostle and bump—as strangers collided in the crowd—felt like pushing through a concert audience, making her way to the front of the stage.

She became increasingly aware of the rich diversity around her—voices, dress, expressions—a collision of cultures.

It felt like she was on a magical world tour.

With her heightened senses, Claire absorbed more.

At first, she noticed the contrast between the pungent aromas of different cuisines—then the subtler layers emerged.

Citrus, fenugreek, lager, spices, colognes, aftershaves.

Then, more specific perfumes.

Her own Armani Code.

The ever-present No. 5.

What scent might he wear?

Her thoughts turned to Fika—imagining what it might look, sound, and smell like.

And then…

Here it was.

She stepped boldly into the doorway and through the entrance.

She was ready.

Mike had arrived at the restaurant twenty minutes early. He glanced inside. Basic. Doubt.

"Somewhere different," she'd said when he'd asked where she'd like to go.

"Surprise me," she'd added.

And he had joked, "I will."

Anders had suggested Fika, claiming it served authentic Swedish dishes rarely found in the UK.

Some friend. He'd said it was rustic. Understatement. Spartan.

Any further clues about the place?

How were people entering and leaving dressed?

Pair after pair of jeans strolling in and out.

He was overdressed.

Would Claire have gone to a lot of trouble?

Every time he'd seen her before, she had dressed well. Tonight, surely, she'd look even smarter.

A glance down the street. Any nearby places? Could he change plans?
Maybe he could meet her here, admit it wasn't what he expected, and suggest the Italian place down the road instead.
But that would hardly be "somewhere different," nor would it prove his ability to "surprise" her.
A single date, then? A short date?
Would she turn back before even walking in, unimpressed by the exterior?
Panic.
Too late now.
At ten to eight, he stepped inside, as agreed.
A member of staff approached him.
"Welcome to Fika. Have you bokat bord... reservation?" she asked, the accent and phrasing immediately marking her as Scandinavian.
"Hello. Yes, my name is Lewis. I have a reservation for two at eight o'clock. I will be joined shortly by . . ."
Mike paused, briefly considering how Claire might introduce herself.
He erred on the formal side.
"Dr Fontrelle," he thought before reconsidering.
"Erm, Claire Fontrelle."
He found himself instinctively smiling at the waitress.
She turned to lead him to the table, and his smile faltered.
The bare wooden tables. The stark uncovered benches. No tablecloths. Minimalist, to say the least.
A sinking feeling. He followed, half-smiling, half-terrified.
The walk to the table felt like a trek.
New anxieties arrived thick and fast.
Where would they be seated?
By the toilets, to seal his fate?
Would it be one of those tables where one person faces the wall while the other looks out into the restaurant?
Years ago, he mistakenly took the outward-facing seat while waiting for a then-girlfriend. She had gone mad.
But if he sat facing the wall, he wouldn't see Claire arrive.

Palpable relief as he was shown to a decent table—against the far wall, where they would be facing each other, side-on to the room.

It even had a candle and some flowers.

Perhaps he would survive.

And—crucially—he could see the door.

He declined a drink while waiting.

No menu on the table left him praying that the food would at least be "different" in a good way.

His eyes scanned the room, trying to spot what others were eating.

Nothing but desserts and coffee.

Another prayer.

His attention returned to the door.

From his seat, he had a clear view of people arriving and leaving.

Can't keep staring at the door.

He reached for his phone, opened the BBC website, and pretended to browse.

A glance back.

And then—

A bright coral-coloured coat.

A woman enters.

The greeter briefly obscured her head.

Then, as the staff member stepped aside—

It was her.

Even more beautiful than he remembered.

She was helped out of her coat, revealing a stunning ivory dress with a floral print.

And then—the finishing touch—

As the greeter took her coat, catching her hair slightly, she instinctively brushed it back into place, a smile spreading across her face.

A vision.

Enchanted.

She mouthed a few words in response to the greeter, then turned toward the room.

Her gaze lifted as she walked through the restaurant.

Their eyes met.

Mike stood to greet her.

He stepped slightly away from his chair, his arms instinctively extending toward her waist—but he stopped just short of touching her.

In a trance, he kissed her gently on each cheek.

As she sat, her hair fell forward slightly.

Beautiful as ever.

But in the restaurant's soft lighting, she was positively spellbinding.

Then—her eyes, her mouth, her necklace, her dress.

He was transfixed.

"You look wonderful," he half-whispered.

She smiled.

"It's lovely to see you," he added.

Another smile.

Her voice was warm as she said, "Thanks."

Mike looked around the room. "Well, it is different," he said nervously.

Claire mirrored his glance around the restaurant.

"I don't know Swedish food, to be honest. I've been looking forward to it," she replied, then added brightly, "Go with the flow."

The waitress arrived, handed them menus, and asked if they'd like a drink.

Mike asked for a copy of the wine list.

A brief silence as they began their exploration of the dishes.

Then—

"Exciting," Claire said brightly.

Mike was immediately struck.

The vibrant tone of her voice.

The enthusiasm she always seemed to carry.

An open, playful, happy openness to what the world had to offer.

And the wonder of it all.

Infectious.

Mike had always been lifted by her energy, even in the work setting where they'd met.

Tonight, it was utterly intoxicating.

"To Sweden, then."
They continued flipping through the menus.
Somehow, Claire had relaxed him.
All his concerns vanished.
Now, he simply wanted to look at her.
To hear her.
Her left hand turned the page of the menu—
Graceful. Effortless. Beautiful.
Her fingers had the dexterity of an artist but also a femininity that stunned him.
He so wanted to reach across the table and take her hand.

*

As Claire entered the restaurant, her immediate feeling was one of relief.
She was on time.
Her clothes made her feel special.
The coat, as it was taken from her, was chic.
She smoothed her hair and caught a glimpse of her dress.
Feminine. Beautiful.
The aromas told her she was in a place of delicacy, not pungency.
To her, the restaurant looked charming.
She loved the simple rustic styling.
She recognised some of the art prints on the walls.
Many were from Swedish modernist and expressionist periods, including the Halmstad Group.
A smile.
She spotted a print of Svanen by Hilma af Klint—a female artist she admired greatly.
And then—
Almost magnetically, her gaze found him.
Her face lit up.
As she strode toward him, she felt the swish of her dress.
She was sure he would like how she looked.
As she approached, she caught his gaze again.

He had been watching her closely as she walked toward him.
Then, she saw him drop his eyes.
Shyness.
A fleeting uncertainty as he stood up to greet her.
Then, a comforting resolution—
A kiss on each cheek.
She felt a momentary warmth where his lips had touched her skin, turning into an inner glow.
She lingered in the sensation.
Her mind spun, barely registering his words—
She only knew that he was trying to flatter her.
His eyes and smile told her everything she needed to know.
"Thanks," she said.

*

And with that, they began to talk.
She scanned the menu.
What starter?
Gravadlax.
Cured salmon with dill and mustard sauce—light, not hugely calorific.
But for the main course?
Meatballs? Curry? Vegetarian?
Several salmon options.
OK, one of those salmon dishes. So, not salmon as a starter...
Then—
"Västerbottenpaj," Mike said at the exact moment she'd mentally committed to it.
"Simply because it's such a great word."
"Not totally sure what it is, but why not?"
She scanned the main courses again.
She didn't want to fuss too much or seem hesitant.
A simple choice.
Salmon with duchesse potatoes, asparagus, and hollandaise sauce.
She settled on it—
"Lax Planka."

They said it in unison.
She laughed.
He laughed.
Oh, how she loved his laugh.
Not booming, not giggly—
But a playful, fun-loving chuckle.
And he looked so lovely when he laughed.
She was hypnotised.
This time, he held her gaze.
His eyes looked like hers—
Full of life.
The restaurant's noise level was perfect—lively enough to convey other people's joy but quiet enough for them to speak naturally.
She left the choice of wine to him.
"Ah, Köpingsberg Blanc de Blancs," he said as if he knew it well, clearly signalling he didn't.
She caught it—another thing she liked about him.
His confidence in genuine humility.
A simple "Cheers," not a cringey "Skål."
Their glasses clinked—
The sound of unity.
She excused herself to the loo before the food arrived.
As she returned, she noticed—
A glance from him.
Not too long, but definitely there.
She shuffled slightly in her chair, crossed her legs, and then noticed—
Her shoes.
She did love that coral colour.
Then, she realised—
Mike's gaze had followed hers to her shoes, then drifted back up to the fall of her dress.
Not lecherous—
Just undeniable attraction.
As she reached to brush her hair back, she caught him watching her hand's movement.
She felt it, too.

A charge between them.

He made conversation so easily, telling her how his friend Anders had suggested the restaurant.

She absently traced her fingers along her cheek, then her hair as he spoke.

Again, the following gaze.

Her hands lowered to the table—close to his.

She so wanted to reach for him.

They stayed at the restaurant for hours.

"It's late. We'd be better off with a taxi. I'll ask if they can call one. D'yer think?" Mike asked.

Claire nodded.

As she climbed into the taxi ahead of him, he watched in awe.

In his mind—

A movie scene.

Lights of London flash past, and the ride is comfortable, easy, and warm.

He wondered what she wanted.

Would she invite him in?

Would she say goodnight?

"Well, thank you for a wonderful evening, Mike. I loved it. What time can we meet in the morning?"

"Late night. Breakfast at 8:30? Yes?"

"Perfect. And I'll think of a surprise for you."

That smile.

That joie de vivre.

And then—

The first kiss.

A responsive kiss.

A kiss that electrified his whole body.

The next day—

They walked hand in hand through Hyde Park and St. James's Park.

They laughed.

They kissed.

Romance.

Chapter 49

Mike arrived at Claire's house at 11:00 a.m., right on time.
He reached for the bouquet from the front seat of his car, stepped onto the pavement, and walked to the door.
Claire answered.
She wore a white skirt, cinched at the waist and fitted at the tops of her thighs, but pleated and flared just above her knees.
Her floral-printed blouson was tucked beneath a delicate white shrug.
And, of course, her smile—
Vibrant. Inviting.
She beckoned him in.
Mike handed her the flowers.
"For you."
He leaned forward and kissed her gently on her left cheek.
"Beautiful. I'll put them in water."
She turned and headed to the kitchen.
Mike followed his gaze, instinctively drawn to the subtle sway of her hips.
Her skirt swished, her hair falling to one side—
That bewitching movement that had mesmerised him since the first time they met.
She reached into a low-level cupboard, bending slightly to retrieve a vase.
Mike swallowed hard.
She filled the vase with water, arranged the flowers, then turned—
Mike was standing right behind her.
As she faced him, her chin tilted slightly, meeting his gaze.
Without a word, he kissed her.
Her right hand found its way to his waist.
He wrapped his arms around her and deepened the kiss.
"That was nice. Lovely."
"You're lovely," he murmured, kissing her again.
Claire responded more passionately.

Their hands explored—fingers gliding across waists, backs, shoulders.
Mike's touch lingered as he traced the curve of her spine, stopping just short of her hips.
Claire stepped back slightly, her lips curling into a playful smile.
"Let's go upstairs."
Mike didn't speak.
He just smiled and nodded.
She turned, extending her hand behind her.
He took it—
And followed.
Her skirt shifted, offering him a tantalising glimpse of her thighs with each step.
Inside her bedroom, Claire walked toward the head of the bed and reached for the docked iPod on the bedside table.
A soft melody hummed to life.
The room smelled sweet, carrying a hint of lavender.
The feminine touch of her bedding.
The soft dusk light filtered through the window.
Mike paused at the foot of the bed, absorbing everything.
Claire sat, her skirt hitching slightly, revealing more of her thighs.
Her shrug sleeves had been pushed up to her forearms, left unbuttoned, the blouson draping over her frame, hinting at the contours beneath.
She placed her right hand on her left knee, tucking a strand of hair behind her ear.
"Are you shy?" she asked, voice soft as silk.
Her left hand cupped her cheek, her lips parting just slightly.
Mike held her gaze.
"No. Not at all."
He took a half-step forward.
Claire's fingers ran slowly through her hair, her smile widening.
Then, she blinked deliberately, lowering her eyes for a moment—
Before lifting them again.
"I've thought about this moment a lot," she whispered, her gaze flitting briefly to his groin.

Mike's breath hitched.

"So have I," he admitted.

Claire's smile deepened, her fingers brushing absently against the tip of her nose.

She looked away briefly, then back up at him—

"Oh, really?"

Her right hand still rested on her knee while her left thumb flicked gently against her palm, her fingers curling, uncurling—

An unspoken invitation.

She stood.

So did he.

Their movements were perfectly synchronised as they began to undress.

Claire slid her hands down the sides of her skirt, pushing the fabric slowly down her hips.

Then, gracefully, she smoothed the front before reaching her shoulders.

She turned slightly to her left, letting the shrug slip off.

It dropped to the floor.

Her hands lifted again, fingers brushing the nape of her neck, unclasping the blouson.

She turned slightly toward him, tugging it over her head, then clutching it to her chest.

A barely perceptible curtsy.

Then—hesitation.

Where should she put it?

Mike's shirt hit the ground.

She tossed her blouson further away, exaggerating the movement with a playful flourish.

He drank in the sight of her—

The narrow curve of her waist.

The flatness of her stomach.

Claire ran her hands down her hips, smoothing her skirt one last time—

This time, over her buttocks.

Then, she reached for the buttons on the side of her skirt.

Mike removed his socks and trousers, acutely aware of the heat stirring beneath his underwear.

Claire's fingers moved slowly, undoing the buttons—
Gently sliding the skirt down to the floor.
She stepped out of it, rising to full height.
His breath caught.
Tight purple panties with a tiny red bow at the waistline.
She saw the way he looked at her.
Anticipation buzzed between them.
Simultaneously, they stepped toward each other.
Their bodies collided.
They embraced.
In perfect harmony, they eased onto the bed.
Mike quickly removed his pants.
The kisses deepened.
Fingers explored.
Breaths grew heavier.
Mike's hands slid to her back, deftly unclasping her bra.
The straps fell forward.
Claire pulled it away, letting it drift to the side of the bed.
The intensity mounted.
He pressed against her, his arousal undeniable.
She lifted her hips slightly, allowing him to ease down her panties.
He kissed her—
Her lips, her shoulders, her breasts, her abdomen.
Their bodies melded, their senses overcome.
They breathed each other in.
Tasted.
Explored.
Until the moment arrived—
The moment when they gave themselves completely.

Chapter 50

At the end of February, Manisha returned to the UK.
Claire drove across to see her.
During the journey, memories of Manisha danced through her mind—
Vivid flashes of her at university, in Florence, in countless moments across the years.
As soon as Manisha opened the door, Claire ran to hug her.
"Oh, Manisha. Manisha."
Manisha held herself together.
"Thank you for coming, Claire. It is good of you."
"Of course. Of course. It's all so terrible."
"Yes. It is tough. I can't deny I am struggling." Manisha's voice faltered. "In so many ways, David... defined me. You know?
"When I was in Mumbai, I kept thinking: 'No David.'"
"Who am I?"
"Where do I want to be now?"
"Birmingham?"
"I don't think so. Not without him."
"Sure. Well, yes," Claire said quickly. "You'll need time to figure out what you want to do. Have WMU been good?"
"Yes, I have been on compassionate leave. I told them I am going to leave the university."
She paused, then added, "They've said I don't have to serve my full notice period. So I will be going."
Claire froze.
"Going where, Manisha? Where?"
"Back home. India. Mumbai. My family. They are my life now."
"No. No." Claire shook her head. "That's too quick. You're rushing things."
Panic.
What to say?
"Yes. I understand. I do. But you do have friends here. Lots. Me. Are you sure you're not . . . jumping the gun?"
Manisha nodded slowly.

"I know. I know it seems that way. But sometimes, you know what is best, Sakhi. Not in a spur-of-the-moment thing, but deep down."
She sighed.
"David was such a big part of me. I cannot fill this void with friends."
"I need warmth. Human warmth. Love."
"For me, that means being back in the bosom of my family. That's all. It's right. It is best."
Claire stepped forward and wrapped her arms around her.
"I care for you, Manisha. I do. I know I don't show it. But I do."
Manisha placed her hands on Claire's waist. Her voice softened.
"Perhaps, once. That might have been true, Sakhi. But now? Maybe not in the way I need."
Claire felt her chest tighten.
"I suppose. But... maybe I do feel? I'm not sure. I'm never completely sure since . . . us."
Her voice caught.
"Tell me you'll think about it a bit more, Manisha."
Manisha eased her hand away.
Claire stepped back.
Manisha looked so sad. So lost.
Claire struggled to think of something positive.
"We can stay in touch, right?"
"You can stay in touch with people here. You know. Yes?"
Manisha barely stirred.
"Yes, of course. I will try."
Claire's voice rushed.
"I know how much I have depended on you, Manisha. You're my guiding light."
"Maybe I haven't been so good to you in return, but maybe I can help you now. You know? Somehow."
Manisha smiled gently.
"I love being there for you, Sakhi. And I still will be. We can talk on the phone and, hopefully, meet up—here or in India."
"I'm sure we will."
"You are kind, Claire."
Claire's emotions spun wildly.

Leaving?
No sane voice?
No caring voice?
She shook her head rapidly, needing a distraction.
"You won't get to meet my new man, Mike. He's pretty special."
Manisha smiled faintly.
"You deserve special, Claire."

*

Claire drove home, a single word tumbling over and over in her mind—
Dependency.
She grabbed her sketchpad, but instead of drawing, she froze.
An image surfaced in her mind—A cutaway drawing of a pregnant woman's womb. Manisha. But inside, not a baby—
Her. Her own body curled up inside Manisha's.
The thought sent a shiver through her.
Another image—
Manisha cradling a newborn.
Except the baby was still her.
Her stomach clenched.
Manisha reaching for the umbilical cord.
Scissors in hand.
Claire jerked back in horror, the sketchpad nearly slipping from her grasp.
Her first instinct was to put it down—
Escape the thought.
Run.
But she didn't.
This time, she picked up her pencil and drew it.
Throughout the week, Claire returned to the feeling of loss.
She knew that being mothered and mentored wasn't love—
But still, the absence felt huge.
She didn't like staying in those thoughts for too long.

*

She welcomed the distraction of Mike's emails.
His light-heartedness was infectious.
They made plans.
He would visit her soon.
Something new.

Chapter 51

Claire told Mike on the phone that "a close friend" was leaving the UK. He had been sympathetic.
They met at Birmingham New Street Station as planned and walked to the Art Gallery together.
"I must have come here twenty or thirty times," Claire said, her voice more animated.
Mike picked up on her excitement. "I've never been to Birmingham, but I'm looking forward to seeing what's here. I've seen other Pre-Raphaelite paintings in London, but as I said when you suggested coming here, these sound great."
They moved through the gallery, hand in hand.
"This is Rossetti's preparatory study of *Una Donna Della Finestre*," Claire said, stopping in front of a sketch. "In *La Vita Nuova*, the Italian poet writes about the lady in the window, looking down at the grief-stricken Dante mourning the loss of Beatrice."
"Right. So, this isn't the finished piece?"
"No, but if you see the full painting, you'll notice how it builds on these depictions of her face and hands." Claire's voice took on a subtle art teacher tone.
They walked on.
"And here is '*Beatrice*'—The Beata Beatrice."
"Rossetti's, right?"
"Yes, but finished by his lifelong friend, Ford Madox Brown, after his death. Dante's courtly love idealised Beatrice as divine—a love that transcends time and space, requiring the pure virtue of the lover."
Mike arched an eyebrow. "A tall order."
Claire laughed lightly. "The Pre-Raphaelites were all about purity and virtue."
Mike turned to the painting again. "And she has your hair. That unforgettable hair."
Claire shrugged modestly, but her smile lingered.
"The model was actually Rossetti's wife, Elizabeth Siddal. She had been his muse for years. After she died, he painted her as Beatrice—a tribute to his love for her."

Mike nodded, impressed. "Fantastic. You're good at this, aren't you?"

"I'll spare you the lecture on the dove and flower symbolism."

"Ha. But seriously, this is lovely."

He leaned in and kissed her gently.

They moved on.

"Ah, I recognise this." Mike pointed to a painting of Morgan le Fay by Frederick Sandys. "She was the powerful enchantress from the Arthurian legends."

"Exactly. The Pre-Raphaelites were fascinated by chivalry, magic, and the romanticised Middle Ages." Claire's voice brimmed with enthusiasm.

"I've seen Waterhouse's *Lady of Shalott* at the Tate."

"Then maybe we should go to Port Sunlight to see Burne-Jones's *The Beguiling of Merlin*."

"Oh, I'd like that. Let's do it sometime."

Claire squeezed his arm affectionately.

She enchanted him.

She felt the beginnings of something real.

They had tea at the Edwardian Tearoom, reminiscing about student days.

When they stepped back outside, they squinted against the sudden brightness.

The summer sun was in full force.

Claire suggested they walk to Brindley Place.

As they climbed the bridge over the canal, the lively restaurants, bright clothing, and the hum of conversation reminded them of Venice.

Suddenly, the squeals of laughter overtook the ambient chatter.

They turned their heads—

A group of children ran through mini fountains in the square, shrieking as the water shot up around them.

Mike laughed. "They're having fun."

Claire caught the longing in his gaze.

"Come on then. Our turn."

She grinned at him.

Mike's entire posture changed.

His head locked straight ahead, and his neck stiffened.

Then, he turned his entire upper body to look at her.
And in a perfect Kryten voice from *Red Dwarf*, he deadpanned:
"It's no good, sir. I just can't do it."
Claire froze, stunned.
Red Dwarf?
The impression was so spot-on.
Before she could react—
Mike bolted through three fountains.
Fantastic.
Despite being dressed smartly, he didn't hesitate.
Claire didn't even think—she ran after him, weaving through the plumes of water.
Now, at the other side of the square, they locked eyes—
And ran back through, hand in hand.
Their clothes clung to them, drenched.
They stared at each other, their bodies pressed close.
If they hadn't been in such a public place—
They might have made love right there.
Instead, they broke their embrace, turned side by side, and walked back across the bridge—
Romantically.

Chapter 52

Mike visited Claire in Nottingham more often on weekends, always bringing his guitar.
Claire had once told him that he not only spoke like Ed Sheeran but sounded like him when he sang.
He wasn't sure how he felt about that.
Did she think that was a good thing?
On a Saturday evening, his eyes landed on a photograph pinned to the cork noticeboard in the kitchen—a place Claire used for notes, business cards, and postcards. The image showed a forest ablaze with vivid autumn colours.
Mike frowned, memories surfacing.
Martell Forest.
He thought back to his walk there after the Randolph conference, to the colours that had reminded him of the girl in the car park—the girl with striking red hair.
And now, here she was.
Claire walked over and caught him staring at the photo.
"That's Martell Forest in Indiana. I took it a couple of years ago."
Mike let out a low chuckle, eyes widening.
"No way. I took exactly the same photograph after the Randolph conference."
"No way?" Claire grinned, intrigued.
"Yeah. I'd seen a girl with beautiful red hair as I drove into the car park. The colours reminded me of her when I walked through the forest."
He turned to Claire and pulled her into a warm embrace, pressing a gentle kiss to her forehead.
"You."
Claire blinked in surprise. "Wow. Some weird vibes in the ether kind of drew us both there."
"It is pretty amazing." Mike smiled softly. "Meant to be."
They spent the evening drinking wine and watching a film.
The next morning, they made love.

Afterwards, they lay tangled together in the bed, wrapped in the quiet contentment of the moment.

Claire nestled against his chest, her head resting on his shoulder. Mike wrapped an arm around her, fingers absently twirling strands of her hair repeatedly, shaping tiny ringlets between his fingertips.

Then—

"Tell me about the other girls."

Mike's fingers paused. "What?"

"The other girls. You once said you had three main girlfriends. I don't mean all your conquests." Claire's tone was playful, but her curiosity was evident. "I was just wondering about them."

Whether it was the intimacy of the moment or his growing trust in her, Mike answered honestly.

"Well, I have key moments that come back to me. It is like they are speaking to me, but I don't know what they mean."

Claire laughed. "Ghosts, you mean. Or are you cracking up, Dr Lewis?"

He chuckled. "Well, first, there was Adele. Not that Adele. We were together for about eighteen months—maybe from fourteen and a half to sixteen. I was devastated when she left me. We got on well. Kissed a bit. She was pretty."

"So, your first love?"

Mike was quiet for a moment.

"Like I said, I think memories come to us in moments, for whatever reason. I can remember a sunset with Adele, walking together, and I know I was gutted when she ended it. I have an image of that. It has come back to me whenever I am sad. Got me writing songs. But love?" He exhaled thoughtfully.

"I thought about it for months. I liked being with her. But honestly, I think a big part of it was how much she liked me. Feeling unliked afterwards—that was the worst part. She admired me. But bathing in admiration isn't love."

"Hmm," Claire murmured. "So, you were a people pleaser even back then?"

Mike raised an eyebrow. "You think I still am?"

"Oh, definitely."

Mike smirked, but Claire only snuggled closer, pressing against him like a child waiting for a bedtime story.

"Who next?" she prompted.

"Lydia. We met through music."

"Music?"

"Yeah. Funny thing—actually met Adele after a gig, too."

"So, what happened with Lydia?"

Mike shrugged slightly, careful not to disturb Claire's position. "I had a few one-night stands in between, but I went to Manchester for uni, mostly just hung out with mates, played open-mic gigs. Then, I wanted to get back in a band. A group was auditioning for a guitarist. That's when I met Lydia."

"Did you enjoy the time between relationships? The independence?"

Mike considered the question.

"I don't know. Time passes. I was fine, I guess. But I think I'm happier in a relationship."

"Uh-huh. Go on."

"So, Lydia and I were together for almost seven years."

"Wow. That's a long time. Were you in love? Did you think about marriage?"

Mike sighed, shifting slightly.

"No. It all went pear-shaped. She got into drugs badly. Another image that haunts me, I stayed. I wanted to help. I thought I had to be loyal."

Claire tilted her head knowingly.

"Ah. But the extent of loyalty isn't a measure of love, Mike. More people-pleasing."

Mike chuckled dryly. "Yeah. I figured that out afterwards."

A slight tension crept into his tone.

"Then there was Sherifat. She was Nigerian. We met at Plymouth. Together about three years. It was good—peaceful. Cosy settees and all that. A relief after Lydia. But…"

He hesitated.

"But?" Claire pressed gently.

"It didn't work out. And anyway, peace isn't love."

"No," Claire smirked teasingly. "And then me. Treat in-store, huh?"

"Yes. You."
Mike squeezed her waist and kissed her forehead.
"So maybe..." he mused. "Maybe I always blamed them when actually... it was me who needed to change."
Claire arched an eyebrow.
"Change how?"
"Believe that I'm liked." Mike exhaled. "Even with Sherifat, I wasn't sure. I knew she wanted kids, but that's not the same thing, is it?"
Claire studied him for a beat. "Well, you know I like you. Surely?"
Mike almost believed her.
Then, he turned the tables.
"And you? Your relationships?"
Claire shrugged nonchalantly.
"Not much to say. All fine. Fun, then not fun. But, like you, I have strong visual memories of key things. Maybe we all do. Not sure I've made sense of them, though."
"Names? Dates? Descriptions?"
Claire grinned. "Yes, Inspector Lewis."
Mike rolled his eyes, amused.
"Alright. So, I was happy being with my bestie, Penny. And life outside. I only really remember being outside. Then, at sixteen, I had a boyfriend—Brian—a bit of a trophy, sort of thing. We did art stuff together. But he had some kind of breakdown. Just being in a relationship isn't love. I remember his jumbled picture of love, though."
"Go on."
"Then I was just... me, again. Until sixth form. Older guy. Caspian. Super caring. It was nice, but I knew I was off to Birmingham, so that was that. Liking being cared for isn't love, either. And then..."
She paused thoughtfully.
"Well. Then . . ."
"Then what?"
"Then... I had a crush on a lecturer. Manisha. She . . . "
Mike raised an eyebrow, intrigued.

"I guess I wasn't sure who I was. I experimented. She helped me—a lot. Helped me figure things out. About me, I mean." Claire chuckled softly, shaking her head. "Figure things out? Ha. Maybe some things."

Mike nodded. "Right."

"She was kind of like a mum. But a dead cool one. And highly affectionate. And a mentor. But..." Claire's voice softened. "Loving being mothered isn't love. She did a lovely drawing of me, and I have one of hers."

Mike nodded slowly, sensing there was more.

"Then Simon. Crazy, mad, drunk, Simon. Four years."

"Four?"

"Yep. All filthy, passionate, and arty. But he didn't know himself. Probably still doesn't. Perpetual drifter. Professional drifter. It made me realise... sex isn't love."

"Wow. Some contrasts there. But hopefully, you were happy at some point?" Mike teased. "Apart from the sex, I mean."

"Water under the bridge." Claire shrugged. "I'm always happy. In myself. People... complicate things sometimes."

She paused before adding, "I've stayed in touch with Manisha over the years. She's still like a mum. Maybe more of a mentor now. But... she's moving to Mumbai."

Mike frowned thoughtfully. "Well, maybe you can still keep in touch."

"I hope so." Claire exhaled. "Anyway. Busy life. Doctorate. Flitting about. Then, a guy called Eddie. My part-time lover from Wales."

"Part-time?"

"Eddie was excitement." Claire's eyes glimmered with nostalgia. "Good fun. I don't think there was a sport we didn't do. Adrenaline rules. But... excitement isn't love."

"Together for a while?"

"Ha. Yes. Another three years of my life, flashing by."

She rolled onto her side to face him. "So, what do you make of all that, Dr Freud?"

Mike chuckled. "Make of it? Well, you seem to have me sussed. People pleaser? I suppose I still am. I guess I do like being in a relationship. And before you say it—no, not just anyone."

"So, what do they call people like that? You psychologists have a name for everything."

Mike grinned. "A name? Well, yeah. I suppose there is." He stretched slightly, eyes twinkling. "I've never thought of myself as a condition, but... people who have to be in relationships, who are scared of being alone... that's anuptaphobia."

Claire snorted. "You're making that up. Anuptaphobia? Next, you'll tell me there's..." She glanced around the room, eyes twinkling. "Curtainphobia. Wardrobephobia."

"Ha. Well, actually..."

"Ha. Ha. No way. So, what am I suffering from then?" Claire grinned mischievously. "Not one of your anuptabods. Probably the bloody opposite. What's that? Un-anuptaphobia?"

"OK, OK," Mike laughed. "I'm sure you're not suffering from anything. Neither am I, thanks."

Claire narrowed her eyes playfully.

"But seriously," Mike continued. "Some people are afraid of relationships. Not just romantic ones—friendships, too. People who avoid commitment altogether? That's called... gamophobia."

Claire gasped in mock horror. "Now, I know you're bullshitting me."

"No, honestly."

She rolled onto her back, staring at the ceiling. "I think we all have these ideas about love, these models in our heads. Picked up along the way, sort of thing. Like the *imaginari* . . . pictures in our minds we've been saying"

Mike studied her face. "Maybe."

"Images of love," Claire mused. "We see them everywhere. Art, cinema... I think they're a big part of what we believe about love."

Mike tilted his head slightly, watching her. "Well, for you, maybe. You're an artist."

"No," Claire said firmly, turning back to him. "For everyone."

Mike pursed his lips, considering it.

"Maybe you're right. We have our notions, don't we?"

What does she feel?
How do I feel?

They made love.

After showering, they returned to the bedroom. Mike's voice was gentle. "I want to be with you forever."

Claire tilted her head, pretending to think hard, exaggerating her expression in playful hesitation. But before she could reply, Mike continued, "But I need to tell you something enormously important first."

Her smile faded slightly as she sensed a shift in his tone.

"It's only fair to tell you... I can't father children."

Claire's eyes searched his face, waiting for him to explain.

"I told you about my childhood leukaemia. Well, three years ago, I had tests. Because of the treatment, I'm completely infertile. There's no remedy."

He hesitated before adding, "If you want children, this may be a big issue for you."

Claire stepped toward him, her voice filled with warmth. "Oh, Mike... how sad. For you. Have you always wanted children?"

As she reached out, Mike exhaled. "I suppose I did. But I've come to terms with it now. The real question is... what about you?"

Claire took his hand and gave it a gentle squeeze. "Me? A mother? No... I shouldn't be a mother. I wouldn't know how."

But then, she saw the sadness in his eyes and the deep sense of loss. And yet, there was also relief.

Her chest tightened. Tears welled in her eyes—not for herself, but for him.

Tears of empathy.

Tears of care.

*

Their weekends together became more frequent. In June, Claire visited Mike's house in Plymouth.

On Saturday morning, she suggested he shower first. She heard him playing *Chasing Cars* by Snow Patrol on his guitar when she came downstairs.

She paused to listen. She always loved it when he played.

Sunlight streamed through the windows. The day was glorious.

"Shall we go for a swim?" Mike asked.
"That lovely beach again? Bovisand?"
"Ah, no. I have a surprise for you."
Claire raised an eyebrow, intrigued. "Ooh. Where?"
"You'll see."
As they drove, Claire noticed they were heading into town, not toward the beaches.
"Oh, a swimming pool? This'll be nice."
Mike laughed. "And then some."
When they arrived, Claire stared in awe.
The sky.
A lido.
But not just any lido.
A dream lido—its shimmering blue waters melting into the horizon, where the sea and sky became one.
"Mein Gott, this is incredible." Claire breathed. "It's beautiful."
As they walked across the ceramic tiles, she yelped. "Scheisse! They're so hot!"
Mike grinned, watching as she half-hopped, half-sprinted toward the pool before diving in.
The water was heavenly.
They swam for several minutes before Mike led her to the far side of the pool, where the water seemed to merge seamlessly with the sea.
They climbed onto the concrete ledge, backs resting against the low wall. Claire closed her eyes, letting the sun's warmth soak her skin.
"This is idyllic." She sighed, turning to him. "Thank you. I didn't realise it was a lido. But it has to be the most beautiful lido in Britain. This setting is… incomparable."
Mike smiled. "It takes your breath away, doesn't it?"
She leaned in as he kissed her. Then she tilted her head back against the wall, eyes closed, as if in a dream.
A few minutes later, she felt movement.
She opened her eyes and watched as Mike dove back into the pool. She couldn't take her eyes off him—his strong strokes, the way he surfaced and flipped onto his back so effortlessly at home in the water.

He's so fit. So, so fancy this man.
Droplets slid down his skin when he climbed out, catching the light.
He walked toward her, beaming. Completely happy.
And that's when Claire felt something she'd never felt before.
Not just her own joy.
But his joy.
And in that moment, she didn't just love how he made her feel. She cherished how he felt.
Total empathy.
They made their way back to Mike's house in a comfortable silence.
Claire found herself thinking that, somehow, they were the complete couple—whatever that meant.
Unknowingly, Mike had similar thoughts. God, we're good. I think she'll stay.
The next morning, they took a peaceful walk through Ramsay Woods. In the afternoon, Mike needed to catch up on some work reading while Claire set up the easel she had placed months earlier in the spare room.
About an hour later, Mike wandered in.
"I love watching you paint." He stood behind her, wrapping his arms gently around her waist. She is amazing.
Claire half-turned, craning her neck to kiss him while keeping her brush strategically away from him.
"Watching someone paint is weird," she mused. "I've done it many times, and it's as if I'm painting with them. Like I can feel the movement, appreciate the stroke, the effect."
Mike chuckled. "Blimey, I don't do that. It'd be funny if I tried to mirror your movements on a painting next to you. I don't think it'd look remotely like yours." He grinned. "More Jackson Pollock."
Claire laughed.
Mike paused, thoughtful. "But what you're saying is backed by science. We have mirror neurons in our brains—they fire when we see movements we can relate to or execute. So, neurologically, part of you is painting along with them."

Claire rolled her eyes, mock-exasperated. "I might have known you'd have an explanation."

She turned back to her painting, pausing for a moment. "But it's true. You can almost project yourself into a piece of art. It's not just about seeing it—it's about feeling it, the process, the movement. You connect with it, almost empathise with the object itself."

Mike nodded, intrigued. "I get that. Sometimes, with a photograph, I don't just see it—I feel it. There are moments when an image captures something so perfectly that it's... complete. It transports you. Like sensing something deeper than just what's there."

Claire glanced over her shoulder, eyes alight. "That's exactly why religious art is so powerful. People relate to it so completely that they imbue it with spirituality. It becomes something more than just an image—it's archetypal."

Mike smiled, watching her. "Ha. Well, I think more and more, I can see you—sense you—in your paintings. That's why I love them."

He hesitated before adding softly, "Too."

Mike left Claire to her painting, her words lingering in his thoughts.

Archetypal.

Yes. Some paintings captured the essence of something, something timeless. That's what he loved about them.

He started preparing dinner.

A little while later, Claire entered the kitchen. She had cleaned up after painting, her hair tied loosely back, her cheeks flushed from concentration.

Mike said, "I was thinking about the paintings that capture something fundamental," she said, leaning against the counter. "For me, it's Rembrandt. The way he uses light—it pulls you in. And the way he paints his subjects' expressions... you feel them. Like I was saying about mirror neurons —this time, with emotions. Empathy."

"Yes, we talk a lot about Rembrandt with our students. You put it beautifully."

"You do the same thing in photography—you paint with light to capture the essence of a moment. Well, I try."

Claire laughed. "Well, I wouldn't go comparing yourself to Rembrandt just yet."

"Fair enough," Mike said, grinning.

"But artists still do it today," Claire continued. "Look at Banksy's *Mobile Lovers*. The glow from the phones is brilliant—it completely changes the scene. You feel the distraction of the couple. It's just as powerful as Rembrandt's light, in a different way."

Mike lit up. "I love that painting. It's like you're there with them—you get it immediately. Well done, Rembrandt... and Banksy."

They laughed.

And then, they kissed.

Chapter 53

By autumn, Mike and Claire had spent every weekend together. Mike still felt like a visitor, even after all his time at her place. One evening, he suggested they take a weekend getaway.

Claire's eyes lit up. "I've heard people talk about a beautiful beach in mid-Wales—Criccieth. The beach is supposed to be lovely. I'm sure we could find a cottage to rent this time of year."

Mike nodded, intrigued. "Sounds perfect. I can drive up to yours on Friday afternoon, and we can head there together. I don't have any lectures that day."

Claire suddenly beamed. "Wait—let's hire a campervan instead!"

"Like the classic old VW ones?"

"Yes! Yes! Let's do it!"

They hired the VW campervan and arrived at Criccieth around 8:00 p.m. on Friday.

"I brought us some food. We could cook together in here. It'll be novel," Mike admitted.

"Well," Claire grinned, "I brought wine. And even croissants for the morning. The booking info said there's an espresso machine somewhere, so we're all set."

They cooked together, eating late into the evening, talking, laughing, and drinking wine. Their intimacy that night felt more profound than ever.

The following morning was crisp and clear, the air cold but invigorating.

"Let's just head straight to the beach," Claire suggested over coffee and croissants.

"Okay. But you're carrying the buckets and spades," Mike teased.

They drove straight onto the beach from the campsite, bundled in thick coats, expecting biting wind.

There was none.

The beach was deserted, the sand untouched, and the low tide stretched out before them like a private pathway.

They walked in silence, hand in hand, their only sound the soft crunch of their boots on damp sand. It felt like their beach. Their moment. Their little idyll.

Mike pulled out his phone. "Where do you want to stand? Just the sea behind you, or the cliffs too?"

"I'm easy. You choose."

A gust of wind swept a lock of Claire's copper hair across her face. As she reached up to push it back, Mike snapped the photo. This beautiful, easygoing woman. This simple, perfect life.

They strolled into town, found a cosy café for lunch, and wandered through quiet little shops.

"If we get back to the van now, we should catch the sunset," Mike suggested.

When they reached the campervan, they saw that all the other cars were gone. The tide was licking at the bottom of the tyres. Mike rushed toward it. "Shit—"

"No, wait," Claire said, stopping him with a hand on his chest. "We need to watch the sunset first."

"But—"

"No buts, Michael Lewis. Kiss me."

*

As the months passed, their weekends became less about being apart and more about where they would be together next.

They booked a hotel in the Lake District that Easter, nestled between Newby Bridge and Bowness.

The 1930s lakeside retreat was quiet and secluded, with breathtaking views over Windermere.

In the mornings, they sat on white-painted metal chairs on the terrace outside their room, sipping coffee and watching the lake.

Claire stared at the dark green hills across the water. "Everything is so simple here. So tranquil."

Mike nodded. "Yes. And beautiful. The mountains seem to declare their permanence—'We're here, we always will be. Today, just for you. Appreciate us.'"

Later, they drove to Fell Foot Park, where Mike stood on the wooden jetty, watching the moored sailboats gently bobbing.

Claire slipped her arm around his waist, resting her head on his shoulder.

"I love our weekends in cottages," she murmured. "But this... this effortless life where we don't have to do anything feels even closer. Does that sound weird?"

Mike smiled outwardly, but inwardly, he beamed. She wants closeness like me.

"Not weird," he said. "We're content."

On the drive home, the radio played *You're All I Need to Get By* by Marvin Gaye and Tammi Terrell.

Claire truly understood what it meant for the first time in her life.

*

That December, Mike and Claire agreed to spend Christmas at his mother's house. Mike thought it would also be a good opportunity for her to meet John Brompton.

"You've spoken about him a lot from your teens. I didn't realise you were still in touch," Claire remarked.

"It's all like *Castle on the Hill* by Ed Sheeran," Mike replied. "We've all gone separate ways, but still have that bond. I still see him—probably not as often as I should. I went to his wedding and kept in touch as his family grew. He trained as a plumber, and his wife Caroline works part-time in their local shop. They live in Reddisham, just a few miles from Ilketshall St. Andrew. You'll like them. He still plays music—not live or anything—but has a great voice."

Before heading to Mike's mum's that afternoon, they stopped in Reddisham.

Mike spotted John and Caroline at the door.

"Shit, you've got a beard!" Mike called out. "Hello, Caroline."

"And a bostin' one at that," John grinned, pulling Mike into a hug before giving Claire a playful wink.

"Better than mine," Claire said, rubbing her chin.

"I like 'er," John chuckled.

Caroline laughed, stepping forward. "Hi, I'm Caroline, and you must be Claire. Come in."

"Excuse the mess. I'm sorting out some architraves around the doors," John said as they stepped over long lengths of wood in the hallway.

"Been promising to do it for six months," Caroline teased. "He works too hard."

"That I do. Mum's dropping the kids off in a minute—you'll see how much they've grown."

"Eight and seven, right?" Claire asked.

"That's right. Little angels," Caroline replied.

John laughed. "When they're not up to mischief. Caught 'em playin' pop stars with my best guitar the other day. That's my job."

"Never too late," Mike quipped.

"You still playing live with that Jennie? Those mp3s you sent were good. Well, she's good, anyway."

"Ha! Yes, but less than before. You still playing and writing?"

"Bits and bobs."

Caroline shook her head. "They're always like this. They'll be singing in a minute. Come help me make tea," she said to Claire.

She was right. Before the kettle had even boiled, John strummed *Shape of You* on his guitar, singing while adding fancy guitar licks. The kids arrived home. John and Mike spent hours chatting, reminiscing, and laughing. Claire and Caroline played with the children but joined in as best they could despite the avalanche of memories Mike and John shared.

As Mike popped to the bathroom before leaving, John took a quiet moment to speak to Claire.

"You won't find better than him," John said softly. "He's one of the nicest guys you'll ever meet."

Claire smiled. "I know."

*

The evening at Mike's mum's was lovely.

Claire couldn't get over how she called him "Michael" every time, but she could also see how much she cared for him. She had never seen a warm parent.

As Mike headed downstairs for breakfast the next morning, his mother greeted him.

"Now, this girl is lovely, Michael. Just lovely. Hang on to her. Don't lose her."

Mike paused.

So much of his childhood insecurity had been reinforced by his mother's traumas. Maybe once, those words would have triggered something in him—She might leave. Not liked enough? Try harder.

But today, he smiled.

"I will."

Claire joined them and turned to Mike's mum.

"Shall we all go out for lunch? What's your favourite place?"

"Well, the *Three Horseshoes* is nice. We'd get in there without a booking."

"Great. My treat for all of us."

"Oh, well. I don't know. No need—"

Later, as they went upstairs to change, Mike hesitated. "You don't have to pay for us all, Claire."

"No. I want to. She's always lovely to me. I feel like I'd like to."

Mike paused, realisation dawning.

Of course. She doesn't relate to her mother. Never has. She doesn't know any other way to show kindness to a mother.

But she is showing it here.

*

Mike and Claire flew into Charles de Gaulle Airport on Saturday, March 31st, 2018, for a short Easter getaway.

Mike had sung April in Paris at least a dozen times since they'd booked the trip. And now they were here.

They arrived as tourists—ready to explore the galleries, cafés, and arrondissements.

Their small but charming hotel on Rue Christine placed them right in the heart of the Left Bank. Close to Saint-Germain-des-Prés, the Batobus stops on the Seine, and dozens of hidden cafés.

They immersed themselves in the city.

By day, they were culture lovers and museum hoppers. By night, they became lovers in Paris.

The street art, the cobblestone alleys, and the warm cafés of Cour de Commerce-Saint-André pulled them in, but Rue de l'Abbaye confirmed it.

Claire had climbed higher on the old stone steps, preparing to take Mike's photo below.

And then—it hit her.

In his effortlessly chic clothes, this handsome man stands against this Parisian dream backdrop.

She was intoxicated.

They dined at Café Laurent, Le Relais Louis XIII, and small backstreet bistros.

And slowly, Paris became theirs. And they became each other's.

When they reached Montmartre, they were spellbound.

Mike leaned in, whispering, "April in Paris, this is a feeling no one can ever reprise" into Claire's ear.

They bought a miniature painting from an artist in Place du Tertre.

And that was the moment they knew—they were committed to each other.

*

Back in the UK, as they were parting, Mike took a breath.

"If I could get a job up here in one of the East Midlands universities, could we get a place and live together?"

Claire didn't hesitate.

"Yes."

*

Back in Plymouth, alone, he wrote her a song, *Morning Light in Your Eyes*.

> *Read about deep joy in the morning.*
> *Lovers waking, opening their eyes.*
> *But no book gave me this real feeling—*
> *See the morning light in your eyes.*
> *Soar to the skies,*
> *Fall in your eyes.*
> *Hear you breathing wakes me up gently,*
> *And your heartbeat brings me alive.*
> *There's just one more thing to enchant me—*
> *See the morning light in your eyes.*
> *Soar to the skies,*
> *Fall in your eyes.*
> *Don't need sunshine, rain will do nicely.*
> *Could be snowfall, and clouds are just fine.*
> *So long as days have light in the morning—*
> *I'll be here to wake by your side.*

Chapter 54

Mike and Claire found house-hunting exciting. They focused on small villages along the Nottinghamshire-Leicestershire border. Mike would drive up on Fridays, and together, they lined up a few properties to view over the weekend.

One Saturday afternoon, Claire drove them to see a cottage in a village called Hickling. The storm from the previous night had passed, leaving a cool, crisp air in its wake.

"This place looks chocolate-box quaint," Mike said as they passed a row of terraced cottages and the village hall.

"That was the village hall we just passed," Claire added.

"I like that. Suggests people do things themselves here."

"Yeah. We're used to living in towns, and while we do things through the universities, we don't, in fact, know much about our local communities."

Claire pulled up outside the cottage.

"Certainly, has curb appeal," she said, admiring the brickwork pattern. "That must be the estate agent waiting in the car."

They approached him.

"Hi, I'm Phil Daniels," he said, extending a hand. "The cottage is vacant—owners relocated for work and already bought elsewhere."

Mike smiled. "Great. So, no chain then?"

"No. And you mentioned you don't have anything to sell?"

"No, we're both renting. We can leave by the end of July."

Inside, Phil led them through the house.

Claire uttered the same word each time they entered a room: "Lovely."

By the time they reached the upstairs bedrooms, they had resorted to admiring nods.

The agent waited at the bathroom doorway as they stepped inside.

Mimicking Alan Partridge, Mike announced, "Do you know what this bathroom says to me? Aqua. Which is French for water."

Claire and the agent burst into laughter.

Mike grinned.
In the garden, Claire's smile widened.
"We like the property," Mike said. "We'll talk it over and let you know."
After the viewing, they decided to walk through the village.
As they reached St. Luke's Church, they stopped in awe.
"Oh my. Just look at that lavender sky," Claire whispered.
Mike pulled out his phone. "That colour. That's rare. The whole scene—the church tower, the light—looks like a painting. Almost watercolour."
"Exactly. As I said, images like these stay with us. They become part of us. It's a sign, Mike. We should live here."
Mike looked at her, then at the sky, and smiled.
"We should."

*

Their separate homes now felt like closing chapters.
Instead of feeling inconvenient, their visits became planning sessions—deciding what to bring and what to buy new.
Mike scaled back his gigs, keeping only a midweek residency with Jennie. By June, Claire visited Plymouth for the first time in a while and saw them perform together.
She enjoyed the first set.
But during the second, when Mike and Jennie sang *You're All I Need to Get By*, a sudden unease crept in.
For the first time in her life, she felt jealousy.
She trusted Mike. But the idea of losing him unnerved her.
She needed this man.

*

A week before the move, Claire wrestled with unexpected emotions.
She had always been free and independent, answering only to herself.
Now? She was merging lives with someone else.
She called Manisha.

"While I am excited," Claire admitted, "I'm scared. What if I lose my autonomy? I've always done what I wanted. Am I even good at showing consideration?"
"You can be. And you're right—these are things we all learn. But from what I know about you and Mike, you already consider him far more than you ever did, Simon."
"I suppose so. I just don't want to mess this up."
"You won't. Mike is considerate. Soon, this will all feel natural."

*

Over the next few days, Claire tried to be more open about her feelings.
As they packed up her house, she looked at Mike.
"It feels like an achievement, doesn't it?" she mused. "Us moving in together. Like, proper grown-up stuff. I'm proud we got here. You know what I mean?"
"Exactly."
"But you do realise I go to my studio when I lose my temper, right?"
"Ha. I've already set up a bed in there for you, anticipating it."
"And I've put another one in the spare room—where I'll go to play thrash guitar."
They laughed.
"Jokes aside, people say you get nostalgic for the 'good old days' once you move in together, but I don't think I will," Mike said. "I'm just glad we'll be together. You'll still be you, and I'll still be me."
Claire smiled.
"That'll do for me."
And just like that, they moved in.
One Monday evening in September, as Mike and Claire walked through the village, preparing for their regular run on the Cross Britain Way toward Hose, Claire spotted a flyer tied to a lamp post outside the village hall.
She stopped to read it.

"It's a fun run. For childhood leukaemia. The Sunday after next. Starts at 9:30 am. It's only five miles, so we'd have to do something different to get people to sponsor us. Let's do it. Heh?"

"Sure, if you like. We can both get sponsors at work easily."

"Wicked."

Mike smirked. "There's a fancy dress shop near my university. I'll stop by this week to get something. It'll surprise you on the day—and for everyone here. I'll tell my sponsors what I'm doing, though."

Claire grinned. "Ace. Right, then... I'll run it with you, holding hands. But I'll do it... running backwards."

The morning of the fun run, Mike retrieved the costume he'd been hiding in the car boot, went upstairs, put it on, and waited for Claire.

Downstairs, Claire was buzzing with excitement.

"Have you put it on? Are you ready? Can I see?"

Mike called back in a playful hide-and-seek voice. "I'm ready."

Claire flung open the bedroom door—and burst out laughing.

Mike stood head-to-toe in a bright yellow chicken costume, complete with a red comb, wattles, a tail, and oversized wings.

He struck a dramatic pose, hands on hips, chest out, before flapping his arms and launching into a chicken dance.

"Cluck-buck-buck-buck!"

Claire gasped for breath between fits of laughter, clapping her hands like an excited child.

"I love it. I love it. Come on, let's go! This'll be amazing!"

And so, they ran.

Claire, laughing uncontrollably, backwards the entire way, holding hands with a chicken.

Every movement Mike made—each exaggerated stride, each ridiculous bounce—made it funnier and funnier.

Can happiness make you tread more lightly? Move more gracefully?

Can it make something as simple as making tea feel intimate?

Can it alter every feeling you have about everything?

Yes.

Armed with vivid imaginations, they often talked about their world together. Their space. Their connection.

In the place where they always had their most intimate conversations—their bedroom—they lay on their sides, facing each other.

Mike tucked a loose strand of hair behind Claire's ear.

"You ever wonder what people would think if they watched us all day? I bet it'd be like a couple in *The Sims*—just floating around, totally relaxed, doing life in some blissful state of serenity."

Claire smiled, mirroring his gesture, brushing his hair from his forehead.

"True. We do." She slipped her hand into his beneath the sheets. "But when we touch, we come alive. It's like we're just in the moment. Spellbound. They don't get that."

Mike's gaze locked onto hers, his pupils making tiny, searching movements.

She was looking into him.

And he felt it.

*

To the outside world, they lived ordinary lives.

They had typical jobs and a routine, and joined a gym in Nottingham in November—primarily for swimming and essential exercise.

Every Friday night, they went together.

And even there, they couldn't stop looking at each other.

One evening, as they stood in the pool, Claire studied him.

"You've still got some tan."

Mike glanced down at himself, then back at her with a smirk. "Jealous?"

"Nope." She stuck her tongue out. "Anyway, you're more yellow than brown."

A few weeks later, Claire noticed something else as they stood by the pool's edge.

"Mike, I think you might be overdoing it. You're losing weight."

Mike patted his stomach. "Do you think? I needed to lose a bit."

But by early December, something felt off.
One morning, Mike woke up violently ill.
"Some kind of bug," he groaned. "I've got diarrhoea too."
Claire frowned.
"You've lost loads more weight. This isn't right, Mike."
The days passed. The symptoms lingered. The pain in his abdomen worsened.
"You're going to the doctor."
He went.
The GP examined him, took blood and urine samples, and scheduled further tests.
A week later, the call came.
"Mr Lewis, you've been given an urgent cancer referral. We suspect something with your pancreas."
Mike swallowed hard.
He told Claire.
"Nine out of ten people referred don't get diagnosed. They're just being thorough."
Claire stared at him, her breath catching.
"But given your history, Mike—" she whispered.
"It might be."
A silence fell between them.
It might be.

Chapter 55

Several weeks later, Mike had his appointment.
In the interim, his symptoms had worsened. Swallowing had become difficult.
He and Claire went together.
On the way there, they spoke of everything—except cancer. Except for the consultation itself.
The closer they got, the quieter the hospital corridors became.
The further they walked, the more the space seemed to empty of sound, leaving only their nervous shoes echoing against the linoleum floor.
Signs. Arrows. Directions. Endless turns. Each new corner made the distance feel both too long and too short—as if the hospital had been designed to make you wonder how you'd ever get out rather than prepare you for what waited at the end.
A knock.
A handle turning.
And then—in.
Mike stepped inside and paused.
For a room holding the weight of a life-changing truth, it looked so... ordinary.
Plain walls. A cluttered desk. A space that did not match the gravity of what was about to be said.
It wasn't a room for death sentences.
Mike's gaze flicked to the consultant—assessing—poker face. No clues.
She gestured toward the two seats across from her. Was that a smile?
They sat.
She began with a recap of the previous tests—efficient and clinical. Then, a pause.
"So, where are we?"
For a second, Mike wasn't sure if he was supposed to answer.
He glanced at Claire—she was already watching him, offering a small, steady smile.
The consultant continued.

"We have confirmation that it is pancreatic cancer."
Pause.
Mike managed to respond before she could go on.
"Right."
"Did you get a chance to read the information sheets you were given before your tests?"
"Yes."
"So, as you know, there are different stages of cancer. One to four."
Claire shifted uneasily in her chair.
"Yes."
It felt like a TV game show, with the host stretching the silence before delivering the verdict.
A beat too long. A breath too heavy.
The consultant lowered the papers in her hand.
She met Mike's eyes directly.
No smile.
"Yours is pretty advanced. Stage four. Metastatic."
Silence.
"We will need to do further scans, but it appears to have spread in several ways beyond the pancreas, which means . . . "
Mike finished the sentence for her.
"That it's terminal. Yes?"
A brief hesitation.
"In such cases, that seems to be true, Michael."
She glanced back at her notes—as if looking away might soften the blow.
The rest of the conversation blurred.
More tests. More scans. More medical jargon. But the words all meant the same thing.
"Managing some of the complications."
The only vaguely positive note was the mention of "outstanding recent pain management developments."
Mike listened, but his mind was somewhere else.
"So... do we have any sort of timeframe?"
There was still hope in his voice.
He was listening for one word—"years."
A number. Something to hold onto.

The consultant's voice remained measured.
"A few months. Maybe a bit more. But as I say, we cannot be precise at this stage."
A pause. Then:
"For now, the important thing is that you talk together, support each other, and enjoy things on a day-to-day basis. That is always the best."
There were more words after that.
Dates. Locations. Further appointments.
But none of it mattered.
Mike had received the only message that counted.
He was going to die.
Their British reserve led them to silently leave the room, walking instinctively through the hospital corridors until they were outside.
Still, no words.
Mike turned to Claire.
He opened his arms.
She stepped in.
They held each other.
After a moment, Mike tilted his head down—their lips met.
A kiss.
A kiss like no other.
An empty kiss.
A kiss that couldn't break through the numbness that had already begun to settle between them.

*

Claire's reaction took Mike aback as she drove them home.
"This is ridiculous!" she snapped, her voice rising. "Were there no steps you could have taken? Why didn't they tell you this could happen? They should have done something."
She was angry. Furious.
Mike sighed. "They never said. I don't think they expected anything else to—"
"Bloody ridiculous!" she cut in. "They should have thought about it! It's not right!"

Mike flinched as the car drifted toward the white line in the middle of the road.

"Let's just get home and talk," he said carefully. "Anyway, we don't have all the information yet. This could all be further away than she thinks. We need to wait and see. Yes?"

Claire took a shaky breath.

"Yes. Maybe."

A beat.

"We need to find out more. And maybe she's wrong. We need a second opinion. That happens, you know. They get it wrong."

As they continued driving, Mike tried to monitor his thoughts. There were too many.

Fleeting moments of fear. Then sadness. Then self-pity. Then injustice.

Nothing settled.

Just two words.

"Why me?"

Then—

"Why now?"

He thought he had only spoken in his head.

But Claire's voice broke through the silence.

"I don't know," she whispered. "I don't know."

Not knowing became their default state in the days that followed.

What to do?

What to say?

Who to see?

Where to get more information?

How do I seek a second opinion?

Each question was infused with guilt.

"What am I supposed to do?"

*

The only answers they got were the ones they didn't want.

The consultant hadn't been wrong.

Mike endured more tests and scans.

He listened to doctors discussing the "speed of progression" as though his body were a racecourse and the cancer was a pack of competing thoroughbreds.
He felt himself weaken by the day.
Claire kept returning to anger.
By day, she clung to denial.
By night, it abandoned her.
The small hours were reserved for nightmares—
Mike dying in agony.
A grief so vast, it crushed her completely.
An injustice so cruel—
How could she have found such happiness only to have it ripped away?
Why Mike?
Of all the people she had ever known, of all the men in all the world—
Why him?
But underneath it all—beneath the rage, the grief, the disbelief—
Was heartache.
A demonic, unrelenting weight pressed down on her.
It stole her breath.
It dimmed every light.
It made every sound hollow.
It emptied the world.
Except when she saw him.
Then, all she wanted was to touch him.
To hold him.
To protect him.
To wrap herself around him so tightly that nothing—not illness, not time, not even death—could take him away.
And so, in their sadness, they held hands.
She would lie beside him, her head on his chest—
Their way.
The way that had always stopped time.
That had always hidden worries.
That had always been their world.

But as the weeks passed, Claire became consumed by one question.
"What can I do for him?"
She knew she would care for him. Nurse him.
But what could she—and only she—give to him?
Then, she knew.
A painting.
For this man—
This handsome man.
This clever man.
This funny man.
This kind, dependable, sexy, infuriating, brilliant man.
The man who had completed her.
She stepped into her studio.
And she began.

*

On March 3rd, 2019, Mike woke again at 2:30 p.m.
He felt weak. So weak.
But something inside him stirred.
He forced himself up—slow, unsteady.
Perhaps Claire was in the lounge.
Or the kitchen.
No.
Her studio?
Determined, he began to climb the stairs.
Halfway up, he stopped.
Breath gone.
He rested a moment, then pushed on.
The door was ajar.
He could see inside.
Not there.
His gaze caught on something—
A bright blue cover draped over her easel.
A wave of instinct.
He moved toward it.
He lifted the cover.

A 'Rembrandt' painting.
Only it wasn't a Rembrandt.
It was a painting that Claire was doing of the two of them.
He is lying in the bed
She, sitting beside him, watching him.
On the bedside table sat a single-stem vase—inside it, a white rose.
The light from the window fell on his face.
It fell on her hair.
That hair.
Casting her in half-shadow.
Her beautiful face—
But no spark in her eyes.
No brightness.
A face of sorrow.
A wishing face.
Her gift.
A final act of love.
He knew, as she must have known, that it wouldn't save him.
But it didn't matter.
It was magic.
It gave him the acceptance of his picture for William.
Not a cure
A gift of love.
His heart leapt—
And then stopped.
As he fell back, he slid down the wall.
And in those final moments, he knew—
He had loved her enough
For her to truly feel loved.
And to give love.
Claire was outside in the garden.
Mulling over her painting.
Something was wrong.
What?
Images from her life that had defined her flickered across her mind.
And then, she knew.

The vase.
Not a white rose.
A lily.
Love—even after death.

Printed in Dunstable, United Kingdom